Skyshooter

Rod Lindsey

The author would like to acknowledge the US Department of Homeland Security, the Transportation Safety Administration, the Federal Air Marshals Service, and others who put themselves in harms way to guard the safety of the rest of us. Thank you for being there.

Sincere thanks to Melissa Watkins Alexander, William Vaughn, Alexandra Panic, and Margot Ayer for their generous critiques and support.

Edited by Nita Lynn with Margot Ayer

Cover art by Megan Rackleff

For my father, Ralph E. Lindsey.
A true Renaissance man in so many ways: a reader and thinker and
kindhearted sufferer of fools (me, in particular).

Oh Sinnerman, where you gonna run to?

Sinnerman, where you gonna run to?

Where you gonna run to?

All on that day

Well I run to the rock, please hide me

I run to the rock, please hide me

I run to the rock, please hide me, Lord

All on that day

But the rock cried out, I can't hide you

The rock cried out, I can't hide you

The rock cried out, I ain't gonna hide you guy

All on that day

Sinnerman (American Traditional)

Don't Worry

"Strings need to be pulled," Mr. Kenneth told Jessica Vega. "I can do that."

I can do that? the voice in her head echoed. *An easy thing for him to say.*

Maybe an easy thing for him to do, too, Jessica thought; this tall dark man without rank or title, she would see what he can or can't do soon enough. Meanwhile, she was becoming worried. She hated that; the feeling something unpleasant was about to pounce and time to do anything about it was running out if not already gone. This was not an ordinary itch of superstition that she felt, nor a churning guilty conscience, although a smidgen or two of guilt probably wouldn't hurt her as her mother liked to remind. No, this was a matter of simple mathematics: bad luck x enough time = bad luck squared with remaining time equaling zero. Jessica had been skating along on luck for far too long, and everyone knows that luck is a poor partner in the long run – a teaser.

Things will turn to shit soon enough, the voice inside her head said, unsolicited opinions of the ominous sort always spewing forth from that dark-hearted hitchhiker without warning.

Thank you so very fucking much for alerting me to something I already knew, Jessica thought, knowing very well that she could depend on the voice to keep shit stirred up. Meanwhile she'd have to stay sharp, stop being so impetuous, and seriously consider Mr. Kenneth's option before it became just another entry on her ever-growing maybe-I-should've list.

He was an enigma, Mr. Kenneth. Tall. Forceful. And dark in every possible meaning of the word. A man obviously accustomed to power, he'd told her that he was one of the good guys; said that he could help with her situation. Jessica was impressed but unimpressed, or at least unbelieving. Good guys had rules and usually played by them. This Mr. Kenneth would have her believe the rules didn't apply to him – therefore he must be one of the bad guys. What's more; she knew perfectly well that good things simply did not happen all by themselves. Not in the real world they didn't. Not to her they didn't. In her experience happiness not only could but actually had to be purchased, unhappiness and disappointment diligently guarded against at all times. There was always a price. The only real question; is it worth the price?

With a heavy dose of irony Jessica wondered who she thought she was fooling. There was never any question – the price always gets paid…always, whether it's worth it or not. It all comes down to whether you pony-up without bitching, or try to hold your ground while assuming the position for something much worse that you know damned well is coming. She was skeptical, and threw the tall dark man a look intended to say so.

"Save your chips," her badass Mexican father had repeatedly admonished when she was a girl, "and always remember you have them. One day you'll need them. Chips are dearer than cash in our world because certain favors cannot be purchased with cash. Not real ones when you really need them."

Gracias Papa. Your advice is appreciated more than you know, Jessica thought.

Considering the idea of garnering chips to spend later on favors; Jessica had realized long ago that it would take more than a few of the real ones to get her out from under the horrific shit she was guilty of. Add to that all the shit others were guilty of heaping on her her whole life, and it was a genuine shitload, she thought with a mirthless inner smile.

Bad influences = bad girls. More math, Jessica Vega style. Inexperienced as she was with anything that could possibly be seen as a normal life through even the rosiest of glasses, Jessica didn't know if she'd recognize a good thing if it bit her on the nose. But she was scrappy, a fighter. And now, an option – Mr. Kenneth's chip on the table.

A good thing? Maybe. Maybe a chance to reboot her life. It was unexpected, and she was certain the offer would not be repeated.

It hadn't exactly been easy, killing the old man…

But necessary just to shut him up, the voice in her head concurred.

Didn't hurt that he'd become a world-class creep, Jessica thought; another disgusting old fart just like his brother had been. And recently he'd begun running his lying lips entirely too loosely – lies and more lies about things he said happened on the trestle. Things he hadn't seen with his own eyes nor heard with his own ears but thought he knew all about, nonetheless; so he had to go. Won't be missed.

Simple, the voice said. *And much easier than the woman was, huh?*

Jessica would rather forget about the woman…

His girlfriend, supposedly…

Not true! She was nobody's girlfriend. A scheming, ruthless whore was what she'd been. Appreciating the woman in the same harsh light that had shone on herself for so long was a curious experience. Jessica often thought of herself as something of a walking paradox; pure as the driven snow in a slightly-tainted way as her mother had so often said.

But the woman hadn't been expected. That was the problem. She wasn't supposed to be there, so she wasn't part of the plan insofar as Jessica had an actual plan, and spontaneously killing her had been very awkward and messy.

Yes, killing the craven old man had been a real joy by comparison.

"Wasn't right!" was all he'd said. Said it repeatedly as Jessica remembered. "What you did wasn't right! Wasn't right! Wasn't right!" he babbled on and on. He was dying by then, and she'd thought that he might have something important to offer, so she listened. But all he wanted to do was bitch and accuse.

He truly brought this on himself, she thought, because I would've gladly stood forever before a scrim of uncertainty around that whole damned trestle incident. She had agreed to meet him – not to kill him…not *exactly* to kill him if encouraging a heart attack doesn't count, but to hear whatever he had to say, only because he'd suggested that he knew more than he possibly could about the day Billiejean fell.

"My brother knew!" he had cried as if this revelation somehow lent weight to the situation.

It didn't.

"Big fucking surprise," Jesse said. "Of course, I suppose it's possible that your brother might've seen something – he was driving the train, after all. But he's dead and you weren't there. That kinda makes whatever you think you know pure hearsay doesn't it?"

"He knew! And he told me all about it!" the sad old man wailed, desperately wanting someone – anyone other than himself – to take the blame for his twin brother's suicide, crying; "He told me what you did, and what your sister told him you did. He showed me!"

"Showed you what, exactly?" Jessica had asked.

"Everything! The whole scene. It's all there – every detail. And real evidence too. He kept a sliver of wood from your cheek – did you know that? And a jacket with blood smears on it."

Bummer! That doesn't sound good at all, the voice in Jesse's head brooded, a spike of agony hitting Jesse right between the eyes.

The jacket, Jessica thought. How could she have forgotten about the jacket?

Crap! Crap! Crap!

***

The 10" Wusthof chef's knife had belonged to Jessica's grandmother, a wedding present from back in the day when such gifts were intended to be durable, thick-bladed and heavy enough to chop through bone. Two-handedly, she plunged it into flesh and drew it back out. Again and again. The blood produced was copious: warm, sticky, and very satisfying to her. Satisfying for how long she couldn't guess, but probably not so long.

"It wasn't right!" he repeated ad nauseam. The dying old fucker just wouldn't shut up…Why is it that dying people choking on their last breath think they need to use it to set some vague record straight? Jessica wondered. Frankly, unless their last words start with 'I hid the money' she couldn't imagine why anyone would give a microscopic shit about what they might have to say on their way out.

"It wasn't right!" The words were little more than desperate, gurgling whispers toward the end, heavy with awful implications and hard to spit out. He was lying in his own mess by then. And then he was dead and they were his last words.

It was Halloween Eve...

Chapter 2

Saturday morning before Thanksgiving the entire commercial airway corridor from SeaTac to LAX was heavily overcast, the snow-carpeted mountains and shadowy valleys far below the cruising airplane obscured by a thick boundless vapor in shades of gray and grayer, the world swallowed-up by a featureless void since the flight from Seattle to Mazatlan took off three hours ago.

Sipping his fifth coffee refill, black and bitter – the way he liked it, Air Marshal Ezra Hooten was beginning to feel a little überamped on caffeine, also the way he liked it – except that being so tuned-in and aware of his surroundings included being fully aware when the slightest adjustments in cruising altitude were gained or lost by the airplane, his pulse quickening by a half-beat every time. Truthfully, the caffeine kick barely raised a blip on Hoot's internal radar: thus, his nerves no more fidgety than usual this morning, his natural suspiciousness combined with the tightly-packed closeness of this particular holiday flight caused only a few of the little transparent hairs on the back of his neck to rise a millimeter or two above normal, but that was about the extent of it; his edge for whatever it was worth.

Diagnosed OCA1 albino, Hoot's complexion alternated between an alarming deep red to a deathly white pallor depending on his blood pressure. Unusual for one suffering with albinism, he was without significant vision loss, but his blue eyes were so pale they were almost clear, light sensitive and ever-busy behind polarized glasses. He had eyebrows…almost – thin and nearly invisible white ones, but expressive. And he was crowned with a full head of straight white hair that in recent years had become the envy of vampire fans young and old. No wolf in sheep's clothing, Hoot liked to think of himself more as a lamb in a vampire suit. A flying, well-armed lamb in a vampire suit.

And then there was the flying part. It was becoming routine, everyday stuff, and Hoot told himself that he was getting more comfortable with the idea of air travel, but he was always fidgety on a flight simply because he was the sort of man who preferred to keep his feet firmly planted on terra firma. At sixty-three-years-old, six-feet-four-inches-tall, and uncomfortable in more-spacious first class seating on principle alone, he was doomed to be physically and mentally miserable in any seat on any airplane. He accepted it as penance of a sort. He was, after all, a lifelong sinner...

Hoot flinched almost imperceptibly when his ears popped. They popped again and he flinched again. Just another normal physical reaction, he knew; eardrums flexing due to changes in atmospheric pressure lost or gained from altitude changes. Takeoffs and landings were the worst. Cruising not so bad. But knowing what caused his discomfort didn't make him like it any better, didn't keep him from feeling as if he were flying with his head caught in the jaws of an ever-tightening vice. Nothing he could do but endure it; chew gum like a madman to work his jaw muscles, try to flex his inner ear canals and maybe ease the pressure, but for the most part, simply endure it. Hoot had become very adept at enduring it. He turned his head and felt a satisfying crack, momentarily relaxing the tension in his neck, used the motion to take another look around.

Matching if not trumping the physical agony of flying, there was always the relentless sound of an airplane in flight; any aircraft, including and especially helicopters. Hoot hated helicopters, had been plagued with a morbid attraction-through-repulsion relationship with the ungainly hoverers since Vietnam, and had flown in hundreds of them during his career with the US marshals. By comparison, the main problem with jet airliners was their thin, aluminum skins as tight as drumheads, the way they transmuted sound decibels with pressurized cabin air until the noise of flying became a nearly solid substance, the neverending background roar from massive jet engines mounted under wings just outside the aircraft's fuselage thickened into something approximating ear gravy. He hated that roar growing more and more insistent until he felt as if his very core could burst.

Can't allow that to happen, Hoot derided himself with a hearty pinch of self-directed sarcasm. Settling back and taking a long slow breath, forcing his shoulders to relax, and willing himself to simply chill, he discreetly replaced the flavorless lump of gum in his mouth with a fresh sugar-free stick and chewed earnestly while covertly looking around.

His nerves obeying Hoot's command to chill like good soldiers accustomed to bad orders, he began to feel a bit more relaxed and in control while remaining very much aware of his surroundings. He considered his charges on this flight; some business flyers as usual, but mostly families and couples, boisterous holiday travelers getting an early start, roast turkey and pumpkin pie their only concerns. Or perhaps, considering their ticketed destination, their sights were set on fajitas and flan instead of the traditional fowl and pastry. For Hoot, this was a study of familial dynamics in action, a little game he sometimes played in his mind to make his job seem less boring than it actually was. The trick was avoiding comparison to his own feckless ventures into the murky realms of Husband and Father at all costs. He idly wondered how many of these travelers were simply hoping to get where they were going safely. How many were worried about getting through the rest of the week past T-day without a major family incident? How many of them had their sights already set on Santa Claus, New Year parties, next summer's vacation? Most of them? All of them?

Most were slouched in their seats with their seatbelts loose, chit-chatting and grinning like certified idiots as the union-made and therefore presumably flawless projectile containing them rushed ever farther southward. Of course they were all maniacs to assume there was any such thing as a flawless aircraft, meaning they were manically grinning idiots, Hoot decided with an inner smile of mild disgust. Still, he appreciated the tenacity of their holiday cheer worn like gaudy beach attire underneath a winter coat, all for the family, even if much of it was bogus.

Have to love 'em. Can't shoot 'em, he concluded in his father's Coastal Maine voice while taking another clandestine look around, a bit of droll humor getting caught in his mental throat. At that same moment a detached part of his imagination was taking little sidesteps, thinking for the zillionth time since he landed this glorified sheepherder's job how sweet it would be to get completely out of law enforcement or anything else that exposed him overmuch to the dark side of human nature. Maybe he could start a charter fishing service out of Ilwaco once the economy got back on its feet. In his experience drunken fishermen weren't bad company to keep, comparatively speaking.

Yeah. That's what I should do; go fishing, he thought, allowing himself a slight but genuine smile. Hoot had a very short résumé – one page with wide margins. Fisherman. Soldier. Marshal. And now...

With barely a full year invested in the Federal Air Marshal Service, the charter fishing idea was gaining a little more traction with every flight he took. Perhaps he had been hasty to take another badge so soon after turning the last one in, the exit wound still raw – literally as well as figuratively. His career-spanning pursuit of a boyhood friend turned psychopath suddenly over, Hoot had hoped to find something a bit more relaxing to do without rolling completely over into retirement. Saw a TSA pitch recruiting discharged military and law enforcement people to become air marshals and thought it could be an opportunity with potential, much as he hated flying notwithstanding. How's that for oxymoronic? he had often wondered since – nobody to jerk my strings so I jerk my own. Gotta stop doing that...

Meanwhile, this sky marshal job was a serious job and Hoot certainly took it seriously; how could anyone not in the age of terrorism? But did it hold his interest and challenge him the way fugitive apprehension had done when he was a US marshal? One hundred and eleven flights later the answer remained – no, it did not.

No matter. Hoot had already outlived his warranty. The rest was gravy.

From his aisle seat he pantomimed reading a book on his Kindle while keeping watch over his maniacally grinning and chit-chatting flock from behind the cover of his photochromic glasses. Watching – he was always watching and appraising his charges. Hoot wanted to feel empathy for these travelers. He really did. After all, for the duration of the flight they truly were vulnerable chicks under his protective wing whether they appreciated him for it or not.

But true empathy was a stretch for Hoot, especially for the intrusive and chatty female occupying the center seat next to him. This was outside of protocol – there should've been an empty seat next to Hoot, but the holiday-season flight was oversold. Introducing herself as a professional exterminator when she first squeezed into her assigned place, her shoulders, arms, elbows, and knees made intimate forays into both Hoot's personal space and that of the college student feigning sleep in the window seat.

"I'm returning home to LA from a training seminar in Seattle," she said after wriggling into place. "Was a great seminar about the latest developments in pest eradication. Traps. Baits and poisons. And, of course, business development through social networking. You wouldn't believe how many otherwise nice homes are absolutely infested with pests…all sorts of pests!"

Hoot pulled his glasses down on the tip of his nose to emphasize his disinterest, hoping to nip the subject of pest eradication with an unfiltered cold look, but instead he found her to be the sort who didn't really need reciprocity to carry on a conversation. He said, "I'm sure I wouldn't," his tone flat, imagining the woman sitting next to him rutting around under the living room floorboards in someone's crawl space, taking out rhino-sized rats and Shelob-sized spiders with the latest developments.

"You wanna switch seats? I bet we'd both have more elbow room with me on the aisle," she said.

"No. I'm good where I am," Hoot answered, tapping his Kindle to a new page.

The ensuing silence was brief. "You aren't really reading that thing, are you?" she asked.

"Trying to," he said, his tone as flat as dirt, suddenly jealous of the college kid's MP3 device with its firmly planted ear buds presumably sending the overriding comfort of music straight to his essential synapses.

"You look kinda pale," she said. "You feel okay?"

"I feel fine," Hoot answered, thinking there are days when rudeness rules and it looked like today was going to be one of them. "Now if you don't mind, I like to read when I fly," he said.

He wondered: had he been truthful – did he really feel fine? What he mostly felt was the ever-present in-flight sense of vibration in everything around him. The physical hum of flying high above the landscape at more than 500 miles-per-hour, or at light speed, or a gazillion miles-per-hour; the sensation of speed losing its relevance once the plane is off the tarmac. The same pressurized, germ-infested cabin air since departure, constantly being filtered and fucked-with from the flight's beginning to its end, every fart, cough, sneeze, and other ill vapors stretched thin but still aboard and accounted for. The roaring jet thrust reminding Hoot of old Roadrunner cartoons from when he was a kid – Wile E. Coyote with a rocket strapped to his back, sure to explode. Trumping it all was the anxious energy of a full load of passengers riding a similar rocket of pure holiday lunacy, everyone blinded by excitement on the cusp.

It's true that Hoot had never liked flying – even before he became a sky marshal and flew almost daily. His father a lifelong commercial fisherman, his mother a school bus driver and Meals on Wheels volunteer, every adult that Hoot knew when he was a kid growing up had been constantly busy with the hard knocks of life. Nobody had ever promised him an easy job – not once, and he sure as hell didn't expect anyone to do so now.

Often during his career as a US Marshal he had imagined how it must've been for marshals in the old times; butt parked for endless hours on a saddled horse, calluses growing thick on the insides of your knees and thighs, kidneys loitering down around your ass cheeks at the end of the day. The planes Hoot routinely flew in were simply today's version of the old-timer's horse and saddle. Could be worse...

Had been worse, actually – far worse. Yet here he was, former US Marshal Ezra Hooten briefly retired and quickly reincarnated as Air Marshal Ezra Hooten, and in less than a year flying had evolved from something he truly disliked and avoided as often as possible to become something he still disliked, but was nonetheless as routine and boring to him as clean socks every morning – thin, ambivalent socks, wearing thinner flight after flight.

Twenty minutes shy of this particular flight's scheduled refueling and customs inspection stop at LAX in Los Angeles Hoot's attention was drawn to an annoyance happening all the way up front in the plane. The first class flight attendant was busy with some guy loitering near the door to the forward lavatory just outside the cockpit door. Hoot remembered meeting the first class attendant prior to boarding. Her name was Marceline and she wore award pins showing that she was a million-miler several times over. From his location way back in row 20 Hoot couldn't hear what she was saying, but he could clearly see she was asking the man to return to his seat. Reminding him, no doubt, that waiting in the aisle for his turn in the lavatory was not allowed. Telling him we would be landing soon and there was no time.

The man hassling Marceline was not a first class passenger. Hoot had noticed him pass by when he walked up the aisle from a seat farther back, so he certainly didn't belong up near the first class lavatory but he wasn't budging. Of medium build with Hispanic features and medium-length black hair, he was wearing a plain gray sweatshirt and baggy black trousers – medium and colorless prettymuch summed him up. Hoot instinctively understood the man would be nearly invisible in a crowd. One of a zillion. Or a hundred. Or even of ten. He would blend in. Except for his nervous eyes – Hoot always noticed a person's eyes.

Time stood absolutely still for a brief instant. No noise. No motion. Everything hung suspended by aluminum wings at 30,000 feet while Hoot looked this troublesome passenger over, registering details. He removed his polarized glasses to allow his pale blue's to be seen. With his almost avian pupils beneath nearly invisible eyebrows and his full head of white hair combed straight back, Hoot often took advantage of his vampire-like persona to make himself more noticeable, to send a message; I'm watching you...you've been noticed, but he was too far away to make good eye contact in this case.

His partner on this flight, fellow sky marshal Jessica Vega, was sitting in row 9, first row of the economy-plus section, much closer to the action outside the first class lavatory. Hoot didn't care for sitting in the plus or first class sections unless he was working a flight solo and needed quick proximity to the cockpit door. Working with a partner he preferred to take a seat midway back in regular economy class, a much better vantage point to observe trouble in the making. He also preferred to board the plane along with the paying passengers instead of ahead of them; just another ordinary fella sucking down copious amounts of coffee while going somewhere ordinary, except this one looked like Death and was discreetly packing a loaded SIG Sauer P250 Compact in a holster under his jacket.

It was impossible for Hoot to tell from his vantage point if Vega was paying close attention to what was going on at the front of the passenger cabin. She'd better be, he thought, but he didn't really know what to expect from Jessica Vega since he'd met her only minutes before they boarded the plane in Seattle. Assigned together as part of a last-minute switcheroo, they'd barely shared a dozen words.

Silas Wilson, the SeaTac TSA director, had intercepted Hoot in the terminal security office, preflight. "Something came up, Hooten," he said. "You'll be leaving for Mexico in ten minutes instead of Alaska in a half-hour," and Hoot had replied with a generous pinch of sarcasm, "Well, shit! Here I went and packed my mukluks and mittens without bringing along my sombrero and sun block..."

Truthfully, Hoot was unfazed by the last-minute flight switch because it was something that happened often; just part of the job, and he was thinking that his offhand sombrero-and-sun block comeback had been hilarious in view of his ultra-gringo complexion and white hair. But Wilson, one of those bureaucratic middle management types who seem to come cheaper by the gross, didn't even crack a smile, a sense of humor considered unnecessary baggage in the TSA and therefore subject to suspicion.

"My orders are to put two marshals on the next flight to Mazatlan instead of one," director Wilson said. "Short notice." He nodded toward the outer office where a petite woman was just taking her leave from a tall black man known in the TSA only as Mr. Kenneth, first or last name unclear. "Vega, your partner for this trip, is the woman walking toward us right now," Wilson continued. "There will also be an ICE agent, Immigration and Customs Enforcement officer, aboard escorting an undesirable back to where he came from. Details are in the folder." He gestured toward a file on a nearby desk, adding, "Read it," before turning his attention to the compact female air marshal approaching with businesslike strides.

...And that's how Hoot first met Jessica Vega. "Jesse, as in Jesse James, the famous outlaw," she quickly explained, expressing

18

her preference for the shorthand version of her name. Seeming even smaller and tighter standing next to Hoot's long-legged frame, she was a thirty-something ex-marine reincarnated as a sky marshal, much the same as he. Very Mexican-looking with curly black hair, she wore a snug, barely-to-the-knee business skirt and a matching navy blue tailored blazer securely buttoned from the center of her breastbone. Above that point a minimal shadow of cleavage was accented by a cabernet-colored silk blouse and a hint of something lacy and black underneath – an altogether too-sexy-for-undercover work ensemble that encouraged Hoot to wonder where she concealed her weapon.

"So you're Ezra Hooten, the famous shooter," she said with a heavy hint of derision in her otherwise sultry voice, offering a firm handshake with a warm hand.

"Pardon me?" Hoot answered, thrown a bit off balance from the one-two combination of Jesse Vega's sexy tough-gal physicality and the sensation of being sucked into her deep, chocolate-colored eyes. Flirtatious eyes, they were sending out a gut-level challenge. This was a rare experience for Hoot, a lifelong alpha male who liked to think himself aloof and above it all – and he liked it.

Skin the color of cinnamon, there was something odd about the skin texture on the left side of Jesse Vega's face, heavy makeup concealing a blemish of some kind – scar tissue – but her eyes drew him past it without close scrutiny. She was the sort of woman, Hoot suspected, who could be trouble without even trying and the tone of her voice combined with the look in her eyes told him that she was probably trying.

"The famous shooter," she repeated. "Called Troubleshooter, the way I heard it. And I've heard all about you; Sky Marshal Ezra Hooten, Ex-Deputy US Marshal Hooten, Ex-Green Beret sniper back in the day as they say. Way back in the day – before I was even born, actually. You are currently the best shot in the Federal Air Marshal Service, they say."

She had a deep voice for such a small woman, almost masculine, her tone sounding like a bass riff in a jazz trio growing ever more insistent until it becomes a solo, she added, "That's something I'd like to see. I'm a bit of a shooter, myself – maybe if you aren't too tired we could meet at the firing range when we get back from our little jaunt across the border with Mister Cartel."

Too tired?

Roughly half my age, Hoot calculated with a lingering look into those lascivious twin pools of melting chocolate, knowing that in his heart and keeping his own best interests in mind, he wanted to be attracted to older, more experienced women, women he could appreciate for their humor and intellect without SEX holding all the trump cards; but he kept backsliding. As Hoot's father had liked to say; the younger ladies were like cupcakes everywhere he looked: sweet and lovely, nicely decorated, and not good for you at all. This one was mocha flavored with a pinch of spice and a large chip on her shoulder. His imagination briefly conjured a mental image of Jesse Vega as a toddler crawling around in diapers and booties at the same time that he was pussyfooting through the jungles of Vietnam avoiding punji stakes. But the image was unconvincing, a badly-executed Photoshop. Nonplussed by her attitude, he brushed aside the implied swipes his new partner was taking at his résumé and age and asked; "You're telling me the escorted prisoner flying with us is a member of a Mexican drug cartel?"

"That's exactly what I'm telling you, marshal. He's one of the worst. A known member of Los Hermanidad. Suspected member of Los Negros – a suspected enforcer in Los Negros, in fact, but no proof of it." Her eyes seeming to sparkle with excitement, she said, "He's a genuine Latino sicario, a death-squad member. And he's supposedly a fallen favorite nephew of the infamous el Lobo, himself, one of the bloodiest men in Mexico. He's a bad man and we're sending him home so that his uncle Wolf can personally spank his naughty ass since the current administration in our country doesn't seem to have the balls to do it."

Hoot scrutinized the expression in Jesse's eyes. She seemed to have a tightfisted grip on the politics of things, certainly beyond the pale of his own fuck me if I care attitude regarding the woes of TSA management, but there was something more there; there was also real fire in her, something unsaid fueling it.

"So we squeeze a professional hitman on a sold-out flight the Saturday before Thanksgiving?" he asked director Wilson, genuinely appalled at the lack of Justice Department foresight this sort of exercise demonstrated. "This surely could've waited until after the holidays…"

"…No. It couldn't," Silas Wilson interrupted with a brief glance at his companion. "Tight timetable. His extradition got rushed through at the last minute as part of the President's holiday amnesty review. DOJ gets busy in the eleventh hour cleaning out dirty corners. Happens around this time every year. It's all in the file – read it," he repeated over his shoulder while walking away with the silent Mr. Kenneth at his side, management excusing itself from the fray.

"Bring it along," Jesse Vega said with a look that left little doubt whom she considered to be the senior member of the team, their relative ages and years spent behind a badge notwithstanding. "Read it later. We have to hurry to our boarding gate…"

***

And now: Carlos Rico, the *undesirable* as director Wilson had called him, was sitting four rows ahead of Hoot, starboard side window seat. The center seat next to him was empty by protocol, his ICE escort sitting on the aisle. Jesse Vega was seven rows ahead of Rico on the left, aisle seat, the shoulder of her tailored blazer just visible.

Hoot didn't like it that his partner was caught between an obnoxious asshole at the lavatory door in front of her and a known hitman seated out of sight behind her, making his own position key. He was also acutely aware that the ICE agent sitting next to the cuffed cartel member had the worst seat of all – too close to potential trouble from his prisoner to see it coming until it was already there. He didn't like anything about it, the whole situation. It was just a feeling like a minor itch, a tic of the eye, but nothing sticks to you like hard-earned experience in the law enforcement business. It makes you cautious, and when you are also six-four and pale as a vampire it seems to make your fangs ache…

Hoot nonchalantly reached inside his jacket and fingered the butt of his pistol, his gut instinct warning him something could easily come unglued in this situation between the first class flight attendant and the lavatory asshole but not knowing what it might be.

Suddenly the lavatory door opened and a portly gentleman sidled out, squeezing past the clutch of people in the aisle to his nearby seat, the obnoxious asshole nimbly ducking inside the now-vacant facility and pulling the door closed before Marceline could stop him.

Foiled, the flight attendant assumed a mirthless all-purpose smile that didn't quite make its way to her eyes and went about checking to ensure passengers' seatbelts in her near vicinity were buckled. She was a grandmotherly gal, this Marceline, but still very much on her game and sexy in a mature way, Hoot thought with sincere appreciation. She looked to him like a cross between Mary Tyler Moore in the golden years of her career and Sandra Bullock today. Compact and tight from long hours on her feet, a sweet-and-smooth-but-no-bullshit flight attendant, she was the kind he liked best except for the phony smile. Moments later she hardly gave mister asshole a second glance when he exited the lavatory and began making his way back to his seat.

Marceline's preoccupation was unfortunate. Had she paid closer attention she might have noticed something odd coiled in the man's hand as he passed – a carbon-fiber garrote as thin and flexible as a length of dental floss, non-metallic, but with razor-sharp edges and enough tensile strength to suspend a metric ton of weight, a sticklike handle at each end. He had been quick to strip this item from inside his belt, the remains of which were left behind in the lavatory trash receptacle. And if Marceline had only noticed it in his fist her expression alone might have alerted Hoot that the event his gut had been warning him of was actually happening. Instead, Hoot was watchful as usual, but not especially so when the lavatory asshole came abreast of Carlos Rico and his escort.

There, the man stopped in his tracks; and then quick as a lighting flash he drew out his garrote in both hands, wrapped it around the ICE agent's neck, and nearly decapitated him with a fast jerk, a gusher of blood immediately spewing all over the trays and backs of seats ahead. Twitching, the body slumped forward while the assassin performed a maneuver like a calf roper at a rodeo, unwrapping the garrote from what was left of the slumping border agent's neck in a single fluid move. He quickly reached across the empty seat and looped his improvised lethal weapon around the neck of Carlos Rico. With a flick of his wrists, he jerked and did Rico too…

Two men dead in two seconds and a rapidly-growing pool of blood in row 16.

A woman across the aisle screamed hysterically. Other passengers were stunned.

It took Hoot less than three seconds to stand, draw his pistol, and fire a single deafening shot to the center of the assassin's back as he dashed back up the aisle, dropping him at Marceline's feet.

Stay down, idiot! Hoot thought, exhaling a held breath. He had not hesitated. His first and only instinct had been to deny the asshole lying prone on the aircraft floor the opportunity to make a hostage or third victim of Marceline or anyone else on this flight.

His flight. His watch. His call.

Still, second-guesses started coming almost immediately – as they always did whenever he'd had to use lethal force: Could I have stopped him before any of this happened? Taken him down without shooting him? These were normal but irrelevant doubts and they bounced off the stone wall of Hoot's resolve like swatted tennis balls. He refused to waste energy worrying about them.

The shot still ringing in everyone's ears, a surge of pandemonium broke loose in the plane – cockpit-to-tail section, terrified passengers panicked. Some tried to regain composure and then totally lost their wits. Most were cowering wide-eyed and hushed. Some were shouting and screaming. Babies wailed.

Hoot walked up the aisle with his SIG Sauer at the ready and all of them were suddenly scrambling in their rows to back as far away from him as possible as he passed. Frightened eyes darting back and forth between the bloody mess in row 16 and the inert body in the aisle at Marceline's feet ultimately locked onto him as if expecting horns to sprout from his head, flames from his nostrils. Camera phones had been drawn and their flashes were firing throughout the cabin like sawed-off shotguns in a silent Quentin Tarantino film.

Jessica Vega had jumped up from her seat the instant Hoot's shot rang out, her weapon drawn, but the main event was already over. She glanced at Hoot approaching, then turned back and looked down at the motionless form lying at the feet of the very pale but otherwise nonplussed attendant. Hurrying up the aisle ahead of Hoot, she knelt and checked the downed man's vitals, and then she turned again and looked up at her partner with a probing expression on her face, looking confused.

Trying to figure me out? Good luck with that, Hoot thought, shaking his head.

There was no way the fool lying on the cabin floor at Marceline's imperturbable feet could've thought he might escape, making this a planned suicide hit from the start.

Explosive vest wearers! Shoe bombers! Underwear bombers! – Hoot could just imagine a radical cell recruiting pitch for that job; we don't know for sure if it's enough explosive to bring down the airplane, but we do know that sacrificing your 'nads for the cause will guarantee you a place in heaven. Virgins galore…praise Allah!

With no 'nads? Yeah, sure, Hoot thought, bring on the virgins!

And now the drug cartels are sending us goddamned suicide dental floss assassins! Imaginative but stupid. He wondered, what makes someone decide to do a thing like that – brazenly kill two airline passengers while midair with virtually no chance of escape?

Suicide hits had never made sense to Hoot. In fact, the very idea pissed him off. The worst sort of indoctrination and manipulation; all forms of radical terrorism were nothing less than the fomentation of mental illness as far as he was concerned no matter how unjust the nest it gets hatched in.

War for the sake of war? Good Guys like to call it war because the word sounds official and sanctioned and necessary…War. The war against terror. The war on drugs. Make a war out of it and now goddamnit you're doing something!

Bad Guys also enjoy the war label; the macho, muscle-flexing glamour of it makes their cause real.

The common denominator is that once notions like murder, torture, rape, and ordinary heavy-handed gang thuggery are seen from the war point-of-view everyone's feelings about them are substantially more okay. From the Good Guy perspective it makes people like Hoot seem almost excusable. Necessary at the very least.

Hoot had had plenty of experience with actual war, and he knew it was no place for psychos even while serving as a Petri dish for psychosis of the darkest sort. Insanity motivated them all: the bad guys and the good guys, and especially the good guys turned bad, the revolutionaries. Ragtag extremists of every stripe were the new faces of evil. In Hoot's opinion, today's so-called revolutionaries were little more than deviants, idiots, and twisted idealists.

Terrorists – he would never understand them. Nevertheless, if that's really what these psycho-assassins for a cause wanted, if it meant that much to them to go out with a blood cry on their lips instead of quietly in their beds, then the infamous Troubleshooter Ezra M. Hooten was more than happy to oblige, as long as it was just between him and them – no collateral damage bullshit; every bullet fired a well-aimed bullet...fired to kill.

Chapter 3

Jesse tossed and turned in her bed at night; sleep had not been her friend for some time, not since the business on the Chartreuse. Killing the woman had been much harder than it should have been — harder than killing the man by far, Jesse thought with her brows creased, beads of perspiration forming in her hairline. This conclusion was hardly the result of some twisted sense of empathy, the laughable notion that simply because a woman was a woman she was worthy of special consideration, of…protection.

Protection is a myth regardless of one's sex, she thought. I've certainly never felt protected because of my sex. Quite the opposite; in fact, I've felt vulnerable — and I hate that feeling more than I can say…

Hard to kill? No kidding! the voice in her head chided like nails scratching an exposed nerve. *Did it matter in the least that it was a woman?*

A little…maybe. Not just, Jesse thought in response. Stupid cunt was aboard the boat because she was worried Harold might sneak a girlfriend aboard and have a little party instead of working on her goddamned autopilot.

Harold Hesse with a girlfriend? What a ridiculous idea…

I had to improvise. Do her first to get her out of the way before I could do him.

Oooh! You're a tough one, you are. Decisive. Don't wanna fuck around with you!

Jesse's jaw clenched. The voice in her head was certainly not the legendary Voice of Reason. Not by a long shot. Instead, it was meddlesome to say the least, the way it had grown from an occasional and relatively easy-to-ignore girly-sounding nuisance to a whining and impossible-to-ignore adult-sounding distraction over the years; an opinionated presence in her mind like the little guy inside the big guy's head in the first Men in Black movie, the pain associated with the voice becoming more and more intolerable as it matured.

Much easier to kill a girl your own age…is that it? the voice said. *Perverted old men or grocery boys with hardons aren't so easy-peasy, are they?*

Just shut up, will you? Let me think.

The old fart was drunk on his ass. Nice of him to wait in the forward cabin while you stabbed the holy crap out of his employer in the galley, don't you think?

The hurt in her head was right…there! She could see it, an inflamed burr tearing away at soft tissue.

He didn't put up much of a fight.

Awful pain sizzled in a familiar place behind her eyes. Spiky and insistent, it came with an intense flash of light like the arc from a stick welder, blinding to look at but impossible to look away from, it was all part of the hurt settling in for a lengthy stay; something shadowy moving in the blinding gap at the source of the light.

It was a nice boat, the Chartreuse. Even though I hated the name, the voice said in the condescending tone of an infantile adult. *A real shame that it had to be scuttled.*

"I told you to shut up!" Jesse said aloud, finally getting a tentative grip on her headache and taking it down a notch. Thinking sarcastically to herself; And now the fucking voice is a nautical expert on top of all the rest of its infinite talent. Thank you, Lord!

To say that Jesse was both disappointed and baffled at how the tone of the voice in her head had not matured as the years passed while she, herself, grew older would be a huge understatement. Recently it had got to the point where it actually hurt to listen to it, a tangible hurt of the sort that left scars behind, hurt that nurtured a seed of concern she might've somehow lost her grip on what was real and what was not without noticing, that she might've quietly slipped into the same pit that had claimed both her sister and her mother long ago – an idea she refused to consider other than to fear it.

Did crazy people actually know when they lost their grip? Jesse wondered. Or, did they go on thinking they were on the verge long after the fact? It seemed the latter was true in her mother's case. The former in her sister's. In Jesse's case – well…maybe everyone is crazy to one degree or another, but no one else Jesse knew was crazy in the same way that she was…

***

In her sleep there were dreams. And memories:

Jesse remembered standing on the shore of a small estuary on the south side of the strait, but she couldn't recall how she got there. It was darker than dark. Just before dawn. And it was drizzling rain. Soaking wet up to her butt and beyond, she had shivered while looking out over the broad expanse of ever-moving water, wondering if it might have been just a little piratey to send the Chartreuse to the bottom of the strait when it would've been so much easier to just set it afire and let it drift away, a boatful of flaming guilt riding the tide.

Numb with cold, she had been as awkward as a club-footed loon clambering into the dinghy to make her escape. Barely got off the boat with her wits intact. Would have been easy enough to drag the cunt's body to the forward cabin before paddling away, she thought, lock them in together; but she hadn't taken even that simple precaution…

That would've been the thing to do, the voice said, whispery and loaded with a heavy dash of petulance, *instead of pacing back and forth from cabin to galley, looking at them as if you expected them to suddenly jump up alive and pissed off.*

"I only did what I had to do," Jesse said aloud, her head spinning. "What needed doing."

Yes, of course. No other choice.

"Can't believe that I did it – both of them! But once I started I couldn't stop myself."

You forgot to lock the cabin door. He'll probably get loose. She will for sure.

The pain behind her eyes intensified and Jesse imagined a wavering cushion of hot air building up over churning water. Here it comes…the awful hissing fire, she thought, massaging her skull and bracing herself for another soul-splitting onslaught; a spreading inferno looking to burn her and getting ever hotter. She clamped her eyes closed and slowly turned her head from side to side while holding her throbbing temples tight, sorting it all out, sloughing away memories and looking for the sweet spot that hurt infinitesimally less than the rest.

It was simple, the way she'd planned to do it: lure the old coot below deck with the never-fail promise of illicit sex and kill him in the master suite with uncut cocaine – or rather, let him kill himself. He was an old fart, so she figured a couple of lines would probably do the job. She was willing to fuck him to kick-start him if she absolutely had to. But he was very old, always griping about his medical conditions, and she figured a little hardcore flirting would send him to dirty-old-man heaven with a smile on his face.

And then the idiot wouldn't even touch the coke!

She remembered stabbing the holy shit out of him. Her too, the bitch just refusing to give it up – had to admire her for that…but Christ!

Then sinking the fancy fucking motor yacht and paddling the inflatable ashore like a castaway. Everything as frantic as a Keystone Cops cartoon with only one cop.

She wanted to laugh out loud but whatever mirth there was inside her seemed calcified and stuck there. Still, the whole thing had been such a farce – everything that was supposed to be easy-peasy lemon-squeezy going straight to hell the moment the woman showed up. Timing is everything when death is the game.

Just like Pablo the supermarket boy? the voice said, an intentional chafe exactly on-target. *Unless you'd prefer not to think about him. No need to remember Pablo. Not if it's painful…*

Jesse refused to think about the supermarket boy or any other incident from her past. It would be too much right now. Right now she had to gather her wits because she knew that when they became scattered they were like clouds before the wind, leaving her entirely empty inside; a hollow vessel, purged but unclean, with little say regarding what may fill it next.

Her breath became shallow and her eyelids fluttered.

Then she found it – the spot, and she lay perfectly still and straight, curling her toes until her feet cramped, pressing her temples with her fingertips until her knuckles ached.

Everything went blissfully quiet. A few moments of sleep…

Chapter 4

It was after midnight, late as hell for Hoot, who was exhausted but still buzzing from the day's events. Shooting someone has a way of tweaking the nerves, after all – even if you're Ezra Hooten the infamous Troubleshooter and you have a reputation. But it was early by LA standards; a city of people constantly on the move, so it was no surprise the Latitude 33 Lounge at the LAX Marriott was a busy lair of vagabond travelers by the time Hoot and Jesse Vega managed to get away from their lethal action debriefing. They claimed a shadowy booth toward the back of a spacious atrium-style seating area and sat side-by-side on a supple red leather cushion, flickering candles providing ambiance while lush tropical plant arrangements nearby offered a degree of concealment from potentially curious patrons.

Several large television monitors were mounted in strategic locations designed to be visible throughout the bar, and they alternated sports clips with news footage featuring the In-flight Shootout Between Homeland Security Sky Marshals and a Cartel Hitman, as the day's excitement was being hyped by the media, making Hoot very conscious of the possibility other patrons might recognize them. With his distinctive appearance it was always a challenge for Hoot to remain incognito after something like this, but no one was looking.

Other booths around Latitude 33's perimeter were equally intimate, the center area containing a scattering of occupied tables with comfortable-looking chairs where flyers on-the-go could grab a quick bite and a drink or two if time allowed. Several people were perched at the bar near the entrance. A few couples and small groups. Mostly singles. YouTube vignettes; flyers zipped in for a quick one and right back out again. Hoot understood the underlying wave action of these patrons. Stragglers from the greater gaggle of holiday nomads, they had surrendered to and were moved by powerful forces – shuttle buses, itineraries and boarding passes – they were like zombies on speed. At this hour they were mostly layovers and cross-country redeye flyers. Several were business flyers. Hoot knew that most didn't give a damn about anything other than their schedules, about getting there. Good for them, he thought, as if he gave a miniature shit about any of them.

That was rude. Must be all the liquor I'm consuming, Hoot decided with little consideration for the ten months of stone-cold sobriety he'd just thrown aside. Prior to mounting the wagon he'd been able to drink just about everyone else under the table since his army days, so, though admittedly flirting with the dark side of the force, he knew from hard-earned experience that his screw-it-all attitude had little if anything to do with liquor.

Maybe I do give a shit and that's my fucking problem, he thought. He raised a small heavy-bottomed shot glass up to the candlelight, admired the oily look of distilled blue agave inside, and then relished the heat as he tipped the glass and let the liquid slide down his throat, thinking; I've given it up before – lots of times – I'll be damned if I can remember the reasons, but I'll bet I can do it again. No Diet Coke for me tonight!

The thing about being a seasoned liquor aficionado at large, as Hoot liked to refer to himself, meaning without affiliation to anyone's multi-step program, was that there was nobody hanging around to be disappointed in him while simultaneously swearing out the other side of their mouths it was okay. There was nobody waiting only a phone call away to talk reasonably with him, to reassure him. There was only himself. So the question always boiled down to; was he disappointed in himself?

Fuckit…he could be disappointed in himself later. Now was no time for a certified troubleshooter to sober up. Now was the time for hard liquor and lots of it.

Still, the thought nudged him in the ribs: Ten months! A wispy thought without traction like smoke on a light breeze, gone by the time it was noticed – almost a record.

A smile played at the corners of Hoot's mouth, not falling for his own bullshit as he shared a few of the more palatable details of his less-than-stellar career in the US Marshals Service with Jesse Vega. This would be the Cliff's Notes version of his life, paring the saga of a twenty-eight-year manhunt for his nemesis and onetime best friend, Norman Carpenter, down to "I'd get close, and he'd vanish again." It was a story he seldom shared, and never in any detail; the resulting hubbub about him either highly exaggerated or entirely false.

"Until?" Jesse prompted, touching Hoot's arm in a surprisingly soft, feminine, and almost coquettish way.

"Until the last time. Until he was dead and I wasn't."

"The infamous Troubleshooter, US Marshal Ezra Hooten, taking him down in the end," Jesse said, leaning-in closer, her voice dropping a decibel, a significant amount of added eye contact.

Here it comes, Hoot thought. The young babe flirting with the old guy because she figures he's a safe bet. Lather him up a little and then put him away with a peck on the cheek and a shot of Maalox.

"Did you always get your man? Or woman?" she asked with a gleaming smirk.

Yes, she was definitely flirting with him. And she was playing it both ways, switching tack from hapless heroine mode to butch bitch and back again in the blink of an eye, her ego playing games with his.

Of course she had been there for the bloodletting on the plane even if she hadn't pulled the trigger. Close enough to feel the bullet's breath as it passed? Certainly close enough to get the buzz. Sharing this experience was like sharing dope – freebasing adrenalin.

With a sudden rush of macho enthusiasm Hoot realized that he liked the way Jessica Vega walked the line, pushing buttons as she passed. He was starting to like her a lot, the way her attention to him made the ol' inner stud stand up and flex its hormonal pecs. Made him think, You haven't lost it yet, old timer. Okay…so a bit more honestly, maybe it had been a while since he'd caught the eye of a woman if you didn't count his ever-warming but absolutely non-romantic, friendship with Maddie Marvel the past year, but there had once been a time when Ezra Hooten got his fair share of female attention.

"Not always," Hoot answered Jesse's slightly-barbed query, thinking; She's a prickly one, no doubt one of those liberal hotties with her hackles up for alpha men on principle, a woman in earnest competition with all the cocks-n-balls in the world ever since preschool.

Looking into her eyes, he could see that Jesse had the BQ – the big question – on her lips, the Is everything down there still working? question that always seemed to slip into the conversation in one way or another by experienced women nowadays, the question that was usually encountered and dissected early in the sizing-up part of any potential relationship even if it isn't actually asked in so many words. But instead of boldly going there the way he expected she would do, with a lowering of eyes that seemed more evasive than coy to Hoot she said; "So…once that lifelong chase was finished – ending up with your girlfriend's ghost killing her killer if I understand it correctly – you simply turned in your star just like that?" snapping her fingers to emphasize the degree of her incredulousness.

Delighted by the way Jesse had cut straight through the bullshit to the nut of the matter, Hoot smiled at her quick rendering of the comedy of errors constituting his life story and said; "Wasn't a hard choice. Once my belly caught the pointy end of Norman Carpenter's knife my career in the field was over. Bosses had been looking for a way to retire me for a long time, anyhow, and getting wounded at my age fit the bill perfectly. Sure, I could've requested light duty, but my pension was already vested so I didn't need the hours, and for me the idea of giving up fugitive apprehension for courtroom protection and serving routine bench warrants had very little sex appeal – too much like giving the old guy an old guy's job."

"Yeah. I get the sex appeal part," Jesse Vega said with a lick of salt, shot of tequila and bite of lime. Her navy blue blazer set aside on the red leather cushion since they arrived, a button on Jesse's blouse seemed to have lost its grip after they started drinking shots, leaving the top two buttons undone and revealing a much bolder show of shallow-but-tempting cleavage to Hoot during the performance of her salt and lime ritual.

Smooth brown curves and a pronounced collarbone. A teasing display of flesh suggesting all kinds of unsaid possibilities. No evidence of a bra in sight, Hoot wondered; when did she slip out of it? And why? Discomfort perhaps…or simply more overt flirting, preferring the latter. He knew he'd be squirming like a worm on a hook if he were strapped into one of the god-awful things all day, but somehow doubted if comfort had much to do with Jesse losing hers.

He caught a whiff of her aroma. She smelled good. Fresh. Something light and herbal with a subtle hint of coconut oil. Something that would undoubtedly smell even better if she were lying nude in the sun on an exotic beach. Yes – there was a mental picture instantly burned into Hoot's archival mind like hot celluloid film caught in a projector, Jesse giving him another loaded glance with those dark chocolate eyes. Keep it up, girl, and you'll be getting the answer to that unasked question real soon, he thought.

"What I don't get," she said, "is why you're still hanging around in law enforcement, still carrying a gun, and still putting yourself in harm's way for a FAMS paycheck instead of doing private work? Corporate or personal security? Or P-I work? Good money there and most of the legwork is Internet-based now."

"Fair question," Hoot replied. But one without a simple answer he thought to himself, the all-too-recent excitement of shooting a bad guy in-flight still practically ringing in his ears, similar incidents preceding this one hanging like grinning skeletons in the closet of his career.

He said, "I've considered private work. Maybe I'll do that. Get licensed and give it a try if this air marshal gig goes south over today's incident. It seems to have become a theme of mine over the years: I'll shoot somebody, doesn't really matter who, or what the circumstances are, and then the shitstrings that are inevitably attached to the incident never break off. They just keep growing, getting more and more tangled with all the other shitstrings that came before. Unfortunately, law enforcement and fishing are the only two things I have marketable experience with. I'm no salesman. And I'm too damned dumb to troubleshoot computers. The art of soldiering has moved into the twenty-first century without me – my lack of experience with gear like drones and live-feed video making me too damned outdated to do the paramilitary thing and become a Third

World mercenary. But I'm not quite ready to cash-in my chips yet. The hitch is that I seem to have what career counselors have long referred to as a very narrow skill set."

Hoot considered his fixer-upper cabin near Port Timothy on the Strait of Juan de Fuca and added; "They're right about that you know, about my skills. I certainly have none for carpentry, as I've recently found out, though I remain a firm believer that any fool can learn to do almost anything with enough effort and a little research.

"How about you, Mizz Jesse James Vega? I could ask you the same thing. About staying in, I mean."

"It's different for me. From my vantage point, I'm not as close to the gold-plated watch and attaboy party as you. Don't have the time invested."

From her vantage point? So many years younger than him – Hoot wondered; was that really all it was in the end…just time invested?

"You know…earlier," Jesse said, "when we were on the plane and all the shit happened? I heard the commotion behind me and barely got turned around in time to see you standing up. Then… Then I swear to God I've never seen anyone draw and shoot so fast in my life." She cocked her head, seeming to refresh her appraisal of him with a measuring glance, and added in a sincere voice, "If I hadn't seen it with my own eyes I would have sworn it wasn't possible."

Something in Jesse Vega's body language screamed a message that Hoot couldn't quite read; shock, or maybe even anger? The suddenness of the whole incident on the plane had obviously caught her off guard. Hell, his bullet had probably passed within two inches of her head; that would rattle just about anybody.

"Time becomes warped under pressure," Hoot stated flatly. "You know that."

"I know what I saw. That's what I know," Jesse said, the expression on her face anything but certain. To Hoot's eyes the expression he saw in hers was defiantly defiant. Angry, the way people accustomed to life on the front line tend to channel their fear into anger. "I guess you really are a genuine troubleshooter, a modern-day Wyatt Earp in the sky," she added with a new edge lurking in the sultry folds of her voice.

Taking another long glance at his randomly-assigned partner for the day, Hoot's eyes eventually locked without reservation on Jesse's brazen show of cleavage. An ordinary-looking stainless steel dog tag chain drawing his attention to shadowy cinnamon-brown curves with no detectable tan lines – no aversion or coy pretension of shy modesty there. Cabernet-colored silk complemented her skin tone, the whole show giving a subtle new meaning to the term natural attributes.

He raised his eyes to hers and said, "No, I'm not really that guy, the man-of-action guy…"

Silence ensued while Jesse Vega gave Hoot another of her overtly-appraising looks; the confrontational, primal kind of look that conveys all sorts of messages subject to being interpreted incorrectly. Hell, the woman practically oozed pheromones!

Breaking eye contact and the smoldering silence with it, Hoot said, "Here's to the quick-draw cowboys of the Old West. May they never die!" throwing back another shot of tequila followed by the usual ritual.

Honestly, aside from Saturday afternoon matinees when he was a kid, Hoot had no particular affinity for quick-draw cowboys, and he wore his reputation more like a hard-earned hairshirt than a crowning achievement. He had learned to kill in Vietnam and brought the skill home with him – those were the only old days he had ever laid any claim to. He recalled that he had preferred orange slices to limes with his tequila back in those old days, sliding into more conventional tastes during the neverending-chase days when shit happened all the time. But this was the new Hoot in a new world. And these were the endless-surveillance-while-in-flight days where shit was never supposed to happen but it did anyhow – for Hoot, at least, it always did.

Toeing the line! Limes are fine! Hoot thought, knowing that rhyming was a bad sign, a sure indication of impending severe inebriation. Worse, a hillbilly ballad was taking shape in his mind and he imagined himself playing tambourine on stage with Susan Tedeschi and Derek Trucks – oh yeah…he was definitely getting drunk!

Hit us again, bartender, please, he thought, Air Marshal Jessica Vega matching him drink-for-drink.

"I never cared much for that nickname, Troubleshooter."
Hoot said after he and Jesse had contributed to a significant spike in
the need for vast acres of agave plants. "Wears me out when I hear it.
I'm actually the quiet type at heart. A good book and fishing pole
kind of guy. Recreational time-wasting was my assumed forté going
into retirement. This was before I bought my cabin. Now it's all
about roof leaks and moss control. Plumbing. Not so sexy, huh?"

They had started off their post-debriefing tête-à-tête drinking
vodka martinis on the rocks – the smoky kind consisting of ice-cold
Absolut vodka over ice, a bare splash of house scotch, and a thin
lemon twist – before moving on to tequila shots. Hoot wasn't sure
how much liquor they had put away so far, but he was very much
aware that he was into at least his forth tequila cruda and he had a
pretty good buzz going.

Ten dry months!

It seemed that Hoot had a few empty places to fill.

Ten months! He thought again, a simmering sense of shame
trying to pop his bubble. Too late to start feeling remorseful now,
Hoot figured. Best to go ahead and wallow in it because guilt is still
guilt in the end, so make it count, as his father had so often said.
Gone to his greater rewards twenty years ago, it was only recently
that Hoot had begun to miss the ol' man's regurgitating repository of
dark-side-of-the-force gems – the Tao of Dad.

Steering his attention back to the matter at hand, Jesse James
Vega was starting to look prettydamned good to him in spite of her
overstated lack of softness, her blunt lack of charm balanced against
smoldering sexuality. She was a scarred woman, obviously, and she
wore it proudly, although in the candlelight Hoot couldn't even see
the actual scar on Jesse's face without looking right at it, and her
mesmerizing eyes were loitering entirely too nearby to allow much of
that. Besides, she had other attractive attributes that stole his
attention, a pair of them still making a tantalizing display of
prominence pressing against semi-sheer silk, A-cup cleavage stealing
the show with the smoothly-unnoticed release of those two strategic
buttons.

One more button and I may dive in headfirst right now.
Right here in this booth, he thought. And then as if reading his mind
and holding Hoot's gaze with her witchy eyes, Jesse brazenly and

lasciviously unfastened a third button on her blouse and adjusted the collar, a quick flash of bare nipple confirming beyond doubt that she was not wearing the black lace bra she'd started the day with.

This was all the sign Hoot needed. It was time to wrap up the evening...

Breaking Jesse's gaze, Hoot felt a surge of restlessness in his gut, the adrenaline spike from taking a life mixed with liquor making a volatile combination that was about to ignite. He might explode soon, he thought, with widespread collateral damage. Understanding that his ability to hold his liquor (though obviously still formidable) wasn't quite what it used to be, and willing to concede that it was probably a good thing, it was getting near what old-timers in his line of work, soldiers, lawmen, and other manly men who worked dangerous jobs sometimes referred to as the score-or-call-a-whore hour.

Had to include the gals, nowadays, Hoot thought, giving his inner self an enlightened slap after clearly seeing a gleam in Jesse's eyes.

"Truthfully, I'd grown tired of hunting for scumbags long before the worst of them stabbed me," he said.

Reaching one hand inside Jesse's open blouse, he cupped a warm breast in his pale hand as if it were the most natural and appropriate thing to do in the world. It felt good, as if an ultra-high level of intimacy was somehow hardwired into this moment, a pre-destined moment of connection that neither of them could ignore...so, why try?

Seeming to read his thoughts, Jesse leaned into the touch, encouraging Hoot to pinch her nipple with an increasing degree of firmness. Her cheek brushed against his, her breath warm on his neck. They drifted into the faintest whisper of a lingering kiss; one that deepened, becoming a tongue-to-tongue duel. It was one of those moments – one of those reckless, lust-driven moments. Hungry with an all-consuming desire like a couple of sex-crazed teenagers, they threw off their remaining inhibitions, and in their shadowy booth, time stretched.

Then abruptly breaking away, they avoided eye contact while attempting to repair their mutual dishevelment; Jesse turning aside and re-buttoning her blouse while Hoot waved toward the bar, summoning the tab.

Scrambling to gather his wits, he said in an awkward attempt at humor while waiting for their waitress to appear; "Back in Seattle I keep reading The Stranger classified job ads; figure maybe I could grab a gig as a high-dollar gigolo."

He laughed a humorless laugh, the kind that sounds more like a bark than a laugh, and added; "This from the same fool who, two months after leaving his hospital bed, his new scar still fresh and purple, applied to FAMS for a job as a fucking sky marshal? Crazy, huh? You asked me why? I can't begin to tell you. Won't even try."

"The gigolo idea sounds interesting," Jesse offered. "You'll need references…"

Hoot repeated his brief bark of a laugh, but with more humor this time, said, "Lots of references." His fingers, twitching slightly, seemed to yearn with a will of their own to return to her breast.

"From satisfied repeat clients," Jessie offered in a husky voice while Hoot handed his credit card to their bemused waitress.

Even though Jesse's enticing feminine assets were now concealed, Hoot had seen them. And he had touched them. What's more, her slightest movement against the semi-sheer cloth that was supposedly hiding them actually made them even more noticeable. Utterly mesmerizing. He could feel a carnal smile growing on his face. It had started in the crow's feet at the corners of his eyes with a familiar to-the-victor-go-the-spoils feeling, and now that feeling was traveling a slow, warm path southward like lava from a supposedly extinct volcano, heading all the way to his toes by way of his groin.

"And a good website…" he finally said, distracted.

"Or you could just spend the last couple years of your law-enforcement career winding down at a slower pace, traveling around on FAMS' dime and seeing the sights," she offered with a broad smile, a loaded twinkle in her impossibly dark eyes. "Nothing wrong with that. It's what I'm doing." She placed a twenty-dollar bill on the table to cover the tip.

"Except it's a lie," Hoot said, standing and gathering their coats along with what was left of his highly-inebriated wits. "Or at least it's a stretch. Airports are prettymuch all I've seen since joining FAMS. Airports and hotels. Mostly assorted Marriott's and Hyatt's."

"…Or lesser accommodations," Jesse finished as if reading from the regulations.

She stood and stepped in closer to Hoot. Close enough to touch. Close enough to share breath. She put her hand on his chest over his heart, looked up into his eyes, and said in a flirtatious, quasi-teasing tone, "But Ezra Hooten the famous Troubleshooter is no quitter, right?"

Touching Jesse's bare breast only moments ago had caused a lingering reaction in Hoot's trousers. And now her touch in return caused movement down there combined with a heroin-high sort of testosterone rush, pleasant but uncomfortably insistent. As sure as sunrise, he could feel himself being drawn into one of those inevitable macho rituals of the sort that he admittedly had been somewhat addicted to throughout his arrogant youth and obstinate middle age.

Easily predictable; a man, or a woman for that matter, kills someone or is close-by when violent Death rears its awful head, and immediately feels the urge to fuck. It's the rape-and-pillage instinct; all very sensible from a historical/psychological point-of-view, a hard-wired hormonal and seminal release without concern for the downside, a prehistoric survival instinct triggered for the propagation of the species. Call it what you will…it happens – often enough in Hoot's case to largely serve his declining manly needs. And it was happening to him right now. He couldn't remember when he'd last felt this horny.

"I decided I'd give it an honest try – sky marshalling," he said, getting caught up once more in Jesse's dark and flirtatious eyes, his words rambling as he leaned back for another lingering look: she was a small woman, tight, over a foot shorter than Hoot without her heels. He took in the way her torso tapered past her athletic shoulders and her boldly-on-display breasts to her slender waist. Below were legs that looked like they were probably fast. Very fast.

Goddamned woman…not shy, are ya? he thought, watching Jesse toss an errant coal black curl aside in order to better observe him through a shoulder-length hairstyle he was beginning to see as more suited to a stripper than a sky marshal.

She looked him in the eye, holding his glance, unflinching, and he could see that she knew exactly what she was doing to him. Furthermore, she knew that she was doing it very well...

"Figured I'd see if I could cram thirty years of field experience and instinct for the criminal element into the cramped confines of what I confess I think of as a big fucking bus with wings," Hoot said, struggling to continue some semblance of adult conversation with his very exotic sky marshal partner, not quite understanding why Jesse had such a profound ability to affect him the way she did other than the usual shell-shock of lethal action, of course. He wondered if he might be experiencing early-onset DOMS, Dirty Old Man Syndrome and found the thought highly amusing.

"You're new. You'll get used to it," she said.

He smiled. Used to what? The constant flying? The airports and hotels? Hoot was thinking he wasn't so sure that he would ever get used to it while he and Jesse Vega crossed the hotel lobby to the elevators, the sexual tension between them nearly palatable. Thinking that the first part of any fling is the best part and it always gets pushed aside rushing-in for the rest.

A clinical ding! announced the arrival of the elevator.

The door opened, and Hoot entered the cozy suspended box after Jesse.

The door closed with barely a sound and suddenly they were alone...together.

"My room, okay?" Hoot asked, his finger hesitating over the elevator control panel.

Jesse's answer was to turn around and face him.

Reaching up, her arms were suddenly and insistently around him. Her fingers in his hair. Her lips on his lips...

Chapter 5

It was dark, drizzly, and cold under a heavy sky: still a couple of
hours before daybreak, and the yacht's inflatable dinghy floated low
on the water. Jesse shivered and willed herself to stop it because she
knew from experience that shivering didn't help. It did no good to
tremble, and even less to start leaping to dire conclusions about shit
you could do nothing about when it was happening: things like cold
or heat, hunger or thirst, getting raped or just getting fucked. Better
to focus on doing something practical about your situation, basic
jarhead survival training coming in handy evermore – Ooh-rah!

Considering her situation, Jesse mentally marked her position
and the relative location of the sinking motor yacht by using the
flashing Diamond Point lighthouse beacon and a rough triangulation
of lights low on the distant Canadian shoreline. She turned south,
rowing for the nearer shoreline nearly a mile away while watching the
big boat sink until it disappeared; a watery magic trick in slow
motion, finally taking the bodies of Harold Hesse and Suzy
Wickerman down with it...at least for a while.

Good riddance, the voice in Jesse's head said without a trace of
remorse.

Jesse had watched the Chartreuse sink knowing that her
fingerprints and who-knows-what other evidence were undoubtedly
all over it, some little something that she might have left behind.

It would've been impossible to clean the whole goddamned
thing, anyhow; blood from bow to stern, it was an enormous floating
fingerpost pointing directly at her and practically screaming Culprit!
Culprit! She had thought about setting the boat afire and simply
burning everything, but knew even that would leave clues.

Furthermore, setting a boat that size afire in the middle of the strait would've been certain to draw quick attention. So she took a shotgun from the master suite down to the bilge compartment in the engine room and blew three sizeable holes in the epoxy-ferrocement hull. Not as easy a task as she had hoped it would be, it took a half box of shells to do it; shotgun pellets dangerously ricocheting this way and that, but still a lot more discreet than a burning fuel slick, she thought.

It had to be done, the voice said, don't fret. All reason and tact, the usual whiny childlike tone stowed away for the time being.

I know it had to be done. Doesn't mean that I liked it.

Sure you did...

"Just shut up and let me row, will you!" Jesse said aloud, shivering, focusing her attention on a landmark on the Canadian side of the strait and putting her back to work pulling the too-small oars, the inflatable dinghy awkwardly making for an uncertain landing spot still a good distance away on the US side.

You didn't even close the cockpit door! That boat's gonna puke-up evidence all the way down to the bottom of the channel. Wait and see. And don't forget this stupid little raft, the voice reminded her. *It's certain to be found...*

The dinghy? Yes; there was that, obviously. Plus, the voice was right; who knows what else the boat might've let go while it was sinking? Loose stuff. The woman's body, left on the cockpit floor with the door wide open, would undoubtedly escape eventually if it hadn't already.

Jesse's eyes kept darting over the surface of the water surrounding the inflatable as if expecting the aging beauty queen to pop up with a big splash and wave bon voyage as the dinghy passed by. She didn't see the expected specter or anything incriminating float to the surface, but nonetheless knew that she was making a huge investment in luck. It had been stupid to sink the boat without taking time to better secure the woman's body, maybe drag it to the forward cabin with the old man's, except she was unwilling to touch their bloody carcasses afterward. She could stab the holy shit out of them until they were as dead as they would ever be, but was repulsed by the resulting mess.

It had been that way with the grocery boy, too, she remembered, the horror of what she was doing always so

43

overwhelming in the commitment of the act that she went blind to it. Blind and mute, and absolutely focused on silencing the scream building in her head; she was a deadly puppet at the end of unseen strings. And then later – what a cartoon! Inevitably unable to remember the details of her fury, everything afterward was always an off-the-cuff performance to cover the blunders she'd made. In short: Jesse was a sloppy murderess. Deadly but sloppy. And lucky…so far.

Never underestimate the power of Dumb Fucking Luck, she thought; knowing with a growing sense of fatalism that she was testing the limit of hers.

***

Jesse spied a cove on the shadowy south bank of the strait just as dawn broke dripping wet and dreary. There were a few desolate piles sticking out of the water where a long-ago pier had once stood, now a rotted leggy ghost. There were no occupied-looking structures or other signs of life in sight. She thought she recognized this place though she'd never seen it from the water before. Near the mouth of the Pysht River, it was perfect; out-of-the way. A long-abandoned lumber mill hunkered on the shore behind a shallow bar that had undoubtedly been left un-dredged for ages, making it difficult for boats much bigger than the dinghy to negotiate a way in.

Jesse landed the dinghy. Dismounting the awkward craft, her back ached from rowing, but otherwise she was numb with cold from her lips to her toes. Knowing she had little time before full light and would need to stay hidden until she reconnoitered the area, she scrambled for cover. Her feet sucking bucketfuls of squishy muck with every step she took, roots and low branches grabbing at her, she struggled to pull the rubber inflatable back into a brushy area where errant fishermen were unlikely to wander, Mother Earth herself seeming to throw up resistance in order to protect the delicate ebb and flow of good and evil at the mouth of the Pysht.

Ridiculous fucking dinghy! Jesse thought. Chartreuse, Eagle Creek Marina, Port Timothy WA, was painted in white on its red doughnut rim. Had her grandmother's Wusthof not been stuck like Excalibur in the old man's back Jesse would've gladly stabbed the holy shit out of the dinghy. Instead, curbing her nerves, she concentrated on hiding the painted part especially well.

There might be snakes, the voice said, regaining its irritating whine.

There are no snakes, Jesse thought with firm resolve. Not poisonous ones at least… Not this time of year… But the voice was fucking with her. It knew how to get her wound up, and a corner of her fertile imagination worried about them anyhow.

Snakes – they slithered, and she hated them.

Frogs were okay, long as they kept their distance – there were bound to be frogs.

And slugs – awful slugs…

Maybe leeches, too. There was no way of knowing what might be lurking nearby in the shadowy wetness. But it was mostly disgust and not fear that she felt; Jesse was actually afraid of very little, and the peninsula backwoods was her backyard. With a little effort she set her worry about all the creepy-crawly possibilities in the area aside and dragged over more camouflage.

***

After the in-flight incident and the debriefing that followed, and after de-stressing from it with Jesse at Latitude 33, Hoot put his impending hangover on autopilot and awoke early Sunday morning from a familiar nightmare – the one where he was struggling to cross a shallow Cambodian river, his M-21 sniper rifle clutched in one hand, a burning bullet hole in his side, and his best friend over his shoulder. But instead of gaining ground, the far bank was getting farther away, the fetid water deepening. He expected to die soon and was comforted by the thought, wanting nothing more than to fall to his knees and get it over with. Instead, in a headachy flash of consciousness he raised his head from his Marriott pillow and looked at the bedside clock. Digital numerals glowed 3:55 AM. He reached over and shut off the alarm before it buzzed at 4.

Jesse Vega stirred beside him and rolled over. Pressing her bulletlike nipples into the middle of his back, her fingers idly toyed with the sparse patch of white hair on his chest before wandering southward to see if anything was happening down there with the little marshal. There wasn't, but soon would be if she kept at it.

"Getting tired yet?" she whispered, her warm and slippery tongue following her words into his ear.

This brought a smile to Hoot's face along with vivid memories of last night's marathon. A whirlwind of activity had greeted them as soon as the jet touched down in LA where the situation was much worse than he'd expected. It had been a TSA circus. Ringling Brothers and Barnum & Bailey on the tarmac thanks to the unavailability of space in a large-enough hangar away from the public's eyes to deplane. Passengers were herded out of aircraft emergency exits in clear view of the North Satellite Terminal; not empty of passengers as advised because terminal security personnel had hopped right to it per their practiced protocol and cleared the South Satellite Terminal for emergency action, standing guard like traffic cones over there instead of being on hand for crowd control where the crowd actually was. Combined with the near-criminal encroachment of the media, the result was the whole unfiltered news-frenzy fiasco of what had started out being called an Attempted Hijacking Foiled in-Flight being quickly revised to Terror in US Airspace buzzing all over the Internet before the last passenger had cleared security. And then it had turned into a late-night fuckfest when Jesse accompanied him to his room at the Marriott, shut the door, and pushed him toward the bed.

Evidently, the night wasn't over...

The woman is insatiable, Hoot thought, his smile growing as Jesse reached under the sheet and gently moved the little marshal aside in order to fondle the posse wide awake. She's either trying to kill me or jump-start me!

Lots of people were like that. He knew this from long experience; the adrenalin rush from close proximity to danger cranking-up all the animal instincts, especially the sexual ones, he was one of them himself, certifiable. Some, he knew, had a fuck-like-crazy-and-forget-it attitude about dealing with the effects of using lethal force. Liquor helped. Drugs for some. But for Hoot, even with the liquor and hot sex taking the edge off, winding down from an incident also meant replaying the whole scene over and over in his mind. Repeatedly. Until it made sense – or not. In this particular case:

The assassin with his carbon-fiber garrote. The single shot. All the second thoughts that he had instinctively held at bay during the heat of the action. The over-the-top hubbub afterward – six hours of it! It was a movie that wouldn't stop looping. And, try as he might, he couldn't make any of it make sense. It just didn't.

Hoot turned over on his side to look at Jesse Vega. Saw her face peeking out of a tangle of bed sheets and blankets looking back at him in the half-light coming from the bathroom vanity. She was still wearing her Marine Corps dog tags regulation-style with one hanging below the other on a short toe chain. He recalled from last night (when he was on his back and she was on top) there was a small brass key hanging with the tag on the short chain, and he wondered what it was that she kept locked up...her heart? He was about to ask when she started to turn away, but he touched the scar on her cheek with his fingertips and she stopped, giving him a penetrating glance.

"That's a significant scar," he said.

And not a new one, he thought, wondering why she hadn't had it corrected with surgery. He lightly stroked the skin; the tissue smooth but irregular, it felt like melted plastic. Hoot had his own scars, plenty of them, all with that same alien smoothness and disconnected numbness, but nothing as large, and certainly not as noticeable as this. A scar like this one must've come with a shitload of pain.

"How did you get it?" he asked.

"It's a long story," Jesse replied, a dark expression passing through her eyes before she looked away, veiling them, "and I don't know if we have time for it."

"We've got plenty of time," Hoot said, very much aware of the little marshal stirring and stretching his only muscle. "You suggesting time is short because of our appointment with the regional director this morning?"

Jesse got out of bed and walked, stark naked, toward the bathroom. Naked, but not precisely feminine – she was nimble-looking instead. Very muscular, with narrow hips. Her figure was boyish except for her small, surprisingly soft-to-the-touch breasts capped with weaponlike nipples. She had sparse, kinky, black-as-coal pubic hair. And she sported an elaborate Celtic tattoo of a winged Z on her upper right arm and shoulder.

Hoot, watching her walk, noticed how the only thing even slightly jiggling was her hairdo, her taut body reminding him that he was a grandfather, that he had changed the diapers and powdered the bottoms of girls Jesse's age long before they became her age. A big age difference between them, him and Jesse…*big*.

She smiled a wicked smile over her tattooed shoulder and said, "You're right – we have plenty of time."

***

The LAX Homeland Security office wasn't nearly as busy at 10:00am on Sunday morning as it was most days, but it was hardly empty – especially not today. The mission a 24/7 commitment and FAMS just one component of Homeland Security, the office was a constant din of activity 365 days a year, computer monitors and fluorescent lighting giving the whole place a US government business lack of coziness. Phones ringing. The low murmur of overlapping conversations. Yesterday's incident still sparking a considerable amount of buzz; the static energy from it lingered everywhere.

"Ezra Monroe Hooten?" the Southwestern District Federal Air Marshal Service director, Leland Popejoy, read from a page on his desk, the inflection in his voice making Hoot suspect that his name must have confused the man. Wouldn't be the first time. Hoot had plenty of experience with so-called lethal force incident reviews like this one. Knew them to be ass-chewing sessions, and this was shaping up to be a good one. His immediate superior, Silas Wilson had flown in from Seattle and was present with the enigmatic Mr. Kenneth.

"…Staff Sergeant Hooten," Director Popejoy corrected himself, stressing Hoot's military rank as if to highlight that he had obviously not been officer material. Not quite up to snuff his ol' man would've said with a heavy application of coastal Maine sarcasm. "US Army Green Beret sniper code-named…Troubleshooter? Number of confirmed kills classified," the director read. "Awarded the Silver Star twice, once with Valor for conspicuous courage in the face of enemy fire. All this preceding an exceptionally-long run as Deputy US Marshal Hooten, assigned mostly to Apprehension Division where you were also decorated. And reprimanded for bringing escapees back dead about as often as alive, it seems. And now you've become Air Marshal Hooten? That's one hell of a career!"

The FAMS director seemed to be genuinely incredulous, and finished reading Hoot's sheet with an audible phew. Hoot was near-incredulous too, at the accumulated titles of his life. Who could have possibly guessed what a gunslinger he'd turn out to be way back when he was an introverted teenager too damned unsure of himself to stick it out in college? When he was too dumb to marry the only girl he'd ever wholeheartedly loved, rushing off to war instead?

Smart kid- no brains, his father used to say. All these years later he still didn't quite seem to fit inside his own pale skin much of the time. His ex once told him that titles were only tags and people wore them like paper party hats, refolding them constantly. Linda was always trying to get him to refold his, to do something more domestic than wear a badge and pack a gun for a living, maybe go into sales – as cockamamie an idea as she'd ever had and she had certainly had some.

"I see you haven't been with FAMS for very long, Marshal Hooten," the director continued, digging deeper into the neat stack of papers on his desk, pausing now and then to read a bit.

Hoot stood before the director's enormous desk. Front and center and two steps back. Hoot's boss and Mr. Kenneth stood off to one side, observing everything and saying nothing. Waiting for her turn in the stocks, Jesse Vega stood off to the other side, an unreadable look on her face.

"Still fitting-in with us, I see. But you served a long stint with the US Marshals Service in a number of jurisdictions," the director continued. "Seems you had some bad luck with partners there...or they had bad luck with you? Says here that you were wounded in action and applied for early medical retirement before deciding to jump aboard here at FAMS and protect the flying public..."

He shuffled back through the file a ways, found the sought-after page, said, "You were...stabbed in the course of an apprehension in which the escapee was killed?"

"I suppose that's technically correct, sir," Hoot replied in a testy tone. "The knife was thrown. I caught the pointed end in my gut, making it a stab wound as opposed to a slicing one."

"Uh-huh. I see." The director paused. He either didn't realize Hoot was tweaking him or didn't care. His brow, devoid of any trace of humor or personality that might confirm he was a human being, was slightly furrowed as he continued. Hoot figured it was always precisely and exactly furrowed, pressed just like the crease in his trousers.

"These records aren't inconveniently classified like some of the military records are," Popejoy said, opening another file from a tidy pile. "If my math is correct, from the information here it appears that you brought in or helped to bring in a total of sixty-nine fugitives during your twenty-eight-year tenure in the US Marshals." He clasped his hands together over Hoot's files, fingers tightly laced together as if fervently praying for divine intervention in the course of performing an exorcism, said, "Sixty-nine! That's impressive. But I note that only forty of them were apprehended alive. Another impressive figure considering how only yesterday you drew your weapon while in-flight and shot a fleeing suspect in the back before your partner," he nodded toward Jesse, "could get to her feet to intervene or assist."

"The incident occurred out of sight behind her, sir," Hoot said, misunderstanding the director's remark to be a criticism of his partner's reflexes. "She reacted very quickly to the gunshot."

Jesse gave Hoot a hard glance then turned it toward Mr. Kenneth, her reaction appearing to be an unsaid query, making Hoot wonder what the fuck was going on here – something that could've been said last night but wasn't?

"You did this without commanding the suspect to halt before pulling the trigger or giving your partner a chance to intercept?" the director continued, his voice heavy, the cold silence in the office seeming to roar.

Hoot offered no response. Remembering the unfortunate ICE agent's blood spurting like a grotesque holiday fountain in the middle of the airplane, the term suspect became stuck in Hoot's craw, the director's high-horse tone telling him there was nothing he could possibly say at this time that would have enough muscle to move the man off whatever opinion of him he'd already brewed – or that had been brewed for him.

Hoot felt the silent weight of the others present, knowing that Leland Popejoy was just another dumb fucking hammer in a huge toolbox full of them. Someone else always did the swinging. He broke his glance away from his hapless boss and looked straight into Mr. Kenneth's eyes – eyes the color of coal – seeing absolutely nothing looking back.

Jesse remained standing aside, her expression inscrutable.

"Our mission at FAMS is to protect the flying public," the director continued as if incanting a solemn ritual. "Specifically, from terrorists who choose to exploit the vulnerability of innocent passengers on commercial airliners." The demon thus exorcised and supposedly cowering, the director unclasped his hands, his brow a bit less pressed. Seconds passed as he picked up and reconstructed his paperwork, apparently diligent in keeping the top of his desk as neat as a drill sergeant's skivvies. Truly, Leland Popejoy was a focused man. In his late fifties or early sixties, jowly but fit, tan, with stylishly layered blonde hair turned gray, he looked like a real-world recreation of Robert Redford. He wore a black suit with a dark red tie and he spoke with conviction. "This country is at war, Deputy Hooten. Every day, around the clock," he said in an authoritative tone as if making a PowerPoint presentation. "And every flight without incident is another victory for the Federal Air Marshal Service in that war."

Rah! Rah! Hoot thought. There should be background music. Flags flapping.

"Since our inception as a small part of US Customs in 1963, through our current and much larger role as the law enforcement arm of the TSA, only one suspect has ever been shot by a sky marshal – in 2005. And that was on the tarmac!" Director Popejoy said. "None on a plane in flight or even on a landed plane while passengers were boarded…until yesterday."

Cue a formation of Blue Angels roaring past overhead, Hoot thought, resisting a quick peek out the director's window to look for them as the man continued, "Victory without roughshod tactics or the need for deadly force is the goal we seek to attain. Do you understand that Marshal Hooten?"

A crescendo of cymbals and kettle drums hushed with Hoot's answer, "I do."

"After yesterday's demonstration, I have to tell you I am unconvinced of that," Popejoy said. "One shot? In the back? Bullet passing through the man's spinal cord, grazing his heart as it passed by, and stopping with some impact against the backside of his breastbone? You couldn't have put one in his leg? His ass, maybe? Better yet, somehow held him captive until the plane was safely landed?"

The director walked around his desk to Hoot's side and leaned against the front edge. Planting his toes not three feet away from Hoot's toes, he said, "The man was unarmed, Hooten! Unarmed!! The press hasn't started running with that little detail yet, but they will. And you have no idea how much it pisses me off that I'll be the one answering questions when they do. Bad enough that a few cell phones managed to slip away from us during the passenger debriefing. Pictures and video clips popping up on the internet, it was all over the network evening news by the time the last of the crew was off the damned plane!"

Detecting no sign of encouragement of any sort coming from either his boss or Mr. Kenneth, Hoot locked eyes with the director, said; "We knew all of this last night and discussed it during the lethal action debriefing. As I understood it, our main talking point was that the cartel hitman had shown himself to be a user of unconventional weapons by killing two passengers with, essentially, a piece of string, and that I was correct to assume he was armed and dangerous. Lethal force was appropriate. What has changed since last night?"

Leland Popejoy broke his stare to take a quick glance aside at Silas Wilson, a brief exchange of eye contact with Mr. Kenneth, then he squared his shoulders and returned to his own side of the desk, pausing as he sat down to minutely adjust the engraved nameplate heralding him the FAMS Southwest Regional Director standing like a miniature shield in his verbal joust with Hoot. "The talking points are fine," he said. "Just make sure you use them. My concern right now is with the action that made the talking points necessary."

"Air marshals are trained for this," Hoot said. "Training that stresses the importance of taking the best shot when it's afforded.

Plus the importance of hitting the intended target instead of unintentionally putting a hole in an airplane at 30,000 feet."

"FAMS training was specifically designed around terrorist and hijacker situations – typically standoff scenarios – not fleeing assassin scenarios," Silas Wilson offered as if pitching-in to build a consensus while the taciturn Mr. Kenneth offered nothing.

"Fleeing? Fleeing to where?" Hoot asked.

Ignoring Hoot's question, the regional director continued toward a climax he clearly felt entitled to, repeating; "The damned man was unarmed. Unarmed! Overnight, the publicity from this one incident is turning into a certified nightmare for FAMS. And it's going to get worse. Lawsuits from traumatized passengers haven't started rolling in yet and you can bet they certainly will. Just wait until the backlash from that hits the fan!"

Typical government bureaucrat, Hoot thought, in his mind reducing Director Leland Popejoy to an authority level roughly equivalent to a fungus. The man was as predictable as thunder after lightening, sitting at his desk and roiling up behind his nameplate, blowing idiot wind out his ass while making a career of pointing his finger at others, saying things like; "At the very least you have demonstrated a convincing argument for those who want to restrict us to using non-lethal ammunition. Hell of a mess you've stirred up…isn't it, Hooten?"

"I stirred up? What about two bloody contributions from a very nasty bad guy? The same nasty bad guy I expediently put down before he could hurt anyone else?"

"Have you seen the news, Hooten? That guy got maybe ten of his fifteen minutes of fame. You'll get all of yours…and more." He opened a drawer, tossed the latest copy of The Washington Post on the desk in front of Hoot, a bold headline reading Sky Marshal Sniper Codenamed Troubleshooter Shoots to Kill, and said; "This is what's all over the news now. Reporters scrambling to come up with an accurate count of your total career kills. Digging around in your Vietnam records. Far be it for any of them to mention that the Federal Air Marshal Service does not employ snipers! Do you realize The LA Times Online is already calling you Skyshooter? I don't like it. Not one bit."

"Neither do I," Hoot agreed, running his fingers through his hair. This was the first time he'd heard about his new nickname, but he knew immediately that it would stick.

"You will be on administrative leave while this incident is reviewed," the director said, closing the meeting. "For now, you have an appointment with Dr. Goode, one of our staff psychologists. Her office. Downtown. At noon. Don't miss it. Then you can hop a return flight to Seattle at your convenience. Just stay available."

"A psych evaluation?"

"It's routine. Part of the standard lethal action review. You should know the drill better than most, Hooten." The director moved his orderly pile of paper a few inches to the left, looked up at Jesse and said, "Vega, don't forget to check the duty roster on your way out. I believe you've been assigned an afternoon flight."

Routine? No attaboy. No good shooting, cowboy. Just you know the drill?

***

"Want me to call you later?" Jesse asked Hoot, stepping aside as they left the director's office together.

"Sure. Though I doubt you will," Hoot answered, a vague distrust for Jesse was growing in his gut side-by-side with lust, and he didn't quite know what to make of it.

"Life is like lobster" Hoot's grandfather used to say as if offering the ultimate pearl of wisdom – "Not something to trifle with. Nasty and mean, even. But sex it up with a little garlic and butter and it boils down to something great!"

Sex is the key, he would say – the old man often referred to as the horny Hooten.

Sex was a lifelong weakness of Hoot's; constantly interested in it, never very good at it…and unlikely at this point to get much better. The thought almost stopped him in his tracks. Hoot barely knew Jesse, but sexually she was already well-entrenched under his skin. Inside and out and on top of it as well, he thought; knowing what an unreliable bellwether sexual attraction was for any sort of relationship, even a sexual one.

"A fucking psych evaluation – again," he grumbled. "For doing my job – again! It's not like this is the first time I've shot someone in the line of duty. Sometimes responsible agents of the law actually use their guns."

"Some of them do," Jesse agreed.

"I do."

"You'd think by now they'd have that part of you all figured out."

"Evidently not yet."

"One more evaluation should do it," Jesse offered with a wicked little smile at the corner of her mouth, the one Hoot was beginning to watch for...

Chapter 6

Early Monday morning it was dark and damp and Hoot was back in
Seattle. Grounded pending completion of his ongoing lethal action
review and already growing restless, he grabbed his truck keys and
loaded-up a few boxes full of books and treasured vinyl LP's from his
SeaTac apartment storage area. He added a framed map of the US
with pictures and notes glued and pinned all over it top-to-bottom
and coast-to-coast, a friend's mounted moose head with a 6' antler
span that Hoot had been storing for him and moving all over the
goddamned country the last twelve years, a framed collection of US
Marshal badges dating to the late 1800's that he valued far beyond its
assessed value, and an unfinished oak side table that had been a
spontaneous garage sale acquisition back when Hoot thought he was
a refinisher. Satisfied nothing else would fit, he covered the load in
his pickup with a blue plastic tarp. And further satisfied that it did,
indeed, make him look like a character straight out of The Grapes of
Wrath, he headed out to beat as much of the peninsula-bound ferry
traffic as he could.

    Hoot's lease was up at the end of the month. His plan was to
get completely moved out of his SeaTac apartment over the
upcoming holiday weekend and turn his keys in without penalty. No
need to hire movers; he could and would do it himself. Tap a friend
or two for the heavy stuff. Too tight with his money to rent a moving
van large enough to do the job in one fell swoop, the trick was to
take quick advantage of rainless opportunities to use his uncovered
pickup without subjecting his few precious possessions overmuch to
the elements. This obviously wasn't going to be the last load he had
hoped it would be. He would need one more trip, probably two if he
didn't sell some old paintings on eBay soon; a couple of framed

Frederic Remington and Charles Russell copies – nice ones but big. In spite of Hoot's gypsy-like frequency of moving every year or so in pursuit of assholes, he'd never got the hang of living small so moving was always an epic event, a growing inventory of certain items moving to the next storage locker without being unpacked from the previous move. At least now, with his suspension in effect, he'd have the time to finish this move – hopefully his last move into a place he could call his own. No excuses.

He stopped at the Coffee Hut for caffeine and a cookie, and then punched a speed-dial contact on his phone after he was parked in the queue for the Edmonds/Kingston ferry.

***

"Am I fishin this weekend? Hell yes, I'm fishin! Ever chance I get!" Chili Hilliker exclaimed, continuously pacing the confines of his office while using his new Bluetooth hands-free device to talk to Hoot with sweeping arm gestures. "A man don't have t' be re-tired t' fish, you know," his voice booming like an old-time revival preacher.

Chief of Police Charles Hilliker was the Big Bear in Port Timothy. Script attesting to that little homily was painted on the door of his cruiser, a reminder to anyone who might've forgotten or was too dense to take one look at his grizzled face framed between linebacker shoulders and make the connection. This morning Chili was an exceptionally growly bear.

"Last chance ya know. Salmon season's about t' close for the winter. Crabs too." he roared, presumably to Hoot at the other end of his Bluetooth, or maybe to the world at large. "Got a half-dozen second-hand collapsible crab traps repaired and ready to set, plus my regulars. Gotta have 'em all outta the water by day after New Year's Day, so there's time for a couple more re-sets, but I don't wanna wait 'till the last minute. You bein unemployed all of a sudden, you gonna be available t' help me do a little crabbin?"

Grace Marvel, Chief Hilliker's office assistant and dispatcher ignored him without ceasing her continuous, lightning-fast typing – tappata tap-tap at over 100 words per minute. A grandmotherly gal, her pinched-lip smile ever present and genuine, Grace no longer bothered to remind her bear of a boss that a normal speaking volume was all the hands-free device required. At least he had quit trying to talk out of the side of his mouth as if he were throwing his words toward it. An antiquated two-way radio the size of a small casket sat atop Grace's desk, it squawked something barely understandable about Breakwater Beach and she briefly interrupted her transcription of evidence reports to answer, pressing a well-worn bar on the microphone base, "Chief is ten-twenty at base, Unit 4. Copy that?"

"Copy," the voice on the radio crackled, and then added, "Tell him the doc just arrived. Wants Big Bear to give him a callback on his cell," the words sounding crackly with static and squelch.

"You hear that, Boss?" Grace Marvel chirped.

Feeling a bit nostalgic, Chili nodded, thinking that the goddamned cell phone companies had put up so many towers so quickly it seemed like every other mountaintop in the Olympics had one of the gangly contraptions perched on it nowadays, they would probably make the two-way obsolete soon, even deep in the woods. He would miss the this is official –pay attention, damnit! squawk of it. Cell phones were entirely too private for police work. Too courteous.

Chili didn't use his cell much except to answer it when he was in a mood to do so. The raw truth was that he disliked cell phones on principal. Was unimpressed with the convenience of them weighed against their relentlessness. Detested call waiting and texting, automated voice mail, and apps of every kind. He considered it very likely that built-in phone cameras and internet connectivity were the work of the devil, and he especially hated seeing school-age kids constantly yakkety-yakking on their phones as if they had something so almighty goddamned important to say that it just couldn't wait.

Grace continued typing; tappatap, tap-tap, tap, tappatappatap, Chili appreciating the fact that she was aware of her boss's fondness for the big two-way radio and seemed happy to use it for as long as he wished. And that'll be for as long as it still works, he thought.

Chief Hilliker's mail waited in three orderly piles sitting atop his desk blotter. Official, Personal, and Bullshit. Pacing the floor, listening to his friend's voice speaking directly into his ear, Chili briefly looked at the single personal envelope and returned it to his desk. Preoccupied, he made a quick scan of the official pile, reorganized it and also returned it to his desk, picked the latest National Geographic out of the bullshit pile and dropped the remainder of that pile into the recycle bin near Grace's desk as he passed. "Listen, Hoot," he said, his voice dropping a couple of decibels, turning, and walking toward the back room while continuing the conversation in a conspiratorial tone; "Fact is a murder victim washed up on Breakwater Beach at high tide early this mornin. Since you're comin t' Port Tim anyhow, I'd 'preciate it if you'd stop by, take a look…"

***

Hoot arrived in Port Timothy shortly before noon to find Chili Hilliker standing on the path above Breakwater Beach beside a big yellow mobile crane with its boom extended. Chili was looking down at his cobbled-together CSI team in action behind a temporary cofferdam hastily provided by a local construction company and put in place by the crane to keep the tide at bay. Over five hours at the scene and they still had not removed the victim's body. Hadn't even turned it over yet.

Good, Hoot thought, Chili was doing it right. Time didn't matter right now – thoroughness did. Hoot had first met Chili early in both their careers when he was assigned to a team working out of the US Marshals' office in New Orleans to nail a counterfeiting ring. Marshals were working with local assets including the Lafayette Parish sheriff's office, and he had become quick friends with the droll, down-to-earth deputy sheriff. It was different then, when Hoot was young and still new to the marshals, when he made friends expecting to keep them. The art of making friends was a knack that Hoot had found to be more and more elusive as the years passed; his growing reputation for shedding partners like a snake sheds skins preceding him wherever he went. Over the long and tangled course of time Chili Hilliker became the only old friend Hoot would bother to claim, or who would be likely to claim him in return. Their friendship recently rekindled by the simple coincidence of proximity; it seemed fated that they had both come by such different roads from one corner of the country all the way to its opposite corner to practically be neighbors in their so-called golden years.

And now, with cold coffee growing ever colder in a Styro cup held loosely in his enormous paw of a hand, Hoot's singular old friend was standing atop a riprap jetty and looking down at a body isolated by a plate-steel cofferdam on the narrow strip of beach below. Nude. Male. Probably late middle-age – hard to tell from here – certainly not young if the bald pate fringed with long remnants of a comb-over were taken as a clue. Lying on its belly, bloodless gray flesh starkly revealed like poached bratwurst on a stovetop, a sizeable knife was protruding from its back.

Hoot, impressed with the size of the blade stuck in the cadaver, walked over and stood next to his friend, saying, "I gather you've ruled out accident and suicide," being a smartass. A full head taller yet a good forty pounds lighter than the bearlike chief of police, Hoot knew their viewpoints of this situation were nonetheless identical – both men understood that they were looking at trouble.

"We go down there, you'll see," Chili said with a wry look. "You've had first-hand experience with knives...I 'spect you'll agree it'd be a real trick to fall backward on the pointed end of what appears to be a sizeable carving knife seven times, the last time hard enough to plant the blade good-n-solid in bone. And we haven't even looked at the front side yet." He tossed the dregs of his coffee into a public waste can, said, "I already told my people t' proceed with diligence above and beyond. They're new to this CSI business. At least where an actual murder is concerned they're new to it. No rubber dummies this time. No fuckups'll be tolerated. No excuses listened to."

Chili was correct, the voice of experience, unimpressed with itself yet loaded with the wisdom of hindsight. This was going to tax his department's resources.

Looking out at the busy water of the Strait of Juan de Fuca, Chief Hilliker said in a low growl; "Assumin this crime occurred out...there," (putting the obvious into words seeming to add weight to the thought), "problem remains that it could a' happened anyfuckin where out there. Floatin trouble tends to chart its own course, you know?"

"So I've heard."

Chili looked over his shoulder at his friend, said; "There was another one…"

"Another floater?"

"Yep. A woman. Washed up just over a week ago out past Port Angeles. A place called Pysht Bay on the road to Cape Flattery. Media never latched-on t' that one – wrote it off as a fishin accident."

Chili's glance went beyond Hoot to a crowd gathering behind the barricade at the foot of the jetty, network news vans taking up temporary residence, their alien-looking antennas reaching for the heavens. He shook his head and said, "They've already latched-on t' this one. I talked to the Clallam County sheriff and he agrees they're connected, that stabbin and this one. Just about gotta be. Both victims stabbed multiple times. Big knife. We figure it's an easy bet the blade stickin outta the beach litter down there is the common murder weapon. Sheriff agreed t' keep quiet about that little detail 'till we can compare other details. Still, a pair a' fuckin pincushions floatin-in less than 30 miles and two weeks apart…"

"You're thinking this is the work of a cold-blooded killer as opposed to some sort of thievery turned lethal or a crime of passion? Maybe a serial killer since this guy is evidently one of at least two victims?" Hoot gave his friend a quick look, over a half-century of experience passing between them in a glance. "

Chili said, "Likely to be a crime a' passion is what I think."

Hoot nodded. "Agreed…"

Chili wrinkled his nose as if catching a nasty whiff. "Bad voodoo in the air," he said, letting his transplanted Louisiana roots show even more than usual. "I fear this is gonna get butt-ugly real quick. And you've got more experience with this kinda thing than anyone else I know."

"What sort of thing would that be? Murder? Or knives?"

"Psychopaths. Wait 'til you see the stab wounds in this guy and tell me if you don't agree it's a crime a' passion. The work of a very fuckin unbalanced killer at the least. A madder-n-hell madman."

"Or a professional hitman?"

"Nah. Don't think so. Pros are typically shooters," Chili said with a cocked eyebrow thick as a rolled carpet. "They're usually throat-slitters if they use a knife. Sure as hell don't use knives to stab the crap outta people like they're tenderizin meat. No, they like a quick double tap to the heart and one to the head. Small caliber. Everybody watches teevee knows that..."

"Unless they're Mexican pros," Hoot offered. "Mexicans seem to enjoy making a mess out of murder. They'll shoot the living shit out of each other just to make a macho statement out of it. The guy I put down on the plane was a Mexican cartel hitman, and you should've seen the fucking mess he made with a goddamned piece of floss!

"Muslims on the other hand seem to prefer bombs, gas, and other creative ways to achieve much larger-scale genocide.

"And, of course, the North Koreans are itching to get their mistreated and misunderstood hands on a nuke they can deliver to DC in a shoebox because they can't get their fucking rockets to fly right.

"Then there are all the unaffiliated assholes we have to be concerned with nowadays; independent terrorists who are in it for the money – or worse, the glory. The moral is that you never know from which direction the shit will fly, so you have to be ready for it from everywhere."

"I still can't see a pro leavin his knife behind like that," Chili said, "much less tossin a body overboard with the murder weapon stuck in it without tyin an anchor to it to make sure it stays down. All I really know right now is that, whoever killed this poor fuck, it's just my rotten luck he had to float-up here in Port Tim."

"Rotten luck," Hoot agreed.

"Yeah. But maybe it's my good luck that you're here, too?"

"Not sure how much help I can be. But, yeah...I'm yours as long as I'm on sabbatical. At least a couple of weeks for the lethal action review," Hoot said, barely giving his weekend moving plans a second thought. "Meanwhile you're still coming for Thanksgiving dinner at my cabin? Maddie confirmed she's coming and I'm thinking about inviting someone else."

Chili grinned and said, "I'll be there. Did you forget that I'm the one bringing the crab? Or we are, I should say; if you're still game t' help me with the pots." He waved at one of his men on the beach below and said to Hoot, "Ready to climb down and join the circus?"

Chapter 7

Jesse and Hoot went their separate ways after the lethal action debriefing in LA. She had hoped for an opportunity to speak to Mr. Kenneth alone without Hoot or Silas Wilson present, but it didn't happen. Instead, she flew to Atlanta on duty and Hoot flew to Seattle on administrative leave. Now she was alone with her thoughts in a plane full of passengers. They were dark thoughts – except for Hoot; the very pale man suddenly standing tall in the middle of everything.

Tall, slender, and white as bone, Hoot was the negative image of Mr. Kenneth who was roughly equal in size and height but as black as Kentucky coal. Hoot was interesting – oddly interesting, actually – a bit older than men she normally was attracted to but maybe not so much, and his ageless vampire-like persona only made him all the more interesting to her. With a smile she recalled fantasizing that she was being fucked senseless by a 1000-year-old minion of the underworld last night. Repeatedly.

Yes…she would definitely give Hoot a call when they got home. The question was; would he fuck up everything that she had going with Mr. Kenneth?

Had he already fucked it up? The business on the plane had certainly not gone well. Not well at all…

"So they called him Troubleshooter in the Marshals and before then, did they?" Silas Wilson had said. "We sure as hell don't need him shooting people over here at FAMS."

Too late, Jesse had thought.

It was getting to be too late for too much, she feared. She looked out the window at Oklahoma passing by below and turned her thoughts in a new direction…

***

She thought she was so fuck-all special. So smart, the voice in Jesse's head said. This was the adolescent potty-mouth version of the voice, refusing to shut up to the point of robbing Jesse's sleep and scrambling her concentration. *Silly cunt. She was a loudmouthed nobody with money. A show-off. And that's why she died.*

No. That isn't right, Jesse thought, responding to the voice in spite of vowing not to. The woman was unexpected. She wasn't supposed to be on the boat – Harold Hesse was supposed to be alone. He was doing some work for her, adding a new gadget to make Soozy Wickerman's pretentious super-canoe even fancier than it already was, and she'd hung around to keep an eye on him. It was a simple case of someone being in the wrong place at the worst possible time and I had to adapt.

She meddled.

Sure, the Wickerman woman was a meddler, Jesse thought. A gossip and a horny middle-aged widow looking for a new sugar daddy because the last one's money was about gone. Then she decided to fix-up her boat to impress impressionable men and got hooked-up with the trainman's brother if you can imagine anything so disgusting. Trading drydock repairs for blowjobs? – yuck! But that doesn't mean she deserved to die. She simply wasn't part of the plan…

Nobody liked her. Took a while for anyone to even realize she was missing for cryingoutloud! So no big deal…right?

Shut the fuck up, damn it! Just shut up. Shut up! Shut up! Jesse screamed silently, her throat constricting until she nearly choked from the effort of restraining actual speech in a crowded commercial airliner.

Getting a grip, she said inwardly in a softer, more controlled tone, Please. I'm working…

***

The county medical examiner/coroner from Jefferson Medical Center in neighboring Port Townsend, Dr. Leo Wolfe, seemed awfully young and over-the-top nerdy to Hoot to be an expert in forensic pathology or much of anything else other than video gaming.

Carrot-topped and freckled; Hoot's first impression was that Dr. Wolfe was hopelessly unsure of himself, the world, and everything in it. Fidgety, the doctor looked like he was barely out of adolescence to say nothing of medical school and residency, and from his body language in the near vicinity of the corpse it was apparent that he had spent very little time at actual crime scenes.

Almost tip-toeing on exposed nerves around the inside perimeter of the cofferdam, the young medical examiner seemed to be overdoing everything, comically-careful to note the smallest of details, apparently bewildered by the untidiness the murder scene presented and unconvinced the dam would keep it dry enough long enough for him to do his job adequately. But even as the boy doctor meticulously examined every square centimeter of the body on the beach with amateur enthusiasm, his intense focus and surprising command of authority made it clear that he would conduct his on-site investigation at whatever pace required to ensure thoroughness, regardless of the cost to his nervous system or strain on the patience of the team waiting for him. Until he was done the crime scene was his and he knew it. So he prodded and poked. Took notes. Took samples. Inched to another position and did it all over again. Now and then he would direct a sheriff's department photographer to take a few specific detail shots of this and that, doing all of these things before allowing the victim to be moved. Once Hoot got a good look at the young doctor's intense green eyes he could see that, in spite of his youth and evident lack of experience, he intended to do this unpleasant job by the book – exactly by the book – even if he had to take the goddamned book out and read it as he went along.

More power to you, Doc. Keep it up, Hoot thought, always amazed that any well-educated young doctor with a wide-open future would take a medical examiner's job. Most of the ME's Hoot had known were smart as hell and regular guys or gals away from the morgue, although most of them he'd known were crotchety old curmudgeons like himself and Chili. This young one showed promise.

"Bloody fuckin Monday," Chili said, leaning against the lip of the steel cofferdam and looking northward across the broad strait. "Bad way to begin the holiday week." He stepped aside and took another long look the other way, back along Breakwater Beach toward his heretofore peaceful community; buildings and streetlights on the main drag draped with gaudy holiday garlands, the milling crowd of onlookers in the foreground ever growing.

Hoot could see the sadness in his friend's eyes. Murder – his town would never be quite the same after this.

"Goddamned shame this had t' happen just before Thanksgivin," Chili said as if to confirm Hoot's thoughts. "Bad voodoo's whaddit is."

"Bad voodoo," Hoot agreed, kneeling in the sand for a lower perspective of the corpse while respecting the young coroner's domain.

The victim had obviously been a mature man. Hoot figured probably sixty-years-old or older. Caucasian. The knife was still firmly planted in his left shoulder blade – it seemed almost anecdotal; stuck there without any trace of blood, submersion in salt water washing everything clean, probably washing any incriminating fingerprints away along with any trace of DNA the killer might've left behind.

The sight of that gleaming blade made Hoot feel slightly nauseous. Made him feel like he was slowly turning cold from the inside out. Made the scar in the middle of his abdomen ache like the devil. And it made him remember his onetime best friend, his onetime nemesis, Norman Carpenter.

…It had happened so quickly. People always say that and it's true. So damned quickly!

Hoot remembered he had gestured to Norman with his pistol. Told him to drop the knife. But there had been no response from his so-called blood-brother. Not a movement. Not a flicker of the eye or change of expression. Norman could have been frozen, a freaksicle on a stick, his complexion slowly fading from dark red to ashen white.

Hoot remembered telling the girl to move away from Norman.

He remembered her sidestepping away.

When she was safely off to the side he remembered glancing over her way for a fraction of a second, asking if she was okay.

She had answered, Yeah, and in the time it took the sound of her voice to reach his ears the knife had traveled from Norman's hand to the center of Hoot's belly. He could see it in his mind's eye as he had seen it a hundred times, over and over the past year. Coming straight at him. Faster than fast, yet almost in slow motion; that wicked unwavering blade.

"…Any idea how long he was in the water, Doc?" Chili asked the ME, snapping Hoot back into the here and now.

Chili received a startled look before getting his answer. "I'd say a week. Maybe two, as cold as the water is. Too soon to tell for sure. Don't worry, chief; you'll be the first to know everything there is to know after I get him back to the lab and have a look inside him. Could take a couple of days. At least three for the DNA report. Be sure you answer your phone."

The young doctor may be inexperienced, but he seemed diligent enough, Hoot thought. A good sign. Yes indeed, he'd be glad to help Chili find this carving knife killer – Chili could use the help. Moving the last of his personal crap, stuff that he should probably just go ahead and donate to Goodwill, from SeaTac to the cabin could wait. This could get interesting…

Chapter 8

Jessica Vega seldom remembered her dreams. But now and then a nightmare...

She needed to pee in the worst way but the car wouldn't stop. She always needed to pee in her nightmares – it's one of the ways she knew when she was having one. Papa was driving and Mama was sitting next to him. Mama was nude, of course. Mama was always naked in Jesse's dreams; like a doll, she was nude but sexless, her anatomy vague, as if she had come that way from the store and nobody ever bothered to remedy the situation. Nobody else was naked – just Mama. And it wasn't a car. It was a rusty old stock truck with rickety wooden sides that she could see through; baked caliche and burnt scrub brush in every direction, mountains standing like stone barricades beyond.

"Where am I?" she asked against a searing wind that was blowing sand and dirt in her face, her eyes crusting with it.

"Nowhere," Papa Flix said.

Papa Flix? She always called him that in her dreams, seldom in realtime.

There were others being loaded into the truck. Surly women with squalling kids. Ugly men with enormous exposed cocks, dirty feet, and loaded shotguns. They crowded aboard, pressing and touching. She hated it; all the groping...

"But I have to go!"

"Then go already," Papa Flix said.

So she did. Standing right there in the truck, she let go and peed down both legs, the humiliation of it so awful that it was actually physically painful to her, tying her gut in a knot. All those filthy men leering at her. Their dirty cocks growing hard...

***

Jesse hopped a redeye from Dallas by way of San Francisco and arrived back in Seattle early on Thanksgiving morning. She stopped by her West Seattle apartment just long enough to shower and change clothes. She fed the one-eared stray cat that had moved in last summer, and then she headed out toward Gig Harbor and the Washington Corrections Center for Women.

This was a popular holiday and visitation was sure to be heavy. Visiting hours started at 10:30 and Jesse's usual policy was to be first in line or not go at all. Get in, then get the hell out – the only way to do it. Today she was first in line at 9:28. Others queued-up behind her soon enough, depressed people waiting in the rain. Mostly they were single women with children. Very few men. A couple of entire goddamned families jammed the line where it funneled through the security station. Tears and hostile attitudes were being held in check for the most part.

It was ludicrous, Jesse thought, and sad, the way they thinly decorated the public access areas in the Treatment and Evaluation wing of the kook block as if pretending it wasn't part of the prison. There was a scrawny fake Christmas tree in the lobby with a strand of multi-colored mini lights and a few cheap and unbreakable ornaments hanging on it, wrapped-up boxes underneath – all bogus.

The wrapped-up boxes were empty; Jesse knew because a sign on the wall told her so. There was a procedure for bringing actual gifts to inmates and it definitely did not include the scrawny tree or shit being wrapped up. Cheapo stuffed animals and jigsaw puzzles with missing pieces were hidden away in a bin behind the reception counter just in case some kid visiting Mom in the joint started bouncing off the walls.

Bogus...bogus...bogus! the voice inside Jesse's head repeated, the voice she thinks of as the Billievoice, her ever-present companion always whining on the cusp of an oncoming headache.

The facemask friendliness of the waiting room area was starting to make Jesse feel itchy all over. Claustrophobic. And topping that off a growing wave of nausea was getting nudged along by the lingering aromas of this place; aromas of drudgery and despair to Jesse, laundry detergent and ammonia holding an avalanche of ever-encroaching mold and mildew at bay, an unpleasant reminder of living in her mom's thirty-six-room motel when she was growing up; endless housekeeping work to be done even during slow times and guess who got to do it?

Finally, her call came – visitor Vega at station number one. Jesse assumed the spread-eagled-scarecrow pose for the guard with the scanner and then she was in – the wrong side of everywhere.

Her sister Christine had lost weight since Jesse last saw her. She looked scrawny and the ever-present dark circles around her eyes had worsened until she resembled a ghoul in a Tim Burton movie.

"Jesus, Chrissie! You look like a skinny raccoon," Jesse said. "Are you eating?"

Christine smiled sarcastically, replied, "You haven't come to see me in what, three months? Four? And you wanna talk about my *diet*? You aren't exactly soft and pudgy yourself, you know. Stick around for a slice of paper-thin, dry-as-dirt prison turkey, tasteless mashed potatoes with watery gravy, and rubbery stuffing, then see what's left of your finicky appetite."

So what if it's been four months? Big deal! the Billievoice said, its usual little-girl whine set aside in favor of gangsta bravado. *Don't listen to this bitch's bitching. Don't let her throw her poor-little-me attitude at you. She's where she is because she deserves to be here. Tried to kill herself what...three times, and couldn't get it right? She's a loser...*

"I've had a busy schedule," Jesse told her sister.

"Yeah, I know. I saw you," Christine said, her restless glance locking onto Jesse's eyes for a long heartbeat. "On the television in the common area where they let us watch the news. First time ever a sky marshal kills a guy in the sky they said, and there's my dear sister on the 6 o'clock news, getting off of the very same plane. Are you the one who shot him?"

"No. My partner did."

"You sure it wasn't you? Is anybody sure it wasn't you? How about your Papa?"

"Don't start with me, Chrissie," Jesse said. "It doesn't help anything."

Christine was always doing that; tossing out moldy crumbs of the same old gripe about how it was Jesse's testimony that put her here. About how her own recollections of the incident on the Queets River trestle didn't quite jibe with the record once she'd had time to think about it. About how realizing the true story behind the story made her crazy enough to try suicide…repeatedly. Crazy enough for them to lock her up and lose the key.

Not true! the voice said. *Chrissie convicted herself when she admitted she pushed me and agreed with you that you tried to catch me. Even if it's all backward – nobody seems to remember who was really doing the pushing and who was doing the catching that day…do they?*

By now the headache was really taking root, sending out suckers and spreading throughout Jesse's feverish brain like a thorny blackberry bush in the woods, choking-out everything else. "I got some news for you, Sis…nothing helps anything," she said, massaging the bridge of her nose. "What we did. What you did and what I did – nothing helps that. You get it? Nothing. It's done! Just do your time and everything will be fine."

Meanwhile tell her to button her loud lip about it, the voice said, and Jesse ignored it.

"I'm sick, Jessica, really sick this time," Christine announced as if slamming the bell after trading for the Pit card cornering the market on illness, "and I know that you couldn't possibly care less…"

"I care about you. Truly I do," Jesse said, the words heavy in her mouth and falling out ungracefully.

"Yeah. Sure you do," Christine said. Then turning her tone of voice 180 degrees on the spur of the moment to the Soft and Pliant setting, she asked, "Paid your holiday visit to mom, yet?"

Temples throbbing, Jesse slowly shook her head. "No. Not yet."

"When you go, please be sure to tell her that I miss her real bad. Tell her that I need her to come visit me."

We don't need to listen to this sad story, the Billievoice offered. *Let's go…*

"Chrissie," Jesse said with her teeth gritted against the escalating pain in her head, "I'm sorry I haven't been to see you like I promised. I'll do better."

"No, you won't. Don't make promises." Christine cocked her head, looking at Jesse as if she was trying to see through her skin to the core underneath, said, "You've got the headaches again, don't you? Are you hearing that voice?"

Jesse silently returned her sister's gaze, their eyes locked.

"Yeah, you are. I can tell," Christine said. "I'll bet anything dead bodies are starting to pile up somewhere. Anyone I know in the pile yet?"

Jesse broke the stare to cast a quick glance toward the door. There were always guards loitering there. Another guard was visible through thick glass at a security station outside. Lots of eyes and ears – not that they cared, they saw and heard so much bullshit in this place. "Listen, Sis…" she started, but was cut off by her unbalanced sibling.

"…Don't tell me!" Christine interrupted. "I don't wanna know. I can't take it. The knowing."

It's definitely time to leave, the Billievoice said to Jesse. *Let this sorry bitch wallow in her misery. The only thing that makes her happy is wallowing in it.*

"Listen, Sis," Jesse repeated. "I have to go, but I'll be back again soon."

"Don't do me any favors," Christine replied. "Just go…"

***

Her headache receding enough for a moment of lucid thought, Jesse stopped her car at the Highway 16 intersection on Burnham Road before deciding which way to turn – turn right and head back over the Narrows Bridge or turn left toward Bremerton. She called Hoot's cell number and he answered after the second ring, saying "This is Hoot" in his distinctive whispery voice.

"It's Vega," she said. "I called your Seattle apartment earlier to see if you were in town. Didn't leave a message."

"Would've crossed paths with the one I left for you yesterday and canceled each other out, anyhow," Hoot said in a guarded tone. "That message was an invitation to Thanksgiving dinner. Frankly I'd given up on you. I'm surprised you called back."

"Good. I like to surprise people. Does the invitation still stand?"

"Sure it does."

"Where can I find you?"

"Remember I told you that I have a cabin near Port Timothy on the strait?" Hoot answered. "I'm fixing it up to be my full-time hangout and I'm working on it while I'm on suspension."

"Yeah, I remember. I know the Port Tim area pretty well. I grew up on the peninsula and still visit my mom in Forks and whatnot. Are you staying over the whole holiday weekend?"

"Looks like it," Hoot answered. "The police chief is an old friend of mine. There's been a murder, and I offered to help out."

"Murder in Port Tim?" Jesse said, feeling genuinely shocked and dangerously exposed.

"Believe it or not," Hoot said. "A body washed up on Breakwater Beach."

"I believe it. A man? Or a woman?"

"Male – stabbed to death."

"Any good clues?"

"Not yet."

The cell phone connection went as silent as deep space for one of those are-you-still-there moments. Jesse broke it by changing the subject, saying; "I suppose you and the chief are looking forward to the famous five course, can't-eat-it-all, turkey dinner at the Myrtle Turtle for your Thanksgiving feast?"

"Nope. We'll be enjoying a fisherman's feast. Plank-grilled salmon, fresh Dungeness crab galore, Caesar salad, and geoduck clam chowder here at my cabin."

"Wow, I didn't know you cook."

"Actually I don't. But I have friends who do, and they're invited too. I'm just the sous-chef and busboy. When do you fly again?"

"Not until after my salmon and crab and chowder. You sure it's cool if I crash the party?"

"You aren't crashing anything. I invited you. Dinner is planned for four o'clock. If that's too early we'll save you some leftovers. I'll text you the address of my cabin."

"Perfect. I'll grab a couple bottles of wine on my way."

I know you want to kill him, the Billievoice inside Jesse's head said as she confirmed the address of Hoot's cabin and punched it into her GPS app.

You should. Yes...I definitely think you should.

You would. You're always ready to kill someone, Jesse thought.

You should fuck him again...and then kill him.

I don't recall asking for your opinion. Why should I, anyhow? It's always the same.

A nice remote cabin would be the perfect place...

"We'll see," Jesse answered aloud, depressing the accelerator and turning left. It's ironic, she thought, the coincidence of Hoot living near Port Timothy, the way she'd been drawn back to the strait so soon after her recent adventure there. Now...of all times!

Evidence starting to float up along the shoreline like tub toys on bath night, the hand of fate was obviously busy stirring things up, making it interesting and testing her nerve, Jesse's luck always seeming to push her back to her father's lair; a place where a single misstep could easily get her killed, or perhaps worse yet. She knew for a fact that she could easily find herself crossing the high and dry country at night in the back of a stock truck – now *that* would be some bad luck!

Stuck in the middle no matter which way she turned, Jesse was largely ambivalent about luck. But she believed in fate, she surely did. Sometimes it seemed to her that her whole life had been knitted together from scrappy skeins of it, and she had had very little control over the raveled shawl produced. Well, that much was changing; she had found a way – or, more precisely, a way had found her – a double-stitch that just might knit something new.

Was it even possible considering the terrible things she had done?

Yes. This time it would be different.

You're playing a dangerous game, the Billievoice said. *I like it!*

"You would!" Jesse quipped aloud, stealing a quick glance into the rearview mirror when the sound of her own voice surprised her. The eyes looking back were the eyes of a cornered animal spying an escape route and weighing the risk. She increased her speed.

"We have to be very careful with Mister Hooten the shooter," she said. "He's unpredictable. That makes him risky. And we can't forget his friend the Port Tim police chief. Together they're bound to be very dangerous. Patience is the key."

I still like it. Oh yeah, it's rock 'n roll and I liiiike it…

Jesse's full-fledged scream, "Shut up!" surely must've made the windshield bulge out. She saw that she was now driving at over 70 mph, took her foot off the gas, and regained a tenacious grip on her calm.

Chapter 9

Jesse had been living her life as carefully and cautiously as she could for a very long time; basically since everything went off the rails while crossing the Queets River when she was fifteen, then another brief detour off the rails to take care of the Alan problem when she was eighteen, but since then always playing it safe. Keeping her mischief under the radar and making as much of an ordinary life for herself as possible, she satisfied her more aggressive urges, bolstering courage over her darker fears by making a badass marine out of herself. This was easier to accomplish when the Billievoice was staying nice and quiet, but the quiet times were always a lull at best, coming and going without advance warning. A few months ago her patience had began to wear so thin that keeping dark thoughts at bay and the voice content and shushed had become a real struggle.

Now the headaches were returning with a vengeance. And the nausea.

Jesse's ill-fated confrontation with Harold Hesse and his employer on the strait had left her feeling lightheaded and curiously invigorated afterward. Feeling safe even, once the jitters had died down. Bottom line – the problem of the Hesse brothers' neverending blabbering had finally been hushed; first, by Howard's suicide on the trestle, and now by Harold's deepwater dive with grandma's Wusthof stuck in his back. Rumors the Hesse brothers had started were still out there, of course, floating around like dust motes in the sun. But now that their source had been silenced they would be more easily ignored and more likely to float away.

Jesse knew she had been pushing her luck with Harold – and most certainly with Soozy Wickerman – but she felt fulfilled because it was fate...obviously. Harold's meddling in the Queets trestle tragedy had been like a sliver left under her skin that could've easily festered at some calamitous moment in her unforeseen future; so dealing with him had to be done. The unbelievable rush of adrenalin immediately after the act had almost caused her to lose her covenant with gravity, but predictably, the good feelings were short-lived and Jesse's feet were now back on the ground. She knew she could never scrub that goddamned trestle clean enough to make it squeak because there was no way of telling who the trainman and his brother had blabbed to. There was no other first-hand account of what happened – except for Christine's.

The voice concurred; *We should take steps to find out. Be watchful. There could be others he talked to...*

Billievoice obviously wanted more. Acquiring the taste for violence is very much like catching a virus; once it takes hold in a person it's nearly impossible to eradicate. Rather than curl up like a kitten after a bowl of cream, the childlike entity in Jesse's head was infected with the violence virus and amped-up by the experience, refusing to shut the fuck up and driving Jesse nuts with her bloodlust. She would get her wish soon enough.

A part of Jesse sometimes wondered if she really and truly wanted the voice to shut up. She feared that she was becoming accustomed to the interruptions, the invasive childlike insistence. Sometimes guilty of thinking of the voice as real; she figured if she could learn to control it, to mute it, wouldn't that put the lie to her own reality, the entity inside her head as tangible and interactive as any?

Reality...what a concept! read a faded 60's-era bumper sticker that had long been affixed to the registration counter at Mom's Motel, one of the few icons of Alison Wonderland's youth her daughter had the slightest bit of commonality with. Jesse thought the problem with reality was that it leaves little room for allegory. Fate and faith are equally scorned. She considered how the whole concept of reality had evolved considerably since the advent of so-called Reality TV. Media-made, promoted, and sold. Reality as a commodity, no more real than professional wrestling had been before it, it makes promises that require no faith and promise no favor, only surrender. Slathered onto the masses, this version of reality calms in a perverse way by making everyone feel that their own secret perversions are just hunky-dory.

And then fate sticks a fickle finger in the mix, and along comes Air Marshal Ezra Hooten and the life that he took on the airplane...priceless! Jesse may have been ambivalent about certain intangible issues like right versus wrong or the existence of God; but she believed in fate, and she knew its coin was blood.

The blood that had been spilled. So much blood!

Getting down and dirty with Hoot afterward had been an exercise in wild abandon. She had wanted to wallow in it. Wanted to swallow him up with her cunt and spit him out again until the burning feeling inside was sated, as if she had any idea what sated was supposed to feel like! All Jesse knew with any certainty was that she did not believe in coincidence. Therefore she had no reason to think Hoot's presence on the flight was any more coincidental than hers had been. Everyone is someone else's game piece, always.

She stopped at a mini market in Silverdale and bought two bottles of chilled wine, a bagful of holistic trail mix from a bulk dispenser, Visine, and a six-pack of Perrier water. Back in her car she opened one of the water bottles and swallowed four codeine-laced Canadian 222's with a fizzy swig of France's best and a nibble of the trail mix, and then she doused her eyes with the Visine before hitting the road again. A few miles later the Billievoice finally faded away and so did the headache, making the rest of the drive to Port Timothy ever so much more refreshing.

Jesse had grown up in Forks, smack in the middle of the Olympic Peninsula, making her a peninsula girl to the bone. She was comfortable in the mountains and the rain forest, and she could handle a small boat. Without landmarks it was easy for people to get lost in the thick fog and rain that were routine occurrences on backwoods trails and roads crisscrossing the Olympics, but Jesse knew the area around Port Timothy very well – Port Townsend and Sequim, Port Angeles, and all the wide spots in between. She knew the old abandoned Forest Service roads, places she had seen with Alan, her perverted stepdad.

Jesse's real father was Felix Vega, a cartel-connected outlaw of ever-growing renown; aloof and demanding, abusive and proud, he lived in Mexico and seldom saw his daughter a world away in

Forks. He was Papa Flix to Jesse, a man to be feared and obeyed and lived in awe of, but to her, still just her father – even if he took perversion to heights Alan couldn't dream of. To everyone else he was *el Lobo*, The Wolf, a ruthless cartel leader according to law enforcement authorities on both sides of the border and a Latin-American gigolo of the worst sort according to Jesse's mother. At the very least he was muy macho, a badass killer, and not someone to mess around with, but for the most part Papa Flix was a stick figure to Jesse, the image incomplete because she willed it so. To consider her father in greater detail was to risk the emotional avalanche that inevitably came with such consideration – the cold undercurrent of objectification that was always present for any female regardless of age or status. Salacious eyes. Hands loitering in inappropriate places…

Other than a nearly two-year stint living with him after the Queets River incident, there was no history of Jesse actually residing with her father – just visiting. And when she visited he was seldom around, his presence felt nonetheless. Antonio Banderas always away somewhere making a movie was how she thought of him, glamorizing his absences while tolerating his behavior when he was around, a trick she had learned from her mother.

On the other hand, Jesse's stepfather, Alan, had been her buddy since age eight, her playdate in everyday ways and in secret ways, and he would probably still be alive today if he'd just been happy with her *happy handiwork* as he called it and left Billiejean and Christine out of the fun. Alan was a truck driver, a timber hauler for Rayonier those last few busy years before spotted owls killed the peninsula timber business for good. Everybody knew it was coming, the end of the gravy years in timber, so they logged the holy shit out of the Olympics in the meantime. Jesse had ridden with Alan all over the backcountry on skinny unpaved logging roads including many that she knew had remained largely unused since those days, becoming overgrown and washed out in the years since the owls got their political mojo up; the woods, though vastly diminished according to radical environmentalists – treespikers driving 120-penny nails into trees and turning chainsaws into logger mutilators. The backcountry was slowly becoming less accessible and more remote than since the old times when loggers ruled with their huge two-man saws and calks on their boots.

Sometimes Jesse's friend Billiejean Wisdom and her sister Christine crowded into Alan's cab with her, all three girls riding along on those hilly hair-raising excursions, but mostly it was just Jesse.

Endangered and supposedly needing every board-foot of timber still standing on the peninsula to survive, the owls ultimately gave loggers the boot with a swipe of President Clinton's pen in 1994. When Jesse returned from Mexico to Forks two years after the trestle tragedy, the logging business in the Olympics was as dead as Julius Caesar, murdered by politics. Unemployed, Alan had taken a detour into booze, pot, and hookers. Drunk and/or stoned all the time, one day he made the fatal mistake of taking a couple of hard swipes at Christine while trying to put his cock in her mouth. He went missing for nearly a month before his mauled body was found by hikers along one of those largely unused backcountry logging roads. Jesse had been seventeen-going-on-eighteen at the time, only recently returned from Mexico when she surprised Alan with Christine, and she'd seldom thought about him since, while her younger sister couldn't seem to quit...

***

Chili Hilliker stood at a sideboard in the oversized kitchen area that comprised the entire view end of Hoot's small cabin overlooking the Strait of Juan de Fuca. He was cleaning a tubful of freshly-cooked Dungeness crab – the edible parts soon to be arranged on ice for the holiday feast – but he was struggling to keep his mind on the task, thinking: Murder in Port Tim!

The very thought was loaded with enough bad juju to derail the Big Bear if he were to let it. In the dark recesses of his Cajun imagination Chili could just see folks making a big goddamned flap while sitting around their holiday dinner tables, ever-embellished details growing grislier with each retelling, the horror of it becoming more and more bloated with all sorts of wild speculations. People were naturally going to link it with the Port Angeles murder if they hadn't already. And they'd be right – the crimes were certain to be connected; Chili would bet his left testicle on it and Cajuns are damned tight about wagering the family stones.

"I have no comment at this time" was all he'd said to eager members of the press; first to the peninsula-area locals who came running with notepads and cell phones in hand soon as the body was discovered. And he said it again when the big city newshounds started showing up. Over and over again, Chili repeating "I have no comment," to redundant questions being fielded as if some staggering new development needing pundit interpretation might have occurred in the last few seconds, the key to solving the case suddenly discovered - no such luck, folks! Nonetheless, he knew the hype would spread quickly enough. There was nothing he could do to stop it.

"Just wait n' see if it don't get worse before it gets better," Chili grumbled. "TV news crews from Seattle with their goddamned antenna-sproutin vans are already double-parked all over town. At Breakwater Beach. Outside my office. My house too, I imagine. Nobody knows about you or they'd be hangin around this place. Slow week for news, I guess."

"Not anymore," Hoot said in grim concurrence.

"Lid's gonna blow plumb off this whole thing soon as we're past the holiday weekend. I'll have to give 'em somethin, then. Goddamned reporters. They're like a pack a' wild dogs after fresh bones – no scruples among em...not a one!"

Chili gave Maddie a shy nod, added, "Present company excluded, of course."

Maddie had thus far been conspicuously absent from the newshounding going on all over town, though she would ultimately get all the info she needed thanks to her inside connection to Chili's office – her older sister, Grace, being Chili's right-hand gal. "Don't be looking my way with those hostile Cajun cop eyes, Chili Hilliker," she said. "You have obviously never read the Graph or you wouldn't call it a newspaper. Mum's the word, here. And you should know that...."

Madeline Marvel was a difficult woman to ignore and she hated being patronized; especially by salesmen, attorneys, and so-called news editors. She had often said that she would gladly launch the whole bunch of them along with virtually all of the world's telephone solicitors into deep space on a one-way quest for a new world even more gullible than this one. Gifted with a lead-singer-in-the-choir style of forthright persuasiveness, she was a mature and attractive gal at an age where her edges were starting to blur a bit while her priorities seemed sharper than ever. She had interviewed Hoot last year after he shot and killed Stephen Mays and another escapee in the forest above Queets. Bad deal, that was. Hoot's partner had died in the shootout, and Hoot had been unwilling to talk to reporters about it…except Maddie. She got the scoop if you want to call it that, and had obviously become infatuated with Hoot in the bargain for reasons Chili Hilliker couldn't begin to fathom. Hoot had started visiting Port Tim often shortly afterward, going fishing and cementing the cracks in his long friendship with Chili, ultimately buying his cabin while building a quasi-romantic friendship with Maddie at the same time, all good in Chili's unsolicited opinion.

"Shame on you for suggestin your paper ain't as valid as any," Chili said. "And it happens that I do read it. Thoroughly. It's insightful and on target. Mum's only the word because your paper's a weekly and the Thanksgivin issue is out already." He pulled another crab out of the tub. With a quick sleight-of-hand the inedible innards went into a garbage pail, the delectable parts onto a sideboard for cracking and separating the meat from the shells – Hoot's job.

"You are very good at what you do, a local treasure, but you're still a reporter at heart, Maddie," Chili said. "Itchin for dirt. I know that…"

"Bullpoop! Tell him I have scruples, Hoot," Maddie said, stirring a dash of Worcestershire into a pot of clam chowder simmering on a back burner atop Hoot's ancient gas range. Lots of twice-tenderized chopped geoduck clam meat, thickened cream, chopped onion, a bay leaf, thin-sliced carrot and celery, bits of bacon and the reserved clam nectar, wine…and more clams, plenty of black pepper, a generous pinch of dill weed, and no spuds! This was Maddie's way to make clam chowder – the best way – and there was no room in Hoot's kitchen for argument about it.

"Maddie has excellent scruples," Hoot teased, giving her a one-arm hug, a cold bottle of Red Hook in his other hand. "They're usually hiding under a sweater this time of year. But I'm sure she has 'em," he said, earning a mocking scowl and a "You're bad!" comment from Maddie.

There was a knock on the front door and Hoot answered it, Jesse Vega crossing the threshold, saying, "Happy Turkey Day, Hoot! Hope you missed me half as much as I missed you…"

Throwing her arms around his neck, Jesse planted a long kiss on Hoot's mouth before he even got the door closed behind her. Anyone watching Maddie right then would have seen her nearly drop her wooden stirring spoon, and might've seen a blush of color race to her cheeks. As it was, nobody saw anything but Jesse taking the limelight.

Chapter 10

In the spring of 1992 twelve-year-old Jessica Vega became infatuated with the Civil War-era outlaw Jesse James after reading a dog-eared copy of Jesse James Was His Name by William Settle Jr., a lucky Bookmobile find that she never bothered to return. She began insisting everyone call her Jesse instead of Jessica, and prettymuch everyone did. Most people around Forks still thought of her as a kid rather than a girl anyhow, ignoring early signs of her sexual awakening thanks to Jesse shunting every outward sign of it that she possibly could into the background.

Sexual ambiguity was Jesse's game. She was the quintessential tomboy, a dyke-in-training according to her mother, and she was in no hurry to be seen otherwise, especially after the incident later that year in October with Clarence/Pablo that had reset her life's compass in a heartbeat – his last heartbeat, as it turned out. Puberty was a bitch for her; tsunami-like mood fluctuations accompanied the on again off again advent of menstrual periods that never really settled into a reliable rhythm, cramps that could crush rock. Her suddenly hypersensitive nipples suggested the eminent growth of breasts that adamantly refused to happen beyond the development of puffier and even more sensitive nipples, and in Jesse's opinion, grotesquely uglier-than-before breasts.

Lastly but not the least of her pubescent woes was the advent of horrifying body hair – underarm hair, leg whiskers, and a sparse patch of wiry jet-black pubic hair that finally sprouted long after she'd given up waiting for it. Other girls her age were camouflaging their meddlesome pussies by turning into young gorillas while Jesse's supposedly-private area remained as bare and noticeable as a happy face button. When it finally came it both alarmed and amazed her to see the pubes knew exactly where and at what length to grow, thankful that the whiskery fur didn't run amok across her lower belly like the weeds growing out of control in her mother's gardens.

1992 was also the year that Jesse's best friend Billiejean Wisdom suddenly lost her baby fat, her personality turning sassier and more flirtatious at roughly the same pace that her breasts grew full and inviting, her legs longer. It was the year that Alan didn't seem to mind Billiejean hanging out with Jessica so much anymore. He even stopped calling her *Stoop* and started inviting her along on weekend hauls. This was about the time Forest Service warnings that it was all about to end started getting real. Rayonier loggers clear-cutting like crazy while they still could, there were plenty of overtime loads to be hauled right before the bottom fell completely out. Jesse's mom was either constantly working on her tan or flirting with the latest itinerant logger to check in at Mom's Motel, so Jesse was largely left alone and footloose when she was not doing mother-mandated housekeeping work.

Smart enough that she didn't need to study and still slide by on C's and D's at school, Jesse had learned the knack of applying what Alan referred to as the MRE, the Minimum Required Effort, at an early age. Not that that she was lazy – she was bored. Tossing aside the odd page of school homework that might've accidentally found its way home with her, she would skip class and hang out with pot growers and backwoods hooligans all over the peninsula – roughly 3,600 square miles of Jesse's personal backyard that had not even been properly explored by non-indigenous people until a Seattle newspaper sent an expedition across Puget Sound to do so in 1890. Jesse liked to pretend she was scouting for that expedition; Port Angeles to Gig Harbor, Bremerton to Forks, she hitchhiked and rode the Rayonier rails to get around.

Mostly going off on these clandestine and dangerous excursions alone, Jesse nonetheless headed-up a girl gang of sorts. They were a posse of three: Jesse, Billiejean, and Christine. Jesse had wanted to name their little gang the Spotted Owls so they could wear polka-dot panties and stage spotted owl sightings for the fun of it, but she settled on James Gang Pussies when finding polka-dot undies bigger than toddler size proved more of a challenge than she'd expected. The word *pussies* dropped away all by itself soon enough, making them simply the James Gang, but without all the bank robberies of the original.

Billiejean was game for the gang idea. Always eager to accompany her best friend on never-boring adventures, she would spend hours conniving reasons to be included in whatever Jesse had going on, weaving elaborate lies for Mamma Wisdom's ears, and doing what she pleased in spite of the old woman's wishes, sassing everyone. An easily-depressed girl, Billiejean tried too hard to be liked, inevitably feeling left out if Jesse wasn't around every possible second of every day for her to cling to, to emulate.

Christine was the odd duck in the gang, almost two years younger than the other two girls but refusing to be left out of the posse, she was prone to fits of pouting and tattle-telling. Considered the official gang whiner because she was; she would threaten and wheedle to be included; "Leave me behind and you'll be sorry!" Sassy Billiejean would tease Christine and get her all wound-up calling her Wiki-Wiki, explaining that *wiki* in the Makah language means no, therefore Christine was No-No in Makah.

Jesse, on the other hand, was Ho-Ho – *Ho* in Makah meaning yes. She was the default mother in all their Mother May I's, the tough love admonisher after every scrape – Don't you dare cry! – the arbitrator of every argument. There were days she could hardly handle the hormonal horseshit constantly stewing within her little gang like enriched fuel. Volatile times were abundant.

Now…over twenty years and four incidents later, her sights set on crashing Hoot's holiday feast, Jesse drove north up Highway 16 past the turnoff to Bremerton and on past the big shopping mall at Silverdale, everything prettified and changed since the days she and Billiejean and Christine thought the whole world was theirs for the taking. She smiled remembering her old nickname, remembering how pleased she was because she thought it sounded like a sexual jibe. At the very least it was a naughty-sounding name.

Mamma Wisdom had explained the K'wati legend, and Jesse started thinking of the Hoh River as her personal river. "*Ho* is not the same as *Hoh*. The Hoh River is Chalak'At'sit to the Makah, meaning Southern River," Mamma Wisdom told Billiejean and Jesse, pronouncing the word *Chalak'At'sit* indigenously from the back of her throat. She said the Hoh people were created by K'wati, the shape-shifting Changer who went around the world during the time of beginnings to remake things into the way they are today, a much more believable allegory to Jesse than a tall tale about a man and his family floating around the flooded globe in a big damned boat with a mated pair of every critter that was or ever would be on board.

The girls were all tangled up in their troublesome twelve's as Mamma Wisdom put it – they needed to untangle and retie themselves. Billiejean, barely able to multiply twelve times twelve, couldn't tell you the capitol of Montana on a wild guess or spell much of anything beyond her name, but she knew her family's heritage down to the roots, while Jesse was firecracker smart but didn't know shit about family – nothing worth repeating, anyhow.

There were other differences: Billiejean was hardly a pretty girl, but she was alluring, with a budding preteen figure and ready-to-surrender eyes. Jesse was slender and compact with smooth olive skin and luxurious black hair, penetrating eyes the color of polished jet. "She was a picture-pretty baby girl – beautiful actually," her mother would say with the heavy sigh of a person certain they had been next in line when the winning lotto ticket was sold.

"Mamma says I'm going to have big boobs and I'll just have to get by on that," Billiejean once said, while Alison Wonderland told Jesse; "Don't count on your looks, Honey. The only thing you can count on looks for is the cold hard fact that they'll be gone before you know it."

Mamma Wisdom told Billiejean and Jesse that when K'wati got to the Hoh River he discovered the people living there walked on their hands and worked their fishing nets with their feet. He went around setting them right side up and showing them how to work their nets correctly with their hands. "That's why Hoh elders refer to themselves as Upside-down People," she said, and the two girls had laughed at each other until tears were in their eyes, getting dizzy mimicking fat old men doing handstands and fishing with their feet.

As much a full-blooded Makah as could be found anywhere at the dawn of the twenty-first century, and a genuine tribal shaman to boot, Mamma Wisdom passed these and other nuggets of indigenous lore down to her darling granddaughter, while Alison Wonderland Vega-Hay-Mackey, Jesse's mom, was what Mamma Wisdom called a backsliding Catholic with a viselike grip on the sin

Catholics love so well, sin they love to be both condemned and forgiven for, she claimed, Original Sin at the top of the list.

Jesse's mom had it alright, tweaked and entrenched; that sin-is-sin attitude – had it in spite of her otherwise unorthodox and uninhibited ways. "You get up in the morning, go into the kitchen for your breakfast, and already you're guilty of so much sin you may as well keep on going straight on down to the hot place," Jesse remembered her mother telling her on more than one occasion – her mother a paragon of hypocrisy, a mother-earther pagan cum fire-and-brimstone backslider with enough sin packed away in her under-confessed heart to cover the earth twice over.

So what difference does a little murder or two really make in a family like mine, Jesse wondered now that she was an adult retracing her adolescent steps.

She smiled, knowing that it had always been about the risk, the pure adrenalin kick of it. Simple. There was no better kick than risk, and she couldn't imagine a life without it – she wouldn't want to, anyhow...

In 1992 when Jesse was twelve-years-old this was dark and dangerous thinking, but not surprising considering her environment, her experience. She rode the rails. She hitchhiked with truckers. She had climbed towering trees using logger's spurs. She had killed. And she could walk up to strange men in the woods without fear, her ego practically shouting that she was the soon-to-be infamous Jesse James Vega...so watch out! Meanwhile, she figured that she knew what she knew and the rest she could learn along the way.

Basic facts-of-life that were passed from Alison Wonderland to her daughters were steeped in unfounded lore more than actual fact, family anecdotes a fabled mishmash of the culture and politics of the time; redneck logger bravado grafted onto a worldview brought to the peninsula by hippies and potheads migrating north out of California and getting sidetracked around Forks in the late sixties – interesting fables that were easily knitted into Alison Wonderland's skein, but without roots. The only roots that Jesse had ever claimed were a tangled mess on her largely-absent father's side of the family tree, and he'd spent the last dozen years demonstrating how little interest he had in his daughter or her heritage.

"Never forget…the dead talk – you just have to listen," was another tidbit of shamanistic wisdom Mamma Wisdom loved to espouse, ever eager to pass native beliefs and histories down to anyone who'd listen. "They don't say much in actual words most of the time," she explained, "but they're talking all the same, the dead. In the sound of ocean waves. Rain falling on leaves and rocks. In the sound of wind in the trees. Even wet tires on the highway and the clickety-clack of trains on their tracks. You have to want to hear them."

And Jesse did. She listened. So did Billiejean, but Jesse was already there. Even at this young age Jesse seemed to have a direct dialogue going with the darker side of anything spiritual, Billiejean hanging back in the shallow end of that pool, but still in over her head. On a lighter note, no one had ever made Jesse laugh the way Billiejean used to make her laugh. Goofy girl; dumb as a fencepost and more annoying than a rash. Long years had passed, and Jesse still missed her friend, the voice in her head a poor substitute even if it did sound so goddamned much like Billiejean Wisdom.

But then…Did she even remember what Billiejean actually sounded like anymore?

No. Not really.

Furthermore, she knew perfectly well that the voice in her head wasn't an actual voice of the dead; a talking ghost of the sort Billiejean's tribal elders might get excited about. Unfooled, she knew it wasn't the same because it wasn't real – Jesse would concede that she might be a little off in her cabeza, but she wasn't crazy – it only existed in her head, and it never made her laugh. The real Billiejean had always been good for a laugh.

Until the incident on the Queets trestle, that is…

It had been so long ago, the incident.

A slip of the hand…

***

Mazatlan, 1993:

Located north of the city center beyond the Marina Mazatlan, the Playa Rocosa Resort stood alone at the end of a long stretch of boulder-strewn beach whose name the resort's original developers had borrowed. This far out of town it was quiet during the daytime and completely secluded from the frantic hubbub of dives and discos in the Zona Dorado at night, miles away from the docks where cruise ships spewed out hoards of bargain-hunting tourists running amok and creating inebriated conga lines wherever they went, and it was out of reach for most of the beach vendors and beggars who incessantly picked the bones of those staying closer to the Golden Zone. Simply put, it was too quiet and isolated and expensive for tourists of a certain ilk, and too far out on the fringe of town for the more affluent. Constructed during the early eighties, by the late eighties, when the original owners were forced to come to terms with the importance of location, they had already added a nine-hole golf course and started construction on a third tower – it was a nice place for a no-place.

The Los Zetas cartel had acquired the property at a bargain price, paying hard cash through a tangled thread of ownership and purchasing the resort that everyone had thought was located too far north of Mazatlan specifically because of its location – isolated; standing like the last sign of civilization at the end of a long stretch of mostly undeveloped beach property. More specifically; it was Jesse's father, el Lobo, and his cronies who'd purchased it for that reason, and then they immediately turned around and hired the same timeshare management team who couldn't make a go of it on their own to continue managing a portion of the property as vacation rentals to maintain a veneer of legitimacy. The cartel didn't view their investment as the last sign of civilization at the end of the road. Far from it – they saw it as the gateway.

When Jesse stayed with her father at Playa Rocosa in 1993 only a few bargain-hunting tourists were staying at the resort along with a fluctuating assortment of cartel honchos and their bodyguard posses. The honchos were mostly heroin-dealing middlemen with connections in the US. Drug dealers and street thugs and tourists – odd resortmates, you might think; middle-class Americans and Mexican mobsters. But not so different from each other in their tunnel-vision views of the world, and remarkably similar in their tastes ranging from fashion to food. Taken as a group, both camps were informed, misinformed, and ultimately defined by the ever-evolving trailing edge of pop culture. The *trailing* edge: Mexico had never been at the leading edge of anything with the possible exception of drug smuggling at this time; the decade before 9-11 when violence was still seen as fun and exciting to those promoting it – entertainment, and life on the streets. Cartels were flexing their muscles in those days but the blood hadn't started to really flow yet, a world of violence just around the corner.

Among the bloodiest of the cartels, Los Zetas was definitely on the way up, having its share of the fun, and high-ranking Los Zetas members and business partners often came and went to Mazatlan via small planes, avoiding attention at the airport by using the resort's private golf course as a landing strip – fucking-up the third hole fairway and no doubt the handicaps of untold numbers of startled golfers in the process.

Preferring to think himself an astute businessman rather than a lucky smuggler, Felix Vega catered to only the highest echelons in any enterprise he undertook. Dimebag drug dealers were discouraged from contaminating the place by leaving their bodies to rot in shallow ditches or hanging from trees and overpasses near wherever they'd come from – not exactly heads on posts at the Playa Rocosa gate, but serving the same purpose. In short, from the local police point-of-view it was largely peaceful at the resort in spite of drug lord ownership…if such a thing could be proven, of course.

Maybe it was a little too peaceful for thirteen-year-old Jesse who was always up for an adventure, but apparently a perfect fit for Billiejean Wisdom, Jesse's hermana del alma, her soul sister and shadow who felt lucky beyond lucky that Mama Wisdom had allowed her to miss a semester of school and tag along. Billiejean, a girl who was lazy to the core, mostly just wanted to lounge around the pool eating mangoes and melon and reading teen romance novels while working on her tan. Nearing the end of their third week in Mexico, it was now nearly March. Jesse and Billiejean had a week left; all thanks to Papa Felix's reluctant invitation after Jesse's mom got busted for selling pot and Jesse had nowhere else to go.

Leaving Christine behind to bounce between Mom and her real father and his family in Port Angeles, it was just a two-girl James Gang on the loose in Mexico. Jesse and Billiejean south of the border, and in spite of being constantly on the cusp of boredom,

Jesse liked it in Mexico. The girls spent most days dressed only in bathing suits and cover-ups, and most evenings in light cotton shorts or skirts and tee-shirts. They'd go into town. Sometimes to shop or to eat, but mostly to affect the demeanors of eighteen-year-old hotties and flirt with tourists old enough to get them into some real trouble were Jesse's father not so resolute about protecting his daughter and her friend in his usual manner. That is to say not with any measure of personal attention, but by assigning an armed posse to shadow them wherever they went.

The Los Zetas escort team assigned to this detail consisted of young sicarios. Muy macho right down to their raw bones, they often complained their honor was being compromised by the task, but they were nonetheless easily manipulated by the rambunctious girls. It was fun, Jesse and Billiejean traipsing around Mazatlan affecting the airs of streetwise sluts without taking any of the risks that girls who were actually driven to the streets were inevitably subjected to: Teasing with sparkling eyes and pouting smiles ruled most days. A flash of panties with a Hello Kitty cartoon on them one day. A semi-sheer thong the next. Peek-a-boo puffies in Jesse's case. Mini-mounds in Billiejean's.

It was all a game. Jesse's new bathing suit was a bikini that made her feel like a total daredevil in public. And she was – this a new sensation that she was becoming pleasantly addicted to. Made of snow white Lycra with a bottom so narrow and thin in the pubic area that a single hair would have stood out grotesquely, the suit shone whiter-than-white against her suntanned olive skin, the string-tied top was mostly string, magically making her essentially buttless and titless torso appear much more voluptuous than it actually was. She wore the Lewd Suit, as she liked to call it, most of the time with a modest long-sleeved white lace cover up, sometimes with her black Chicago Art Institute sweatshirt if the weather was chilly in the morning. But sometimes when the mood was on her…

They often traded clothes back then, Jesse and Billiejean, and they had done so the night Billiejean was grabbed from behind by Hector Lopez. Hector was an eighteen-year-old member of the escort team, and a not-so-secret admirer of Jesse's who recognized the sweatshirt and grabbed the wrong girl's breasts by mistake. Expecting a warm response from his favorite little caramelo he got a terrified scream instead. Startled by Billiejean's scream and confused by the different feel of her compared to Jesse, he started backing away the instant he touched her, dragging Billiejean along with a vice-like grip on her tit that made her scream even louder. Billiejean said later that she had wanted to stop screaming but couldn't. Not until another young man in their entourage raised a nickel-plated Dirty Harry-sized pistol and shot Hector Lopez in the center of his forehead.

It was a deafening blast.

The side of Billiejean's face was instantly splattered with Hector's blood, still hot with life, cutting off her scream at its peak and setting off a psychotic shock wave inside the head of one of the most co-dependent creatures on planet earth. This unfortunate incident precipitated a quick end to Jesse and Billiejean's Mexican holiday when the proverbial shit hit the fan about two seconds after Felix Vega learned that one of his best young sicarios had killed another of his best over his flirtatious daughter and her friend. His roar of rage a thing of legend, echoes were still peeling off Playa Rocosa stucco weeks later, certainly several of his favorite prostitutes had a rough evening or two, and Maalox stock was sure to peak. Ultimately, family or not, business was business, and the girls were bad for business. Their stay cut short, Jesse and Billiejean were returned to Forks.

Jesse had never been so scared in her life as the moment when she saw that cannon-like pistol pointing at Billiejean and Hector, had never felt so utterly vulnerable. Even so, it wasn't until later that night that the true nature of the soul-sucking wickedness moving through her world was revealed to her; her father interrupting Jesse and Billiejean in their bath, standing as naked as a Spartan warrior beside the big whirlpool tub, sporting a sizeable and conspicuously-erect spear, and asking if they needed anything. Billiejean had hiccupped and turned away like a mumbling zombie. But Jesse faced him, saw wickedness spinning like terrible dust devils in his eyes and said without a falter; "No Papa. We don't."

Her father had retreated, but Jesse's dreams were still sometimes haunted with the vision of his cock, poised like a cantilevered Sword of Damocles; looking like it was reaching out for her, like it wanted to murder her. This was the first time in her life that she had felt terrified of her father and the dark power he wielded

– terrified knowing that the same darkness lurked inside her, the proof of it in eight very graphic sketches hidden away in her treasure chest, sketches drawn by the same bloody hands that killed Pablo the grocery boy in a frantic fit only last year.

Cold blood ran in her veins; truly it did. Jessica Vega was her father's daughter – he would expect her to swell with pride to think it…and maybe she did. This was the turnaround point for Jesse. The moment she decided to become a certified badass. The moment she decided she wanted to become a Marine and learn to kill properly. Minimum enlistment age, eighteen – she figured she had five years to toughen up…

Chapter 11

Early Saturday morning after Thanksgiving Hoot was standing in the
bow of Chili's 32' aluminum fishing boat. They were about a half-
mile out under low angry-looking clouds on a slow eastward bearing
along the south bank of the Strait of Juan de Fuca, cold wind blowing
from the southwest. The chilled hull of the boat making Hoot feel
like he was riding the chop in an oversized ice cube tray with ice still
in it, he was shielding his eyes and carefully scanning the water ahead
for marker buoys. A normal human being would be miserable under
these conditions.

For Hoot, this was exhilarating. Miserable, yes – but
exhilarating. He hollered over his shoulder to the cockpit where Chili
was at the controls under the ridiculously-slim protection of a canvas
rain fly without side curtains; "We gotta be nuts! Out here with the
wind hawking up the strait like it is."

It was definitely getting colder on the water with a needle-like
spray blowing off the chop, and both men were wearing their foul-
weather gear. Bright orange Helly Hansen slickers with hoods and
rain pants. Filson gloves. Chili's Hunter boots undoubtedly keeping
his feet a good deal warmer than Hoot's Red Wings.

Chili hollered back, "I don't 'spect the weather'll get better
any time soon, and these last few pots gotta be checked and reset,
plus the new ones. Besides…we ate all the fresh crab Thursday at
your place!" his voice booming to be heard over the wind, "so it's
shut up and suffer or we get canned tuna surprise for dinner at my
house tonight!!"

"Aye-aye, Cap'n, I'm shutting up," Hoot answered in his
normal soft voice, words barely escaping his thin smiling lips. Numb

lips. He didn't really mind the cold – but the wet; he didn't care for the wet. Could put up with cold as long as he stayed dry.

Chili slowed the engine when he figured they should be getting close to the last buoy. "You think the dead know what cold feels like the same way they're supposed t' know about hot?" he asked.

Hoot answered with furrowed brow, "No…I don't. Don't figure they know about hot either. What makes you think otherwise?"

Chili's eyes looked tired. He said, "You know…Hell and all."

Hoot was thinking canned tuna surprise sounded prettydamned good when he saw what he was looking for bobbing in the chop and called out; "There it is! White buoy at two o'clock!"

***

"You bringin her for dinner?" Chili asked Hoot, the less than satisfactory day's catch of crab packed on ice, the boat secure in its slip and their rain gear hanging up to dry in the marina's boat shed.

"You mean Jesse?" Hoot said. "No. She's flying this weekend. I'll ask Maddie to be my dinner date."

Chili hunched his massive shoulders, growled, "Oh no ya don't!"

"Why not?"

"Because it's too effin late to invite a lady t' dinner if you haven't already – that's why. Don't you know they don't like that last-minute-decision bullshit? Besides, it's my goddamned party this time, and Maddie's invited with or without you."

Hoot looked into the Big Bear's eyes, said, "All right buddy, exactly what is it about Jesse that has you asking me about her like it hurts your hemorrhoids to broach the subject?"

Chili lowered his head, adjusted his winter cap, said, "Aside from her age, you mean? And you knowin diddlysquat about her?"

"What about her age?"

"Nothin."

"Say what you want to say, Chili. I won't ask you again…"

Looking up at Hoot through bushy eyebrows made bushier by his cap corralling them as if they were rambunctious pups in a

96

fenced yard, Chili said, "She's only what, four or five years younger than your own grown-up daughter? But that ain't it. Every old cur wags his tail at the frisky young bitches from time t' time. Can't help it – it's just the way we're wired. It's just that there's somethin 'bout your flyin partner, Jesse, as in *Jesse James the outlaw*, don't seem quite right to me. That's all I'm sayin."

"Hell's bells, Buddy! You know anybody who is quite right these days?"

"While I was in the office yesterday I did a quick check," Chili said, reacting to the sudden expression in Hoots eyes as if waiting for thunder after witnessing a bolt of lightning. "No disrespect intended, old friend, but did you know she has a sister doin time at WCC down in Gig Harbor?"

"Yeah, I know. Jesse stayed over at my place after the party Thursday night, and she mentioned it then. Said she'd been to see her sister before coming to my place for dinner. And for your information, her sister is in the psych wing, not the hard-timers block."

"Uh huh. Figures she stayed the night," Chili grumbled. "Maddie knew it too…"

"Is *that* what this is all about…Maddie? You think I'm two-timing Maddie with Jesse? You have it all wrong. Maddie and I have become damned good friends this past year, but that's all we are – just friends. You should know that."

"Yeah. I know, but sometimes I'm not so sure Maddie does. The woman is crazy 'bout you for some goddamned reason. I admit I can't quite figure her out."

"She's not crazy enough about me to be jealous of Jesse. Trust me, Chili. It's like I said; Maddie and I are just friends – that's all we've ever been. She knows it as well as I do. In fact she's the one made the boundaries clear shortly after we met."

"Shortly after you met? Well…you do grow on people," Chili said. "Sometimes. After they get past the rough edges. The halo hair. The whole vampire look. Maybe she's changed her opinion 'bout boundaries since then – women do that."

"Forget it," Hoot said. "Me and Maddie are okay. Anything else about Jesse got you tweaked?"

"I guess it's just her body language."

"What exactly is it about her body language?"

"Well, it's kinda…loud."

Chili threw Hoot one of his Bayou wisdom glances and then amended himself, saying, "I gotta admit she's got a hellava cute shape for such a little gal – maybe I just don't trust grown-up women built that tight. I 'spose it's the fuck-you-if-you-don't-like-it attitude of hers that bugs me the most – gets hard t' take from a woman without a little sugar now and then. And how 'bout the scar on her face? What's the story with that?"

"I don't know yet."

"Listen, Hoot, I'm just sayin that if you weren't so distracted lookin at her instead of seein her you'd know what I mean without me havin t'remind you."

"Remind me of what?"

"What happened after the plane landed in LA, for one thing. You do understand that what happened between you and her after the shootin was just a normal, caveman-type reaction, don't you?"

Hoot looked away.

"All the badasses you've put down? You should know better than most – you shoot somebody in the line of duty, you go get drunk and fuck somebody. No big deal. Happens all the time. You take a life, and then you celebrate life with a killfuck. Keep it simple in your head and it won't get outta control. But Thursday night after Thanksgiving dinner? That was a slightly different situation. That smacked of premeditation…"

"A year ago I would have agreed with you," Hoot said. "But I don't see these things quite so clearly anymore. The line between what's right what isn't right seems to be getting fuzzier the older I get. Maybe all the assholes I've dealt with have spoiled me for anyone true and decent, and that's why I always fall for low women; too many blighted trees to appreciate the best part of the forest, that sort of thing."

Chili gave Hoot's shoulder a maul-like squeeze, said, "All the different types people I've come across my whole career as a lawman. All the crazy and the sane people. The good people and the despicable people. Outta all of 'em, I've never met anybody who don't believe that they are really and truly decent people in their own hearts – even if their definition of *decent* is a bit askew from most.

And they want others t' believe it, too. Most of 'em work damned hard at pushin that notion. The upshot is; mostly, their kin feel the same way 'bout 'em, even the really despicable ones. Their friends – and especially their lovers – seldom see the dark side. Blind love is a real honest t' god thing. It's a human flaw, that shortsightedness, and it backfires on us all the fuckin time. Nothin to be done 'bout it except watch out for it."

"And you don't think I'm watching out?"

"Bingo! I do not…"

"I'm supposed to be retired," Hoot protested. "Taking it easy. Just working a side job with FAMS, flying around in soda cans with wings like it was all good fun. There aren't supposed to be any fucking suicide assassins or terrorists or hijackers on the planes because they know I'm there. Or I could be. Just the possibility of my presence making them tinkle in their explosive underwear – that's the way it's supposed to work…right?"

"Supposed to? Yeah."

"Well, it seems the game has changed now that I've gone and killed one of them in-flight and upped the ante. Do you realize they're starting to call me *Skyshooter* on the internet thanks to that asshole at the LA Times? As if the *Troubleshooter* tag weren't already bad enough. My picture has been all over the news. Video of me on YouTube walking up the aisle with my SIG at the ready. They'll sure as hell know when I'm there, now. So much for flying undercover – don't do me any favors, folks – because there are plenty of assholes and terrorist-type bad guys out there who'd love nothing more than to hang a target on my ass just to score a point, a goddamned line of them stretches around the block and it's getting longer."

Hoot's shoulders slumped a bit and he said, "Truthfully Chili…I think I'm finally getting old. Can you believe it? Me – old, and weary of the hunt?"

"Gets tiresome, watchin out for assholes all the damned time," Chili said.

"It eats at your empathy," Hoot said. "I'd had more than enough of it the night I got stabbed, and it isn't getting any better."

"You say that you were ready to turn it all off even before Norman Carpenter's dyin carcass finished bleedin out? I don't blame you. But I don't believe you, either. What you're telling me is that before you ever looked into Jesse James Vega's witchy eyes or glanced at her tight little tush you'd already started turnin off all the instincts that've kept you on your toes and alive all this time? Just turned 'em off like changin teevee channels when the program gets borin? I guess you must be feelin kinda vulnerable about now, comin down with AIDS for Instincts the way you have…"

Chili was pacing as he spoke. He would lumber away a few paces, then abruptly turn and walk back as if he'd hit the end of an invisible chain. "So the retired, instinct-handicapped Skyshooter just shut it all down?

"Had a bad day at the office. Got his ass chewed for it. And because of that he's all unplugged now – is that it?"

Lumbering away again, Chili pushed his thick fingers through his salt-and-pepper mane and said, "If I understand you correctly, I think what you're tryin t' tell me is the younger Troubleshooter would a' been more tuned-in? Would a' somehow stopped that fuckin airplane assassin before he could do the deed?"

Chili stopped pacing and looked around as if to confirm no one else was present. Then he looked straight at Hoot and said, "And you're tryin t' sell *me* this bullshit?"

***

They'd been cruising the strait aboard the Chartreuse all afternoon and deep into the evening, presumably so that Harold could fine-tune the autopilot speed control interfaces for the boat's new variable-pitch propellers. Jesse had blatantly played one of her favorite gambits – the promise of hot illicit sex – garnering an invitation to come aboard and assist. She hadn't expected Soozy Wickerman, the onetime Port Angeles Founder's Day princess and the boat's owner to decide at the last minute she'd come along and muddle things up. Soon as the sun started to set everyone hunkered down below deck because it was too blustery up top, Harold nervous and drinking like a proverbial sailor while Soozy shone the spotlight of attention on herself.

"I think we should make a deal," Soozy finally said as if she had just opened the candy jar, sugary sweetness wafting on her voice.

"A deal?" Jesse asked and the Billievoice in her head echoed, *A deal?*

Just look at her, Jesse thought. I remember she was a lot prettier when she was younger and the Billievoice added, *A few too many chocolate caramels will do that – set a princess up for gravity's revenge.* She'd had kids, too, Jesse remembered, and that probably hadn't helped in the looks department, either. She had definitely possessed a much tighter ass at one time.

What a pity, Jesse thought. She would never let herself go like that.

Evidently the old man thinks there's still some sass left in that ass, the new and assertive Billievoice said. No whiny baby-talk, now.

Meanwhile, Harold Hesse was holed-up in the princess's private forward cabin like the chickenshit Jesse knew he was.

"We need to talk!" he had phoned two days ago and said right out of the fucking blue as if whatever was on his mind was an unbearable load that had to be jettisoned immediately.

"Some things have been on my mind recently" he'd said. "Things that Howard told me. Things that bothered him until…well – you know. Really, we should talk. Privately."

Uh-oh! Shit's on the loose and heading for the fan! the Billievoice had cut in, sounding joyfully alarmed. It was one of Alan's favorite sayings that Jesse had always hated – "Shit's on the loose and heading for the fan!" – and it set Jesse's nerves on edge to hear the nagging Billievoice repeat it now, but she had no time to be dragged into Billie's bullshit and bit her allegorical tongue.

Meanwhile, passed out cold from sampling the thermos of pre-mixed Bloody Mary's and a plate of cannabis-infused peanut butter cookies that Jesse had brought along to kick-start their little cruise, Harold's rambling mouth was shut for now. Their floating party had evidently been entirely too lively for the old coot to keep up – a cheap date, and he didn't even do any of the $300 per-gram coke that Jesse had provided for the occasion. Couldn't get him to touch it, he seemed afraid of it, and he was probably smart to be scared; good shit was known to stop a weak heart, and Harold had an exceptionally weak heart, everyone on the peninsula knew it. Hell, a dime bag of ordinary, seriously stepped-on, street coke would probably have been enough to kill him if she could've got him to snort it. Instead, he'd sat openmouthed and watched his employer suck the good stuff up like an Oklahoma tornado, saying; "I never realized what a party girl you are, Soozy," over and over with a nodding head, a drooling smile, and another nibble of cookie.

Obviously wanting some time alone with Jesse, Soozy the aging beauty queen sent Harold to the forward cabin to sleep it off, saying to Jesse; "As I understand your situation; you'd like Harold to keep his big mouth shut, and I can see to it that he does," Soozy suggested, popping the cork on a chilled bottle of champagne to celebrate their eminent collusion.

I'll just bet she can! the Billievoice said. *In exchange for what? Your deepest gratitude? Don't forget, you don't have any money.*

...Will you please stop your interrupting, Jesse silently implored the voice in her head while asking Soozy Wickerman, "What sort of deal do you have in mind?"

Soozy smiled a well-worn smile that had once caused countless boys' zippers to come undone, said, "Your mother is one of the biggest brown heroin dealers on the peninsula. Everybody knows it. Quality shit for Mexican. Gets it straight from your papa; I happen to know that, too – don't ask me how. But she doesn't like me so she won't cut me in on the deal. I want what she's got. Without having to get it from her..."

She wants to retire Alison Wonderland! How's that for a ripe idea?

"You're assuming my mother'll cut you in on her action if I tell her to. I don't think so."

"...I didn't say I wanted anyone to cut me in. Oh no, I no longer have the slightest interest in being part of her business. I couldn't begin to care less what your mother does – lazy old hippy. Or, for that matter, what *your* thoughts on any particular subject might be," Soozy Wickerman interrupted with a tight and especially unbecoming pucker of her lips, the high-end Bolivian firing squad that should have killed Harold all nice and clean and easy-like getting his employer pumped up and prickly instead.

"I just love a little bubbly with my blow, don't you?" Soozy Wickerman said with a broad smile, pouring two glasses. She passed one of the glasses to Jesse, picked up the coke straw, pinched her nose, and sucked a generous snort of white powder to somewhere beyond the back side of her sinus cavities, took a moment to compose herself, and said; "Now, here's the deal…I want you to set me up with your papa. Directly. Once I'm set up, your mother can lie around with her tits hanging out until she turns brown to the bone – I don't care. Just hook me up with her source, and leave the rest to me. Make this happen, and I'll ensure that Harold stays quiet about certain details his brother might've shared regarding a native girl falling off his train."

"Sure," Jesse ventured, feeling a sudden flush from her scalp to her fingertips as clarity rushed in, a building sense of dread in her gut warning her that her world was ripping loose. "I suppose it could work." Except it requires trust, she thought, biting the side of her tongue until she could taste fresh blood in her mouth. Both hands buzzed with the need to grab at something, eager to tear something to shreds…

You're not very good with that trust business, the voice reminded. *Good thing you brought Grandma's knife along, huh? That was my idea.*

Jesse seriously did not want to do this, in spite of prior experience. She hadn't been sure she could even go through with her plan after Harold dismissed her offer of a little quality coke…not until this very moment – the point of no return. But her purpose was perfectly clear now.

The Wickerman bitch wasn't even supposed to be on the fucking boat for cryingoutloud!

The heavy-bladed Wusthof was only three steps away in Jesse's bag. But the champagne bottle was sitting right there on the end of the bar – much closer. And as the beauty queen leaned down for another snort of the costly blow Jesse closed her fingers around the neck of the bottle, saying; "Actually Soozy, I think I'll just go ahead and deal with the Harold problem myself, if you don't mind. As soon as I'm finished with you…"

Chapter 12

Jesse's hands and arms were covered with blood, her face and hair heinously splattered, and her last nerve was teetering on the verge of panic when she returned to the forward cabin to deal with Harold Hesse. Hesitating at the bulkhead, turning, and then starting back, she forced herself to stop a moment and gather her wits, get a leash on her frustration and anger from having to deal with Soozy Wickerman.

Queer that Jesse's memory of Soozy's... *killing* was so full of lapses. There wasn't a shred of doubt in her mind that she had killed the woman. But she had no real memory of it, either. Heart pounding, she'd edged around the lifeless form on the cockpit floor, and helped herself to a couple lines of the coke that had been left in an untidy heap on the bar before getting on with what she knew she had to do.

Jesse took a moment to catch her breath, then, using her thumb and forefinger to pinch her nostrils, she let go a mighty snort of heavenly snot to the back of her sinuses, saying; "Alright, now!"

She negotiated the corridor leading to Harold with the dubious advantage of coke-powered sea legs, bumping from side-to-side and leaving a Rorschach trail of blood to the next crime scene. The pain in her head clawed at the tender insides of her skull with ravenlike swipes, but the sensation was becoming muted by an increasing cocaine buzz that was obscuring certain details of what she had just done.

Obscuring some. Highlighting others.

Can't let him live. The man is untrustworthy. Completely unable to keep his mouth shut, the Billievoice said.

Yes. And thanks so much for handing my words right back to me, Jesse thought, feeling little interest in mollifying her inner demon in the midst of everything else going on at the moment. She paused, hand on the door handle, feeling the buzz sweep through and set everything right in her head. Her ears deaf to all but the sound of her own heartbeat and her fingers itching with renewed purpose; she pushed open the door...

Harold, obviously drunk and stoned beyond reckoning, was sprawled across the king-size bunk as if he'd been dropped there by a passing storm. Tormented by a secret that wasn't his but was killing him anyhow, he wrenched his eyes open and looked up at her with a pitiful expression when Jesse entered the master cabin.

"Now for you," she said.

He moaned.

Honestly, the man has no dignity – killing him is merciful, the Billievoice offered.

Closing the door behind her, Jesse almost felt sorry for Harold Hesse. Almost but not quite.

She was a dreadful sight, she knew, a murderous ghoul wearing the grisly horror of what she had done like a foul weather cloak. Soozy had not gone without a struggle; even after a skull-shattering whack from the champagne bottle, the woman had put up a fight, grabbing at Jesse as she fell, getting her fingers tangled in Jesse's hair and clothing while being repeatedly stabbed with Grandma's heavy knife.

Jesse turned...

Harold's eyes were glazed and unfocused. He blinked as if mocking a child's awkward efforts to wash away the Sandman's work: blinking away a memory or a dream. Then he focused on Jesse with renewed terror and cried, "Howard told me all about the Queets River trestle! He told me all about everything. Everything afterward. And everything before, too!"

"Now, you see Harold," Jesse said as if addressing a naughty schoolboy. "That's where you get into trouble...right there. You and your perverted brother sticking your noses into other people's shit, and then getting bent out of shape when something doesn't smell right?

"You shouldn't have listened to Howard's babbling. But you did. And, of course, you were horrified by what he told you. I can't even imagine how terrible you must've felt when he hung himself in the exact same spot where Billiejean fell. But it was none of your business – less your business than his, anyhow.

"People rode the logs all the time.

"The James Gang girls rode the logs all the time. No big deal.

"It was a tragic accident, what happened to Billiejean. And if your weepy brother hadn't taken Christine aside for a chat before I was able to talk to her, it would've stayed a tragic accident forever.

"Was all hearsay anyhow, what Howard thought he knew. Killing himself over it doesn't prove a damned thing. But it fucked-up my sister, bigtime.

"...And you, too."

Jesse came two steps closer, idly wiping the Wusthof blade clean on her shirttails.

Harold cringed, seeming to become smaller and even frailer than before on the red velour bedspread.

This was more like it, Jesse thought; the feeling of being in command of the situation. More like what she had planned all along – though she was beginning to appreciate how over-valued the necessity of planning could be if a person was quick-witted and determined. That was the key; quick wits and determination. No more puking her guts out in a corner for Jesse Vega!

"Don't misunderstand me, Harold" she told him. "I'm not here to settle the score for my rattled sister. And I'm certainly not here to unburden myself of some idiotic notion of guilt for shoving Billiejean off the train."

She said; "I'm only here because you've made a complete nuisance of yourself, Harold. You've become a 'loose end by proxy' as my papa Felix Vega would say. And if you knew my father, you'd know how we Vega's feel about loose ends."

Harold slammed his eyes shut tightly, so he didn't actually see Jesse raise the Wusthof. But he seemed to sense it coming down; saw it in his mind's eye, his doom riding on the tip of that heavy blade. He started to scream an instant before it touched his flesh.

***

106

Saturday evening Hoot watched the sun going down from the vantage point of Maddie Marvel's hot tub overlooking Port Timothy, a picture-postcard town full of vintage architecture anchored on the south bank of the strait, Canada hunkering in the northern distance. A mild evening with streetlights coming on, it was a soothing view, and Maddie was good company; the most gregarious woman Hoot had ever met, melding into almost any conversation with natural charisma and genuine interest. Even their conversations in the tub with both of them naked below the waterline, neither precisely *looking* but also not looking away, were comfortable experiences for Hoot – the nudity and the conversation.

Maddie was not a person that Hoot would call *talkative*...not precisely. His ex had been talkative. Maddie *engaged* people. There was a difference. Only four years younger than Hoot, compact and deceptively youthful-looking, but beyond the appropriate age to be called petite, she was full of energy and enthusiasm for everything life had to offer. Hoot often felt a little sluggish by comparison to Maddie, though he probably could've outrun a tsunami while lifting her off the ground with one arm forty years ago. Now, long hikes on local beaches and trails left him feeling breathless and her feeling revived in spite of his long stride and her much shorter one. Deep excursions off the trails and into the woods in search of wild mushrooms were hard on his knees and challenging to his stamina, invigorating to her.

"You make me feel my age," Hoot told her. "That's a new sensation for me, and I don't think I like it much."

"Oh? I make you feel old?" she queried with a challenging frown.

"I didn't mean that it was *you* making me feel old, but keeping up with you does," he said with a joker's smile and a quick peek below the bubbles, appreciating the inherent calm of non-sexual nudity with the opposite sex for the first time in his adult life. "I just am – that's all. I've grown old. I'm certainly not bitching about it; numerous doctors have confirmed a suspicion I have that I've outlived any reasonable expectations, all things considered..."

He and Maddie were entirely different, from different backgrounds and with different interests, but they were also the same in unexpected ways. The thing Hoot most appreciated about Maddie was the way she made him truly want to let go of the tension that was packed into every nook and cranny of his being. If only it were that easy; if tension hadn't been the secret fuel keeping him going his whole adult life since Vietnam. Part of him was afraid to let it go, because it was also the glue that kept his courage pasted together. He feared that he'd stall and come unraveled without it.

"You're an action person. I'm a word person," Maddie explained as they sat knee-to-knee in the hot tub like a headhunter's dinner in a cauldron. Discussing differences and similarities in their world-views and the responsibility writers have to their readers, Maddie said, "You always go straight to a fight without a second thought. And I'll always try to talk my way out of one. But we're both engaged in the fight; each in our own way, and hopefully to our best advantage. The only odd thing about me is how non-political I am for a journalist. People think I'm copping-out because I use more colorful language than most to give stories in the 'Graph an intimate local flavor instead of standing on a soapbox. I don't really care what the critics have to say because I know what my readers expect and enjoy. That's what matters to me."

Hoot knew this to be true. He had read several of her feature articles and Maddie always threw in details and snippets of personality that the big boys and girls working for the big publications overlooked. She was much the same face-to-face. Yes, it was funny how they were so different in so many ways, and yet they got along so well – especially, it seemed, while stewing in a cauldron.

Hoot recalled that his ex-wife, Linda, had once called him a taciturn man, teasing him with the word, saying it described him perfectly with the minimum number of words – one; saying he was always hard-pressed to lay-on extra words even on an exceptionally verbal day. And Linda would know. She had made up for his silences in spades until the day she simply wasn't there to contribute anymore. There were still days when he missed her constant jabbering.

Maddie was that way too, in her own fashion; always able to provide a running dialog during their time together without much help from Hoot. The difference was Maddie was more patient with him than Linda had ever been. What she talked about was more relevant somehow, and sex didn't have to be part of it. Weird how that worked. Maybe it was just his age kicking in at last; hard-won experience finally amounting to something. But he was pleasantly surprised at how sex never seemed to ruin the moment between them, even when they were sitting naked together in the hot tub.

"I'll take the potholes and speed bumps out of our conversation as long as it doesn't drive you nuts, me talking so much," Maddie said.

He responded, "I like the sound of your voice. My voice is mostly in my head."

"Nothing wrong with a silent thinker," she responded with a lingering look at the view; the sun a radiant mime taking a long slow bow before exiting the scene.

The house that Maddie shared with her sister was one of a dozen cantilevered stilt houses along Bayview Street in Port Timothy. With Butler Street far below on the view side, the sunset view from the deck was unimpeded. The sun was dropping faster now, sunset reduced to a blazing orb diminishing into the Pacific beyond the long gullet of the strait. The day was done, but the waning glow of twilight would linger on, the sky streaked with ribbons of backlit clouds in colors ranging from pink to deep red and purple following the prevailing airstream. The strait shimmered with reflections of the fiery sky above.

Looking at Maddie, Hoot found it impossible to make what he knew about her align with any notion of the press as he'd understood it his entire career. She simply didn't fit the mold of either the dirt-digging crusader on a quest for truth at any cost, nor the self-promoting narcissist after attention. And in spite of her position as editor and owner of the PT Telegraph, she promoted that distinction. What she told Hoot confirmed to him that her heart was essentially in step with his on the stuff that mattered; the brutally honest stuff that always has a way of popping up.

"I have the advantage of being so far out of the so-called mainstream press that I don't have to grub for headlines," she said as if reading his mind and responding to his thoughts. "They've become lazy, these so-called reporters snooping around. They're certainly not the investigative reporters they pretend to be. They're not even proper ambulance-chasers. And right now they're desperate because the holiday weekend is all but over. They see this as lead story material for a wrap up before they move on to the next headline, but they still have a measure of dirt to dig if they want it to pop."

"That means they'll be sleuthing around town tonight and probably tomorrow, interviewing locals who don't have a clue to offer and hoping to stumble over something linking Port Tim's murder to the one out past Port Angeles in Pysht Bay," Hoot said. "Maybe then they'll move on to PA and give Chili's nerves a break."

"They get desperate quickly," Maddie agreed. "If these so-called newshounds don't find something to chew on soon they'll start pulling theories out of their bottom-ends and selling them as 'likelihoods'. Most audiences won't know the difference."

"Don't I know it," Hoot agreed, the voice of experience talking. "They've been behaving themselves so far, but Chili doesn't trust them on principle. Don't forget; Cajuns still use newspapers to wrap their fish guts and other garbage. They have a word for editorial conjecture; it's called bullshit."

"Don't worry," Maddie said. "Grace will help. The reporter who can hoodwink my big sister hasn't been born yet. You know she took the train to Portland to be with her kiddos for Thanksgiving, but she's back now, and already down at the police station with Chili. She'll have an updated cheat sheet with talking points about the case to hand out, and that's all they'll get. Period."

"Good gal, your sister. Makes a horrible cup of coffee."

"Most print media reporters nowadays get their leads from either the internet or television, anyhow, all of them reporting the same story with the same hook like good little toddlers crossing the street on a rope," Maddie lamented. "And television news reporters are the worst of the bunch. They're puppets; not reporters – hair-gelled, bleach-toothed, teleprompter-reading puppets primping around Port Timothy like prostitutes on the dock when the fleet arrives.

"Television talking heads are most definitely not writers of the news, or anything else. It's all written by unseen hacks nowhere near the scene and read before studio cameras as if it were gospel. With green-screen technology using cut-and-paste graphics, they don't have to go anywhere near a location if it's inconvenient and still be seen live from there. News with FX! No wonder so many people get their news from the internet nowadays. The power of mute and delete makes all the difference. Free television as we've known it is as dead as hardcover books, vinyl LP's, and public phone booths. Get ready; free air and deep thought are up next!"

She had a point, Hoot knew. One of the things he enjoyed most about Maddie was the way she saw past the superficial sheen of everything, and she was very opinionated about what she found underneath. From her deck he could see vans from three different networks stationed at the entrance to Breakwater Beach Park a half-mile away, their easy-to-spot antennae raised and locked on invisible communication satellites loitering in near orbits as if their human operators were expecting the killer to stop by the crime scene any second now and explain himself.

She leaned closer, saying, "The good thing is they'll give up and go away even faster than they got here in the absence of a fresh corpse to pick apart; you're right about that. Give it a day. Two at most."

"As a fellow newshound you don't feel left out of the fun?" Hoot teased.

"Hardly! I admit I'm not above profiting from hometown troubles, but I live here, so whatever happens here happens to me. I don't see any reason to rehash in my paper what the network people have already spewed out. They're empty words, anyhow, for the most part; words without real meaning in my opinion. But sometimes a really big story comes along. Say an earthquake in Japan for instance. Or a terrorist attack on American soil. And maybe Big Media will try to put a human face on it. But, if the story is big enough, the ante for advertising dollars gets raised so high so quickly they can't help blowing the original story out of proportion. They overdo it and politicize it, networks trying to outdo each other by putting a Big Issue spin on everything, including the original human face that has, by now, been reduced to an icon for selling products and opinions. No matter how bad any situation is, it can always be trumped by how much worse it's about to get; that's the slant they're all looking for. It sells today's big news show and it sets up tomorrows."

"But your stories are different..."

"I think so. My slant is more personal. I look for some heart to put in my stories, a bit of romance whenever possible."

"Romance? In everyday news?"

"Sure…why not? Romance is good; every day needs a little romance in it to keep us from going completely nuts."

"Interesting that you would mention romance. Chili seems to think that's what's at the core of our friendship, yours and mine," Hoot said. "And he thinks you weren't too happy when I invited Jesse to dinner for Thanksgiving – because of the romance between us. Is he right?"

"Don't be silly," Maddie said. "Jesse was very interesting. Different, and interesting. I enjoyed her being there."

"I do feel attracted to her. I think you should know that," Hoot said.

Maddie smiled, said, "Of course you're attracted to her…obviously!"

"If it's a problem…"

Madeline Marvel laughed that take-you-in-and-nurture-you laugh of hers and said, "Pay no attention to anything Chili Hilliker says about relationships. I've heard it's very difficult for Cajun men to mind their own business, and that seems especially true of Chili. Makes him a very good police chief and a very nosey friend."

"Maddie," Hoot said, his pale blue eyes as serious as he could make them in the waning twilight, "If I've ever said or done anything misleading…"

"Don't even go there, Ezra Hooten," Maddie interrupted. "You've become a very dear and good friend this last year and I'm happy about that."

"Truly?"

"Truly indeed. Do you think I'd sit naked as a fish in this hot tub, talking truth with someone I didn't trust and feel completely at ease with? This works just fine for me…for now. What's more, I've come to know you well enough to suspect that anything more than *friends* may not wear well on our friendship."

Hoot smiled and said, "You've been talking to my ex-wife behind my back?"

Maddie gave him a light kiss on the cheek. "Never!" she replied and then quickly hopped out of the tub, grabbed her towel, and retreated inside to change for dinner at Chili's, leaving Hoot alone to enjoy the last minutes of the fading view from her deck. Mesmerizing and relaxing. Hoot could never express how much it

112

meant to him to feel so relaxed, how grateful he was for this simple peacefulness. Peaceful was not a natural state of being for a man who had spent his lifetime chasing bad people.

Hoot used the guest bathroom to shower and change. When Maddie returned, she was wearing a rose cardigan sweater over black wool slacks that flattered her slender legs and made her look taller than her actual 5'-2." Hoot couldn't help noticing she had some softly-interesting business going on underneath the sweater, and appreciating her feminine charms made him yearn to curl up in front of the fireplace and stay indefinitely; not a reaction he was accustomed to, and certainly different from his recent reaction to Jesse's commando-like attributes and attitude. Maddie wore a dab of makeup, her cheeks bearing a fresh hint of color that seemed to be inspired by the sunset. As a finishing stroke she had applied some lipstick; nothing shocking, it was the perfect shade of pink to compliment her sweater, the result dividing Hoot's attention between her slender-yet-curvaceous figure and the curve of her smile. She had a nice smile. Her hair was a springy mass of silver curls shot through with threads of auburn that seemed to catch the lowering light and hold it.

It hardly mattered to Hoot that Maddie might be considered a hottie for her age. Not that he hadn't noticed, but in his opinion her best attributes were her intelligence and sense of humor. Smartest woman he'd ever known. After sitting highbrow-naked with her in her hot tub for a half-hour, he couldn't imagine her flaunting her feminine attributes in a duel for attention with Jesse or anyone else. He had never wondered about Maddie that way before: if she might be the jealous type. He didn't think so, but what did he know about any woman's motivations? On the other hand, if Maddie had gone to these small troubles to push his buttons, it was working. And he was flattered by it.

"I'm starving," Maddie announced. "Did Chili tell you what's on tonight's menu?"

"Said it's a secret. The catch this morning was light, but he said to come hungry anyhow. The man can certainly cook, so it could be anything."

"I happen to know he's serving a stuffed pork loin with risotto and mesquite-grilled vegetables, toasted crab-and-cheese slammers for appetizers. And a cherry torte – my small contribution – for dessert."

"He told you?"

Maddie smiled and said, "I have ways of finding things out."

Yeah, Hoot was beginning to see that she did. Giving Maddie an appraising glance, he admitted to himself that something about this woman stirred him. But she was undoubtedly correct about anything beyond friendship between them only fucking up the friendship.

Chapter 13

Jesse returned to Seattle early Friday evening. This was sooner than she'd expected thanks to pure luck; she drew a short rotation, a quick round trip to Vegas and she was thankful she wouldn't have to take a sick day for what she knew was coming. Another visit to her own personal purgatory...

This one was going to be a bad one, she could tell, and she knew from experience there was no way she could've pulled a full rotation before the nausea and headache hit. Arriving home not a minute too soon, she went directly to her West Seattle apartment, showered with the water as hot as she could stand it, and then fell into bed in the grip of killer cramps.

She stayed under the covers until late Saturday afternoon when she finally resurrected herself. Her headache wasn't precisely gone – Jesse's headaches always seemed to leave traces like cobwebs in her cabeza. Dimming, but not fading away; disconnected shards of a nightmare floated around in her skull and merged with memories to form something entirely new, something dark, and menacing. Still, she felt much better now. Her nausea eased the instant blood started flowing from her cunt, she was like the Nile during flood season, dead endometrium sloughing away in torrents, her cramps finally letting go as her uterus surrendered to the inevitable hormonal siege. To her relief, she got through it this time without doing something rash.

She marked her calendar: 42 days.

After the Queets trestle incident, two people were recognized by WA State Social Services as Jesse's mental health monitors; two annoying people who'd still be more than happy, almost twenty years later, to express their disappointment and concern if they learned that she had suffered another bad one without reaching out to them, never once offering Jesse credit for sweating it out on her own. The Mood Gestapo, they were 1.) Her mother, always first on the list to care about being first on the list without giving much of an additional fuck; and 2.) Dr Hill, the shrink assigned by the county to evaluate Jesse after the Pablo incident – a fast-acting shrink, quick to offer his card and flee from both Jesse and her mother. She would not inform either of these long-term shirkers. There was no need. Instead, she texted Hoot, **What's up, Skyshooter?**

Hoot immediately responded, **I'd rather you didn't call me that.**

She phoned him; saying, "You don't like Skyshooter? Everybody's calling you that, now. It's viral on the internet, if you haven't noticed."

"I've noticed," Hoot said, his voice as flat as the phone in her hand.

"You put down the first bad guy in-flight, and that's what people want to see; reliable ol' Bruce Willis dying hard and shooting harder to keep them safe and secure in the skies."

"Bound to happen, I suppose," Hoot said matter-of-factly, not sounding especially proud – nor bitter or remorseful for that matter, obviously unwilling to engage the issue, the whole 15-minutes of fame thing something of a hot button with Hoot. "Keeping busy?" Jesse changed subjects as quickly as changing channels with a remote.

"Yeah, I'm plenty busy. Thanks for asking," Hoot said. "The ME report finally came back on the Breakwater case and it's quite the appetizing read. Blood tox. Viscous liquids. A bunch of well-focused images of a putrefied liver, waterlogged skin, and matted hair. The usual tasty menu; Chili and I will probably discuss it over dinner at his house. Manly stuff."

Jesse could hear the smile of boyish glee on Hoot's lips. She ignored his lame effort at testosterone-infused humor by asking, "Any new clues?"

"Too soon to say. We're still waiting for the lab to analyze a partial print we found on the knife."

"A print?" Her gut clenched.

"Not much of one, but it's amazing what they can do with digital regeneration these days."

Jesse took a deep breath and said, "Listen Hoot, my rotation got changed at the last minute, so I'm off a couple of days. I thought I'd make the obligatory holiday visit to see my mom in Forks. I could ferry and drive around the top of the peninsula instead of my usual bottom-end route through Hoquiam. Stop in and see you on the way if you like."

"Do you want to meet for dinner, and share in the manly chit-chat at Chili's?"

She offered a phony laugh at the suggestion, "Ha!" and said, "I've noticed that you don't like to eat alone..."

"It's not the eating alone as much as the cooking alone."

"I bet you're one of those people who eats straight from a package of cold wieners while standing at the sink. Don't worry, I am too. No...I don't think dinner this time. Maybe afterward? Just the two of us, if you don't mind?"

"Works for me. What time?"

"If I catch the 7:15 ferry out of Edmonds I should be there by 8:30 or 9:00."

"Somewhere in town for a drink then?"

***

It was dark and drizzly at 7:30. Jesse stood shrouded in her raincoat and scarf at the bow of the Edmonds-Kingston ferry, leaning against the painted steel deck rail and feeling the chill of it through thin black leather gloves. She watched the deep, dark water of Puget Sound sliding past. Lights scattered along distant shorelines. A few fishing boats heading home and a tug pulling a loaded barge. The return ferry from Bainbridge Island to Seattle lit-up like a Christmas ornament and gliding along its route a few miles away to the south.

So much water! Staggers the imagination; water a constant force to be reckoned with around here, and that's what people did, largely without a second thought for the inconvenience of it:

The rain. The humidity.

Moss and mold. Slugs and snails.

Stormwater runoff up the wazoo.

A moody climate, but Jesse liked it. Especially today. It suited her mood perfectly today – standing with the wind and rain in her face, holding onto the safety rail and thinking about her sad excuse for a mother…Alison Wonderland.

Mother. The word bore down on Jesse like a thick and musty blanket; something you'd expect to be comforting but suffocates instead. Her gloved fingertips tepidly touching her scarred cheek, she considered simply blowing-off her annual holiday visit with Mom and spending her free time with her new man-toy, Hoot, instead. But she knew it would be easier in the long run to just get her butt to Forks and get it over with.

Mom can wait, the Billievoice in Jesse's head said. *We should take care of your sky marshal buddy. We need to do that…*

No, Mom can't wait – that's her whole problem! Her capacity for self-pity is a boundless force that resents being ignored. You know how she can pitch a bitch, and I'm in no mood to listen to it. Mom needs people for holidays, you know; she needs an audience for her stoned reminisces of better times, wallowing in depression over her entire life turning to shit. Besides, Hoot's not going anywhere. We need an actual plan for him, nothing off the cuff the way we've been doing it.

We've been careful…

"No, we haven't. We've been lucky," Jesse said aloud, and then finished in her head; Good luck sucks because it never lasts – my daddy taught me that; but it was you who made it stick. Remember? A lesson learned the hard way is a lesson learned forever…

I get it. You're talking about the time we were all playing hobo on the train; you, me, and Christine hitching a ride down on the last log train from Black Pass. The time when Christine freaked out halfway across the Queets trestle. I remember it very well. I remember screaming at her to shut her mouth or the Luckraven would hear and come knock us off. Told her what my mamma always told me. Told her that good luck always runs out…

"You were right about that part, as it turned out," Jesse said aloud.

…I told her the Luckraven aid loves to peck a chickenshit on the head, and I told her she should shut up before he looked our way and pecked us. Not my fault the bird pecked the wrong head – that's all I meant.

118

No, it didn't happen that way. You were showing off to impress me, and lost your balance. And that's all there is to say about it...

The Billievoice was silent for a long moment, and then said in a tone that had whiplashed back to pre-adolescent petulance; *I think what you meant to say was that I was showing off and someone pushed me...*

Jesse sucked in a deep breath of moist air, filling her lungs with the coolness of it. Minutes passed, diesel engines churning; and then a long stretch of relative silence was broken by an enormous blast of the ferry's horn, the docking signal. She replied in a whisper, "You pushed Christine first..."

Arriving...Kingston Ferry Dock. All drivers please return to your vehicles. blared over squawky loudspeakers.

Alright then, the Billievoice said. *If you're so determined to go see your crazy bitchy mamma I guess we'll go see her....*

***

Maybe she shouldn't have teased Alan so much, that summer of '92, Jesse thought, but it was so easy. Alan was such a hornytoad and a stupid man, much more entertaining than Vincent, Christine's dad. Maybe she only did it to spite Billiejean...

She remembered teasing her that summer. A lot.

The Vacancy sign had been on at Mom's Motel ever since Jesse's abusive and unfaithful but romantically muy macho father departed. Her mother's ensuing boyfriends, potential stepfathers each and every one, passed through the place like second-string members of a minor league ball team. Most of them were short-timers and easily ignored by Jesse who figured there was little point in wasting effort getting close to the obvious losers. Jesse instinctively understood that her mother fell in love for recreation. Unable to find the long-term profit in it she claimed she deserved, but determined to find a keeper in the clutch, Alison Wonderland sifted ever-hopeful through whatever male chaff drifted her way. Meanwhile, whether intentionally or not, she was one piss-poor role model for an impressionable daughter on the cusp of her teens and eager for anything extreme.

The awful summer of 1992, twelve-year-old Jesse's erratic menstrual periods began and so did the headaches that went with them. It was the summer when she moved into her own room in the C wing at Mom's Motel, far enough away from her mother and Christine in the office apartment to largely ignore them both and to be mostly ignored in return except for Chrissie's neverending nosiness.

This was also the year when her mother, a self-described free spirit in a moment of weakness, gave Jesse a genuine artist's easel for her birthday. A huge one that had been custom built of straight grained oak for a long-dead portrait painter and resurrected by one of Mom's boyfriends-between-boyfriends. It was the best gift Jesse had ever received from her mother; the only one suggesting that her mom even remotely understood her. It should have been the spark, the key element that would turn her around toward a better future, a less troubled one at least.

It could have been better…couldn't it? Jesse had asked herself this question countless times.

Maybe not if her compass was already set and she could do nothing about it. Not if her path was a treacherous one from the outset. Not if it was too…*tilted* – too upside-down according to Billiejean's Mama Wisdom.

…Not at all in other words.

This was a condition Jesse understood only too well, the hard lesson being the well-learned lesson. There was blame to be laid, no doubt. But even as much as he may have deserved it, the blame could not be entirely laid at the feet of Jesse's Mexican drug runner father. He had seldom made an appearance in his daughter's life, treating her like a whore in training whenever he did. Papa Felix hardly deserved all the credit for Jesse's starch. Not entirely. Alison Wonderland was a piece of work in her own right. Stoned morning, noon, and night; she was the one who had allowed Papa to get away with it, all that bad behavior with his own daughter. Step-pappas too. Acted like she never even noticed.

Mom, ever busy being Mom and the rest of the time being out there, had paid Jesse and her sister minimum wage for housekeeping work they performed as regular chores at the motel. Cheap labor, keeping it in the family. Jesse was able to purchase enough art supplies with her earnings to dabble in various mediums, searching for one that fit. She was determined to shine; until that happened, she was largely determined to keep to herself, so she sketching and painting. Landscapes and buildings, including Mom's Motel and the gardens. Ordinary objects. Birds and people. Places in the woods few eyes had ever seen.

People were complicated. She had trouble with people and decided what she needed was a model, a real person to pose for her.

She quickly found one. He was older; sixteen. Dark-haired, and very pretty for a boy. He dressed in bluejeans, a tucked-in white shirt and a clip-on tie, and he had big dark eyes that always seemed to be looking around like crazy without seeing much. His name was Clarence but Jesse called him Pablo, and he worked at the IGA next door to Mom's where he stocked shelves, shagged empty shopping carts, and helped customers load groceries into their cars. Once or twice every week he would help Alison Wonderland and/or her daughters carry their bags to the motel next door, making idle chitchat while covertly angling for peeks at Mom's braless hippy assets. Easily flattered, Jesse's awkward preteen flirtations seemed to catch his eye almost as much as her mother's unrestrained breasts; her bohemian artistic notions seeming to intrigue him in spite of her youth. He had potential...

Jesse started volunteering to do the shopping alone, the chitchat between her and Pablo becoming bolder with more privacy. He answered her initial dare-you invitations for him to model nude for her in an exaggerated huff of brusqueness that she easily saw through. Pablo saying, "Huh-uh! I don't think so," later adding, "You're just a kid. It's indecent what you're asking," and "How old are you, anyhow?"

She knew these were only shams to hide his embarrassment at considering the idea. He was curious. She could tell...Pablo was a hornytoad right down to the bone, the way all boys are; she could see it in his eyes. Even at twelve-years-old Jessica Vega knew that look, had seen it in her own father's and stepfather's eyes many times. She knew how to reflect it right back at him and take it up a notch.

He blushed and smiled, saying, "You're kidding!" and "No way!" Then later still, he blushed a deeper shade of pink and grinned, saying, "Sure, why not? But nobody else can know. And, if I get a boner…"

She met him on a Sunday afternoon at her recently claimed studio, previously a kitchenette unit converted long ago into a storage area at the far end of A Unit at Mom's Motel. Not quite as bold as he had let on, once Pablo was actually there in her studio and realized that she was serious, his commitment to go through with posing in the buff vacillated. He started making stammering excuses, saying things like, "If anybody found out…" and, "It's a sin…" until the back of his skull met the business end of a rusty old golf putter that had been left in the closet since the heyday of the motel garden.

His body immediately collapsed on the dirty linoleum floor as if he'd been a puppet all along and someone cut his strings. Mad, disgusted, and suddenly excited to her core, Jesse hit him a few more times; making a mess of his head just to make sure he was dead.

He was easy to pose after that.

She took her time drawing a set of eight highly-detailed sketches. She locked them away in her secret treasure chest, and then ran to the office, crying rape.

It was all her doing, this first incident. And the overwhelming experience of it laid her low for days with a crippling headache and the onslaught of a heavy menstrual period nearly two weeks early.

Years later, when Jesse was a lance corporal in the US Marines military police, she read about philosopher Martin Heidegger's claim that whenever an object or a desire passes from concealment into revelation, truth appears. Heidegger was right, she knew, it does. She knew this from personal experience in 1992, even though she had been immature and confused; too young and too vain to understand much of life or anything else at twelve-years-old. But she nonetheless understood that the truth about Jessica Vega had appeared on that day in her studio, the day her life changed forever. And the truth was that she was wired all wrong from the start; her heart disconnected from her soul without a spark to bridge the gap.

With an odd combination of pride and shame, Jesse finally came to understand that she was, indeed, her father's daughter; remorseless, the blood in her veins running dark.

She could detest the Billievoice in her head all she wanted and it wouldn't matter one iota, except to make it worse. She knew this because she knew that she had created it herself; her own little demon. The ever-intrusive voice a manifestation of Jesse's own overactive guilty conscience posing as Billiejean Wisdom's ghost – it had to be.

...Jesse knew this, and struggled to believe it.

Chapter 14

Early Monday morning the sun would've been rising over the North Cascades if there were any sun to be seen. There wasn't, not that Hoot or Chili would notice – they were ensconced in the windowless back room of Chili's office where they had already been hard at it for four solid hours; cross-referencing crime scene notes and photos from Dr. Wolfe's ME report and other case files on the Breakwater Beach murder with the similar murder at Pysht Bay near Port Angeles, comparing details and pinning notes on the board. Basically, this was old-fashioned police grunt work done the old-fashioned way with a bit of computer-age assistance, not exactly cutting-edge, but technology the two old-timers felt comfortable working with; hard copies were best, and slides, but slides were so outré now that finding a working projector or light table might require an archeological dig. Instead, files had been emailed from offices and labs participating in the investigation, archived on a memory stick, and printed by Grace Marvel for her boss, everything neat and tidy before Chili and Hoot attacked it in much the same way an old-time cavalry unit would've hit an entrenched artillery position…head-on and furiously.

The Breakwater Beach case was a few days fresher than the Pysht Bay case, and related files were already thick and growing thicker with law-enforcement agencies near and far answering the call to take part in a combined investigation, leaving Chili's conference table stacked like it had never been before. There were reports from two separate police departments plus the big combined report from the Clallam County sheriff's department, the waterway manifest from the coast guard including satellite imagery, and two complete medical examiner reports with extensive photo documentation. Immigration, ATF, FBI, and Homeland Security. Even Fish and Game had opinions and their reports were also on the table. Last, but hardly least, was an uploaded and printed file from the WSP crime lab in Seattle.

Tight-budgeted and understaffed as always, the Port Timothy police department could manage routine stuff; the occasional quick-mart heist, the usual drunks and druggies, speeders and stop sign runners. They could deal with the occasional wife beater and the hardly-ever husband beater, the trespassers, the shoplifters and burglars, but murder was something else, and multiple murders were bound to be hellish. The paperwork alone would soon be enough to fill a barge. By next week the case would probably have its own dedicated mainframe computer storing data while generating enough heat to incubate dinosaur eggs because nobody in Chili's office really trusted the so-called cloud for data storage.

Chili certainly did not begrudge the Clallam County sheriff for taking the lead role in combining both cases into what would soon become known as the Juan de Fuca Murders. But Chili being Chili, he wasn't about to entirely relinquish his interest in what he saw as nothing less than a murdering psychopath's assault on the character and soul of Port Timothy, and by Cajun logic, an assault on his personal self as well.

Yes…Chili would remain very much involved. And what's more, he had an advantage the sheriff's department didn't have: he had Ezra Hooten, the relentless Troubleshooter, working off the clock.

"We know our guy was seriously stabbed t' death. Strugglin with his attacker as evidenced by the cuts on his hands and arms before he went in the water t' soften up a bit," Chili said. Reading from the Clallam County sheriff's department summary, he added, "Looks like the Pysht Bay victim was also stabbed t' hell and back and spent about a week in the water, but her stab wounds were shallower than our guy's, and none appear to be defensive, suggestin she was unconscious early in the attack. Had a dent in the back of her skull that would've killed a cow. Exsanguination was the actual cause of death; bleeding-out within a few minutes of getting bludgeoned and tenderized." Flipping the page, Chili read; "Identified as Soozy Wickerman of Sequim. Age 33. A young widow. She was the heir to Wickerman Lumber in Port Angeles – possible money motive there, but her connection to our guy is…" He shuffled through more papers, bunching his eyebrows and scanning the sheets with experienced eyes, said, "Unknown."

Chili tossed the file on the table, surmising; "So…Soozy Wickerman of Sequim was bludgeoned before she was stabbed? Seriously stabbed like our guy was, I might add. Whaddya make of that?"

"Bludgeoned. With what?" Hoot asked.

"Club of some kind – left a sizeable indention in the back of the young widow's skull. A fisherman found her body tangled in the brush near the mouth of the Pysht along the road out t' Neah Bay, a local surfer spot with some good-sized rocks at the shoreline, but the ME report shows no water in her lungs, so she was dead b'fore she got anywhere near the rocks."

"No defensive cuts on her hands or arms…" Hoot pondered. "That makes the Pysht River gal the likely first victim and our guy sloppy-seconds."

"Pardon me?" Chili said.

"Assuming it's the same perp and the victims were together when they were killed; if we're dealing with a serial killer's mentality, my guess is that the buzz was inadequate without the struggle. A common motivation among serials is the buzz they experience through their victims' suffering, hence the defensive wounds on our guy – struggling the whole time he was being killed. That's why I suspect the Pysht Bay gal was the first victim, but the killer's buzz was unsatisfactory, so our guy took the brunt of it."

"So the killer's ginger snaps for some reason," Chili said. "An argument with Soozy, maybe, and the killer kills her in a fit of passion, alerting our guy, who then tried to defend himself when it was his turn."

"Sure, I'll buy that," Hoot said. "But the woman had money and plenty of it – a very popular motive for murder."

"Soozy Wickerman owns a huge boat that is presently MIA according to the Coast Guard's marina report, and I don't think that's a co-incidence," Chili said.

"Fair enough. Both crimes fit the same general timeframe. We'll nail that down tighter as soon as we get our guy's verified TOD from young Doctor Wolfe," Hoot said, taking a long sip of the coffee Grace made and wincing with acid-fueled satisfaction.

"If it was a cold-blooded professional hit; say one of those drug smugglers the Coast Guard has been seeing so much of since the border with Mexico tightened up was involved, then I figure the Pysht Bay gal was clubbed and tenderized to send a message to someone, another smuggler, and Breakwater was the same message with exclamation points. Hot-blooded murder would be the same basic scenario but with more passion. Either way, I agree with you; the victims were most likely killed onboard Soozy Wickerman's boat, and she got it first. We need to find that boat."

"You really think knockin the woman out before stabbin the holy crap outta her was an efficient way t' kill her, but unsatisfactory for the perp?" Chili asked.

"If it's a serial killer, or some other kind of passion-fueled killer…then probably yes. Passionate murder is always about satisfaction. Professionals, or commonplace killers; makes no difference. In the end they're all just fucked-up people with a skewed perspective on what's what. The thing they all have in common is the way their methods don't change much with their circumstances, both pros and amateurs.

"Pros are doing a job and that's all there is to it. To them, getting paid to put a bullet in someone's head is simply a better gig than driving a truck or selling shoes. Satisfaction has nothing to do with it – easy money is their only motivation. Cagey and proficient killers, methodical; they're very predictable people once you know their methods. What I know of amateur killers tells me they are inevitably poor strategists; they do their crimes off-the-cuff and they usually give themselves away very quickly on the lam.

"I haven't got a lot of experience with psycho killers per se with one distinct exception, but enough to know the basic difference in the way they think and behave. Psychos are different critters altogether, motivated by their own inner demons. Geniuses, some of them. They're predictable only because they're basically junkies at heart, satisfying a need, and they're often very creative about it. They get satisfaction, albeit briefly, by inflicting grievous harm on others," Hoot said, adding, "including torture," with a distasteful expression. "It's not uncommon for them to kill to satisfy a specific theme, linking their victims in ways that can seem vague to others but not to them. For example, we know the gal in the Clallam County ME's cooler was quite a few years younger than our Breakwater Beach victim, so the question is how are they connected other than the number and size of their stab wounds?"

Chili waved his hand to encompass the disheveled tabletop and bulletin board, said, "So, what we have is a sizeable pile of circumstantial shit and reasonable deductions connecting her to my guy, but nothin certain. Sure as hell the same sorta knife wounds – stab-n-stab-again. Forensic tests to determine if it was the same knife have been ordered by Dr Leonardo Wolfe," Chili read from the ME report. "Ordered Friday but results are not yet available."

"Good news is that we actually have the knife. Should be a simple matter to see if it fits the PA woman's wounds. Wasn't so many years ago guys like us would just stick it in and see if it wiggles instead of waiting for digitally-plotted x-ray wound comparisons. We already know it's going to fit, so let's proceed on that assumption until it's proved otherwise."

"Patience, Marshal Hoot. Got nobody for you to shoot...yet," Chili said with a grim smile. "The investigation's the tedious part. Not that you've ever been much of a thumb twiddler. Right now we're obviously up t' our butts in bait and no fish, but you're the one said it was a good thing the young doctor is a...how'd you put it – a meticulous man? Give him time. We're all meticulous on this one, lookin at every possibility."

"If the knife matches I'll agree we could have a serial or psycho killer on the loose," Hoot said, "but it still doesn't rule out a professional hit."

"You actually think a pro would use a goddamned kitchen knife?" Chili said, flabbergasted.

"Why not? I happen to know they're using dental floss nowadays."

Chili shot his friend a scowl, grumbling; "A single goddamned partial fingerprint on the knife – partial bein a generous description for a smudge. And no DNA. We do have the dinghy from Soozy Wickerman's boat found in a brushy mud bank at Pysht Bay, still bein processed for prints while our guts scream bloody deuces because the info we need is too damn slow comin. Ain't it great, law enforcement here at the very peak of the Information Age? Swear t' God it was a hellava lot easier doin what we have to do before we had to be so fuckin informed first!"

"Careful, you're starting to sound a lot like me," Hoot said, taking a long look at a series of photos in the Port Angles file. "Let's confirm the Clallam sheriff still has the Pysht Bay site cordoned-off and find out where they took the dinghy for forensic processing. I'd like to drive over and have a close look at that crime scene."

"Good. I'll call and set it up for you."

"Tomorrow mid-morning would be best. I might take a little side trip afterward and meet-up with Jesse and her mother in Forks."

"Meet her mother? You're joking!"

Hoot shook his head and said softly with a smile, "No. I'm not."

Chili wanted to take the bait about Jesse and her mother, but knew he wouldn't get far with it. Instead, he pushed his chair back in tired exasperation, said, "Jeezus Howard Hughes Christ! Port Tim used t' be such a nice and peaceful town. Bad voodoo's what it is. Bad voodoo…"

Twenty-two years in the Pacific Northwest as a lawman: sheriff's deputy, and highway patrolman, finally ending up as the Port Timothy chief of police – and Charles Hilliker still spoke with a drawl that made him sound like a freshly-landed tourist from a sultry climate. A misplaced Cajun, bits of Louisiana clung to his raspy voice with the tenacity of cold molasses, especially when he let his frustrations run loose. No matter, Chili knew the lay of the land in and around his jurisdiction better than any lifelong resident. He dug his troubled fingertips through the mass of graying black curls piled atop his head, massaging the spikes of blood pressure he felt racing through the roof of his skull, said, "I gotta stay here and deal with the goddamned press tomorrow. You see anything over in PA or Pysht Bay needs my immediate attention just call and I'll break away faster 'n a Bayou crock durin crawdad season. And I mean anydamnedthing that might give me an excuse."

Chili un-mussed his hair with a quick pat and then hid it all away under his cap, grabbed his keys, said, "Let's back away from this happy horseshit for now and go to lunch – I'm hungry for somethin deep fried and bad for me…"

Chapter 15

By the time Hoot met Jesse, he'd long been accustomed to thinking
of his sex drive as being a lot like his spleen, a minor organ he'd left
behind in Vietnam after a VC bullet removed a sizeable chunk of it.
"A spleen is something that may be handy to have, nice even when
it's working the way it's supposed to, but not mandatory in adults,"
he remembered the army field surgeon who removed it explaining.
"Your life may not be exactly the same without a spleen. How could
it be? The changes, the vulnerabilities? But you'll go on until,
eventually; as you get older you won't even miss it."

  The surgeon had been right. Hoot got on with his life and
hardly missed it: the spleen or, ultimately, the sex. Odd, because until
then sex had been plenty important to Hoot his whole life beginning
in his teens; his wildly-lustful teens his ex-wife, Linda, would tease
him, knowing that he was a romantic at heart and shy about his
albinism in spite of the bluff he put up about it like a suit of chain
mail, the way his entire body would blush and burn with
embarrassment. The Vietnam experience had extinguished anything
remotely satisfying romance-wise for Hoot, and Donna Messenger's
murder had trampled whatever shards remained. Physical sex had
ultimately become his exclusive conduit for love, a fickle hunger that
was never quite satisfied.

  Maybe Linda had been on target when she called Hoot a
romantic psychopath, saying he was incapable of distinguishing
between love and lust, forever convincing himself one was the other.
"Truly, with you, if Lust isn't at bat, Love isn't even in the game," she
had claimed and he'd never figured out if it was meant as an insult or
not because, to him, that was just the way it worked. At least, in the
beginning, it had been mutual: the lust and the love.

The weird thing to Hoot was the way there hadn't been anyone serious in his life after Linda, though he would gladly commit grievous bodily harm to himself before admitting it out loud in public. To this day he wouldn't dare to even think it in Linda's presence, the way she had always seemed to know his thoughts before he thought them.

Theirs had been a fierce love affair without bounds, his and Linda's – this was before the freeze came and turned the sheets icy; but back when it had been hot it had been reallydamned hot. Being with Jesse reminded Hoot of that long-ago time with Linda. All the passion and the heat – intense shit! And the sheer fun of it! The difference was that in Linda's case it was genuine wild-child abandon that drove her, while Jesse's passion seemed more calculated, as if there was a scoreboard somewhere nearby.

Odd that Hoot would take the slightest note of these differences. Maybe it was just another sign of Ezra Hooten getting older, he thought; the price an old fart pays for all those years of chasing after hotties half his age to unwind from chasing an endless parade of assholes and nasties – the neverending loop.

If Hoot became a bit zealous for sex after his return from Vietnam it was Linda who showed him the way. She was the real deal back then, and he'd bet she still sizzled today. His favorite memory of Linda was a warm summer night early in their relationship – must have been almost forty years ago; he and Linda were walking through the woods on the east side of the U of Maine campus where she was a post-graduate student, and on a dare she had stepped behind an elm tree, slid out of her skirt and sweater and everything else, and stood there in the dark as naked as she had ever been in her life. Giggling about it, she double-dared him to put up or shut up...so he put up and damned-near got them both caught.

Yes, Hoot thought, Linda had certainly been the real deal back then, a true hot-blooded flower child of the sixties, turned into a driven liberal in the seventies, striding around the eighties in high heels and short skirts with a post-grad chip on her shoulder. And then the fire died; slowly enough that Hoot hardly noticed until the embers were cold. Even then they'd hung on for some years, routinely patching their marital malaise with promises of better times.

They were thin promises wearing ever-thinner with indifference, Hoot using plenty of liquor for ointment.

That was prettymuch it for Hoot romance-wise. Not sex-wise, precisely, but even as good as it had once been, after a while Hoot didn't yearn for the sex so much. The pressure of his job taking an escalating toll, just hanging on for the kids' sake required too much emotional investment to leave energy for much else.

Then came the shell. Like a callous, it slowly formed around whatever soft places he'd once possessed, hardening and numbing him. It had taken a goddamned long time to form that callus, but he only became aware of it when Linda suddenly informed him in no uncertain terms; "We have an appointment tomorrow night with a marriage counselor and you should do whatever's necessary to be there."

Hoot barely heard Linda's ultimatum – her words hard and brittle as hailstones.

This was August 19th 1992. Hoot was scheduled that evening to join a chartered US Marshals flight heading for the famous fracas at Ruby Ridge in the remote woods of northern Idaho. He missed his appointment with the marriage counselor.

***

"Tell us about your new girlfriend," Maddie said to Hoot, a devious twinkle in her eye, but otherwise wearing a strict poker face. They were standing with Chili at the oversized sink in his undersized kitchen, and she was choosing tidbits of leftover crab meat, piling it atop lightly-toasted English muffins with grated cheddar and pepper jack cheese, thin slices of red onion, everything held in place with a dab of mayo. Two minutes under the broiler and dinner would be ready. Fried okra and Chili's private reserve pickled asparagus spears on the side, this was Cajun comfort food. Ice-cold strong black tea with lemon. Notably no beer or wine – Hoot and Chili were cutting back on the booze and losing all restraints on caffeine while working the case.

Brushing aside any hint of innuendo that Maddie's words might've been loaded with and ignoring the girlfriend bait, Hoot answered; "Not much to tell. Actually, I hardly know her," and his words landed as politely unnoticed as dust motes on an otherwise clean floor. After a pause while he ground fresh beans for coffee, Hoot responded to Maddie's doubting glance and Chili's arched eyebrow by elaborating; "You both know that my personal life has largely been a comedy of errors. Some considerably more serious than others, but all of them taking bites out of my backside – the moral being don't look back; you may not like what you see."

"…And don't have expectations lookin the other way," Chili added.

"…And don't speculate," Maddie offered, unwilling to be left out.

"Hoot's rules," Chili said. "Numbers 8, 9, and 10, I think, of hundreds."

"So I take it we've had this sort of conversation before?" Hoot said. "Maybe I'm moving beyond limiting my observations about Jesse to the superficial."

"Any luck with that?" Chili said.

Hoot smiled that well-practiced changeling smile of his and said, "Asking as friends?"

"Of course," Chili answered with a wink at Maddie. "Friends who know what a to-the-core pessimist you really are."

"Fair enough."

Drawing fresh water for the coffeemaker and drying his hands with a towel while considering his answer, Hoot finally said; "I admit I've been a longtime believer in the notion that no one else would be able or willing to light my fuse the way my ex did. Haven't been looking for anybody nor expecting anyone to step up to the challenge. So I let it go, the whole physical aspect of relationships." He loaded the coffee beans in the grinder and hit the magic button – it was going to be a strong pot of java.

Maddie and Chili exchanged an exaggerated look and Chili said, "Preachin to the choir, here, buddy."

"Truthfully," Hoot said with an appreciative smile, "that was an easier door to close than I ever would have expected. Pardon me if I'm getting into uninvited territory here, Maddie, but to me it was like a man's version of menopause. Call it embracing the concept of male menopause on a personal level, a slowly developing check-your-balls-at-the-door attitude, and being okay with that. Then…boom! Without warning here comes someone fun and different, and it's exciting to have the old testosterone flowing again. What else can I say?"

Maddie glanced at Hoot with an expression suggesting that electro-shock treatments might help if he got them soon enough, and Chili said; "Different, huh? No shit, Sherlock. One look an' anybody can see that she's different."

"I'm curious," Maddie said. "How did she get those facial scars?"

"I'm not talking about her scars," Hoot said. "I don't even see the scars."

"I'm not talkin about her scars, either," Chili said. "There's just somethin about her sets my warnin bells off."

"…Ditto that," Maddie offered in a low voice.

***

It was the tall black man, Mr. Kenneth, who came to Jesse with a proposition. Early in the spring of 1997, when Jesse returned home from her two-year stay with her father after the Queets River incident, one of Mr. Kenneth's minions took her aside at SeaTac as soon as she stepped off the jetway.

Mr. Kenneth wasn't with the DHS back then as there was no Department of Homeland Security, leaving it unsaid exactly to whom or to what agency he reported, but his authority seemed unchallenged. "I'm not precisely with anyone. I'm more of a freelancer – department-wise, at least," he explained later, but at the time he was an enigma.

"I'm interested in your father," he said to her after introducing himself with a bogus-looking smile so void of warmth Jesse figured the frost from it must surely hurt his teeth. They were in a private concourse pilot's lounge, empty except for the two of them standing near a window overlooking the runway and the docked jet that she'd just arrived on; Mr. Kenneth, tall, dark, and thin as a stick, and Jesse, a petit teenager wound tight, the scar on her cheek fresh and mean-looking.

"So? Who isn't?" Jesse answered defiantly, seventeen-years-old, angry from the inside out and full of derision for anyone presenting the slightest show of authority.

Mr. Kenneth, seeming to gauge the depth of her scorn with his silent eyes, changed course as quickly as a master chef revising a basic recipe on the fly, adding a pinch of personality, a dash of muscle, and saying, "He's not a nice person, your father. I think you already know that…"

Something in his attitude caused Jesse to realize that Mr. Kenneth was one of those shadowy political creatures her father often railed against, one of the clowns behind the clowns, sanctimonious gameplayers who seem to know everything there is to know about everybody and feel free to use the knowledge indiscriminately.

This worried her because Jesse kept some tight secrets. It simply would not do to let them unravel. So she'd hidden them away with their loose threads in her treasure box in case she ever needed them; safe but out of harm's way and temptation's reach.

"You don't have any idea what I've been through the last two years. What has happened to me," she said, realizing, with a spike of dread that, of course, he knew. He knew about everything he wished to know about because Mr. Kenneth was one of *them*; the legitimacy of her father's constant paranoia validated.

Them.

They watched.

And they listened…always.

"I'm happy to listen if you want to talk about that," Mr. Kenneth said, gesturing with a file folder in his hand. "Help set the record straight?"

"Are you here to arrest me?" Jesse asked, successfully swallowing the lump rising in her throat. Her eyes were captured by the file.

"No, of course not!"

Mr. Kenneth's smile was a wee bit warmer, though not precisely compassionate, Jesse decided – and still thin.

He said "I admit I've been doing some research into your history. I found some interesting circumstances here and there in the data that has accumulated on you. You surely must realize that your circumstances are unusual. But as you can see, it's not much of a file." He dropped the folder on a tabletop and continued, "Details are obviously missing, and I wonder if you could help fill-in some of those details rather than leave me to make assumptions? What do you think?"

Jesse looked at him with all the contempt she could muster, but said nothing.

His eyes were what made Mr. Kenneth look so intimidating, she decided: cold, intelligent, snakelike eyes, the eyes of Thulsa Doom, the 1000-year-old snake-worshipping villain in the movie Conan the Barbarian, one of her father's favorites played frequently at Playa Rocosa.

"As I said, I'm interested in your father. That's the only reason I'm interested in you; because your relationship with him is…unique. And while researching your records some concerns came to light," Mr. Kenneth said, opening the file and pulling out a page, taking a seat at the table and silently regarding Jesse for a moment. He gestured for her to sit across from him, continuing only after she was situated, "For example; I'm sure you remember Clarence, the grocery clerk who tried to rape you five years ago but was killed by you in self-defense instead? Must've been very traumatic for a twelve-year-old girl."

He set that page aside and leafed through a few more pages, running his serpentine eyes over them while saying; "Maybe not as traumatic as seeing what was left of your best friend smeared all over the trucks of a railroad car three years later. I can understand why an impressionable girl would need a long respite with her father in Mexico away from so much violence at home." He smiled without including his eyes and said, "A shame what your sister endured while you were away. Institutionalized for life, most likely."

Mr. Kenneth quietly closed the file, giving the cold lump in Jesse's throat a moment to wrestle with her determination to stay calm. The ensuing silence verging on uncomfortable, he said, "The rail car incident was obviously a tragic accident. Tragic. And I sincerely hope time away with your father tempered the shock. My only real concern about all of this past history of yours is that the clerk-rapist investigation was such a sloppy investigation. Very sloppy. And brief." He tore the single sheet he'd set aside in half, twice, and said, "It should be tidied-up for the peace-of-mind of everyone involved, I think. Don't you?"

"What do you want from me?" Jesse asked, the lump in her throat melting into a puddle of anger, expecting that she'd like the answer only if it was a lie. Then again, this Mr. Kenneth had the air of someone for whom lying is simply too far beneath their dignity to consider, the burdens of unsolicited truth other people's problem.

He closed the file and said, "As troubled a girl as you obviously are, and much as you may need my help whether you realize it or not, I sincerely have no interest in you, Jessica, other than to be helpful if possible. Your father, however, is another matter. I do have a significant interest in him, and I would hardly have the time or resources at hand to thoroughly investigate a sloppy five-year-old investigation about you if I were giving proper attention to him."

Giving Jesse a moment to digest what he was suggesting, Mr. Kenneth continued; "Law enforcement is all about resource allocation these days – computers doing all the thinking even if someone has to tell them what to think; the irony is that much of the time it's actually more complicated and expensive to get needed information than ever before!"

His tone became as warm as buttered biscuits. His eyes hooded, he said; "If there were someone close to el Lobo whom I could trust to provide me with timely information about certain things, I'm confident I could use leverage from that information to turn resources away from other more irrelevant matters and get down to business with your father, The Wolf. Do you understand my dilemma, Jessica?"

Yes. She understood. The light had come on and Jesse understood only too well. She had done her stint as Felix Vega's little whore-in-training the last two years; the parties, one-after-another at Playa Rocosa until it was one big neverending bacchanalia, glazed eyes and rough hands taking liberties with her, all with her father's blessing; ultimately with his participation. For two crazy, terrifying-yet-fascinating years she had seen first hand the power her father wielded over the lives of everyone around him, and now this skinny black man without a boss thought he could flip her?

Her mounting anger as clear as White Lighting in a shot glass, she laughed and said; "You want me to rat my father out? Hah! Not gonna happen, Stickman…"

Chapter 16

Clack-clack, clack-clack…clack-clack – clack-clack, clack-clack…the thirty-car Rayonier logging train snaked its way downhill from the sizing and grading yard at Black Pass to the sorting and holding yard in Hoquiam, its steel wheels seeming to tap coded messages as they rolled over joints in the track, the rails telling tales of trees from long ago, survivors of fires floods and pestilence eons before man and axe ever saw these woods felled and hauled away in a mere blip of earth time; this particular tale was being tapped-out on a warm and humid evening in the summer of 1995:

Twilight had arrived. Full dark was coming. And Jesse Vega's three-girl gang was riding the logs, a strictly-forbidden favorite pastime of theirs. Thirteen-year-old Christine was sitting up on top of the load and holding onto log loose bark for dear life. Bolder and braver Jesse with tagalong Billiejean, both fifteen-years-old, were down lower on one of the lengthier logs that extended well past the cradles where they rode like perched ravens. Their log cantilevered out over the couplers between cars where it almost touched the longest logs on loads ahead and behind, the space between them a treacherous place that was constantly alternating wider and then narrower as curves were negotiated by the train, rough stobs swiping past each other with the promise of Poe's pendulum.

"What do you think the rails are saying?" Billiejean Wisdom asked Jesse, practically yelling her head off just to be heard.

"They're saying if this train doesn't get across the skinny Queets River trestle before full-on dark somebody's gonna go pee-pee in her panties."

"I'm not scared!" Billiejean protested.

"Oh yes you are! No fibbing allowed…"

Jesse stood up and turned loose with her hands. Balancing atop the cantilevered end of a sizeable log, she looked up at her white-knuckled sister sitting on top of the load. Filled with wicked glee, she glanced back at the last few cars following them around a bend. And then with a little hop she turned and looked ahead as they entered another curve, seeing the train stretching out both ahead and behind, the entire quarter-mile-long rail-car ribbon of logs that had been living trees only a week or two ago. Mimicking a soaring raptor staking her claim in the forest she extended her arms out to her sides like wings with fingers instead of feathers at their tips. The wind in her face dusty, smelling of cedar and tamarack, she screamed like a screeching hawk, her spirit guide according to Billiejean's grandmother – "Skeee! Skeee!"

"Cut it out, Jesse!" Billiejean cried. "You'll fall!"

"Not me! Watch this!"

Without further warning Jesse took two quick steps and leaped across the treacherous space between cars onto the rough stob of the longest log protruding from the car ahead, waving her arms to catch her balance as she landed.

Billiejean screamed, "Jesseeeee!" at the top of her lungs while the rails kept on tapping out their code, repeating clack-clack, clack-clack – clack-clack, clack-clack over and over.

"Hey! What's going on?" Christine demanded, raising her head up like a blind gopher in a shooting gallery, long blonde hair blowing all directions in a zillion tangles, her eyes squeezed shut.

"Jesse jumped! She jumped ahead!" Billiejean yelled hysterically, pointing and tattling on her friend. "She could've fallen!"

"I'm not gonna fall, you big chickenshits!" Jesse hollered back to her so-called posse. Then she leaped across the open space again, returning to where she had been before, Billiejean grabbing and hugging her furiously while beating her fists against her back.

Christine peeked out from under a hand shielding her eyes and yelled "Stop showing off, Jesse!" with all the overdone petulance she could muster considering the chaotic circumstances.

Jesse laughed, plopping down to sit on the log while Billiejean wailed, "Not funny!" giving Jesse's shoulder a hefty girl-gang punch for good measure and sitting down beside her with her brows knitted into half-hitches.

Jesse had often wondered since that day how differently things would've turned out if Billiejean had just stayed put and pouted. But the path never is a straight one, and even the best of minions will sometimes wander...

Chrissie's climb down from her perch while the train was in motion was tedious but successful. She was obviously scared shitless and madder than mad when she got there, saying; "Curses on you for this idea, Jessica Louise!" She was working herself into a good sniveling whine but was quashed by the blaring loco horn blew indicating the last grade crossing before the Queets River trestle was coming up just ahead.

Honk-honk! Clack-clack, clack-clack – clack-clack, clack-clack...

"I hate the part over the water!" Chrissie complained with all the volume she could muster. "Why couldn't we just ride home with Alan in his pickup?"

All three girls were now standing up and straddling a couple of long logs. They balanced by grasping the bark of another lengthy log. "This is more fun," Jesse said. "Besides, I thought you wanted to keep Alan's dirty man-paws away from Billiejean's little kitty."

"What little kitty?" Billiejean asked, clambering onto the stob end of their precarious perch to make more room for Chrissie.

"Your little kitty, Kitty-kat!" Jesse said, her voice thick with derision, then in an exaggerated aside to Chrissie; "She's hopeless. Honestly. The girl's as dumb as the log she's standing on."

Billiejean's face seemed to break, eyes shiny with tears ready to spill. "You're mean, Jesse! I hate you!" she cried, winding up to give her friend a swipe on the shoulder but losing her balance and giving Jesse a hard shove instead of a pulled punch.

Jesse went flying past her sister. Legs and feet scrabbling for balance. Arms akimbo...she fell! But instead of falling completely off the train Jesse somehow managed a quick step and a leap. A miraculous maneuver even if lacking the coordination of her previous leaps, she fell short, barely grabbing hold of the longest stob sticking out from the load ahead. Fingers digging into bark that may or may not be secure, she hugged the splintery end of the log for dear life, her feet dangling mere inches above the deadly coupler while a dozen

141

knifelike slivers protruding from the end of the log tore at her cheek like a rabid grizzly.

Suddenly feeling very alone in her predicament, Jesse's senses became heightened to a nearly unbearable state of hyper-awareness of her surroundings: changes in the sound of the train on the trestle, the sound of all that tonnage passing over water, she could even smell the curiously-soothing aroma of cedar slivers that were tearing her face apart, could taste her own blood as those razor-like slivers raked and ripped the flesh from her cheek. It was as if time itself shifted to an entirely separate reality and she completely lost her awareness of the other two girls left behind on the logs, of everything but the oddly-connected sensations of flying and being torn apart like a field mouse in the clutches of a winged raptor. She didn't hear Chrissie's piercing screams, didn't see Billiejean drop from the log onto the track below immediately after her own lucky leap because her eyes were clamped shut. But there was never any doubt in her mind that the jacket she had grabbed hold of at the last instant, the jacket she threw aside and climbed over to save her own hide was Billiejean's...

Maybe it's true that the rap Christine took for the whole affair was a bum rap, the quick lie coming to Jesse's lips fully-formed and bulletproof before the train cleared the far bank of the Queets – the notion that Chrissie had pushed Billiejean after Billiejean pushed Jesse.

Or maybe not. Maybe Billiejean simply slipped. Got scared and slipped by herself. If so then maybe the rest of it really happened the way it was told. Maybe Jesse didn't grab for her best and most loyal friend in the world, dragging her off the train in a mad scramble to keep from falling when she lost her own damned balance for the first time in her life. But that's the way she remembers it in her dreams, the scar on her face a constant reminder that she pushed her shadow off the train one frozen-in-time nightmare ago while being nearly eaten alive by a demon stob...

***

Penance due and penance paid. Though not in full. Never in full.

That's the way the Billievoice tells the story. Repeatedly, Jesse's shadow in life always taking credit in death for being Jesse's number one victim, making Pablo the grocery clerk a well-buried secret.

If only they knew. If only they all knew.

Knew what? Jesse asked with words unsaid. Think it helps to know that my sister and I are just different living versions of our mother's garage sale puzzles, all cut up and scrambled?

Maybe some pieces missing? Maybe some extras?

We have to sort ourselves out and put ourselves back together, because sure as hell nobody else will, Jesse thought.

The Queets River trestle was a quarter-mile-long steel and timber trestle spanning low across neck of the Queets – not a bridge; bridges were wider and they had edges, curbs, sometimes even handrails, but the trestle was so narrow and Spartan that it totally disappeared beneath the train, making it seem as if the whole thing, the workhorse locomotive and its entire thirty-car chain of logs on cradles went flying off the track into unsupported space over ever-churning river water. The train didn't actually leave the track, of course; but it certainly seemed as if it had to the three girls riding the logs. And that's when shit happened…

The instant Billiejean fell Chrissie screwed her eyes shut and screamed the entire rest of the way across the trestle, Jesse stuck and hanging-on for dear life while lethal log stobs shredded her face down to the cheekbone. Neither girl was ever quite the same after that day, the day their friend joined the spirit world.

The rest happened in a haze: Being airlifted to Harborview Hospital in Seattle, the surgeries, the accident investigation. Jesse was whisked away to Mexico by her mother soon as enough questions had been asked and answered, files closed.

Eventually folks around Forks stopped asking about the girls. Most thought Alison Wonderland was crazy as a loon anyhow so it all seemed easily predictable in hindsight.

Second-degree manslaughter charges against Chrissie were quashed due to her age. Instead, she was committed to the psych facility at Evergreen, and eventually Gig Harbor…and that's where she started falling apart, her mother's jigsaw puzzle.

Chapter 17

"I saw you!" Christine cried with wild eyes and an accusing finger, so she and Jesse slipped inside one of the Hoquiam Yard maintenance sheds to sneak a cigarette and have a little talk out of the rain. This was early in December of 1992 and the timber business on the Olympic Peninsula was on its knees, so there were only a couple of trucks nearby, loaded and idling, their drivers chugging coffee and waiting for manifests inside the scale house.

"Don't try to deny it!" she continued after a quick look around while lighting a Camel.

"I'm not denying anything," Jesse chided. "He wanted to kiss me and I let him. So what?"

"You were standing in the middle of the loading area where anyone passing by could've seen you...just like I saw you – that's what!"

"Yeah? I still say so what?"

"So he's our stepfather...that's what!" Chrissie said, passing the Camel like a joint with a glance toward the scale house. "Even if he acts kinda goofy and unfatherly, sometimes."

"Because he is goofy and unfatherly..."

"People talk..."

"Duh! Always have, always will – why should I care?"

"Jesse! It's wrong. You know that as well as I do. As well as everyone does."

"Settle down, Sis. We didn't do anything bad, me and Al. All I was doing was saying goodbye, thanks for the ride and for lunch and all that. A little stepfatherly kiss isn't wrong."

"Stepfatherly? Didn't look very stepfatherly to me," Chrissie said, shaking her head. "The way you had your arms all wrapped around his neck? The way you were pressed up against him? And after all that flirty business with your leg and the gearshift knob in the truck – disgusting! What if Billiejean had seen you two kissing?"

Jesse made an exaggerated kissy-face, took a long hit off the cigarette, and passed it to her sister, saying, "Soooooo?" drawing the word out like verbal taffy. "There was no touching. No fooling around."

"You know how she feels about him. She practically worships him, and it just kills her when you flirt with him."

"Tough titty, Kitty…"

"I'm only saying that maybe you should stay away from Alan for a little while."

"Huh-uh! I don't think so. He's too much fun to leave alone. I say if Billiejean wants him she should put some effort into getting him instead of sharing every little pity-pat of her lovesick heart with us every time he walks past. Maybe she should sit in the middle by the stick shift sometime. Rub her fat boobies against his tattoos since she's the only one of us who has any."

"You're terrible, Sis! Don't you know that Billiejean adores you?"

"Not my fault. Everyone isn't as dumb as Billiejean – thankfully…"

"Jesse! Are you really that mean and coldhearted or are you just on the rag and being bitchy today?"

Jesse blew smoke out through her nose the way Alan always did and gave her sister a cross-eyed look instead of an answer.

"You wanna know what Alan calls you behind your back?" Chrissie asked, staring past her stepfather's idling truck at the scale house through the neverending rain; more of a mist, really, falling in nonstop slow-motion, "He calls you a C-word."

"You mean a *cunt*?" There was plenty of volume and no tremble in Jesse's voice.

"Uh-huh. He spells it out. Says you're a cold little C-U-N-T. First time I heard it I didn't really understand what he meant, but I think I know what he means now."

"Yeah? I had no idea you two shared secrets," Jesse quipped.

"He calls Billiejean well-developed for a girl her age. What do you think that means?"

"Obviously, it means he likes feeling her ta-tas rub against his tattoos."

"That's what I've been trying to say! He's a pervert – the real deal. You and I live with him and we both know that, but Billiejean is so…so naïve!"

"Yeah. It is kinda fun to watch, isn't it?"

***

Hoot returned to Port Timothy after a quick trip to the FAMS office at Homeland Security and a slightly lengthier visit with the professor, his contact at the Washington State Patrol Crime Lab in Seattle. He entered the Port Tim police station with determined strides, plopped his lanky frame into the chair opposite Chili's desk, tossed the ME report he had in his hand into one of Chili's in-boxes and announced, "Forensic DNA turned up zilch."

Maddie's sister, Grace, standing at Chili's side, gave Hoot a look that suggested either; A), the coffee was probably entirely too fresh and acid-free for his peculiar tastes; B), the jury was still out on his potential undead status in Port Timothy and she was among the undecided; or C), he should never presume to know the proper place for anything in Chili's office. She shook her head, moving the ME report to another in-box and depositing a pile of paperwork in its place, then returned to her own desk.

"Not surprisin," Chili grumbled after a quick glance at the document.

"The professor at WSP said that, considering the guy was in the water nearly two weeks before floating up on Breakwater Beach, the likelihood of his attacker's DNA hanging on for the ride was slim, so no surprise that there was no CODIS database match. But we do have a positive ID for the victim," Hoot offered, taking the file back with a stern look at Grace before reading the WSP fact sheet: "He's Harold Hesse. Age sixty-eight. A fishing boat outfitter from La Push."

"Not exactly local," Chili said.

"Jesse would probably disagree. She sees the whole Olympic Peninsula as one big backwater community. She grew up near La

Push in Forks, and her mom still lives there. An hour-and-a-half drive and she talks about going to see her mother like it's just up the road, but still entirely too close for comfort."

"It's a bit of a drive. 'Round the mountains and through the rainforest on the wet side of Hurricane Ridge. So what I wanna know…if Mister Hesse was killed there, how'd his body get here? And if he was killed here, what was he doin here b'fore he tripped and fell on that knife a dozen times?" Chili shuffled through the hard copy of the Clallam County sheriff's report looking for any connection between Mr. Hesse and the Wickerman woman, saying; "Or, from an altogether different perspective, did he simply fall overboard from a boat that sank or hasn't turned up in any marina for some other reason, insurance scam, or a smugglers' scuttle for example – after one hellava accident fixin dinner in the galley, I might add – and then bob around in the strait completely unseen for a couple weeks before turning up on my beach? The question remains; from where? He sure as hell didn't float to Port Tim from Forks – Forks ain't exactly located on the strait or on the coast for that matter."

"I know. I've been to Forks before…briefly."

"Even if we include La Push, a tribal community out on the coast a few miles west of Forks, there's still a lotta currents and tides between here and there. Most of 'em goin the wrong way."

"So you're saying Mister Harold Hesse's body didn't get here by floating all the way from either Forks or La Push no matter how waterlogged it was? Even having two leisurely weeks of bobbing along in near-freezing water to do it?"

"Not possible. At least sure as hell not very likely – not without help. He was killed a lot closer to Port Tim than La Push," Chili said, scanning a document from another file and massaging his brow, scrunching acres of furrowed flesh and thick eyebrows as if he were digging for an epiphany. "No, Hesse didn't float very far. You're a fisherman – you know how the sea works. I got a dollar says he was killed and got hung-up on the bottom of the strait somewhere nearby; puked himself up just in time for the holiday."

Hoot said, "According to the professor it makes sense."

"…Listen to this," Chili interrupted. His interest piqued, he read from another document, saying; "Hesse owned a small marine outfittin business in La Push, did work for smalltime commercial fishermen. Autopilot retrofits. Refrigeration repair. Prop conversions and stuff like that. Contract work at marinas on the strait. It ain't much of a lead, but still…floatin trouble"

"…Tends to chart its own course – I know," Hoot finished for his friend. "Okay, I agree he was most likely killed a whole lot more nearby than La Push, but he could've been killed anywhere and the body dumped here. The reason he's dead may very well have roots in La Push. Crucial details. Somebody's gotta check 'em out."

"We got nothin else to go on," Chili agreed. Finishing his cranial massage by combing his fingers through his hair and patting it into place like a pile of brush, he added, "You know, a lot of the oldtimers livin out here used t' say the peninsula had a special community feel about it, separated from everywhere else the way it is. People used t' say it made them feel safe."

"Not so much anymore I'll bet," Grace interjected, entering the room with a new Clallam County Sheriff's Office report in her hand. She gave the report to Chili.

"Thanks, Gracie," Chili said. "Ray Rogers over at Clallam has all of our files?"

"Yep. The exchange has been made. They now have everything we have and vice-versa," Grace replied. "It's all in the cloud."

"My Breakwater Beach case is slippin away to become part of a much bigger deal," Chili said. "Ray'll have deputies crawlin all over Forks and La Push for a day or two lookin for connections. I show up out there now, they'll give me a number and a line to stand in."

"View's a little different from the back seat, isn't it?" Hoot said.

"It is," Chili responded with a smile like someone just farted.

"Meanwhile it'll be after Christmas before FAMS puts me back on the active flying roster. So if it suits you," Hoot offered, "I think I'll meet up with Jesse and her mom in Forks tomorrow and stay a day or two. I could take a quick run out to La Push and have a quiet good look around separately from whatever investigation the sheriff is conducting. See what I can turn up about Mr. Hesse without stepping on too many toes."

"I'll call Sam Ellis, the Forks police chief and my good friend," Chili said. "Let him know you're comin to town."

***

Mom's Motel was once a cheerful wayside respite on Highway 101, the Pacific Loop Highway-to-nowhere, but it had dilapidated over time into a run-down dive on Forks' main drag at the south end of town near the airport. Originally built in 1945; it had been repeatedly remodeled, added-to, and face-lifted over the course of the following three decades, and then left to wither away for four more. Currently, Jesse's mom Alison Wonderland Vega-Hay-Mackey, was playing the role of Mom, her grandmother and great-grandmother each taking their turns before her.

It was Jesse's great-grandma, Alta Brown, who planted the elaborate but now overgrown gardens fronting the property, Alta's husband Dexter creating the concrete-and-Astro Turf miniature golf course and the winding sidewalks that wandered throughout. An illuminated letterboard sign atop a rusty pole by the highway featured a big red sheet metal arrow on top accented with flashing yellow light bulbs pointing the way to Mom's office for weary travelers who might otherwise miss it.

Starting out as The Olympic Motel back in its heyday, Mom's had been one of a scant handful of post-war roadside respites in the heart of the rainforest. It was sagging into the twilight years of its decline now, meandering rooflines charting the history of its remodels and repairs.

"Sad, ain't it?" Alison Wonderland said, giving Hoot the grand tour of Mom's, Jesse quietly tagging along, obviously uncomfortable. "The place went to Hell in a handcart after my third husband, Alan Mackey, was killed in a trucking accident."

"The handcart had rolled well past Hell long before then," Jesse said.

A long glance between Jesse and her mother followed, and then Alison Wonderland turned and said to Hoot with a radiant smile and heavy-lidded eye contact; "Did I mention that my daughters and

I are directly descended from the original Mom on the maternal side?"

Alison Wonderland was a weathered woman, known around Forks as a certified weird-o. Flirting shamelessly with Hoot from the moment he arrived, her tightlipped mouth flashed brilliant vegetarian smiles loaded with semaphoric eye contact, fluttering eyelids punctuating her words like a ship-to-shore signal. With blonde-from-a-bottle hair showing steel-gray roots, she was in her mid-to-late fifties Hoot figured, but he thought the bleach job made her look much older. Her skin was browner than brown from a combination of half-Puerto Rican genes and a confessed obsession with sun tanning. "I'm so very pleased that my Jessica invited her new boyfriend to meet her mom!" she said.

"Hoot and I work together," Jesse told her.

"Excellent!" Alison Wonderland sang out as if her daughter's visit had just morphed into a flash musical on the spot. She wore an out-of-season flowery sundress with a low neckline showing off acres of suntanned cleavage looking to Hoot like a pair of worn leather saddlebags had been fastened to her chest; otherwise, she resembled a wrinkly stick of pepperoni with feet tucked into yellow gardening clogs. A fringed black shawl clung to her determined shoulders, the too-short sundress exposing long legs that were ingrained with ridges of varicose veins marking boundaries here and there.

Alison said she had lost a lot of weight after Jessica's father ran off, answering unasked questions: yet another intimate detail of several she offered up as if she thought Hoot should know, as if it explained why her skin was creased and sagging in places you wouldn't ordinarily think susceptible to creasing and sagging, making her look like she was wearing hand-me-down skin that had belonged to a much larger woman in a previous life. She had attractive facial features, an older version of her daughter, endowed with the same mischievous eyes and high cheekbones. She removed her sunglasses periodically during their conversation, teasing and reading Hoot with those eyes.

"It was his fault – your good-for-nothing stepfather, Alan," Jesse's mom said to Jesse with a hard look on her brow, words evidently meant for Hoot's benefit because Jesse was obviously not listening. "He was supposed to take care of all this shit and fix the place up. Did a half-assed job of it. See how it's all falling apart now that he's gone? It was hard enough to get that lazy log hauler to do anydamned thing around here. It was impossible to get him to finish it."

She guided Hoot around the gravel parking area where his pickup was one of only three vehicles, saying with a menacing gleam in her eye; "Just take a look at that chickenshit lattice he nailed onto the roof overhang," sweeping her arm to indicate the foot-wide strip of mildewed latticework that was barely attached to the tails of all but the last few porch rafters of Building A, a precarious support for an optimistic planting of a dead-looking vine in flower boxes at the support posts. "Of course the place was a dump when I inherited it from Jessica's grandma. I wanted to sell it right off, but the economy was so bad. And then Alan said he was gonna fix it up. Look at it now – worse than ever!"

Hoot agreed it was in bad shape. Indeed, the whole place looked on the verge of collapse yet somehow hanging in there for a final death knell or one more resurrection, neither of which seemed eminent.

They crossed a long-neglected garden on a concrete walk that meandered toward C Building. Ducking through a broken lattice archway entrance, a weathered sign at the apex proclaimed **Mom's Grandma's Garden, Miniature Golf free for guests. Visitors - $0.50.** There were lots of weeds and neglected plants, and Hoot figured there must have been at least two-dozen badly weathered birdhouses fastened atop poles leaning this way and that as if caught in the slow-motion act of falling over.

Jesse loitered near a battered gazebo in the middle of the garden and said in a surly tone, "You guys go ahead. I've seen it…"

Alison Wonderland put her arm through Hoot's, moving them both along, and saying, "Have you known my Jessica for long, Hoot?"

"Not at all," he answered.

Later, when they were out of Jesse's earshot, she added; "There's a room over in C. I'm not quite finished repainting that one yet, but I use the no-stink paint – know what I mean? It stinks a little…but not much. I could put you up there if you don't wanna shack up with my daughter in her usual room."

Shack up? Thanks for the frankness, Mom, Hoot thought, feeling a curious tension in the air almost as palatable as fog while Jesse stood silently aside. Hoot was certainly not guilty of cataloging of Jesse's quirks and faults like his friend Chili seemed to be doing; nonetheless, seeing Jesse and her mother together made him feel certain that he was in the presence of something volatile if not downright explosive.

A few steps later Alison Wonderland smiled, adding, "Watch out for Jessica's mood swings if you aren't already. Girl's always been moody. Musta got it from her daddy – I'm much sweeter by nature..."

"I'm sure," Hoot agreed.

"Of course, you *do* know about her troubled sister, don't you?"

Hoot looked back and saw Jesse sitting on a rickety garden bench, her eyes dark and unreadable. It was like seeing a gemstone in its natural setting, unpolished; Jesse as untended as her surroundings, diminished and yet vibrant in spite of it. Now there was a troubled woman...obviously – trouble he didn't need to share but was anyhow.

Changing the subject, Hoot asked, "I wonder if you happen to know a man named Harold Hesse, from here in Forks?"

"Sure! Everybody around here knows Harold. Has a place out at La Push, actually. Useless peckerhead, that Harold Hesse. Useless, I tell you. I hired him to do some handyman work way back in the summertime and he vanished before finishing the job. See over there? He barely got started."

Mom nodded toward the back side of Building A where sizeable patches of siding had been replaced with mismatched material painted in discontinued colors; "Has something of a patchwork-quilt ambiance if one applies enough imagination, don't you think?" she said. There was a broken window, piles of building materials scattered around a slightly elevated deck area, weeds encroaching.

"Men!" she said. "You can give em a job, but you can't make em work at it!"

Showing-off all that cleavage as tan as Italian leather, Alison Wonderland bent low to pick up an errant cedar shingle and toss it on a nearby pile, leaving Hoot to wonder whether she was putting homegrown originals on display, or accessories she had shopped and paid for back when times were better. Looked like original equipment to him. She had a nice shape for her age, had to give her that much if you didn't look too closely. But she desperately needed to do something about her hair. Maybe go for a more natural look instead of clinging to bottled blonde like a polar bear on an ice cube. Take twenty or thirty years off her and you'd have something. Far too tan, though. Hoot didn't like women so tan that they seemed overcooked. He was busy wondering if there were granny tan lines under her sundress when she stopped in her tracks and turned so fast he almost bumped into her.

She asked, "How are you with a hammer and nail, Hoot?"

"Not good," Hoot answered without hesitation. "Not good at all."

"Liar!"

Another twinkle. Sunglasses off, her semaphore eyes were flashing. Maybe it was simply the quality of light here in the heart of the rainforest. Maybe something entirely hormonal on her part. Or maybe it was a fundamental shift in his own point-of-view regarding women, beginning with Jesse – whatever it was, Hoot noticed that a distinct youthening was beginning to occur in Alison Wonderland's body language and he couldn't stop a disgusting-yet-compelling mother-daughter ménage à trois mental image from popping-up in his mind.

"You seem to be an enlightened man, Air Marshal Hooten," she said. "Lunchtime's coming up soon. How about we wander over to the patio and eat au naturale?"

"Excuse me?"

"Let's get naked for lunch, Handsome. It'll be fun. We've been doing it here at Mom's for years. Me and my girls. Alan too, when he was alive." She regarded Hoot's reddening facial expression with a gleam in her eye, said, "Don't worry, marshal – I doubt if anybody'll see anything that hasn't been seen before. Besides, nobody ever comes back here…"

Unable to respond, Hoot simply stared at her in mute astonishment. His ears unwilling to believe what they were hearing, the flashing image in his mind went viral.

"I'm a year-round sunbather, if Jesse didn't tell you," Jesse's mother said. "I live for the days I can come outside in the afternoon and soak up some honest-to-god rays instead of lying under a sun lamp like roast pork for dinner," she continued as matter-of-factly as if discussing the relative merits of hybrid tomatoes. "I'm an Aries, and I've always been a nudist at heart. My first husband, Jessica's Mexican daddy, Felix Vega, even encouraged it…but, of course, he liked to flaunt himself, anyhow. My second, Vincent Hay, was a Taurus to the core and terribly jealous. Vincent didn't care for Jessica's daddy one bit, and he didn't like my nudist tendencies either. But my third, Alan Mackey, a Pisces, was fine with it, and often joined in. Still…air and water – we mostly made steam."

Finding his tongue at last, Hoot said, "Well now, Mrs. uh…Mom. I am surprised."

"It's Alison, please! Alison Mackey, technically, since I'm a widow way before my time," Jesse's mom said with overstated flair. Wearing her widowhood like a boa, she took Hoot by the hand across lumpy grass to a low deck where a couple of vinyl chaise lounges stood out like characters in a Disney 3D movie. Shining whiter than vanilla ice cream after Sunday school, they were arranged side-by-side in the chilled sun like a little girl's garage-sale thrones. The deck was weathered but newer and in better repair than anything he'd seen so far. Hoot thought it lent a sacrificial altar appearance to this tidy spot in the weeds and clutter of a dying roadside respite. Stepping onto the platform with caution, he soon saw that the structure was sturdy, a propane outdoor heater standing tall and shiny in the middle like a gargantuan bird feeder.

"Natural rays are so much better than ultraviolet whenever you can get them around here. Come on and try it! It's good for you. Breaks down the inhibitions. Eases stress. And I honestly suspect you're harboring plenty of inhibitions and stress that could use some easing."

She turned a knob and hit an igniter switch, starting the heater with a low whoosh sound. A wave of warmth lapped Hoot's cheek as Jesse's mom, the widow Alison Wonderland Mackey, flashed yet another gleaming smile in his direction, said, "That's better." Then, unbelievably, she stepped back and pulled both the mini sundress and the shawl over her head in a single motion!

Released from the confines of the dress, the saddlebags immediately spread out like a pair of water-filled balloons ready to burst. Much larger and heavier breasts than her daughter's by far, they were uniformly tanned on their tops, bottoms, and sides. Dark brown nipples with areolas the size of small motherships puckered and hardened when they simultaneously caught a chilly breeze and Hoot gawking at them.

Suppressing his astonishment, Hoot pragmatically considered that at least his unspoken query about her tan lines had been quickly and unquestionably answered, and he simply stared.

Mrs. Mackey wore a thong that seemed whiter-than-white against her sun-worshiper flesh and exceptionally salacious on a woman her age. Just as his eyes focused clearly on that minimal bit of snowy Lycra, she hooked her thumbs under the waistband and slid it off too, tossing it aside

…No tan lines there, either! The unbelievably brazen woman, standing in the thin midwinter sun as naked as the day she was born, struck a lewd pose. Her natty pubic vee, every bit as trim and well-plucked as her eyebrows, seemed to look up at him; the face of a small feral creature, checking him out, a bit of spongy pink labia sticking out of its fur like a teasing tongue.

It was a perversion, no doubt, but Hoot felt himself growing hard. Shame burned his cheeks, turning his pale complexion a bright shade of crimson. This just isn't right, he thought – she's Jesse's *mother* for crissakes!!

"I'll ask Jessica to join us, and bring out some sandwiches and chips," Alison Wonderland said, turning and reaching for her cell phone. "If you wish, I'll look away while you remove your things…"

***

Opting out of Alison Wonderland's invitation to expose his delicate hide to the weepy-but-nonetheless-hateful Northwest sunrays, Hoot seized the opportunity to go check in with Sam Ellis, Forks chief of police. "I'm not much of a detective," he told Ellis. "Never had to be. But I'm a good tracker. I find 'em – I catch 'em. That prettymuch describes the sum total of my contribution to Chili Hilliker's investigation. With the Clallam county sheriff's oversight, of course," he added in a lighthearted sarcastic tone. Sam Ellis was a large man. It amused Hoot that he so strongly resembled Chili Hilliker. Thick hair like Chili's, trunklike limbs and big hands.

"How long you known the Big Bear?" Chief Ellis asked.

"Long time," Hoot answered with a slight smile. "Met him in '78 in the middle of a sweltering Louisiana swamp. Snakes and insects everywhere. We were chasing counterfeiters, and both of us were a lot younger then..."

"Amen to that," Chief Ellis said. "The road's a long one, and looking back gets a little harder on the eyesight year by year."

"Looking back is one bad habit I avoid whenever possible, Chief." Hoot said.

"Chili warned me you're one of us..."

"You mean the OFC – the Old Fart's Club?"

Ice broken, Chief Ellis laughed out loud and said "You can drop the Chief – just call me Ellis. Everybody around here does.

"Ellis it is then."

"Chili mentioned you're in town with Jessica Vega? Hope I'm not out of line to mention it, but there are accommodations in town with a few more stars than Mom's, if you'd like a recommendation..."

Hoot smiled, said, "I'll keep that in mind."

"Twin sons of different mothers. That's what Chili calls me and him," Ellis said and Hoot thought that he was absolutely correct. Their roots about as far apart as they could possibly get and still both be anchored in American soil, they had obviously been cast in the same mold, nonetheless. The differences were in the details; Chili was a misplaced Cajun, Ellis was from Alaska – a fallen North Slope oilman, as he described himself. Both men were broad-shouldered, essentially neckless and slightly bent from too many years spent behind their desks. Chili looked half grizzly, while Ellis wore a slack-jawed expression on a ruddy face, making him easily underestimated; an advantage in his line of work, Hoot figured – and he was a damned good lawman by his reputation. "I'd be rich instead of respected nowadays if I'd stuck it out on the slope," he claimed.

"Gotta love that 20-20 hindsight," Hoot agreed, and then got down to the business at hand, asked, "You knew Harold Hesse?"

"Sure, I knew Harold," Ellis said. "Just about everyone around here knew him. I was sorry as all hell to hear about what happened. Damned unlucky family, the Hesse's. Did you know that Harold was a registered pedophile?"

"I didn't see anything in the file about him serving time," Hoot said.

"He didn't. Actually, the whole pedo thing was bogus. People were confused about Harold because his brother served a bit of time in juvie during his teens – even though not for pedophilia. Harold was half of a set of identical twins, see? Couldn't tell them apart, Howard and Harold, except Harold was a pussycat and Howard was a bit of a rounder. A drinker and a brawler with an eye for other guys' gals. Always pushing the bad-boy envelope. In high school, Howard got popped for some minor shit now and then: car theft, B&E, and selling reservation booze off the reservation. Served six months of a one-to-three in Boy's Town and missed his graduation.

"In my opinion, if either of those brothers was a pedo, it would've been Howard. He seemed to suffer from recurring deafness when underage girls told him no, even when he was a middle-aged man…supposedly. Retired early from the railroad – I'm sure they asked him to retire since they were shutting the rails down, anyhow. A year later he hung himself off the Queets River trestle. Exact same spot where the Wisdom girl fell and died. Terrible accident, that was. Howard was the engineer of the train she fell from, and he evidently felt responsible."

"Responsible enough to kill himself?" Hoot said.

"It was a damned hard pill for Harold to swallow."

"The accident? Or his brother's suicide?"

"His identical twin's suicide. The accident was bad enough. Young girl getting killed – shook everyone up around here. And then Howard's suicide stirred it all up again; got the rumor mill working overtime and made it worse. It changed Harold down to the taproot. Reclusive to start with, his brother's suicide made him downright hermitlike and he quit coming to town altogether. People out in La Push claimed he was hanging out around the waste bins with the ravens, talking to them. I went out there to check on him and he wouldn't look me in the eye. A bit later he came into the station and registered as a pedophile. He insisted, said everybody knew it and he wanted to squash the rumors, make it official. We'd never done that before – register a volunteer pervert, as it were – and we didn't exactly have a procedure for doing it. That's why it doesn't show on his official sheet; it wasn't court-mandated. But he was determined, and swore he was a danger to the community."

"Not anymore he isn't," Hoot offered in a tone of finality.

"Sheriff's deputies have been out at La Push all morning, interviewing the wife and others," Ellis said. "Chili'll get copies of their reports, but he thought you might care to have a look around, yourself. Could ride out with me now if you like."

"Thanks. I would like to make a couple of house calls and see how Harold's widow is taking the news…"

Chapter 18

The road to La Push followed the Sol Duc River west from Forks through hunkering rock-faced hills forested with red cedar and fir, evidence of a moist environment everywhere. Tall cottonwoods and thick copses of vine maple crowded the riverbank. Chief Ellis drove his SUV past all this roadside scenery with barely a glance, a man bent on a familiar errand. La Push was a tribal town, a tiny place unable to afford its own sanctioned police department; it was part of Ellis' jurisdiction. "A stingy Clallam County sub-contract, but a steady one," he said. "My biggest problem is the profusion of meth labs in the area and no budget to go after them.

The twisted and churning path of the Sol Duc finally joined the Bogachiel and became the more sedate Quillayute River for a short and relative straight run to the Pacific. At the river confluence, Hoot quietly smiled when Ellis drove past a well-kept campground resort with a large sign out front proclaiming they were crossing the Treaty Line beyond which vampires were not allowed. The air was cold and fresh and filled with complex earthy aromas, a hint of sea breeze blown through an abundance of greenery.

"Twilighters," Chief Ellis said, explaining the sign. "Those Stephanie Meyer books and movies about vampires and werewolves and high school kids all took place in and around Forks and La Push. Ever read 'em? See the movies?"

"I'm afraid not," Hoot confessed, giving a moment's reflection to Madeline Marvel and her newspaper. Maddie probably knew all about the Forks-Twilight connection. She always knew the important/unimportant stuff about people, politics, and pop culture, the trivia that sticks-to and shapes just about everything. She had a sharp eye, always seeing past the superficial stuff straight to the soul of just about any issue without a blink. Hoot revered Maddie's opinion, and while he was considering all this, something inside himself – something he dared not examine too closely – clicked into place with the snap of a hole card being played face up, ratcheting-up the tension like a gambler's fix. For better or worse…he was in bed with Jesse, now. That was a fact.

To be entirely honest, Hoot had instinctively shied away from thinking overmuch about his affinity for Maddie even before he met Jesse. If you don't notice it, it isn't there; the modus operandi of every potential relationship with the opposite sex since his divorce. He cared about Maddie deeply. And he thought she was attractive in countless ways, but for now his attention was fixed on his current situation with Jesse instead. Knowing that he was a hound at heart, he gave himself credit for being a one-bitch-at-a-time hound, at least; a man-dog with principles. In the midst of this homo-sapiens-canine soul searching, Hoot felt a momentary twinge of…what – guilt?

Impossible! He and Maddie were good friends. That's all. And they both liked it that way. Jesse, however, was a romp. And yes, he liked it that way, too. Very much in fact. He hadn't heard any complaints from Jesse, either – quite the contrary; and at his age that was definitely a plus. Surprising even.

For some years now Hoot had wanted to be attracted to older and more emotionally stable women. And he was…honestly he was, including Maddie to say the very least. But it was that cupcake thing of his father's: while he wouldn't go so far as lumping Jesse in with a bunch of empty-headed cupcakes – never that – he nonetheless suspected her name was high on any number of no-no lists for a man of his age and experience. Made him feel old. And, sure as Hell…he was getting there.

"Vampire novels? I don't keep up all that well with pop culture," he admitted.

"I've read them," Ellis said. "All those Twilight books. In fact I suspect just about everybody 'round here who can read has read them. Goofy, sexy stories. All the movies, too. The tourism from it's a big-damned deal around Forks. You have to understand how people here were desperate to grab onto something after the logging died out. Twilight was perfect for Forks. A one-stoplight town, and did you know that our high school is brand new? Mostly built with online enrollment money from kids who seldom or never set foot in the building. TwiFan Twits they call 'em – self-absorbed students from all over the world who wanna graduate from Forks High, with parents willing to pay for the privilege."

"TwiFan Twits? That's a new one for me," Hoot said. "Gotta love today's jargon at the very least."

"The face of the whole peninsula is changing," Ellis said. "Mostly for the better I think. But to get here we've lost a whole lot of what made us special in the first place. I'll still take the TwiFans and their vampire twits over the meth-heads any day." He looked at Hoot with a tight smile, said, "You recently bought a place over in Port Tim? You should explore the rest of the peninsula, check out the rainforest. You're a part of it now, after all. And, no offence intended, but with your…unique appearance you may find yourself something of an attention-getter around this neck of the woods."

"Actually, I've been in the rainforest before. Got a pretty good taste of it not far from here," Hoot said, remembering his first experience on the peninsula barely two years ago as a US marshal. It was somewhere deep in the forest on the wet side of hell as Hoot remembered it, an abandoned hunter's cabin in the Quinault watershed where he'd killed Steven Mays and another escapee. He'd also watched a partner die in the line of duty – again. The Olympic Peninsula; Hoot hadn't cared much for the area at the time, but it was starting to grow on him now that he was getting his bearings, now that he was a resident so to speak…

***

Less than a mile square in total area, La Push was the one and only Quillayute Indian Reservation community. Located literally at the end of the road and mouth of the river, the entire town consisted of a scant cluster of fishermen's flop houses and cabins, a one-burner seafood canning company, a tribal fish hatchery, a revamped marina with a convenience store/post office/gas station, and other small businesses mostly catering to the needs of fishermen: all owned by tribal members. Weathered houses and hunkered-down mobile homes crowded short streets. Population fluctuated between 80 and

180, plus charter fishermen and day visitors to the state park across the estuary.

"You said you like to fish?" Ellis asked. "Charter fishing's a big deal in La Push. Maybe not as big a deal as other places on the coast, and John Wayne never parked his boat here like he did at Sequim, but about as big as big deals ever get in these parts. The mouth of the Quillayute dumps a hellava lot of water into the Pacific, straight downhill from the heart of the rainforest. It's like Mother Nature's lunchbox, a spawning salmon's idea of heaven. What's more, the 'Yute's got a gentle bar to cross so seasick-prone landlubber fishermen love to go out from there. There are a handful of local commercial guys too, but they're strictly small-timers as commercial boats go."

"I'd like to talk to all the skippers we can shake loose, charter and commercial both," Hoot said, filing away the info about local charter fishing in his mental back pocket to compare with Ilwaco as potential locations for his charter service pipedream. "Meanwhile, tell me more about Harold Hesse...how'd he fit in?"

"Harold was always something of an oddball," Ellis said. "A rumormonger and junk collector. I doubt if he ever threw anything away his whole life as you'll see when we get there. His brother, the ex-railroad engineer who hung himself, was a hellava model train nut so there's a bunch of tiny trains running around, too. As tribal as they get – the brothers were full-blooded on their mother's side. Quarter on their father's. Rumor has it the great-grandpa on their father's side of the fence was a bona fide American Nazi during World War II, and was under FBI surveillance, but you can't prove it through the bureau. I've tried."

"The whole family probably went to Woodstock too," Hoot said dryly.

"Harold owns – or, rather owned – a shop at the La Push Marina specializing in custom freezers and ice-making equipment for small commercial fishing boats. Autopilot retrofits. Stuff like that. La Push is an out-of-the-way place for a business like that, but he had clients from Kodiak Alaska to Monterrey California. I assume his wife owns the shop, now. Or the tribe does..."

***

"Harold spent a lot of time out of town?" Hoot asked the widow Hesse.

"Yes, he did. Was gone all the friggin time," she answered.

Her name was Rose, a singularly ugly woman in the waning half of her sixties with teeth so awful it made Hoot's own teeth hurt just to look at them, and she was not ready to accept that her husband was dead.

"Ain't the first time Harold's turned up dead," Rose claimed. "Used to happen a coupla times a week."

A moment of awkward silence ensued.

"I believe he's actually dead this time, Mrs. Hesse," Hoot finally said, breaking the silence with his soft voice and a sidelong glance at Ellis. "I've seen the body, and I really don't think he'll be coming back."

"Dead, huh? That's what the sheriff said. And old Mort the tribal elder. But I'm not so sure."

She invited them in, saying "Want some coffee? It's bad…"

"Love a cup," Hoot answered, admiring the impressive array of clutter in the Hesse brothers' shop.

Ellis excused himself to interview others, leaving Hoot alone with the not-precisely-grieving widow.

"You know, you don't look all that good yourself — you could be as dead as my husband for all I know!" Rose said in a conspiratorial whisper with a squinty examination of Hoot top to toe.

Her laugh sounding like a raven on a fencepost, "I sure as hell won't miss him," she said, smiling with those god-awful teeth and serving Hoot a reheated cup of sludgelike joe. "Harold ain't been around much lately. Been busy some years now, in fact. Gone all the time. Nobody buys new gear anymore. Independent fishermen in this friggin economy? — they spend what little money they've got keeping the old shit going, and that kept Harold going. To Seattle. To Port Angeles. To Alaska quite a bit recently."

"When was the last time he was home?" Hoot asked.

"Been awhile…maybe three or four weeks ago. We can check the routing board. See when he last ran the trains."

"Trains?" Hoot said.

"Yeah, trains. Little ones. Harold promised his brother he'd run 'em. Keep the layout dusted and clean. Big friggin layout – it's a hellava job!"

Rose led him to the rear of the refrigeration workshop where she pushed open a wide sliding door. Inside, a model railroad layout to rival anything any museum might have on display spanned the whole 40' width of the shop. An eight-foot-tall panoramic photomural of the entire Olympic Range backed the layout, curving through the corners and extending forward some distance along both sidewalls. The background image had been created from dozens of Photoshopped images blending into the foreground scenery, giving the entire miniature scene an amazing sense of depth, of realness.

"This was Howard's life after he retired," she said. "And a good portion of it before he retired. Did you know that Howard was a railroader? He used to brag about being the last engineer to drive a working Shay steam loco in the Aberdeen yard before they switched to all diesel-electric switchers. The Northern Pacific Railroad ran all the way out to Moclips back then; of the line. Rayonier owned the logging railroad that connected with the NP in Aberdeen. Running all over the hills, it was a separate track altogether and delivered over 200 loads of logs into Aberdeen every day back in the day. Trains of up to 70 loaded cars sometimes, Howard said. Down to Chenois Creek, and then by barge across the bay to the sorting yard. Truckloads too. They were moving so many logs they couldn't count them all!

"The last regular train to run on the Rayonier track didn't carry logs – 100 empty cars to be scrapped. All the track and most of the bridges and trestles were gone within the next ten years. Broke Howard's heart to see them tearing it all apart.

"Everybody said Howard was retired. Even Howard said he was retired, but he wasn't...not in his mind at least. He stayed as an on-call retiree, helping Rayonier salvage whatever they could, driving the scrap to the scrap yard. Taking out the trash, he called it. Couple of trainloads a month.

"His last load of actual logs was when that Indian girl got killed. The company blamed Howard, and he took it hard, but he never quit driving the trains. He reproduced the whole Rayonier line in exact scale right here. Kept runnin' the logs down you see? They just got smaller.

"Look at all this happy horseshit, would you?" Rose said. "What does somebody do with something like this? Left the whole thing to his brother Harold – my husband. And now, if what you say is true about Harold being dead I suppose it just became my friggin job to keep the damned thing clean and running!"

She sighed with such volume Hoot practically felt asphyxiated, said "Meticulous man, Howard was…for a drinking man. Practically the whole history of the peninsula is here if you know where to look." She took a feather duster off a hook and used it as a pointer, said "This train sitting over the Queets was the last run for Howard, and it was the last scene he completed on the layout." She pointed to a remarkably-detailed miniature train of thirty log cars loaded with scale logs being pulled by a diesel switcher. It was frozen in the act of crossing a long trestle over water, and the center log car included three tiny figures on top of its load. Hoot had never seen such detail in miniature before.

Rose handed Hoot a magnifying glass, said "Howard made all the logs and the little people out of Fimo clay. Take a closer look, marshal."

Bending close and focusing the magnifying glass, Hoot was impressed with the detail of expression captured in three-dimensional caricatures less than an inch tall. Three children, all girls, were realistically rendered in clay atop the logs:

One was falling.

One seemed to be screaming.

And one was either pushing or trying to grab the one who was falling…

Chapter 19

Jesse figured Hoot would be busy chasing clues around La Push all afternoon with Chief Ellis, leaving her abandoned with her spontaneously naked and constantly irritating mother at Mom's Motel for several hours. She had grown up in this dump, raised by a crazy woman who thought she was a forest nymph, and she hated returning here even for a little while; her mother's earth-mother naïveté inevitably driving her into a terrible state of mind within minutes of arrival.

And then there was the Billievoice – that persistent little demon; always lurking in a dark corner just out of Jesse's mental peripheral vision, waiting to complicate things.

Easy to kill him, Billie's ghostly voice would whisper inside Jesse's skull, bypassing her eardrums like the sneaky fuck it was and going straight into her brain.

Easy, a tease heard only in the deepest recesses of Jesse's inner ear. She ignored it. Refused to listen.

Jesse knew it was dangerous being here in Forks, no doubt. It was actually fun in a twisted way, but unfuckingholy dangerous to be here with Hoot. She and Hoot wallowing together in evidence thick as tide pool muck, he was bound to pick up a whiff or two. It was almost too much: Fucking him, touching his ghostly-white testicles with the same hand that left grandma's knife embedded in poor Harold's shoulder...

It was overwhelming, the thrill she felt.

White, warm skin, with blue veins just below the surface...

Jeezus! Could it get any better than this?

Doubtful. Very doubtful. The Billievoice said.

166

This was bad-girl fun on a cellular level. Just thinking about it made Jesse's lips numb.

Careful now...careful!

Her mouth formed a mirthless smile. She'd got herself in a fine fix this time...

A fine fix? No shit...

Nothing new here, she told herself. Certain the headache that had been nipping at her all morning was about to pounce in full force, Jesse's nerves were stretched taut. Something could snap.

Physically, she was starting to experience vague surges of abdominal pain accompanied with an underlying urge to vomit; usual manifestations of a body woefully weaker than the spirit it contained – the price Jesse paid for simply being Jesse. All she could do now was suffer through it...

Why, she wondered for the zillionth time, did she always end up back in this depressing place? Was growing up here really better for her than growing up in her father's whorehouse?

Her mother had always claimed it was – but was it?

She smelled garlic. Saw the light wavering.

Soon the vertigo would come. This was going to be a bad one...

***

Jesse retired to her room; number 310C, where she shut the curtain, kicked off her shoes, and lay down on her lumpy mattress. She counted backward, figuring how long she had slept on this same no-frills bed in this same bland room kept bare of the slightest personal touch just in case a full house made its rental for a night or two eminent.

...Years?

Yes. Years and years of dreaming dark dreams; one dream in particular – the one where she was falling. The clickety-clack of steel wheels over rail joints. Billiejean screaming...

Jesse drew a long breath, held it in, and then let it out slowly. It was crucial that she get it right, her memories. She had recollected every teensy detail of that one single moment – that single horrible turnkey incident – so often it had become a tangible part of her. A venomous bug trapped in the resin of her dreams. Trapped and hardened into amber, the flaw defining the gemstone, venom still deadly. Her entire life from then to now had been too heinous to consider in any detail, yet too enticing to turn away from.

What other choices did she have? She was the bug after all, trapped in her own skin, her own…resin. She only had to touch her face or glance in a mirror, to simply feel the ever-present tightness in her cheek to remember it.

She had so often dreamt of that moment, the moment when she fell.

When someone fell, the Billie voice said.

She had daydreamed about it often, and had countless nightmares about it. In short, she remembered it all the time, constantly thinking about it in vividly-detailed mental pixilation. Always the same but never the same – it was maddening.

Jesse ultimately came to understand that her memories were irreversibly corrupted by her own wicked imagination. They were unreliable memories because she knew that the scenes had been revising and replaying themselves in her mind, constantly rewriting and justifying until she was no longer certain which versions were the originals.

The original moment when she fell – it was crucial that she remember it right because her life was defined by it.

As was her sister's.

And even her mother's.

Inevitably, the Billievoice came along and added her two-fucking-cents-worth, saying; *what happened happened and you can't change it no matter how hard you try. So let the past go and think about your shooter. This is a good time to kill him. Easy-peasy-lemon-squeezy. Just kill him. Make it look like your crazy mother did it…*

Shut up! Jesse thought.

Shouldn't play around with him. It's dangerous…

"I told you to shut up and I meant it!" she cried to the empty room. "Just! Shut! The Fuck! Up!!"

***

Hoot turned his attention to Harold Hesse's widow, said; "All this actually happened?" pointing at the miniature railroad scene by extending a pale finger on the hand holding the magnifying glass. His other hand keeping the tails of his jacket from touching the display, he bent close and examined the minute details of the diorama with the exaggerated focus of Sherlock Holmes reborn.

"Oh, yeah – every bit of it, I'm sure," Rose answered, flipping a switch that turned overhead spotlights on the scene. "Howard never actually talked much about that day. Couldn't make him talk about it. But he was the one driving the train. The one got blamed for everything. And he's the one created this whole friggin shrine!" She waved her arm to encompass the miniature layout, said, "Talented old fart, Howard was. Crazy as a flea-bitten coon hound, but talented. Anything he had to say about what happened that day is laid out right here for anyone to see who wants to look."

Hoot looked, taking it all in, the remarkable detail.

"A shame he had to get mixed up with that girl gang," Rose said. "Jesse Vega and her sister. And the girl who died – the Wisdom girl. Old man runnin 'round with those young girls. Too young. And too loose, if you ask me. Was there bad business goin on? You betcha there was! Stuff I don't know about and don't wanna know, but there were always rumors...

"Howard was the one who was a bit creepy if you know what I mean. Not Harold. Howard liked to hang around the young girls way too much. Was bound to end badly. Everybody knew it..."

"Did you say Jesse Vega?" Hoot asked. His attention suddenly grabbed by what Rose was saying, he spun around and looked with more focused concentration at the miniature scene, saying, "You mean Alison Mackey's daughter, Jessica Vega, from Forks? She was on this train?"

"Uh huh. Alison Wonderland's girl, Jessica...everybody calls her Jesse, like Jesse James, the old-time outlaw. Oh, yeah, she was there. She 'bout got chewed to death by a log stob, herself. Girl's a real piece of work, always has been, used to come around La Push chasing after older tribal men for their pot and booze."

So...Jesse knew the Hesse brothers? His interest piqued, Hoot asked; "What else can you tell me about Jessica Vega?"

"You should talk to her if you haven't already. She got her face chewed up and her sister's in the kook house for her part in the very same little incident you're standing there looking at. Guilty of some sorta manslaughter, they called it, for throwing the Wisdom girl off the train after she became enraged beyond control as the newspapers had it. Temper issues with that one, apparently. Mental issues. Started trying to kill herself as soon as she got to Western – a real shame; she was the nicest of the three girls, if you ask me."

Hoot had asked Jesse how her face became scarred; now he knew, and his instinct warned him there was more to the story...

"'Course, old Howard would never say anything for fear of drawing attention to his fun and games, but he knew better than anyone what those girls were capable of. Turned what little hair he had left on his head nearly as white as yours. Turned him mute just to think about it.

"Shoulda put both of those Vega girls away, except the younger sister's confession tied the whole mess up nice and neat for Jessica – who went kinda mental over the whole thing, anyhow. Musta blamed herself same as Howard blamed himself. Everybody said she tried to catch the Wisdom girl at the last second and failed, damned-near fell off the train. Grabbed a stob at the last second and tore a grievous hole in her face instead of getting killed.

"Jessica went to Mexico to live with her daddy for a couple years afterward. To get away from it all and heal up, her mamma said. But I heard that her daddy's a bad man. Real bad – Mexican Mafia, some say. When papa sent her back home to mom, she'd gone from bad to worse, you ask me. Had a frightful scar on her face from the train incident – the sight of it scared the crap out of guys who used to chase her tight little tail around like hounds on a scent. Next thing I knew, she'd enlisted. Became a Marine. Now there's a frightful image, you think about it."

Rose attacked a nearby dusty spot with the feather duster, saying; "Couple of bad girls, those Wonderland girls. Trouble on a good day, they were. Shoulda put their loosey-goosey mother away, too, far as I'm concerned..."

The small hairs on the back of Hoot's neck were standing at full attention. He bent closer and trained the magnifying lens on the unbelievably realistic miniature scene, focusing on expertly-rendered details.

Yes!...now that the idea was planted in his imagination, he could clearly identify which of the modeled figures represented the adolescent Jessica Vega – the one with the wounded cheek, of course; a detail he had dismissed as a simple flaw in the Fimo before. And it also seemed clear to Hoot that the tiny clay figure of Jesse was pushing, not attempting to catch her tiny clay friend.

Chapter 20

It was late afternoon and deep shadows gathered ahead of a weather front heading toward the Washington coastline in a gargantuan counter-clockwise spiral, remaining daylight taking on a darkening hue as the surrendering sun made a beeline for the deep end of the Pacific. The wind had started gusting from the southwest, hardly noticeable before now; it was getting more bothersome as the day ebbed. Gray curtains of falling rain were forming-up like ranks of hunkering fusiliers on the horizon, waiting for the worst possible moment to march in and dump torrents on the Olympic Peninsula – flash floods of Old Testament proportions were imminent, no doubt.

Hoot and Chief Ellis had only three names remaining on their persons of interest list for La Push. Everyone else they'd talked with thus far said they knew the Hesse's, sure, and they were generally sorry to hear of Harold's murder, though nobody seemed to know diddlysquat about his recent activities: "Brother's suicide hit him hard."; "Got real deep into the bottle." All seemed to agree that Howard was the better bet of the two brothers, generally, but evidently neither brother had enemies who might wish Harold dead.

Hoot got more interesting answers when he started asking about the brothers' relationship with Jesse and her gang: "Grown men slobbering over girls who were barely teenagers!"; "It was disgusting."; "Disturbing."; "Nothing but trouble from the get-go."

So much for hindsight. But something about these tidbits regarding Jesse and her gang rang disturbingly true to Hoot.

What the hell's going on, here? Hoot thought, his mind spinning with a whole new perspective of Jesse and an unexpected light shining on Harold Hesse's murder. All he really had to go on was a tiny clay rendering of an incident that had happened almost twenty years ago – an incident that may have provided a motive for murder – and the woman with whom he expected to spend the night had been involved. His day turning dark from the roots up, Hoot's cell phone vibrated. He gave the caller ID a glance and loathed answering the goddamned thing, but did anyhow, saying; "What's up, Jesse?"

"Sorry to bother you while you're working," she said, "but the weather is turning bad here in town and I figure it must be worse where you are."

"I'm glad you're awake. Get a good nap?"

"Yeah, I think so."

The hawking wind, moist but gritty, was scrubbing the skin on Hoot's face like an unwelcome exfoliation. He turned away seeking shelter behind a nearby shed where he could talk, still fishing without bait. "Feeling better?" he asked when the wind and background noise were more tolerable.

"Definitely better. The headache is easing, and the nausea, but I can't think about eating yet. When do you and the chief expect to be back in Forks?"

"Hard to say," Hoot answered evasively. "We're still interviewing people. Could be a little while if the weather doesn't kick us out sooner."

"Find anything?"

A piece of plastic sheathing blew past flapping like a wraith on the wind, and Hoot waited for it to pass, then said, "Maybe…"

It was a terse conversation, quick, empty, and not particularly warm. Skeletal words, but loaded with enough tension to punch holes in the thin fabric that was them, start a run and threaten a rip.

What am I thinking? Better yet…what am I doing? Hoot asked himself, after the call.

A wave of lucid thought washed Hoot's concerns well enough that he could see things more clearly for a second or two and he wondered; Worried about pinholes? Potential rips? Hell, whatever *us* there ever was or could possibly be is already shredded…

"Let's wrap it up," he told Chief Ellis. "We're done here in LaPush. What I'm looking for is in Forks."

***

Hoot rode quietly back to the police station with Ellis, thinking to himself along the way; What in the lowest basement of Hell is Jesse into?

Was it simple coincidence that she'd known Harold Hesse? Known him very well as it turns out?

Maybe, he thought. Unlikely as lips on chickens…but maybe.

The whole damned peninsula was one big extended community as Chili Hilliker had so often said, sparsely populated but closely tied; everyone living out here seemed to be much closer to each other than mere physical distance might suggest – hence, practically everybody knew practically everybody else. Still, it was sure as hell no coincidence that Jesse hadn't mentioned this knowledge to him, and it irked him to the bone to consider that she must have known the Breakwater victim's identity all along and stayed mum.

Jesse must've known that her subterfuge would be blown the moment Hoot started poking around Forks and LaPush. So if this was some kind of game, what were the rules? The stakes seemed high. And why flirt with discovery at all if she were guilty of anything significant? Something about her simply didn't add up.

Jesse… What did he really know about her? Hoot asked himself.

Precious little. Except that she was an alpha-type personality to the core; the way she seemed so eager to challenge him at the shooting range, test his stamina when they were in bed. Unafraid to a fault, danger obviously excited her. She was an ex-marine, trained for combat, and she had a sister in the nuthouse. She was sexually exciting as all hell, and her mother was certifiably mental. Okay, so maybe she wasn't the sort of girl Hoot could've ever taken home to meet his mom. And up to now all that had been just fine…

Hoot knew that his interest in Jesse had been instinct and lust-driven from the start. Seasoned with a generous dash of testosterone from the in-flight shooting plus a sizeable backlog of suppressed manly needs thrown in for good measure, his attraction to her had absolutely nothing to do with shared interests as Maddie would say – aside from a fondness for marathon sex and experience with violence, that is. Shared interests in food, movies and books, leisure time, weren't a big part of the formula between Hoot and Jesse the way they were between him and Maddie. With a bit of self-inflicted snark he realized that he didn't even know if Jesse knew how to fish!

Not surprising. He hadn't known Jessica Vega even existed a week ago! The little that Hoot knew about Jesse was cockeyed from any other woman he'd ever known, and he enjoyed it being that way. He liked the leap-of-faith feeling of abandon that came with it. He certainly liked the sex. Liked the compact tightness of her. Her tiny breasts and tight ass. He even liked the tattoo, although it only just now occurred to him where he'd seen the design before; the winged Z...

It was a cartel tat – Los Zetas.

Jeezus! Hoot browbeat himself. He was off his game entirely!

For what...sex? Sex hadn't mattered much to him in a very long time. So why now?

Why not now? He immediately thought. What if I've always been weak and wicked, just holding it back like a good little Dutch boy?

No excuses, Gramps! Hoot knew that if he'd had his head screwed on right he would have noticed the significance of the winged Z the instant he saw it. Was he having one of those infamous Oprah-style midlife crisis, male hormones spilling out from under the lid of his libido like old-fashioned popcorn at a matinee?

...As disturbing and ridiculous idea as he'd ever had. Pop-culture theories like midlife crises meant nothing to Hoot. He certainly didn't want to be guilty of actually having one. He had zero interest in playing the role of a man intimidated by looming sexual dysfunction, a Viagra 'scrip with his name on it getting cozy next to the packet of condoms in his billfold. The few surviving members of Hoot's little tribe of manly hormones had been standing up and beating their chests ever since meeting Jesse. Suddenly unable look at a passing pretty woman without lascivious thoughts, without feeling the pull of a smile in the corners of his eyes, these nearly-forgotten reactions were crackling with new life. Ridiculous, but admittedly fun.

Maybe he was reaching for the brass ring here, but Hoots recent increased interest in the opposite sex showed no signs of wavering – the little marshal was back in the game in a big way and liking it! Made him a tidbit anxious because this had all the signs of one of those all-too-familiar Famous Last Stands, in his trousers at least, if not his heart, and he was far from ready for that.

Hoot knew he was fortunate to have loved profoundly once; Donna Messenger – talk about deeply-shared interests paired up with mutual attraction! But that had ended tragically half a lifetime ago, and he'd only recently found peace with it. Maddie sometimes reminded Hoot of Donna, the way she seemed to know him to the core and could anticipate his moods. Maddie was good for him – he knew that...

He had also enjoyed a reckless and passionate love; Linda, his ex-wife. Thus, experience had taught him that the reckless sort of love was a hellava lot easier on the soul, even at the risk of being a bit harder on the body in the long run. Maybe that's why Hoot favored the reckless; the body healing so much faster than the soul, it was fundamentally safer in his bullheaded opinion. Jesse often reminded him of Linda.

Just thinking Linda's name put a welcome smile on Hoot's face – had to give his ex kudos for straightforwardness, at least. The woman would get all over his ass at a moment's notice if she thought he had it coming, and usually he did – there would be a big fight about something stupid and then they'd make up and make love. He missed it, that feeling of physical significance with another person. That spark...

Hoot figured this was the crux of what Chili and Maddie considered to be his utter abandonment of all good sense regarding Jesse. Maybe because he had enjoyed fifteen years of Linda's ever-ready sexual nature, sex had never meant the world and everything in it to him the way it did to so many other men he'd known. But he definitely liked sex. He even dated occasionally. And sometimes he got a little taste of that ever-so-elusive spark.

When it was a really good taste he liked it. He missed it.

Hoot had observed sparkless relationships, couples hanging together year-after-year like love zombies, not dead...just too lethargic move on. He knew he'd tested the limits of his luck to find two women who truly made the spark ignite for him: the spark of true love with Donna, and the spark of hot sex with Linda. He couldn't imagine himself lucky enough to get a third chance at bat, and yet that's what this thing with Jesse had felt like from the very beginning. Maybe this was a dangerous place for him to let his imagination wander. Foolish even. But there was definitely heat when he was with her. And it had been such a long time...

Meanwhile, even as much as Jesse reminded Hoot of his ex, that aura of reckless abandon she wore without excuse the same way she wore the scar on her face and the tattoo on her shoulder, she was nonetheless an entirely new experience for him, different from Linda in every way but one – the sexual one. Jesse certainly did like sex: she apparently liked it a lot; more even than Linda had. She'd had fun in bed and expected him to have fun too. Dangerous stuff, undoubtedly, but Hoot suspected that what was really dangerous about Jesse was something in her he'd yet to see, something that she was shielding from him – or him from it. He'd see flashes in her eye telling him that she would confide in him if she could. Jesse most definitely was a woman of secrets.

Unsure what the word *dangerous* actually meant in Jesse Vega's case, Hoot was nonetheless certain that getting close to her in any sense of the word was risky business. Potentially fatal, but irresistible, she seemed to give off a pheromone affecting only certain others of her species – those primed with sexual prowess and a hair trigger; other primitives like her, in other words...Ezra Hooten most definitely included.

That must be it! Hoot was just a hapless old hound tripped-up by a whiff of Jesse's alpha-bitch scent, leaving him in a state of uncontrollable excitement, peeing on every shrub and tire.

...In a pig's ass! For a man with killer instincts stuck in the dead-end role of an Air Marshal herding sheep, it was an idea that struck a nerve, threw him off his guard and made him vulnerable.

But did he care?

No. He didn't. Danger be damned!

Jesse made Hoot feel alive partly because she made him feel out of control, a feeling he hadn't appreciated before. But, starting in Vietnam and continuing all those years while he chased Norman Carpenter and other shitheads like him, partners dropping like Star Trek characters in the wrong-color shirts the whole way, danger had always been part of the mix for Hoot. Didn't mean he was deaf or immune to criticism for his direct methods and hair trigger.

...And now?

Great! Hoot thought. This is all I need – I'm turning into a late-blooming thrill seeker and sex addict! And why not? The rest of my life has been a bit sordid, too…

Chapter 21

Hoot wasn't surprised to find Jesse gone from Mom's when he returned to Forks. What he couldn't figure out was why he gave a shit that she was gone...

Simple answer; he cared because he couldn't not care. Jessica Vega was obviously a much more complicated and troubled person than he had realized before now, but was she actually guilty of anything? Anything like murder for example?

Probably...

There was no hard proof that Jesse had anything to do with Harold Hesse's murder. Not yet: A pair of victims yielding meager clues. Hearsay and innuendo from locals. Tiny clay people on a tiny toy train. And, of course, Hoot's hunch hovering like a belching elephant in the corner. No actual proof to hand a jury – but hearsay and innuendo suggesting there was plenty of motive. Proof would come. It always does. In the meantime...

Jesse was a killer. Of that, Hoot was now certain. He'd known more than enough killers during his long career as a marshal to recognize a certain look in the eyes, a look that people who've never taken another person's life simply don't have, and he'd seen it in Jesse's eyes. Just flashes, but it was definitely there. He'd always considered it a good thing in a partner, someone watching your backside equipped with a lethal skillset and experience using it – maybe not so much in a wife or girlfriend.

Girlfriend? That's where it gets complicated, Hoot thought.

What the fuck? He honestly couldn't conjure Jesse in the role of girlfriend in any lasting sense the way he could easily visualize the view from Maddie's deck with Maddie in it. He should have his head examined...

Wait just a minute and hold the hotdog! Hoot thought with a grim inner smile; he did have his head examined…recently. The paradox of Dr. Goode's psych evaluation after his lethal in-flight action had hardly been lost on Hoot. "You've had intimacy issues in the past, Marshal Hooten?" the good Doctor Goode had said, making the statement of fact sound like a question.

Hoot had answered; "Intimacy issues? I don't think I understand what that means," his answer more honest than he realized at the time.

Maddie would know what he meant. They had talked about this very thing. "I understand your reluctance to open up," she once told him. "All you've seen. All you've had to give up to do the job you've done. It must wear on the soft spots."

And then she'd sat with him…silently. He could've almost fallen in love with her for that alone, that one timely silence.

That's what I need, he thought. A peaceful place, and the time to think. But instead of a peaceful and quiet place to ponder clues, here he was; empty-handed back at Mom's Motel.

Hoot's instinct teaming-up with a nugget of common sense and his basic disbelief in coincidence, he was now certain in his own mind that Jesse was involved in the murder of Harold Hesse and the Pysht Bay woman. To him, it explained some of the off-kilter things about her, her empty empathy and familial loathing, signs of a powerful cruel streak lurking just below the surface as if she were constructed on a fault line and another headline-grabbing tragedy was only a matter of time.

But he needed to know… Was she actually guilty of anything?

If the foo shits, Hoot thought, remembering the age-old footwear parable with a dab of brittle humor. He had been a meddler of the official sort all the years he wore a badge – he yearned to be a civilian now, to turn a blind and blissfully ignorant eye, to be able to say *not my problem*.

Was it even possible? He wondered.

Chili would say that he'd fucked up bigtime when he let Jesse get away. And the man would be right to send him on his way. Hoot justified it as giving her a fair head start. Pure bullshit, of course. Experience told him that both the official and the personal responsibility for his little lapse in judgment were unlikely to grow lighter over time.

"She took off. Didn't say when she'd be back," Jesse's mother, Alison Wonderland, said, telling him this fully clothed, Hoot noted with some relief.

Her fingers toyed with a beaded amber necklace at her throat: a clunky sterling-silver peace sign and a room key hung from it on a leather thong. "This is a master key. Gets you into any room you like." She lifted the necklace over her head and handed it to Hoot, saying, "You can let yourself into Jesse's room. Or choose another…"

***

Alone in Jesse's room, Hoot took a good look around without knowing exactly what he was looking for. Anything that might shed some light on Jesse. Anything that might explain why she would intentionally hide her knowledge of Harold Hesse's identity from him other than involvement in the murder, or to play some sort of a game with him…

It was a dingy room and there wasn't much to see. Pressboard drawers in the low dresser/TV stand were empty. Bare hangars in the chifferobe. Hoot had noticed her shoulder bag earlier, but hadn't concerned himself with what was in it; probably the basic travel kit that every air marshal kept close at hand – whatever she had brought, it was all gone now. All that remained at Mom's was a small selection of giveaway toiletries that were left behind on the bathroom counter. A toothbrush in a glass. A razor in the shower. There was a single chair at a writing table, a blotter and ice bucket on top. An outdated local phonebook and an old Gideon Bible in the drawer.

Hoot's mind kept returning to the idea that Jesse was certainly capable of killing. But then so was he. So were a number of other people he knew who were not murderers. For some, life and death are more immediate than for others – that's just the way it is; anyone who has been to war knows this. But did Jesse actually kill Harold Hesse? Did she kill the woman? That's what Hoot wanted to know; whose hand did the dirty deed – it was the difference between whether he'd been fucking a murderer or a manipulator...or both.

He already knew the answer to that question, didn't he?

The bedcovers were slightly rumpled. Hoot sat on the edge and then lay back across the thin bedspread, cotton sheet and polyester blanket underneath. The pillow smelled of Jesse, he noticed. She'd lain here in torment.

He got up and moved over to the chair, sat down and looked around. He could feel it – a wrongness in the air like a vague itch, a familiar tic telling him he was missing something. He wasn't seeing something, but what?

There was nothing else but the bed – the only stick of furniture in the place that would have any meaning to a girl like Jesse.

Hoot stood and turned his attention to the bed and pulled off the bedspread. He lifted one corner of the mattress and looked underneath, springs squeaking.

Nothing there.

He went to another corner of the bed and did it again.

Still nothing.

Lifting the third corner revealed a small rectangular tag on a short beaded chain hidden between the mattress and the box spring. Aluminum, with curled edges and rounded corners, embossed on the tag was the name; Vega J L, followed by Jesse's blood type, social security number and USMC. The word Catholic seemed a stretch to Hoot. A familiar-looking brass key was hung on the chain with the tag. Neither an especially old key nor a shiny new key. Smallish, it wasn't a car key or an ordinary door key. Hoot had no idea what it fit. His first thought was that it looked like a padlock key or a locker key. And then he remembered – she had told him about her treasure box; the place where she said she stashed all the shit that matters.

...The big bright light in the back room of Hoot's mind came on. He stuffed the key in his pocket, grabbed his jacket, and headed out the door for his truck.

He knew exactly where Jesse hid her treasure box. She had told him about it in the bar. And he had seen the tattoo...

Chapter 22

Back in Port Timothy, Hoot made a few calls and answered a couple, giving Horner a chance to tell him in no uncertain terms that he'd be entirely on his own if he went after Jesse; making it clear that if he was giving any thought to chasing her across the border into Mexico as a private citizen to apprehend her – or to shoot her – well then…

He sat for long hours on his deck telling himself that he was considering the situation with Jesse from all angles, but he wasn't. Honestly, he didn't dare to dwell on Jesse for too long. Instead, he distracted himself by watching the big container ships glide past heading for wherever-the-hell, lethargically imagining what they contained, a bottle of Absolut in a bucket of ice at his side. It was Maddie who finally broke through to him after two days of effort; moved him from his deck to hers in a thin ploy to get a good meal in him.

Hoot gratefully accepted Maddie's invitation. It was the respite he needed; no Chili Hilliker coming around barking about leads and pouring endlessly over his ever-thickening case files like a driven sorcerer, claiming that Hoot was out of his mind to give "that murderin fuckin headjob three fuckin hours head start b'fore lettin anybody know what the fuck was up" as he put it, always a little heavy with the fucks when he was frustrated.

"I had no hard evidence," Hoot had told the Big Bear.

"Hard evidence? When in Methuselah's fuckin lifetime have you ever seen any hard evidence? Cases are built from the evidence we have – it's our job to make it hard!"

Chili's eyebrows were bunched-up like overworked bookends on either side of the deepening creases in the center of his forehead; it was a tough job, containing the force of his fury. Hoot was drunk enough he could've laughed at his friend's obvious angst, but sober enough not to.

"All I really had was a hunch," he said. "A vague one. Not enough to hold her."

"Let me remind you, my old friend," Chili said. "From day one you haven't had the authority to hold or not to hold anyfuckinbody for anyfuckinthing regarding the Juan de Fuca case – that's my job. Your job was to help my investigation. Not to sabotage it…"

"Sabotage? That's pure bullshit and you know it!" Hoot answered, taking umbrage before he could stop himself. Chili was correct, of course; Hoot was not the lead dog in this particular pack of hounds, and he couldn't help nipping at the heels of those who were. Sensitive to the idea that he might unintentionally derail Chili's investigation, he softened his tone and said; "What I'm saying is that nothing I found or saw, nor anything that I suspected I found or saw in La Push would impress a prosecutor. The case remains exactly where it would be even if I'd ratted my suspicions about Jesse to you and Ellis before I left La Push."

"Ya think?"

"We need evidence – the hard sort that doesn't exist? We just need to find the boat," Hoot said. He understood Chili's anger. He'd be angry too, if the tables were turned.

"I had to pull more than a few smilin crocks outta my ass to keep us both from gettin busted over your involvement in the Breakwater case in the first damned place," Chili said. "A little Cajun voodoo makin me even more responsible than I already was for your mistake in judgment, as the big badges prefer callin Jesse's escape."

"Don't think I don't appreciate it." Hoot said. "My service record doesn't need another hit given my leave status at the moment."

"Was it an escape?" Chili asked. "Or did you hold the fuckin door for her?"

Hoot knew there was nothing he could say in his own defense so he said nothing.

After a few long seconds of silence, Chili told Hoot with a note of finality, "I'm afraid we aren't gonna be lookin for any boat. It's bein looked for by others…"

Hoot watched while a Greek tragedy played across Chili's face, and then his friend continued in a tone of resignation, "Law enforcement has always been a young person's game. Older people with any brains advance through the ranks to private offices with doors, or they move on to a second career. Retire early. Do somethin different. Most who stay in long enough to retire turn into bureaucrats with badges – buck passers…the smart ones do, anyhow. You bucked the tide and I always respected you for it, but this time I'm afraid you went too far my friend. Allowing a suspect to take flight? And not the first time t' boot…"

"Just chill, Chili. You don't wanna go there…"

"Fuckit Hoot! You should've shot her. Everyone'd understand that!"

"Are you trying to fire me?" Hoot asked.

"Not me. The Clallam County sheriff," Chili said.

***

Now it was just Maddie and Hoot and Hoot's bottle of ice-cold Absolut hanging out on Maddie's nicer-and-larger-than-Hoot's deck overlooking the strait. Her hot tub gurgling nearby. A big platter of pasta with spicy meatballs on the table under a large umbrella. And, thankfully, no rain.

"I like thinking of you as a grandpa," Maddie said, picking up a conversation they had started in the kitchen about Hoot's grandson, Jeremy, visiting for the Christmas holiday.

"I'm not a very good one, I'm afraid," Hoot replied. "Never had the knack for it."

"Horsefodder," Maddie replied.

"It's true. I drink too much. And I smoke."

"True and true again. But what's all that got to do with being a good grandpa?"

"Obviously, I'm a bad influence. Haven't exactly been close with my family. I was gone a lot. Haven't even seen Jeremy since he was a kid. Now he's eleven-years-old and he's going to spend his Christmas vacation with me? I'm not sure how that'll work out."

Hoot looked away and muttered "Sure as hell could be better timing…"

"Timing's always a slippery eel," Maddie said. "You may not get another chance if you don't grab this one. Besides, I bet you could be a terrific grandpa. You just haven't put in the minimum required man-hours. Wait and see; you'll both have a great time…"

The conversation seemed to trip on itself and fall flat. After a long silence Hoot said in a hushed release of breath, "I let her go. I don't know why I did that…"

"I understand. Don't worry about it." Maddie handed Hoot a bottle of wine, a corkscrew, and said "Let's eat instead…"

***

"It's a fact. I fucked-up and let her go," Hoot confessed in a tone of unrepentant surrender after putting away two enormous meatballs and enough spaghetti in scratch-made marinara sauce to sink a submarine, plus two bottles of wine. "I let a murderer escape. I could have easily nabbed her before she got off the peninsula, and I didn't even try. Instead, the instant I realized who Jesse was and what she'd done I went as numb as a rookie without a clue. Something inside of me just couldn't – or wouldn't – believe what I knew to be true."

"They say love is blind and desire is shortsighted if it's any consolation," Maddie offered.

"I was too close. Too involved."

Maddie reached across the table and took his hand in hers, said, "It isn't like Jesse actually killed anybody on your watch. No need to beat yourself up."

"…Not yet."

"I'm serious," Maddie said. "Just because you didn't throw on your superhero cape and foil her escape doesn't mean that you personally let her go – it isn't the same thing. You connected all the dots. You did your part. Jesse's a Clallam County sheriff problem now, isn't she?"

"She's a Person of Interest to them, sure. And to Chili. But Chili's so pissed-off at me for letting her get away he forgets that I'm also the one who found her. I'm off the case. Suspended twice in a month's time? Halleluiah! I believe that's new a record for me."

"You're absolutely right. You aren't a marshal anymore Ezra Hooten," Maddie said, retracting her hand and doing a less-than-perfect job of masking her frustration with Hoot's bullheadedness. "You're a grandfather. It'd do your image some good to act like one now and then."

Hoot stood and started to pace the deck, saying "Of course, I know that. I'm working on it…"

"So it isn't your job to track down Jessica Vega, is it?"

"Don't you see, Maddie? That doesn't really matter. I'm culpable for letting her slip away in the first place," Hoot said. "Not the first time I've been sucker-punched by someone close to me by the way, as Chili pointed out. It may not be my job, but it is my responsibility. Besides, I know something they don't – I know where she's hiding."

Hoot stopped pacing, looked Maddie straight in the eyes; his expression tired but determined, and said, "I'm the one who'll find her."

Chapter 23

"He'll come," Jesse said in the tone of an unrepentant sinner on a hot pew; wary, but determined to get it done and be done with it. She was alone with her constantly busy and preoccupied father on the clubhouse verandah or she would not have had the chance to tell him much of anything. He certainly had no interest in hearing about a determined ex-deputy marshal chasing her to Mexico for reasons having nothing to do with the meticulously planned, somewhat botched, but nonetheless successful mid-deportation execution of his nephew by Marco; not even if the ex-marshal doing the chasing was Marco's shooter. In spite of his reputation, Felix Vega wasn't the sort of cartel boss who throws a macho fit and starts killing people if a plan didn't go off exactly as planned…as long as it worked, success inevitably measured on a sliding scale at Playa Rocosa.

Don't make promises you can't keep, the manifestation of Billiejean Wisdom said inside Jesse's head.

Close had never been a word to define Jesse's relationship with her father aside from inappropriate physical closeness when the mood was on him. The two years spent playing the role of daddy's-little-whore-in-training while she recovered from the Queets trestle incident was the longest she had ever lived with him, and it was more than enough for Jesse. Away on cartel business more often than not during her few visits with him in Mexico, throughout her entire life Jesse's father had been cold, dismissive, and abusive to girls and women – with the singular exception of his ailing mother. That he didn't go so far as to deny Jesse's existence seemed to be about the limit of Felix Vega's parental affection. The rest was an altogether different story…

"Seguro?" Felix Vega asked his daughter. She was a stranger, now all grown up; blood the only bond between them.

"Si, I'm certain of it, Papa Flix," Jesse said, testing the water by using the familial Flix reserved for only a few. "I haven't known this air marshal long enough to know him well," she added, "but well enough to know that he's more than a shooter. Much more."

"When has my only daughter ever needed longer than three seconds to know someone down to their roots?" Vega asked pointedly. There was little if any pride in the Anglo word daughter as Felix Vega said it. After all, he had four living sons sharing the Vega name and who knows how many bastards who didn't. Jesse counted herself lucky to get invited to the table at all.

"He's a tracker," she said, addressing the likelihood of an ex-deputy US marshal following her from Washington State to Mazatlan with or without official authority to do so. "One of the best when he was in the Marshals."

"So?" Papa prompted as if his posse was filled with ranks of equally talented trackers.

"Wouldn't surprise me if Hoot went rogue," Jesse said. "He does everything from the gut – and permission is the last thing he ever needs. Also, I'm sure he has a bit of what some call the vision even though he doesn't seem to know how to use it. He blunders a lot and gets lucky, claims to have a vague spirit guide connection from a pact when he was a kid. Mostly, he's persistent; I swear the man had a dog-on-the-scent look in his eye the moment he arrived in Forks. I knew as soon as he and the local lawman went to investigate La Push that my association with Harold Hesse and his moronic brother would be discovered."

"Yes. I remember this La Push from when I was a young bracero living with your mother in that cheap rainforest motel of hers. A reservation town, right? Very small? For all I know, Gota, you could have been conceived on a poncho on the beach at La Push! Of course you would know these men from there – everybody knows everybody there. Knowing them proves nothing…"

How appropriate! the Billievoice scorned, *Everything comes full circle. The notorious Jesse Fucking James-Vega's undoing in the very place of her conception? Still don't believe in fate?*

Jesse crossed her arms, looked off toward endless Pacific waves crashing against Mexican rocks, thinking; no, I don't believe in fate…but I do believe very strongly in Karma. She said to her father; "Hoot's a very simple man with predictable ways, a creature of those who made him. But he has sharp instincts, and it would be a mistake to ignore his spirit guide connection. He can be hard to read, making it impossible to second-guess what he'll do without a moment's warning – except to shoot first and discuss it later; like the way he shot a man who was running up the aisle in a jet plane without hesitating. You say he is odd-looking, and he is. But he's also different in ways beyond his appearance. He has the instincts of a man who's been living on the fringe a long time. I knew he wouldn't be happy with a phony coincidence story about me and the Hesse twins, so I didn't offer one. Besides, proof isn't a required element for Hoot to act any more than it is for me or you."

"Mi comprende, daughter. I understand. You are more than capable of handling your own affairs. You told me that you had to deal with the trainman – that was not a problem. But I also remember telling you that I do not wish to know details about unpleasant things that have nothing to do with me," Vega said in a tone of finality, a small door into the inner sanctum of Felix Vega being closed with a reverberating boom. Controlling the conversation, he asked; "No hesitation when your sky marshal partner shot Marco?"

"None."

"And my idiot nephew? Marco had already killed him?"

"Si. In sight of everyone on the plane, including the air marshal."

The plan had been for Marco, one of Jesse's bastard half-brothers, to be captured after executing his cousin, and for his interrogation to reveal certain embarrassing entanglements between the US government and the Los Zetas cartel – entanglements that could seriously destabilize drug control efforts on both sides of the border. And then Marco would be routinely extradited back to Mexico in his turn, his family cared for during the full term of his absence.

"It was a perfect plan. I devised it, myself," Felix Vega said. "Including putting you there as insurance…and then your loco shooter fucks it all up? Hah!"

His laugh sounding well-practiced and definitive, no response had been called for and none was offered.

"So one could say that my nephew has been avenged – correct?" Vega continued. "That's good. People respect vengeance. What we must do now is take credit for this air marshal's actions. Play up your part as if it all went off perfecto and let those Los Hermanidad nutsacks wonder how we pulled it off. Let everyone wonder…"

"And how do we do that, Papa? Take credit, I mean…"

"This air marshal – he's the sort of man who appreciates serious money?"

"Don't count on it, Papa. I don't think Hoot is a very practical person."

Felix Vega took a focused glance at Jesse, and then repeated the name, "*Hoot.* I think I like him," he said. "I like his direct methods. And he seems very fond of you."

"For now, maybe. He doesn't know me yet," Jesse said, and Billievoice mocked, *Not yet?…You think?*

"Fond enough to come here looking for you?" Felix Vega said, the glance at his daughter turning chilly in a blink. "Yes, I like him, but I don't think I'd like him so much here,"

"I wasn't sure enough of his interest in me to stick around and see how he took my connection with the trainmen."

"So you bring your little problem to my door?"

"Perdóname, Papa. Yes. I'm certain he will follow me," Jesse said with a concealed smile. "As I said, he's a hound dog, so he must. Think of him as un regalo, Papa – for you."

"A gift? I'm in the middle of a winner-take-all turf war here, and you bring me a burned-out marshal as a gift?"

Felix Vega's demeanor warmed a degree to one of tentative approval, looking his daughter over with the same leering macho eyes he would use to size-up any other female who crossed his path. "Mantenerlo interesado, mi gota," he said, turning away before reverting to English. "Keep him interested. This Hoot could be useful to us…"

Chapter 24

As far as Hoot was concerned there were no good flights, only a few
blessedly short ones. He seldom slept on airplanes, never
comfortably, but he slept like the dead on the plane to Mazatlan.
Suspended from active duty while the Skyshooter Incident as it was
now being called throughout the known universe via the internet was
investigated, Hoot was free to travel if he wished, and he had
suddenly wished to visit Mazatlan. So here he was; snoozing his way
south…

Hoot could've flashed his sky marshal credentials and hopped
a free flight, but he didn't, paying for his ticket to Mexico with his
own hard-earned dinero instead. Aside from taking rare advantage of
an upgrade to first class and the vodka martinis that came with it,
Hoot was just an ordinary passenger on this flight, and being
unarmed while on an airplane left him feeling curiously naked. He
couldn't remember the last time he'd flown as a total civilian –
sometime after Vietnam but before joining FAMS. He probably slept
through much of that flight too, because he'd long ago discovered
the less of any flying experience that he actually experienced the
better; it was just a hard thing for Hoot to manage because sleep was
not his friend while he was suspended in air.

Liquor helped…sometimes.

A more honest reflection would be that liquor was helping
out quite a bit recently.

Eyes closed, Hoot's inebriated ego nudged his over-active id
toward a soothing memory of sitting with Maddie in bubbling water
up to his armpits and telling her that looking forward to senior's day
at Kroger's wasn't for him. He remembered telling her he was going
to buy a nice, new, fifth-wheel tenement-on-wheels, and a Dodge

three-quarter-ton pickup to tow it with, saying he wanted to spend a full year touring the off-the-interstate parts of America, the few quiet places that were still left, and end up where he'd started out in Pleasanton Maine, saying he wanted to do this without constantly watching the shadows for scumbag criminals, saying he figured he'd be looking at so much that's bright and right for a change he may need darker glasses!

Sharing this little daydream with Maddie, they both laughed. Hoot had always liked the sound of a woman's laughter and Maddie had a nice laugh.

"Good plan," she said. "You just need someone to share it with."

She had unobtrusively moved his vodka glass aside to set a steaming cup of black coffee in its place. She added sugar and a splash of cream to her own cup and asked, "Did you think Jesse could be the one?"

"The thought might've crossed my mind." Hoot said, glancing at Maddie with an unguarded expression.

"Any others on your list?"

It was a bald-faced challenge – and a flirt. And Hoot couldn't resist serving up a warm smile in response, happy to roll around in Maddie Marvel's attentions like an old hound in a cool mud puddle, eager to get some on the hard-to-reach places. She had come to the rescue. Her mission, she said, was to drag him out of his funk – and sitting together in her hot tub as naked as two lobsters in a pot, he appreciated that she was doing a fine job of it. "I don't actually expect anybody with good sense to join me," Hoot answered, skirting the question.

"Maybe you could downsize your plans a bit," Maddie said. "Cash-in right now and hit the road in a used mini-van with a Coleman stove and a sleeping bag, instead of a new travel trailer towed behind a behemoth new pickup. That might not be too bad a setup for a retired bachelor on the road…if he wasn't expecting company."

"Plan A is better," Hoot replied with a tight smile, and she gave him a look full of unstated meaning.

Or maybe she was just baiting him? No. Maddie didn't play that sort of game…

"What about you?" he asked, genuinely curious. "What do you want for all your tomorrows?"

"Whirled peas?" she ventured with a teasing grin, and Hoot grunted his approval.

"Seriously," Hoot said, "I'm not one of those naturally gregarious guys at heart as you've noticed. I've been told that I'm slow to warm-up to new faces. But I'm loyal." The urge to peek under the water suddenly almost irresistible, he glanced away at the distant strait instead, continuing; "What I'm trying to say is that, even though I've only known you for a year I already feel like I know you far better than most people I've ever known, and yet I still feel like I've barely scratched the surface. I want to know more…"

"Oh?" Maddie said. "This is starting to sound less like ordinary hot tub chit-chat and more like an actual conversation. But you already know everything there is to know about me. The important stuff, anyhow; the rest is detail and excuses."

"Okay then. Forget the excuses and dazzle me with a few new details that I don't already know," Hoot said, challenging her.

Maddie smiled indulgently, said; "I married late in life…twice, as you already know, because the first time was just plain silly even though we were crazy about each other at the time. Funny…he wasn't gay, Robert told me he was <u>asexual</u>. Not that it matters, because I admit I'd had my suspicions from the start that that part of it wasn't going to work, though in hindsight it would've been nicer if he'd come out of the closet with his little revelation during the five years we were dating before the wedding and not the night of it."

Hoot couldn't help laughing, said, "Dating for five years and it never came up?"

"Oh, it came up often enough while we were dating, just not on our wedding night – nor afterward. The ring made all the difference. He said legitimacy killed the thrill for him. Anyhow; after my divorce I took a year and wrote my first novel, and then I became the On the Town correspondent for the LA Times for ten years, as you also know."

"I remember you telling me that writing is the only job you've ever had," Hoot said. "But I've never read any of your novels. All I've read of your work are a couple of articles in the Telegraph."

"It's Romance, tough guy…Romance. Might be a little sweet and predictable for your taste," Maddie said. "But yeah, writing is all I've ever done. Stickwithitness seems to be a trait we have in common."

"All hail stickwithitness!" Hoot chimed.

"My mother raised me to land a good husband and be a good wife. Isn't that hilarious?" Maddie shrugged her naked shoulders and Hoot smiled at the naïveté of their cauldron-like situation. She said, "I moved here from LA after my second divorce to escape the routine of that awful place before it made a complete zombie out of me – or worse; made me feel like a Hollywood hooker for spending my time writing Romance novels instead of meaningful literature. I even wrote a joke about it on my blog – Question: Know how many Romance writers there are in LA? Answer: One less.

"Ralphie, my second husband, could never concede that a Romance writer was a real writer, though he was more than willing to enjoy the financial rewards of being married to one. After strike two, I decided I wanted to live near my sister. Wanted to find some new friends and lose the old ones, so I put down fast roots here and bought The Port Timothy Telegraph a year later.

"It wasn't so hard, changing course. I guess what I'm saying is that picking up the pieces and starting your life over isn't such a bad gig, if you're following your heart." She gave Hoot a sincere look with a hint of smile in her eyes, said; "I know it's none of my business, but I just want to suggest that if your heart tells you you still have unfinished business with Jesse…then you probably do."

Stretching an arm over the tub rail without revealing much that wasn't obscured by bubbles and steam, she dried her hands on one end of her towel before handing him a paperback book titled This Summer's Love by Eveline Baxter; handed him another titled Prince Trueblood's Secret by Margot Maguire, said, "I know you're not a series Romance reader, but take these…remedies in case of sleepless nights."

Hoot knew that his eyes were full of question marks.

"Both mine," Maddie answered his unasked curiosity.

Hoot carefully took the books, looking them over. On the back covers were two younger and subtly different photos of Madeline Marvel accompanied with heavily-hyped and salacious praise for the books' pseudonymous authors. Gushing reviews. Stars galore.

"Each day needs a little romance in it to keep us from going completely nuts," she had so often said. "I write women's fiction," she'd said without elaboration when they first met, and Hoot simply wasn't the sort of man to pry into a friend's private business, just as he would resent a friend prying into his.

He resisted laughing and said, "So you're a real honest-to-god Romance writer…"

"Uh huh, a certified romantic to the core. I'm kinda-sorta famous in my own little corner of the world. Three times over, you might say. You wanted new details – here they are. Not precisely new details, but new to you. Actually nobody around here knows much about my 45-minutes of fame except my sister and a few others. Chili knows, but I don't think it matters to him because he's a certified non-reader. Anyhow…I've kept a low profile since leaving LA, but I still write at least one, sometimes two or three novels a year under three different pen names for two different publishers. Plus I've started self-publishing my backlist. I'm sharing this with you because you asked for details, and I don't want there to be any secrets…"

These were the first of Maddie's books that Hoot had actually seen. He asked, "How many books have you written?"

"Nineteen so far. Two of them optioned for movies. It's how I make my living – the 'Graph certainly doesn't return enough profit to live on."

"Incredible," Hoot said with a low whistle through his teeth only he could hear, a sincere feeling of respect for Maddie washing over him. He'd seen her heavily-laden bookshelves many times but never gave the books a close look. He was a nuts-and-bolts non-fiction reader at best: histories and biographies and work-related stuff. Newspapers with comics topped his casual reading list, while Maddie wrote two or three entire books a year! She was obviously unafraid of hard work.

"You mind if I smoke in the tub?" he asked, handing the books back with undisguised admiration.

"Not at all," she answered, "but I bet I could help you quit smoking forever inside of a week." Her smile was very mischievous-looking to Hoot, suggesting the cure had something to do with sex –

lots of sex, possibly a fully-researched romance novel full of it. There was a bold gleam in Maddie's eyes saying; Yes, I might surprise you, you old curmudgeon.

Hoot stretched a long pale arm across the top of the tub enclosure and reached for his cigarettes. Sure, I could quit smoking for the right reasons, he thought. Hell, I should quit, right reasons or not. If he didn't cut back a bit on the drinking and quit smoking Hoot knew he probably wouldn't live long enough to make it all the way back home to Maine, anyhow. His kids, his brother, his ex, friends and colleagues, and every goddamned supervisor as far back as he could remember had expressed various versions of precisely that same dire sentiment at one time or another. He hardly disagreed with them, was surprised, really, that he had lived long enough to be seriously considering retirement. Hoot had always assumed he would die young on the job.

The drinking and smoking were more deadly than the job, he knew, and the job had nearly killed him a couple of times. It's crazy the way a dangerous job inevitably leads to other dangerous behavior. Being a marshal and wearing a gun made him fair game for any turd on a collision course with the cosmic karma fan. Hoot didn't waste a lot of time thinking about it, but he knew that he was rated high risk in prettymuch every category from an actuary viewpoint.

It was the drinking that made the smoking so hard to quit. Nothing quite as good as a cigarette with a vodka martini – unless it was a cigarette with a vodka martini after wild and passionate sex.

…There was that sex thing again! The Jesse thing. God help him…he'd loved it, no question. But how long could a man his age expect to ride that carrousel? It just wasn't respectable, as his father would've said.

Hoot knew he should follow Maddie's example and put down some quick roots. Could he do that? Could he ever feel truly at home somewhere – anywhere?

Taking a long, unflinching gander through rising steam at Maddie sitting opposite him in the tub, Hoot appreciated how she was a beautiful woman in a comfortable, check-it-out, this-is-the-body-I-live-in way that made maturity seem sexy. Hoot saw her as a woman not easily satisfied by men, yet her interest in him was obvious, her never-give-up attitude infectious – what's more…she was fun!

Could a good woman really turn his compass around?

He honestly didn't know the answer. He only knew that further involvement with Madeline Marvel was likely to be fraught with all kinds of…complications. Serious relationships always are.

Chapter 25

Hoot dared not go chasing after Jesse in Mexico without a damned good reason to return home – or so he told himself.

His ex, Linda, provided it. She called and said, "I'm thinking that Remy might like to come visit his grandpa for Christmas. Get away from all the horseshit back here while Missy's divorce is finalizing."

"Horseshit? Back there?" Hoot parroted.

"Divorces always come with a load of it," Linda said. "Ours did, and it was supposedly civilized. Naturally Missy's would be a very unpleasant affair. You marry an attorney, that's what you get. I just thought it might do Jeremy some good to get away."

"When?"

"ASAP, I guess. Can you take some time off during the holidays?"

"I have plenty of time off right now," Hoot grumbled. "I'm just not sure if I'm the right person to watch after Jeremy. As you know, I don't have much experience with kids."

"He's not exactly a kid anymore," Linda said. "He's eleven; practically a full-fledged teenager who could use a positive role model. Look Hoot, Missy could use a little help with Remy for a few days – a week at most." Sounding suspicious, she suddenly put on the brakes and asked, "What do you mean you have plenty of time off right now? Do those damned marshals have you on admin leave again?"

Hoot didn't answer. He knew his ex didn't watch the news…so how did she always know when his tit was in the wringer?

Needing Hoot's confirmation no more now than ever before, Linda asked, "So, who'd the great fugitive-tracker shoot this time?"

"You forget, Linda, I'm not a deputy marshal anymore."

"That's right! You're a sky marshal, now. I did forget. That's funny considering you don't even like to fly!" Linda was having herself a little chuckle 2300-miles-away at Hoot's expense, then she paused and said; "Hey…wait just a minute! I remember seeing something on the internet about a sky marshal shooting a cartel hitman on a flight to Mexico. Name of the sky marshal was being withheld. That was you…wasn't it?"

Hoot said nothing.

"Yes, of course it was!" Linda said. "For Chrissakes, Hoot! Why do you always have to shoot somebody?"

"It happens."

"No shit? It happens to *you*…"

"Look, Linda," Hoot said, knowing that he sounded defensive as hell because he was on the ropes with the ex, but unable to change his tone even if he tried; "I've got one or two things going on here. You know, moving into the cabin and such. Give me a few days to get organized and I'd be happy to look after the boy. I suppose Remy might like to spend a little holiday vacation time with his grandpa, have Christmas together."

"I don't know, Hoot. Now that we've talked, I'm not so sure it's a good idea."

"Of course it's a good idea," Hoot said, his guiltload shifting just a bit. "Get him out of harm's way back there for a little while. I know it's about time I shouldered a few family obligations. And besides, I could use some younger muscle at the cabin. I'll take him fishing."

"Fishing? Real grandpa-grandson stuff…with a Christmas tree? Promise you won't be taking him on any manhunts or stakeouts? No high-speed car chases?"

"Come-on Linda! Give me a little credit, please…"

If Hoot crossed his fingers behind his back, he hoped it didn't show over the phone.

"That was you, wasn't it? On the plane…"

"Yeah. It was me." Hoot replied, breaking his confidentially agreement without hesitation. This was Linda, after all – what good would secrecy do?

Long-distance silence ensued for several long seconds and then Linda said with a sigh, "I should've known the moment I heard about it. You okay, Hoot?"

"Yeah. I'm good. Thanks for asking…"

"Alright," Linda said. "I'll talk to Missy. But you'd better be goddamned sincere about keeping Remy out of your business or I'll come out there and slap you up the side of your head like you've never been slapped before…"

"I just need a few days," he said.

Hoot remembered the year his father died. It was a year before his divorce from Linda, they were living in Kansas City and he was breaking in a new partner named Mark Cooper. His previous partner, Phil Olson, the second deputy marshal to die backing up the soon-to-be infamous Troubleshooter, had been killed in action only a month before when he entered one of Norman Carpenter's booby-trapped hideouts.

Hoot was still reeling from Olson's death. Slowly sliding into an ever-growing shoulda-been-me pit of despair; the same anguish eating at him since Christ was a corporal. Linda, desperate to find a chink in Hoot's mood before it became another callous on his heart, decided it would be a good idea to invite Cooper to dinner one Saturday night, one of those get-to-know-ya affairs the wives of lawdogs always seemed to be cooking up back in those days. It was early fall, when the oak and maple leaves were turning, and no one could have guessed that Cooper would be as dead as Phil Olson before Christmas – skeleton number three hanging all smiley and unforgiving in Hoot's closet. This was the beginning of Hoot's now-legendary reputation regarding partners – the beginning of the bad years, the jinx years – before the very idea of get-to-know-ya affairs suddenly seemed akin to standing on a hilltop and flipping-off the gods during a lightning storm.

Cooper was a young deputy marshal, still new to the star, and when he arrived at the house the kids were all over him, driving him crazy. So real smooth-like Hoot invited his new partner to run down to Sears with him and do a little manly shopping before dinnertime. Get away from the Wild Bunch for a while. "I want to pick up a leaf blower while they're still on sale," he'd said as if reciting a well-rehearsed infomercial. Instead, he took his new partner to a bowling alley with a card room in back.

Cooper didn't gamble, said he was raised a Bible Belt Baptist and didn't know how to play cards. But he knew how to roll a bowling ball, so he subbed on a league team while Hoot played poker. Three hours later Cooper was long done bowling and Linda showed up. She was clearly pissed off. And she walked straight over to the table where Hoot was playing. He was up by about $500, a big stack of chips in front of him.

"Ezra Monroe Hooten, you shit! Get your sorry ass out of that chair right now, you're coming with me!" she said without a Hi, howya doin Honey, or anything else that might end in a lilt. Linda was a compact woman. In time, Hoot came to realize that lots of small women are forceful, but from the start Linda set the standard. Quick-witted and volatile, she could roil herself up like a pissed-off Komodo dragon if she thought the occasion warranted it – and apparently this one did.

Hoot had always considered himself a man of keen survival instincts, his entire adult life testimony to that fact, and at that moment his instincts were telling him he was in trouble with the wife. But he'd only just broken an evening-long losing streak, was on a roll at last, and the devil inside didn't want to leave. He replied, "Just let me finish this hand, Sugarbiscuit, and then I'll go."

Hoot had been drinking pretty heavily while playing cards, remaining just sober enough to remember to hedge his bets, sober enough to respect the shortness of Linda's fuse, but evidently not sober enough to remember how much she disliked the endearment, Sugarbiscuit. He quickly assumed his best just-mellow-out-a-little-and-everything'll-be-alright expression, his never-miss smile happy and bright, and as ill-fitting as a top hat on a tomcat.

Linda hated that look. Without warning she started hitting him with her purse, calling him a lying bastard, telling him where he could put his goddamned biscuit and demanding that he get up right now while complaining that dinner was completely ruined.

Others in the card room stopped playing cards and looked on with expressions ranging from high alarm to low amusement. Hoot, thinking it was hilarious his pissed-off pint-sized wife was swatting him with her purse, ducked the blows and fended her off with his free hand, trying in vain to protect his chips and his drink with the hand holding his cards.

"But I'm winning, Linda," he said. "I can't just quit in the middle of a hand when I'm winning!"

"Like hell you can't!" Linda whacked him again.

"That's my money you're playing with there, Hot Shot." She said. "So gimme those chips!"

…And that's when a wild swipe with her purse knocked Hoot's pile of chips off the table.

"Okay! Okay! I think I'd better fold, guys," Hoot said to the other players, laughing-off his embarrassment and scrambling down to his knees to gather his strewn wealth.

Linda paced around Hoot on the floor like a mad avenger, cussing him out. Cursing the other players at the table, and men in general by proxy, she raked him with severe verbal broadsides, flaying his back with the purse every time she came near. Her anger insatiable, she took out his rudder, his ego, and she was going for his mainmast – his pride.

Hoot finally got his act together and cashed-in, gave Linda the money, and Linda stomped out of the card room with the loot in her fist. At the exit door she stopped in front of Cooper and hissed in a stage whisper that could've easily reached the back row of Freedom Palace on Main Street, "I don't care where you take that man, but don't bring him home!"

Hoot had made Cooper drive him home in spite of Linda's ultimatum. Insisted his new partner stay and eat the ruined dinner, too: burnt pot roast, dry and stringy as charcoal-flavored beef jerky, withered potatoes the texture and taste of leather. Hoot ate gleefully, raising his voice and praising Linda's cooking, swearing that it wasn't burnt too badly while she fumed in the other room, refusing to sit at the table with them.

It was awful, but as soon as Cooper left, as soon as the dishes were done and the kids were in bed, Hoot and Linda made up and made love with passion appropriate for penitence. They used to do that a lot – make up by making love. Sometimes, he missed it.

…And now: here he was, on a freelance manhunt of sorts.

Looking at his phone Hoot saw a text from Linda reading; **H – Missy says thanks Remy says cool Will send info – L.**

Oh well, he thought. Shit's always on a collision course with one cosmic fan or another. He figured he could do a good-enough job of avoiding high-speed car chases and stakeouts for a while.

Meanwhile, there was Mazatlan, a seaside gem sustained by tourists and drug lords!

December in Mexico was dry and sunlit; a completely different world from the Pacific Northwest six hours ago. Flying in over sheet metal rooftops on plywood shanties, the countryside below was brown and dusty-looking, the General Rafael Buelna airport a sun-baked oasis of paved civilization waiting in the sparse chaparral ahead. The Pacific Ocean lay flat and endless to the west, scrub brush everywhere else: tumbleweeds and scrawny cattle. And then a city built along a broad crescent bay...

Landed and deplaned, Hoot stood in line with his meager baggage like everybody else, and it was a long slow line to the stop/go light at the customs kiosk. Getting past the light on green a half-hour later, he left the hubbub of touristas milling around the congested terminal and ran a gauntlet of cabbies hawking 'free' rides without acknowledging any of them.

Confident that the man he was looking for would be standing aside, Hoot's eyes searched the shadows for Reuben Ocho. Never eager to draw attention to himself, Ocho was an unattractive man with ratlike mannerisms that added an especially unsavory aura to his appearance. He seldom mingled. Ocho was one of those people who easily blend into their environment because nobody really wants to see them in the first place. Still, Hoot knew that Ocho would make a big deal out of it; the risk he was taking by showing his rodent-like face on airport security cameras in order to tag Hoot at the airport; he would snivel about how it would've been better to meet later, somewhere else, somewhere private...all bullshit.

Hoot knew that Ocho led a precarious life – all his kind did. That's just the way it works when your entire life is lived in the underbelly of the underworld. But he also knew that Ocho was hardly taking a risk because of the sheer amount of wonky shit going on daily at the Mazatlan airport. Security largely farcical to the point it was rumored to be safe to do drug deals while waiting in line for customs. College kids getting scared and selling their stash instead of flushing it down the toilet.

Ocho had a tendency to over-react. An interesting paradox about the drug culture in Mexico is the Robin Hood aspect of it; drug lords providing far better job opportunities and community support to communities under their control than legitimate officials had ever done or could possibly do. Everyday life was a daily hustle for the essentials for most Mexicans. Negotiating his way around some of the pitfalls of this uncertain environment, Ocho fled Juarez in favor of his Sinaloa contacts in Mazatlan after the gunrunning shit three years ago, making him the best off-the-grid contact Hoot had in Mazatlan.

Of course, Hoot was off-the-grid himself. In Mexico for the first time as a civilian, he had no badge, no official privileges, and no backup in uniform. He also had immediate needs that couldn't be met with a quick shopping excursion to the public market or the Gold Zone, hence the call to Ocho, a man who owed him a favor or two.

Hoot had first met Reuben Ocho in February of 2010, when he was assigned to a US Marshals team in Juarez helping ATF agents investigate escalations in turf wars between drug cartels and the likelihood of danger to American tourists and interests. Specifically, they were back-checking the paper trail of guns used at the massacre at El Aliviane, a Ciudad Juarez rehab center where eighteen young men being weaned off heroin had been killed in September, and the more recent massacre of fourteen teenage students at a birthday party in Juarez's upscale Villas de Salvarcar neighborhood. Among the victims at both places were innocent people including teenagers having nothing to do with any cartel, but nonetheless wounded or killed with weapons purchased in the US and allowed to walk across the border via the Justice Department's famously-botched Fast & Furious operation. Bad business all around.

A small-time heroin dealer and smuggler who'd had nothing firsthand to do with either massacre, Ocho had managed to get stuck crosswise in the mess by simply being one of several mules who'd sneaked the guns used in the shootings into Mexico in the first place. In the hot seat for smuggling weapons and dope, felonies on both sides of the border, Ocho was more than happy to turn snitch to get his precious personal pecans out of the roasting pan as soon as someone made him an offer.

Nine men were at the table for Reuben Ocho's interview with US Justice Department assistant prosecutor Zack Bitters: Ocho sitting in the hot seat, Bitters with the questions and the deal, two Mexican policemen, two attorneys, a Mexican army officer with issues and complaints but without valid opinions or comments, a silent man from Homeland Security Hoot hadn't met before named Mr. Kenneth, and Hoot. Bitters and Hoot had just spent the last hour interviewing Reuben Ocho about his role in the El Aliviane and Villas de Salvarcar massacres. The Justice department's dick hanging out over what should have been a simple sting operation – allowing a few guns walk across the border in order to identify the top-tier buyers on the Mexican side. A perfect example, Hoot thought, of Justice's unfailing ability to fuck up anything they touched; too damned many lawyers involved.

"You look uncomfortable. Are you uncomfortable?" Bitters stood and asked Ocho. "Tough spot, Huh?"

Ocho looked up, his ratlike overbite exposing a snag of crooked brown teeth that may or may not have been an attempt at smiling, and then he looked away again without comment.

"Yeah. You're in a tough spot, Senior Ocho. Not comfortable at all. I'll bet you're sitting there shitting razorblades just thinking about the mess you're in," Bitters said, mock empathy expressed in thick blonde eyebrows over heavily-bagged eyes.

"It's okay if you're scared – you should be, amigo," Bitters continued, walking behind Ocho and giving his shoulder a squeeze. "Relax if you can. I'm done talking about the eighteen junkies in rehab last year. Now I want to talk about the sixty teenaged kids at a birthday party last month. Kids who had nothing to do with your friends' business but got hit by them anyhow just to make a statement hombre-a-hombre? Loco, huh? So, your nuts are in the roasting pan because what happened was this: guns that you acquired across the border and smuggled into Mexico for your friends killed fourteen of those kids and wounded a bunch more – plus the junkies!

"Your guns, Reuben. Yours…"

Bitters sat down across from Ocho and produced a pouch of sweet-smelling tobacco and a packet of rolling papers. With deep concentration he commenced rolling a fat cigarette, Ocho watching him with sidelong glances and nervous hands. Heavy silence ensued, and then Bitters said "Several of those individual guns were traced directly back to you, Reuben. Purchased in illegal transactions in Oklahoma and Texas and smuggled into Mexico through a tunnel network in California."

Bitters put fire to the hand-rolled fag and handed it to Ocho, who immediately took a long drag.

"You're smarter than you look, not to waste my time denying it," Bitters said, a backhanded compliment that was spot-on. "The whole thing was part of a justice department sting and your skinny little butt is stuck right in the middle of it. ¿Queda claro? This is bad business, Reuben. Very bad."

Bitters pushed a rusted can full of mangled cigarette butts from previous conversations with desperate men toward Ocho, said, "You understand the severity of your situation with the US Justice Department?"

It was a rhetorical question; Ocho's eyes answered for him.

"And then there's the problem with your cartel buddies. The other side of the dilemma," Bitters said. "You know what I mean? I'm saying that if word gets around that we've talked, you and me – the cartels'll want you dead. They probably want you dead already for all I know. The way things are shaking out, your old buddies in La Linea – they aren't your friends anymore. And you sure as hell aren't theirs. Not even Los Zetas…

"What do you think, Marshal Hooten? Is Mister Ocho sitting there shitting razorblades?" Bitters asked, including Hoot in this friendly little eight-on-one before he slapped the collar on his new snitch and handed over the leash.

"Must be," Hoot answered, his tone heavy with bogus empathy. "I know I certainly would be if I were in half the trouble he's in. All those dead kids? From nice families, too – that's the sort of thing elevates this chickenshit war between the Sinaloas and Tijuanas to a whole new level."

"…Gentlemen, please!" one of the attorney's present started to object. But Bitters cut him off with a wave of his hand, nodding to Mr. Kenneth who spoke for the first time, saying succinctly, "Let me remind you, sirs, that you were offered an opportunity to observe this interview. Not to be part of it unless asked. If anyone speaks again without first being asked, you will all have to be content with reading a transcript when it becomes available. Am I clear?"

After a brief, room-filling silence Bitters continued with Ocho, "Bad business. Bad times. For everybody. Border rats like you don't have many friends, Reuben. And in times like this...you need good friends."

Bitters turned to Hoot and said, "Consider how all of the deadly dudes Reuben has ever done business with would sooner see him dead than wonder who the fuck he's lined up with now. We'd be doing everyone favors if we just let the Mexicans put him away on what we've got. Take him out of the equation." He glanced at Reuben Ocho and continued, "I've got a five-spot says mister toughguy here won't last a week inside."

"I'll take that five-spot," Hoot said. "You've got it all wrong, Prosecutor; Ocho won't last a week outside. The guys inside'll wanna play with him a whole lot longer than a week..."

Ruben Ocho moaned.

Hoot turned and trained his pale blues on him, and with all the sincerity he could muster, said, "I know it'll break your heart to hear this, amigo, but the truth is you're a very small fish in a pond full of sharks. Very small. Easier for everyone involved to cut you loose than waste time giving the smallest fuck about you. The problem for you is that you've got no friends, other than us. It's like the man said – you need friends, Ocho."

***

Two days later, Hoot was riding with Ocho to a meeting with La Linea honchos at a warehouse to discuss possibilities for getting back to the business of moving the brown sugar north, as usual. Hoot's job was simple: keep his eyes and ears open, and try to keep Ruben Ocho alive long enough to be useful to Bitters' investigation. Ocho was unarmed and wearing a wire. Hoot was armed with his usual weaponry: a Glock 9mm, and a Beretta 25cal backup.

Hoot thought Ocho's biggest problem was his face; it was untrustworthy-looking, narrow and varmint-like, with a bent nose and a nervous tic that made him look like he was sniffing the air for something. Simply put, he was not an attractive man. Even so, it wasn't so much his appearance that was off-putting; it was his demeanor, a sniveling, defensive way of expressing himself that made him seem constantly conniving and untruthful. Whatever it was – maybe something that Ocho said, or maybe the attitude it was said with: whatever it was, things turned ugly the moment they arrived…

There were four of them: one standing behind the counter, one standing at the door and two hiding among stacks of crated freight. A bloodcurdling scream set it off when the man at the counter slammed the point of a gaffing hook through the back of Ocho's hand, impaling him on the wooden lid of a shipping crate. At the same time, one of the assassins hiding behind a crate stood and stuck the business end of a shotgun in Ocho's face, but before he could commit to the deed, Hoot drew his Glock and put two quick 9mm slugs in the center of the man's chest. Hoot's third shot dropped the man at the counter.

His hand still pinned to the crate, Ocho had struggled to take cover when the bullets started flying; slugs being fired by the man at the door slamming into whatever was inside the box he was pinned to.

Hoot turned without hesitation and dropped the third shooter with a single shot.

The forth assassin fled without firing a shot.

Now, over three years later, Reuben Ocho was still looking over his shoulder, and Hoot felt certain that Zack Bitters, never one to let a good snitch off the hook, still felt free to jerk his strings at will.

Karma is a fickle bitch, Hoot thought. He had saved Ocho's miserable life that day. His rotten luck it couldn't have been someone a bit more worthy of being saved. If not worthy, then at least wealthy and generous, or maybe a gorgeous babe with loose morals. But, oh, no…he had to go and save the life of Reuben the Rat!

"Hola, amigo. Been a long time," Reuben Ocho said, stepping out from the shade of a palm near the end of the airport entrance veranda, turning his eyes in every direction except at Hoot. A lopsided sneer permanently affixed to the man's face, Ocho had not become any handsomer since Hoot last saw him.

"Mi taxi está allá;" Ocho pointed at a haggard-looking Toyota van parked at the far end of the taxi queue. "Please to carry your own bag, senior? I cannot." He showed his hand where the gaffing hook had affixed him to the crate. Disfigured with a large puckered scar in the middle that made it look like he had been crucified; to Hoot it looked like a corned beef brisket with splayed fingers.

"Qué coño? What the fuck, use the other hand, cabbie," Hoot said with considerably more force behind it than his normal feather-soft delivery.

Ocho flashed Hoot a bucktoothed smile making him look as if he'd just suffered a groin injury, muttered, "Por supesto." He hefted Hoot's bag with his good hand and led the way...

Turning the wrong direction at the highway; right toward the dry chaparral instead of left toward town, they would take a longer route than the tourists, bypassing downtown Mazatlan and the Gold Zone.

"What'd you bring for me?" Hoot asked.

Ocho pulled back a blanket on the floor of his taxi revealing a Glock 19 similar to Hoot's pistol left at home and a sawed-off AK-47 full auto with a banana clip – a Fast & Furious favorite. Hoot picked up the Glock, checked the chamber and clip and stuck it under the waistband of his trousers at the small of his back where it was hidden by his linen jacket. He flipped the blanket back in place to cover the AK, said, "If I need to use that, I'll need more ammo. Lots more."

"Si. No problema."

"Take me to the resort. I want to see it."

"Not too much to see from the road, amigo."

"Just take me."

"Como desea. As you wish, senior. But I cannot go there with you."

Chapter 26

The Los Zetas cartel was the newest gang in the game not so long ago. But they'd recently developed a genuine badass rep, controlling a drug empire that extended throughout Mexico and into several major cities in the US; principally straight up the I-5 corridor from San Diego to the Canadian border, Atlanta and Jersey on the East Coast, and Chicago in the Midwest. It was a reputation they had worked hard to achieve. In the Body Count and Gruesomeness categories alone they deserved it; consequently their concern for security at home was high. They had purchased the Playa Rocosa resort north of Mazatlan specifically because it was isolated toward the end of a long stretch of mostly undeveloped ocean front property, simplifying security concerns. It was a landscaped mini-oasis inside a walled compound enclosing a five-story terracotta and concrete tower that contained thirty two-bedroom condo units plus four luxury penthouses on the top two floors. Nearby, incomplete foundations for a second tower waited for money and renewed interest with rusting rebar reaching skyward. There was a private 9-hole par-3 golf course with a clubhouse. Outbuildings included water purification, housekeeping and laundry, security, and landscaping buildings. A generous swimming pool overlooking a rocky beach completed the scene with waves crashing beyond. The bottom two floors of the tower were maintained as rental timeshares for the look of legitimacy to those not looking too close; the rest was the cartel's playground.

Hoot thought Reuben Ocho's assessment was correct – one good look from the street told him that getting into Playa Rocosa resort unnoticed would be nearly impossible day or night. There was no way to get anywhere near the place without a long approach to the guard station at the main gate, a chained and locked delivery gate off to the side. Walking patrols and 'lifeguards' kept eyes on the beachfront below a six-foot seawall with CCTV cameras strategically placed on poles along its length. He told Ocho to drive him to the south end of the Zona Dorado where he checked into a hotel that had taken the hard dive from being a not-quite-luxury resort to well-past-its-prime some years ago. He sent Ocho away until after the dinner hour, and went shopping. Even at sundown it was still warm and humid in Mazatlan the middle of December. Gringo heaven, Hoot figured he may as well soak it up.

***

There were two bright green benches at the bus stand in front of the Señor Frog's restaurant on Mazatlan's main drag. Hoot was seated by himself on one of the benches and a young American family was seated on the other: mom and dad in their middle thirties, two preteen kids. All except Hoot were wearing balloon hats in bright colors on their heads, souvenirs of their recent fun-filled dining experience inside. The dad was also wearing horn-rim glasses with clip-on sunglasses that were flipped up. Altogether they looked like neighbor Ned and his family from an early episode of The Simpsons. Hoot was wearing a straw Panama hat with a wide brim and a brightly colored Hawaiian-style shirt he'd purchased earlier. He didn't know who looked more ridiculous, the family with balloon animals on their heads or the albino with the godawful shirt and sombrero. The idea had been to blend with el touristas, cruise the avenue on a city bus, and shadow the family from the condo while they shopped the Gold Zone, but Hoot didn't have a lot of experience with blending. His physical appearance too noticeable to blend very well anywhere, he'd always been more of an in-your-face kind of guy back in his fugitive apprehension days.

Didn't matter so much with people like this, anyhow, he figured. After tailing them the past three hours he decided they were a walking American family cliché, heads so far up their asses they had to breathe through their armpits while ambling through paradise inside their individual cones of contentment, add the overall family cone and they were impervious to reality. Dizzy with dullness, they probably didn't even realize they were vacationing in a cartel hot-spot, nor would they care if they did. All that mattered to dad was the price was right. He liked the nine-hole golf course on site, he said, and the pool for the kids. It wouldn't surprise Hoot if the man turned out to be an upwardly-mobile corporate attorney or management level techie from a much colder climate, maybe a salesman from Wisconsin or Maine. Sitting there with a squeaky octopus made from what appeared to be hot pink and blue condoms perched on his head, his middle class dignity staunchly unfazed.

"Fabulous hats," Hoot told the mom with a smile that he hoped radiated warmth well beyond what he actually felt. "May I take your picture with your camera – the whole family?"

They were thrilled and posed for several shots.

"You mentioned the Playa Rocosa resort," Hoot said. "You're staying there? What a coincidence! So am I."

"It's a bit far. Very quiet so far from the Zone without much of anything else around," the mother said. "The kids think it's dull. Too far away from the excitement downtown – so…what do we do? We ride a crowded bus into town every day because cheapskate decisions have been made regarding the cost of taxis." She said this last part with a toothy smile that didn't include her eyes.

"Back home we drive a Mercedes," she added. "A nice one."

"I like the quiet," Hoot said, noticing the woman's young daughter glance his way as if he'd just farted.

"We're heading back now," the dad said.

"Me, too. Soon as a bus comes by that isn't packed to the gills. Or, we could share a cab if you like," Hoot said, flashing a subtle wave at Ocho waiting in a taxi queue just up the street.

***

The best disguise is none at all, Hoot thought. Nonchalant and unnoticed.

Barring that; be obvious. In a gaudy Hawaiian shirt and straw hat, for example – so that you were too damned obvious to be worthy of notice. Not that Hoot had a lot of options with his towering height and unusual complexion, so he assumed an easy smile and continued chitchatting with the upwardly-mobile Americans while exiting Ocho's cab with them; all in a group, walking past the security station at the Playa Rocosa Resort entry without a second glance.

She'd better be here, he thought, because getting back out may not prove so easy.

It was past dusk. Outside lights and beach beacons were starting to come on.

Hoot found an unoccupied first floor condo and let himself in with a quick pick of the lock. From here he had a good view of the pool and clubhouse, the rocky beach for which the place was named was ahead behind a low seawall, chairs and chaises on the lawn off to the right. He waited until a couple of hours after midnight while a few guests and the occasional staff member prowled the grounds. Then, when all was still he ventured out.

Fifty yards to the clubhouse. A hundred yards to the seawall. Keeping as much as possible to the darker places, he walked across the lawn to the seawall and looked up and down the beach. Moonlight on the tops of waves, the tide was in. Watchful cartel eyes could easily spot him at any second. He thought of his new cheapskate American friend with the balloon hat and mimicked the man's inebriated posture.

There was a beach floodlight off to his right. Hoot went left, toward the clubhouse. Walked a few steps, took a moment to admire the view of waves breaking over rocks, then turned and went on. He adjusted his sombrero the way a goofball tourist might do and walked a straight line to a side gate as if he knew exactly where he was going. He knew no such thing, of course, only that he hoped to get into the clubhouse office and search for any sign that Jesse was here.

…She had to be. It was the only place that made sense with the clues she'd dropped. He expected to find Jesse's treasure box inside, with a lock fitting the key in his pocket.

The gate was open. Hoot cautiously passed through.

Ahead was a vista of ever-present Pacific Ocean waves crashing against hunkering rocks bigger than some of the outbuildings on the property, slowly wearing them down as they had been for eons. First tee of the resort's private golf course was in the foreground.

Hoot stopped at the edge of the patio and stood very still. He heard the whispery sound of a heavy sliding glass door opening behind him. He didn't turn. There was no need; he knew who it was...

Chapter 27

Jesse had been certain that Hoot would act the instant he made the connection between her and Harold Hesse. Not a complicated man by any means, Hoot's track record made it clear that he was very predictable in that way. The question was, as her father had pointedly put it, how would he act? Usefully...or not? Took him longer than she expected, but here he finally was, alone in spotlighted darkness on the deck of the Playa Rocosa Golf Club, looking entirely out of place and determined as hell; just as Jesse had expected he would be – a relentless two-legged hound on her scent.

"Do you golf?" she said to Hoot's shadowy shape, the glare of spotlights in the mist backlighting his tall and slender form without revealing details.

"No," he answered, still facing the beach. There was the slightest breeze out of the southwest, the underlying aroma of the sea.

"Then I can't recommend this golf course for you," Jesse said. "Isn't a good course for beginners even though it's only par-three."

"Yeah? All the bad guys with guns make it hard for a newbie to concentrate?"

Jesse snickered and replied, "Nothing so exciting. A strong crosswind often blows here, exaggerates hooks and slices."

"Hooks and Slices," Hoot parroted. "Sounds serious."

"Very serious if you're serious about the game."

"It's a goofy game, golf. Never really could see the point of it."

"Maybe that's because the point often has more to do with being in the game and very little to do with actually playing the game."

"Precisely why it isn't my kind of game."

"What is your kind of game, Hoot?"

Hoot stood silent a moment. Pale and still as carved marble, he could be some kind of ethereal stone sentry, standing guard. Then he slowly turned to face her and said, "Solitaire. Sometimes I win at Solitaire."

"Now there's a rigged game!" she said.

"Most are," he agreed, taking a step toward her and thus stepping out of his halo of light. She could see his face now, the eyes looking at her from the shadow of his hat brim were so cold-looking they looked as if they might be glacial – fitting in such a relentless man, she thought.

Though relentless to a fault, Jesse suspected that Hoot was a blunderer at heart. This was disturbing because she didn't know if she could trust him to stay alive long enough to be truly useful. "Knew you'd come," she said.

Hoot held out the key he'd found under her mattress in Forks, said, "You left this to ensure I would, didn't you?"

"My locker key…"

"I remember you told me it was the key to your treasure box when I first saw it on your dog tag chain."

She smiled with satisfaction and said, "So I did. And so it is. That's one of the things I like most about you, Hoot. You know how to listen. And you always remember what people say. The details. Few people really listen. Fewer still remember details."

"It's a curse," Hoot said. "Constantly being tuned in to the shit that's always around in ever-increasing degrees of stink. Seeing and hearing shit you'd rather not. Remembering shit you'd rather forget. But I'm getting better at forgetting, I think."

"Are you?" Jesse smiled wickedly, took a tentative step toward Hoot and said, "You?…forgetting? I seriously doubt if you've ever forgotten anything in your life, Deputy Marshal Ezra Hooten. Especially the details. You hardly know me for example; but you knew me well enough to find me 2,000 miles away in Mexico."

"I got lucky."

"Bullshit. You told me you don't believe in luck."

"Ah yes…you're right. In the cab from LAX to the Marriott – I believe what I actually said was that I consider relying on luck to be unreliable," Hoot corrected, causing Jesse's smile to grow wider.

"I like you," Jesse said. "I like your attitude. Is it a problem for you that you like me, too?"

Hoot threw Jesse the hottest Ezra Hooten say-it-to-my-face look he could manage, said, "You're not going to tell me, are you?"

"Tell you? What? Ask me anything – I'll tell you whatever you want to know. And I'll never lie to you, Hoot…so be careful what you ask."

"I have to know, Jessica…did you kill Harold Hesse and Soozy Wickerman?"

Jesse looked at Hoot with an expression he hadn't seen before: something between scorn and pity? Something complicated.

She said nothing.

A seventh wave crashed against the Playa Rocosa rocks, sending a spectacular spray up into the spotlight. Another large wave followed.

Jesse watched the ebb and swirling backwash for a moment, and then she turned and said without looking at Hoot, "Bet my room is nicer than yours…"

Chapter 28

Hoot awoke at 4:00 a.m. just as he had every other morning of his life for as long as he could remember, always reasoning to himself that it was 4:00 a.m. somewhere in the world twenty-four times a day and the best he could do was get his own personal ass out of bed on time to take care of his own shift; let others worry about the rest. This morning he woke up to discover for the second day in a row that, yes; he was lying next to Jesse in her bed at the resort.

She slept indecently: naked, sprawled out in tangled sheets. She snored a little, sounding like a purring cat. And she slept with her fist at her lips, as if blowing a kiss; or maybe, when asleep, she reverted to a more innocent Jessica Vega and was tempted to suck her thumb. He thought it was sexy.

...What an understatement! Hell...everything about her was sexy – that was the problem!

Hoot eased out of bed, walked across marble tile to the sliding glass door. It was warm in the room, and a ceiling fan was stirring a breath of humid air. He reached above his head to move aside a heavy window curtain and peek outside. Dawn had yet to break, the sky above clear and starry, a nearly-full moon hanging low in the west like a beacon reflecting off wave tops. He opened the door and looked out, pushed his fingers through his hair, and stretched up on his toes. He sucked in a double lungful of fresh air, closed the door, and headed for the bathroom – unbelievable bathroom...Jesse was right: her room was definitely nicer than his.

Morning ritual complete, Hoot ventured a rare critical look at himself before turning off the light, squinted his pale blues, and silently told the fool in the mirror; You deserve every ounce of shit you're gonna have to eat for this...every ounce!

...He was sleeping with a killer, he no longer had an doubts about that. But then...so was she – right?

Hoot remembered the first night: the night he had asked Jesse if she was a killer, and she had not answered because she said she wouldn't lie to him. Like a Siren of the rocks, she had lured him to her penthouse suite, opened the bar, and made the first of several vodka martinis and tequila crudas with high-end liquor until he had only the dimmest memory of tumbling into bed, Jesse all over him and he all over her.

Help me, Lord, for I have evidently sinned...again, he thought.

How's that for pure horseshit? Hoot said to himself.

Coffee! That's what he needed...

Black coffee, he thought. Extra black. It's my last vice and I treasure it.

Crossing the bedroom barefooted, he looked back at the bed where Jesse still lay as naked as the day she was born. Arms and legs tangled in the sheets, she was all akimbo, but definitely sexy in spite of the pose. No...lewd. That's the word. Jesse was more than sexy – she was lewd. And he loved it that she was. Made him think of another L-word. Can definitely put lust back on my Favorite Vices list, he thought, shrugging and wearing an ironic smile as he looked down at his pale and semi-stiff nakedness practically glowing in the moonlight. Yep, he was a lucky dog alright; emphasis on dog.

"Thank you very much, Jessica Vega," he whispered, his thoughts turning nonetheless to Maddie Marvel.

Maddie, practical to the bone and irrepressibly opinionated if she felt she could help a friend no matter how personal the subject matter, had recently explained to Hoot how nowadays keeping a Viagra prescription on hand was a good idea for a sensible man.

"Just in case...you know – if you really need it" she had said with a charismatic smile, "to help keep the ole manly stamina up," and he'd responded; "I'm not exactly having trouble in that department..."

"That's a relief to know," she had said. "But I'd think a guy like you, with a macho rep the size of yours, would want to be prepared in case of emergencies. Seriously, there's no excuse for a man your age to be unprepared these days. The Boy Scout motto and all…"

She was teasing him. So he got one – a boner 'scrip – just so he could say he'd done it already the next time the subject came up, though he hadn't taken any of the little blue diamonds yet. They required a man to plan ahead with the precision of a well-organized sex fiend, and Hoot hadn't felt the need with adequate forethought combined with enough certainty of success to commit. But he had to admit he was curious what would happen if he did. Romance, after all, was not exactly Hoot's strong suit – never had been, even if he liked the fireworks show at the end.

A thorny issue, romance. In spite of Maddie's admonition that every day needed some in it, Hoot knew it was best in his case to keep his romantic meanderings as shallow as possible; easier for everyone involved that way. After his best friend had married and then killed Hoot's first and truest love, the whole idea of dating took a long hiatus before he felt ready to stick his emotional head up again, and when he did, it was Linda who jump-started him out of his funk. During the long lonely years after his divorce from Linda, romance kept spiraling downward for Hoot, finally depreciating into more hassle than it was worth more often than not.

Always the eternal relationship quandary; a quickie, or the more serious, and perhaps dangerous, commitment? Sex or friendship – choose quickly!

How about a friendly sexship?

Nope? Sorry about that…

Relationships with the opposite sex had always been hard for Hoot to maintain; they came loaded with expectations that were impossible to meet. After Linda, sex had devolved into simply taking care of a need. It was like an animal licking salt. Hunger and thirst. The need to pee. Simple as that. Ever consider how much effort is actually required to feed yourself? The hunting and gathering and the preparation? Compare that to the effort that sex requires and it becomes obvious old folks don't lose interest in sex because they aren't as pretty as they used to be, or even because they're tired – they lose interest because sex is a rigged game the house always wins; it wears you down until you're ready to go all-in and be done with it, just to say you played. Mostly Hoot went without and didn't waste a lot of time thinking about it.

Yeah sure. Dog.

Hoot recalled telling Jesse that he preferred non-committal attachments.

"Definitely!" Jesse had concurred with his ground rules vehemently, adding "The sort that quickly evolve into comfortable, dependable, no-nonsense satisfaction," while toying with buttons, obviously flirting with him.

Hoot remembered the flirting – completely outrageous! Like the outfit she had worn on the flight, skirt and blazer looking as if they'd been melted and vacuum-formed on her. She obviously wanted to be noticed but was ambivalent to the attention she garnered. It was sassy and very sexy, unexpected from a woman who otherwise portrayed herself as a tough customer. Hoot had applauded her sensibilities or lack thereof, said, "People like us want simple, attainable goals in our intimate relationships."

"Including easy access," Jesse had added.

"Mutual lack of expectations," Hoot had offered as if by rote.

"No encumbrances. And control of frequency – that's of paramount importance," Jesse had concluded.

Hoot agreed that control was good. Impossible. But good.

And certainly, the last things he needed in his life were encumbrances. In his experience, most women came with a load of them, and he seldom felt the need to share his. More precisely, he didn't feel that he was particularly adept in the art of sharing. Aware of his romantic shortcomings, he avoided overly needy women as if they were carriers of the plague. Tendencies like that could complicate a hasty departure to attend to business, and Hoot's business was prone to disruptions. Self-starting sex machines who made him feel like he was one, too – these were the sort of women Hoot looked for nowadays.

Yeah. Good luck with that, he thought.

Giving Jesse in the rumpled bed another glance, Hoot had to admit; so far Jesse seemed to fit the bill perfectly. More perfectly than Maddie, who was intelligent, opinionated, sometimes stubborn, and certainly more mature? Maybe Maddie wasn't a sizzler in bed the way Jesse was. Hoot didn't know about that. And he was hesitant to admit that he was curious. But something could certainly be said for experience, especially the laid-back, self-confident, take-your-time sort of experience that Maddie espoused. About as free in the encumbrances department as a man could expect from any woman, Maddie was far too self-reliant and well-centered to be a clinger, but she was far more likely to have those dreaded expectations.

So why was he thinking about her?

Not getting any younger, pal. Wiser maybe?

Seemed unlikely. After all; in the quick span of their romance he'd come to know intimate details of nearly every square-inch of Jesse's body. The location of every tat. The feel, texture, and taste of her from head-to-toe. Her scar. The wetness of her cunt and tightness of her ass. He even knew that she had killed at least two people even if he couldn't prove it. But he still didn't know what was locked away in her treasure box at Playa Rocosa, and that was something he felt he needed to know: if there was proof, it would be there – probably more than he'd care to see right now.

Hoot slipped out for a long walk on the beach to clear his mind. Jesse was up by 6, and they enjoyed breakfast on the penthouse patio: scrambled eggs with chorizo and avocado. Finishing their fruit plate, there was a commotion below, and they looked down to see Felix Vega, arriving through the compound gate in a hustle of black Chevy Suburban's. Men in dark suits and sunglasses accompanied him.

"Shit!" Jesse said, watching the group entering the Playa Rocosa lobby.

"Those people are a problem?" Hoot asked.

"It's my father…" Jesse said with obvious scorn.

"And the men with him?"

"His posse. And others I don't know. You need to get out of here. And I need to get ready to switch rooms if his guests are staying."

"May be too late for me to get out of here…unnoticed," Hoot said, lifting his shades and making distant eye contact with Felix Vega. Nonetheless, it was time to get his Casper-white ass set to grandpa mode and back to Seattle, pronto. Christmas was upon him. And Remy was coming…

***

It was goddamned wet back in Seattle; seemed extra wet to Hoot after his three-day jaunt to bone-dry Mexico. Chili Hilliker unexpectedly met him at the airport, immediately turned his grizzly eyes on him and said, "You find what you went lookin for down there?"

"You mean trouble? I don't have to go looking to find trouble. It finds me."

"Come on…let's get outta here," Chili said. "I hitched a ride with a friend. Ridin back with you in your truck, if it's okay."

It was 4:30 pm and the day was darkening by the time they were on the road; windshield wipers, set on delay, periodically making a blur out of the stop-and-go traffic ahead. Hoot finally broke his preoccupation with the last three days, sniffed a rat in his friend's cagy-Cajun demeanor, and said, "Okay…give it to me straight. What has your boxers in such a bunch that you're willing to set up all this need-a-lift horseshit just to have a little private man-to-man time on the way back?"

"Horseshit?" Chili said, pretending surprise.

"Yes. I believe so. You are a driver, my friend – not a passenger – and you asked me to drive you? Very suspicious behavior for a hardheaded Cajun."

"I'm that obvious?"

Hoot glanced at Chili's overdrawn bushy eyebrows knitted together like knots from a Boy Scout manual, suppressed a laugh, and said, "Yes. You are. Tell me what's up? Early Christmas surprise? Death in the family? Most folks couldn't tell the difference from the look on your face, but I know you wouldn't go to this much trouble just to warn me that my boss is pissed-off because I left on short notice."

"You're right, I wouldn't. And he is…"

"So, give it up or you can hitch the rest of the way home from the ferry terminal. I promise."

Chili feigned surrender and said, "It's about your grandson…"

"Jeremy? What about Jeremy? He's okay, isn't he?"

"Fit as a fiddle, I'd vouch my left nut on it," Chili said with the haste of a man squashing a hot cigarette butt.

"Yeah…well? You know that he's coming for a visit," Hoot said. "Should be here by the weekend. Is there a problem?"

"Not a problem exactly…"

"Goddamnit Chill, fess-up. I happen to know that you don't have a left nut – a Louisiana mule kicked you when you were twelve. You lost the left one and the right one grew huge to compensate. Kept you out of Vietnam…right? So out with it, you growly fuck. Is Remy really okay? Or not?"

"Actually, the thing is…he's here. Now. As in today," Chili said, always blindsided by Hoot's ability to remember offhand conversational details like the contents of his nutsack from forever ago, even when liquor was involved. "Seems he got in this mornin on the DC redeye. Your ex called my office at 8:30 sharp. I remember Linda, and she hasn't changed. Woman got straight t' the point – she wanted t' know where Casper the Friendly Bastard was since Jeremy was due to land in Seattle within the hour and his grandpa wasn't on the radar. I take it you weren't monitoring messages from your home phone forwarded to your cell while you were busy in Mexico?"

"Shit!" Hoot said.

"Yeah," Chili concurred, concealing a smile at the Casper the Friendly Bastard jibe somewhere in the rough terrain of his facial creases.

"He's early…"

"Seems like it," Chili said, the deep furrow embedded in his forehead growing still deeper. "She said she wanted me to put the boy on the next plane home if you didn't show up, pronto."

"Where's Remy now?" Hoot asked, the focus of his attention suddenly making a hard U-turn.

"The friend I rode in with was Maddie," Chili confessed. "She took him back to your place."

"You didn't mention that I hadn't returned from Mexico?"

"You kiddin? Nary a word."

"Good. At least you didn't lie?"

"To that woman? Unh-uh! – I remember Linda from back in the day. I ain't gettin fencepost-stupid in my old age…"

225

The queue for the ferry was at the bottom of the hill. Rush-hour backup would soon be building in the curb lane. Nothing to do but wait. He nabbed one of the last few spots remaining in the holding area before the overflow outgrew the capacity of the boat.

"My father once told me that I never seem to learn a damned thing except by the hard way," Hoot said.

"There's an easy way?" Chili asked."

"I'm the wrong person to ask," Hoot replied. Then after a long pause he groused; "Slow fucking ferries. Give a man too much time to think…"

Chapter 29

Everybody had always told Hoot that he could do it. Whatever he wanted – he could do it. His father especially loved to push that button; "Just set your sights on it Son, and give it all you've got!" he would say until blue in the face.

As if determination was the key.

As if determination and hard work would always win out.

But what if he couldn't?

What if he was already functioning at his best, or long past it? What if determination and hard work didn't actually trump a goddamned thing in the everyday world? Or, what if one day, in spite of Hoot's best efforts his entire life, the fuck-ups simply outnumbered the attaboys by a noticeable margin?

"Rule the day!" his father would say, confusing the word *rue* for *rule* without realizing how right-on he actually was. Hoot didn't rule a damned thing, certainly not a household, or some vague notion of a career, and he sure as hell didn't feel remorseful about much of anything either. Quite the opposite – he felt it was better by far to slam the door on the past; bar it and lock it tight before too much unpleasant personal history escaped from the then into the now. Told himself that it kept the load on his bony shoulders a bit lighter.

Barely an hour on the ground in Seattle and Hoot was already jonesing for Jesse in the worst way. Maybe this was his manly ego's way of retreating from the immediate and very real problem of his visiting grandson. Maybe it was simply because he dreaded looking Maddie in the eye just yet. Or maybe the sex with Jesse really had been so goddamned good he just couldn't stop thinking about it. Whatever the reason, the itch was deep, the coward in him wanting nothing more than to return to Mexico and scratch it. He wouldn't do that, of course. Still, just the idea of presenting himself, fresh-fucked and plucked from a sunny place to his grandson and Maddie in the place he called home, somehow made him feel dirty.

"Maddie says I'm a verb," Hoot told Chili as he pulled into the driveway of his cabin. It was dark except for the automatic photocell porch lights and a couple of inside lamps on timers. A whole day spent traveling; 2400 miles in the air, and Hoot hadn't felt like his feet were back on terra firma until just now – Buck Rogers to Mars and back!

"Meanin that you're a man of action?" Chili asked.

"I'm not sure what she meant. You know Maddie – her meaning could've been a bit obscure, but still to the point."

"Such as?"

"I don't know. I was just remembering," Hoot said, looking past a living scrim of ferns and cedars toward the front porch of his cabin. Porch lights on. Windows glowing with warmth where he knew Maddie waited with Jeremy.

"…She told me that verbs conjugate."

***

Jesse arrived in Seattle two hours after Hoot and made a quick stop at her apartment to shower and change. Throwing open her refrigerator like it was a long-forgotten tomb, she discarded containers of sour cream and tuna salad looking and smelling more like science experiments than lunch. She ate a glob of peanut butter straight off a spoon and washed it down with a hefty chug of milk bearing a date on the carton verifying this week was the last safe week. Shrugging, she poured the rest of the milk down the drain, tossed the carton in the recycle bin, and hit the road for Port Timothy. Now, finally nearing the end of her clandestine mission for Papa, she parked a quarter-mile away and sneaked through heavy underbrush to Hoot's cabin.

Careful now! the voice in her head warned, and Jesse put a little extra caution in her step. There were no streetlights fronting Hoot's property. No traffic on the road. The place couldn't have been quieter if it were a mortuary.

Jesse advanced carefully while keeping her attention firmly riveted on the cabin ahead. A pair of LED porch lights illuminated the front porch with weird diode whiteness compared to old-fashioned incandescent lights – appropriate lighting for Hoot, she thought.

A strait-facing spotlight fastened to the back of the cabin revealed how precariously it was perched over a low bluff, fishy smells of the strait wafting up on fog from down below. There were musty woods all around the other three sides, ferns and blackberries, everything damp by degrees that led up to and included soaking wet.

She paused to remind herself, once more, that no poisonous snakes lived around here and was thankful for that knowledge.

You're a big reptile pussy, the voice said. *Isn't it about time you got over that, as much time as you spend in the wild?*

Not reptiles, she thought…just snakes. Jesse wanted to believe it about the snakes: that there were none. She hated snakes; she hated just about anything that crawled, actually, including spiders and all sorts of other bugs, but mostly she hated snakes. "Too wet for 'em west of the Cascades," Alan had once told her. "Water gets in the pit vipers' pits and they drown in their lairs." But Jesse had always known that Alan was a liar as well as a pervert, so a corner of her fertile imagination itched with worry about snakes whenever she was out in the woods in spite of his reassurances.

Jesse knew all about lying. She knew everything that came out of Alan's mouth was a lie – empty words, without truth; like his promise to keep his filthy fingers out of Christine's panties if Jesse would give him a blowjob…

Liar! Liar! Liar!

All her worry about snakes did seem silly now that she was probably the deadliest thing in the woods, wolves and bears and cougars being tagged and well-controlled these days, but she couldn't help it. No snakes supposedly, but frogs. And slugs – awful slugs. Spiders galore. Maybe leeches too, for all she knew.

Nature could be a real bitch of a place, and it gave Jesse deep satisfaction to know that she could be the baddest bitch in it if she chose to be. She was wearing a black zippered hoodie over a black polo, fingerless gloves, and Tommy Hilfiger low-heeled combat boots. She left her pistol behind in the car – this was just a recon –

but her ever-present knife was folded away in a rule pocket in her cargo pants. One must always be prepared, she thought, fondling the knife in its pocket, a lightweight tactical Gerber switchblade with a serrated edge, wickedly lethal in the right hands, and hers were.

A good thing, too, because there's no way of knowing what may be lurking nearby in the dark around here, the voice offered. *Nothing deadly like in Mexico where your aversion to snakes and other crawly things is only sensible. But plenty of slime…*

Truly; there, you could count on something crawly and deadly lurking within striking distance day and night. By comparison, the whole Olympic Peninsula seemed designed to slowly rot you to death. This was a terrifying idea to Jesse, to be slowly consumed by anything or anyone. Not by life. Or by death. She'd prefer go out in a hot flash if she had anything to say about it. Maybe that was why she always bounced back to Mexico in spite of her father's presence there. Mexico was dry, the whole place as dry as her father was, while her aging hippy mother in Forks was every bit as suffocating to Jesse as the rainforest that she lived in – Alison Wonderland rotting away in her dilapidated old motel.

Jesse refused to be the next mom at Mom's, waiting in an ever thickening fog for the foundations to crumble. Nothing ever rotted in her version of Mexico. It burned up instead. Much better!

Maybe that's why I'm drawn to dangerous men, she thought. The fast burn winning over slow decay any day.

Picturing her father, the infamous and ever scheming Felix Vega…

Picturing Hoot, the impulsive shooter…

They were two men who couldn't be more different from each other, yet to her, they were the same. Both were lethal men who disdained any idea of authority above their own. Dangerous men, they were ageless men of roughly the same age. She wondered; when she fucked Hoot was she fucking her father?

The idea brought a bitter smile to Jesse's face.

With some effort, she set her worry about irrelevant things aside, and put her mind back on her reconnaissance. She had a job to do – she would do it and more. Count on it.

It took nearly a half hour for Jesse to advance to a better eavesdropping position. From there, she watched the police chief and newspaper editor say their goodbyes. Heard the Marvel woman say, "I'm so happy to finally meet you, Remy. I'm sure you'll have a great time here with your grandpa," and saw her give Hoot a hug and a chaste kiss. Saw the boy at Hoot's side take a shy sidestep away.

So that's the grandson old Hoot said was coming for a visit, the Billievoice said.

Apparently so. The boy around whom they would have to cool it, Hoot told her before boarding his flight back to Seattle.

Telling a woman who's been fucking his brains out the last three days to cool it? No wonder he can't keep a girlfriend long enough to score hangar space in her closet!

No problem, Skyshooter, Jesse thought, an idea taking shape – I can cool it…

***

"Watch him," Felix Vega had instructed his daughter, his familiar tone of unassailable authority making a reply unwise. So here she was…watching.

Sure Papa, she thought, I'll watch him. I'll watch the holy shit out of him while I slice him up and bury the pieces miles apart if he makes a move to hang Harold Hesse's dead carcass around my neck before I can work a deal with the tall dark man. She would have to be very careful dealing behind her father's back, because she knew that most of the pictures on her father's mantle were of dead men – even the newer pictures.

"I like this Skyshooter of yours. This air marshal," her father had said, smiling without smiling. "I like it that he broke Homeland Security ranks to follow you here," saying this while studying his daughter with the same eyes used to size-up the whores he kept himself surrounded with. "You should follow him back to Seattle. Watch him. Closely."

Turning and walking away, Jesse had replied, "Don't worry Papa. I'm on him."

Chapter 30

Jesse was fourteen when she lost her cherry.

Lost it? – Ha! She laughed. She had always thought it was a hilarious idea, the idea of losing your cherry. How could you lose something when you're the one knows better than anyone else who got it? Okay...say maybe a brush handle or two, a slender green gherkin, and a few fumbling fingers had stretched and rent the way in advance of the big event...you still knew the lucky bastard who got the grand prize, didn't you?

In Jessica Vega's case it was Hugo Ford, a pimply-faced half Salish-half hillbilly new kid at Forks Junior High. Hugo had been held back at his previous school, making him the oldest boy in Jesse's 9th grade class.

Punk tough; Hugo's bad-boy attitude preceded him wherever he went, his persona amped to the max with tattered Levi's and a promising swagger. Logger boots with thick Vibram soles and enough grease in his hair to take the squeak out of the wheel of time. Zero effort to hide his cigarettes. But, in spite of the neverending show, Hugo wasn't really a gangbanger. Gangs were a big-city thing, and hadn't begun to stake-out their territories and cook meth in the woods back in those days.

A fifteen-year-old lone wolf, then? She had mused – yeah, sure...why not?

Hugo's angst was real enough.

As real as hers? Unlikely...

Jesse met him after a school football game. She was excited, expecting experience, expecting something considerably more satisfying than the slobbering kisses and hickeys she'd been getting from boys thus far.

Sadly, Hugo turned out to be all swagger. Sure enough…he got what he came for, but it was hardly a triumphant conquest. It was more of a door prize scenario; a wreath on the head of his cock for getting past the tattered security guard at the gate and depositing a huge mess of pent-up semen both inside and outside Jessie's cunt and all over the backseat of his mother's car.

Not really surprised by Hugo's fumbling, Jesse was nonetheless disappointed, her passage from silly girl to sexy chick so very much less than she had expected. Her disappointment contagious, she infected her mother and younger sister to the extent that an impromptu visit with Papa during the heat of September in Mexico was necessary.

Jesse had loved it, Indian summer in Mazatlan, even if tainted by her father's domineering presence. Mexico was an altogether different world from her mother's little niche in the drenched woods of Washington; the shimmering glare of midday Mexican sun reflecting off hard-baked caliche, warming her skin. And then there was the spicy-hot food. Heat of every kind; she loved it all. She especially loved the heat she felt when her father's young sicarios gave her the look.

At fourteen, Jesse had the figure of a stick but a sassy style. No longer a virgin and proud of it, she liked to overplay a streetwise attitude that encouraged salacious looks and bold approaches from macho males much older than she, and she quickly found the experience she'd been looking for. His name was Raoul, the sicario she fell-in with…

Fell-in – what a quaint way to put it, she had thought so many times in later years. They were her father's words; "You are proud to be a real woman, now?" he said, clearly not counting his own excursions into forbidden places starting when she was eight. He was her father and had special privileges, after all. "You must not fall-in with the men who work for me," he had said. "I believe women and girls should be allowed to choose their own lovers and losers. But not you. Not with these men."

"Why not with these men?"

Felix Vega had looked at his daughter with hard, unblinking eyes, and said, "You are your mother all over again…"

Pacing across his office floor, he turned and added; "Did your mother ever tell you that when I first met her she was a teenager not much older than you visiting Tijuana, and I stowed away to follow her home? Did she tell you that she was in Mexico for the fix? You know what fix I'm talking about? Of course you do – the one that daddies and lovers are always willing to pay for.

"You see, I understand you better than you know. Now, you need to understand me. These men work for me, Gota. Some of them are your cousins and uncles and half-brothers. My brothers and nephews and sons. All of them are my brothers and sons in spirit. All of them are family to me..."

He paused at a beamlike mantle atop a massive stone fireplace opposite his desk. His back was as straight as a steel rod, his shoulders as broad as ever; in his mid-thirties Felix Vega was a man in his prime, and he knew it. He took a moment to regard the hodge-podge of framed photographs displayed there on the mantle. Felons and family, all together and all the same.

"If any of them were to hurt you," he said. "If you were molested or harmed in any way I would have no choice but to kill the man responsible – honor would demand it. I cannot afford to do that, Gota. And I would not enjoy it. But I would do it," he snapped his fingers, "like that! You understand?"

Cousins and uncles and half-brothers...Jesse's father had said those words the same way he might have said profits and losses, or collateral.

Yes. Jesse understood. It was all about keeping score. Everything had value and it was all relative. Her busy imagination considered the idea that the leathery boys and dirty old men who'd been catcalling and eyeballing her during her stay in Mazatlan might've easily been her kin, and she found the notion more tantalizing than repulsive. If there was a single nugget of fear residing inside her it registered as a tingle of excitement for the unknown, not the hair-raising kind of fear. In Jesse's case, any nugget of fear that might dare germinate in her imagination was like a grain of sand inside an oyster – a pearl could form over time. A black and terrible pearl.

"You see the position you put me in?" Felix Vega pointed his finger like a pistol at Jesse and for a moment she was certain it was

234

loaded. Speaking to her without a hint of regard for age, kinship, or gender, he said to her as if speaking to a sicario, "If you don't cut Raoul loose, I'll have to kill him. It's that simple, so leave him alone. The rest of my posse, too. I'm telling you to leave them alone…

"You want to fuck? Fine! You should go into town, find yourself a horny gringo tourist and fuck like minks until you can't fuck any more. I don't care. Just don't make any part of it my problem!"

Jesse turned to go, but paused to look back at her father. He waved her off dismissively and said in parting, his voice rising through a carnivorous smile, "Just like your mother – Jesus save us!"

***

Somewhere during the course of Hoot's meandering adulthood, he had evidently evolved from being a nitpicking perfectionist who could never please himself into a minimalist who couldn't care less about pleasing anyone…including himself. He saw evidence of the transformation everywhere, including the fact that he never fixed anything until he was certain it was broken, a truism he applied to everything from fishing gear to relationships, but it applied in particular to his cabin.

There was however, a list…

"There are a couple of chores we need to take care of, and then we'll go fishing," Hoot told Remy.

"Chores?" Jeremy asked with somewhat more enthusiasm than his grandfather had expected.

"Takes a sizeable bite out of the fun of fishing if chores that should've been done first are still waiting for you afterward. A little work up front makes the fun more fun."

"For money?" Remy blushed and turned his eyes aside, saying; "Mom said I shouldn't ask you for money. But she said you might pay an allowance if I did chores."

"Your mother told you that?"

"Uh-huh. Said she never got a nickel from you she didn't earn the whole time she was growing up, and I probably wouldn't, either."

"She said I was cheap, did she?"

"Not cheap...tight. She said you were tighter than the crack of dawn."

Hoot grinned, said, "Yeah? I taught her that one...

"Okay Remy, listen up – there two kinds of chores; yours: and everyone else's. You do yours without pay because that's just the way it is. Making your bed every morning. Helping with the dishes. Stuff like that. But there could be some money in helping me with mine. Helping Maddie with hers. Chili with his. Everybody can use a little help from time to time, and most don't mind paying if the help is good help."

"What sort of chores are your chores, G-pa?"

"Cabin chores mostly. Lots of cabin chores. For example, that second step on the back stair...the one with dry rot that you already found – how's the ankle, by the way?"

"It's okay," Jeremy said; his words slathered with the ill-concealed pride in injury that is rightfully reserved for the young. "I'll get your tool bucket."

Hoot smiled with a degree of contentment he had absolutely no familiarity with, watching his grandson walk back from the garage and shed with a limp only slightly more exaggerated than it had been going the other direction, though he was pretty sure it was the same ankle, at least.

Hoot's separations from his family while he chased bad guys had often been lengthy ones – especially the last fifteen years spent on the west coast; his kids and grandkids back east. Consequently he barely knew the boy, though it seemed that somehow he knew all there was to know about him. Eleven-years-old and on the cusp of puberty, his grandson was so very similar to Hoot at that age, it was startling for him to see. With one thankful exception – other than the very fine, blond, and presently too-long hair hanging in his face like a silky mop, there were no signs of the albinism that had been Hoot's lifelong cross to bear. Jeremy had a warm complexion with a bit of color, a spatter of freckles, dark blue eyes with actual eyebrows. Not especially tall but solidly built, Hoot didn't think the boy looked much like he did at that age...but the way he acted: his mannerisms and the way he approached things, his quiet persistence and the way he could zero-in on something exclusively – signs of these familiar traits of Hoot's were amazingly strong in his grandson. To Hoot it was like looking into a mirror and seeing himself as a kid except reflected from the inside out, unrecognizable at first but definitely him to the core once he noticed the details.

Jeremy was a good kid. Hoot could tell. Much better than Hoot had been at his age, of that much, he was sure. At least, he hoped he was sure. After a lifetime of traipsing around the dark side of humanity, Hoot was uncertain that he even knew what good really was anymore – except for Jeremy.

And Maddie. Maddie had a good heart…

Jesse, however…

Hoot knew that Jesse was a killer. But then so was he; multiple counts. The difference, of course, was that Jesse was a murderer. Hoot hadn't murdered, had he? To be completely honest; he really wasn't sure. Motive was everything…

Hoot looked up at a thickening sky and then out across the strait. Certainty had been his most prominent trait his whole adult life, and it suddenly hit home that that rock-solid Ezra Monroe Hooten certainty was gone: built up over the years like a thick callous, but somehow diminished by Jessica Vega. It seemed there was a new Hoot living inside his old skin; one lacking in conviction that his was the right action, and much less likely than the old Hoot to shoot a person like Jesse if she so much as twitched while he put her in restraints.

Thinking about the way Jesse had played head games with him in Mexico was very distracting and unsettling to Hoot as he watched Remy struggle back with the heavy tool bucket – damned woman, she just wouldn't stay out of his head! And then, suddenly feeling very confused; Hoot felt certain for a moment that he was standing in a low, smoke-filled sweat lodge, the smoke dense and sweet-smelling. And someone was chanting…

The sweet feeling of pride in his grandson that Hoot had been wallowing in like an old dog was suddenly slammed aside by a vacuumy sense of utter disconnection. Vertigo swept over him with such force that he had to sit down and take a breath. He dared not speak for fear of throwing up. And his tinnitus had become a deafening roar in his head. The accumulated ballast of a life lived more wrongly than not was pressing him down, a dead weight suffocating him. The world spinning out of control.

Meanwhile, Remy was still grinning ear-to-ear at his grandfather. Lugging the bucket a few steps at a time. Putting it down. And then changing sides to pick it up with the other hand and go a little more. Determined kid.

Every time his grandson set the bucket down, it became a little harder for Hoot to see him. Then Jeremy began spinning around with all the rest...

Chapter 31

It was sunny and hot. Blistering hot. And Hoot and Jesse were together atop a huge boulder surrounded by roiling surf, icy spray from crashing waves cooling their naked skin, while they coupled like animals without care that someone might catch a glimpse.

This was pure lust.

The deafening roar of relentless energy all around them.

The pull of the moon. Reckless sex. And then the boulder began to sink...

Fingernails on the blackboard! Something was all wrong here...

Hoot's head was spinning. No, that's not quite right; it was the world that was spinning and Hoot was trapped at the center of it, the sky spinning shades of black above, ocean currents in a swirling whirlpool all around, it was inescapable...

And then he was sucked into the belly of a waterspout, everything spinning madly all around him; a convergence of force beyond control. Jesse had vanished. Wind and spray buffeted him. Until, finally, gravity began to release its slippery hold and darkness teased. Promising comfort...

Hoot knew there was comfort to be had in darkness. He had been on close terms with it all these years. Had flirted with it. Used it...

His stomach lurching, he was thinking that he might feel better if he just went ahead and threw up...

The spinning vertigo slowed and then finally stopped, but Hoot didn't trust it. He stayed as still as stone in the darkness, convinced that the slightest movement would set his head spinning again until it burst into tiny pieces like a dropped snow globe. He almost laughed at the idea but stopped himself. Laughing would be hard on the stomach.

Lying perfectly still, Hoot imagined that he was floating on tepid water. And then he was sinking…fast, like a rock tossed overboard, racing for Davey Jones' infamous locker.

It occurred to Hoot that the increasing pressure of descending so rapidly would soon burst his eardrums. He held his breath…

***

The darkness faded to light, and then Hoot was back.

…Back to where he didn't know.

Gaining a tentative grip on his bearings, he realized that he wasn't lying at the bottom of a bottomless pool as he had supposed he might be. And he was evidently not dead – being dead surely wouldn't come with such a killer headache and lurching stomach.

He was lying in a bed.

His own bed at home?

No. Definitely not…

***

Knew you'd come, a voice deep inside Hoot's head said. A faceless voice. An echo from long ago. It was Norman Carpenter's voice, the voice of most cold-blooded killer Hoot had ever known. Norman had said those same cryptic words to Hoot in Vietnam back in 1968, both men wounded, and both prepared to go down fighting rather than surrender.

…Snipers never surrender. Darkness had been in the mix in those days, too.

***

Knew you'd come…

It was the same thing Jesse had told him in Mexico. So how did they know this, Norman and Jesse? How'd they know that he would come for them? That he would always come?

Had they really known, or were they just grabbing for credit after the fact? And if they really knew, was it because he was being reliable? Predictable? Or had he simply faded beyond white to transparent and become that easy to read? Had Hoot's skin become thinner, a see-through sheath like a living Visible Man, leaving his innards exposed down to the cellular level? Was everything but his deepest thoughts on display? And were they next? This was Hoot's childhood nightmare realized…the skinny, queer-looking, extra-white kid with nowhere to hide.

**

Hoot felt chained down, and that was probably good because gravity was all fucked up. It was as if he was strapped to a centrifuge and his spinning brain was pushed up against the right side of his skull, leaving a void on the left. From somewhere in that void a voice had spoken; the sort of voice you hear with actual ears instead of only in the mind, and his ears were evidently out of service. He strained to understand it and failed.

Rallying his concentration and sweating bullets, Hoot realized it was his own voice that he was hearing. He was speaking, repeating the same words aloud, over and over: "Ma Bell, Ma Bell – Alpha-Bravo-One… This is Troubleshooter. We are Deep Serious!"

Yes! He remembered those words from years before, in combat…

Repeat. We are Deep Serious…

**

Hoot thought the weird thing about time was the flexibility of it; the pull of gravity so persuasive throughout the universe that even time was vulnerable, black holes and whatnot distorting both light and time and fucking everything up on a galactic scale.

Wasn't it Einstein who figured all that out? Hoot wasn't sure...

An unknown amount of time passed in blackness and then Hoot realized that he wasn't where he thought he should be. He smiled, wondering precisely where that might be, and then the smile evaporated off his face as it occurred to him that he had absolutely no idea.

The blackness faded again, and there was light.

Just a little, and it was wavering. He tried to shy away from it because light was where the pain and confusion were. Blackness sheltered him.

This is Troubleshooter.

Requesting Dustoff...

Chapter 32

Hoot awoke feeling confused and dizzy. Eyes open, but struggling to focus, he thought he heard the screaming roar of a pair of prop-driven A-1 Skyraiders flying like bats out of hell. Except they must've been flying down a long corridor just outside a nearby open door, their prop wash tearing everything apart that wasn't nailed down.

With them came the unmistakable music of M-60 machine guns and the distinctive whup-whup-whup of a Huey rotor…

What the fuck? If he could only see!

Goddamnit, the dizziness just wouldn't let go. Hoot fought it, but it fought back and it won – twice; sweeping him away in overwhelming surges of nausea both times. And then there was that ultra-black darkness again. Comforting, cool darkness.

But it didn't last…

***

"What happened to me?" Hoot said aloud, the words gummy and hard to spit out.

He heard a familiar voice respond, but couldn't quite make sense of it.

Struggling to focus, his throat feeling as dry as dirt and his voice a rasp, he said; "Am I dead? I feel dead."

"No, you aren't dead. If you were, you'd feel better." Maddie's voice answered from a wavering corner.

Carefully moving only his eyes without moving his head, Hoot saw that he was in a bright room that he couldn't quite comprehend the purpose of. But clues were becoming clearer as details began to register and he didn't like what he was seeing; an antiseptic place loaded with intravenous devices and electronic monitors.

"I expect you feel kind of empty about now?" Maddie said, her voice sounding thin behind the roar in Hoot's ears. "Like you've had a real doozy of a headache and it isn't quite finished with you? Don't worry, it'll pass."

"What happened to me?"

"In a nutshell, your a-fib and high blood pressure conspired against you. A loose blood clot got stuck inside that hard noggin of yours, and you had a stroke."

"A stroke?"

Vertebrae in his neck cracking like marbles in a paper bag, Hoot slowly turned his head to better see Maddie, instinctively suspecting that his skull may explode from the effort but figuring it was worth it.

It was – she looked great!

She looked…safe.

Maddie glided across the room to his bedside and said, "It was a small one, your stroke. I had a couple of the little buggers myself a few years ago. I call them popcorn strokes. They're manageable with medication, so no extra sympathy for you. Don't see any flowers hidden behind my back, do you? Don't even ask."

"Sympathy? I'm in a hospital….where?"

"Olympic Med Center, Port Angeles. Chili brought you yesterday. Should've seen him fly! The man left his escort behind and practically carried you into the emergency room in his own two arms."

Hoot's blurry mind raced, trying to make sense of this news. Last thing he could remember with any certainty was Jeremy fetching his tool bucket. He said, "Remy was just…"

"That was before." Maddie said. "Right now he's downstairs with Chili and can't wait to see you. He's telling everyone that his grandpa is actually a Jedi knight and the Jedi are in cahoots with Cajuns – this would be Chili's influence, I presume. Says the two of you are doing battle with the dark side of The Force and you'll win; no problem."

Maddie smiled and put a warm hand over Hoot's. Reading his expression, she said, "I know this is all very confusing right now, but you're going to be okay. Trust me."

Giving his hand a squeeze she said, "You just concentrate on sorting-out Jeremy's Star Wars nonsense – if you can get that straight, your head is just fine. I advised your doctor when you started mumbling about Ma Bell, and he's on the way. So, if you'll excuse, me I'll go tell your grandson and Chili that you're awake. Then we'll see what we can do to break you out of this joint…"

***

Jesse reported to her father via cell phone at least once daily.

"How is your shooter?" he asked.

"I don't know," Jesse said. "He had a stroke, so I guess he's lucky to be alive, but they're releasing him. Maybe he's not the best choice for your plans, now?"

"No, Gota." Papa Felix said. "If he can walk and talk, he'll do fine. He has access. He knows the system. And his sudden problema médico can only make him better. Weaker and more manageable. He's perfect for his part."

Jesse's phone was silent at her ear for a moment, but she still thought she could hear a faint sound like shuffling cards, her father's neverending manipulations falling into place.

He knows! the Billievoice said with alarm. *Everything! Your father always knows!*

"I want you to go to him," Felix Vega said.

"Now?"

"Yes, now" Papa Felix said. "Find out his true condition. Comfort him. You must convince your air marshal to do this small thing for us. We have very little time, and I've already taken steps – be ready."

I'm telling you…he knows! You have to break it off with Mr. Kenneth. You have to kill Hoot. It's not too late…

The call ended. Instructions had been given, and game pieces were in motion. Action would follow. It was all so simple yet so awful. Jesse knew that nothing could stop Felix Vega once his mind

245

was made up, no matter how horrible an atrocity was planned; her father so fucking confident that his smallest desire was everyone else's command, his every action defendable if not honorable.

"No problema," Jesse muttered in a disgusted tone of voice; "You want me to get kinky with him, Papa? Or do you think an ordinary suck-n-fuck will do the trick?" She dared the device to refresh connections and bounce the comment off whatever relay antennas and satellites necessary to get it back to Felix Vega while it still sizzled, her father so cold and unwavering in his Mazatlan fortress.

Chapter 33

Hoot was relieved to be out of the hospital and out of the woods for now as his doctor had bluntly put it. He was at Maddie's house, where he'd just finished a two-hour conference video interview intended to wrap up the investigation phase of his lethal action review. Present via video were his immediate superiors in FAMS and not-so-immediate superiors in the TSA, a ranking Homeland Security aide, an über-liberal senator with his aides and lackeys bent on reining-in the TSA, attorneys for everyone involved including a sizeable cadre from the American Civil Liberties Union, and ultimately God himself, no doubt.

Chili Hilliker was on hand with Maddie to support his friend, but pacing with his thumbs hooked into his belt as if ready to pop a grenade and feeling for the pin; he seemed more frustrated than Hoot by the cyber lynch mob that had been assembled for the interview. "That was no interview!" He exclaimed afterward. "It was a witch hunt by proxy – fuckin unbelievable!"

Hoot said nothing, but couldn't agree more.

"The senator and that squealin shoat from the ACLU have you singled out t' burn, ol' buddy. They didn't even wanna discuss the Skyshooter Incident as they seem t' love callin it. Glossed over their own agenda an' went straight to your fuckin partner's sudden disappearance and you goin after her. Her connection with the man in Mexico – and don't tell me that doesn't have somebody's tit at the TSA stuck in Homeland Security's wringer. The senator givin you a load for followin Jesse down there on your own time-n-dime as if you were under house arrest? Somethin here stinks..."

"Skyshooter Incident," Hoot echoed. "They do love calling it that, don't they? As if it was the latest entry on the Guinness list of

Infamous Shootouts. The OK fucking Corral. Ruby fucking Ridge…"

"Actin like somethin has t' be done before it gets outta hand," Chili said with one eye scrunched shut, the other searching Hoot's face as if taking a bead on him with a pistol. "They won't be happy 'till they've got ya danglin. Ya know that, don't you?"

"They've got a point," Hoot said, suddenly feeling very tired. The lingering effects of his stroke amplified to nearly beyond tolerance: he could feel them, ranks upon ranks of little blood clots queuing-up in the general vicinity of his brain stem, getting ready to throw him down again.

This was a bad deal, letting the bastards get to him with that so-called interview. His doctors. Chili. Maddie. Everyone claiming to be on his team had put him against the wall and told him in no uncertain terms that he had to control his stress – much more easily said than done. He wondered if it would always be this way. Would his brain feel like a plate of scrambled eggs with avocado and chorizo from now on?

Hoot pinched the bridge of his nose right-handedly, left arm hanging as numb as deadwood from his elbow to his fingertips after an excruciating morning physical therapy session. He said, "It's already out of hand, old friend. All the criminals I've apprehended? They were bad people, each and every one – all those I shot…and those I didn't. The shit I've put up with for doing a dirty job? And now it seems that I'm hanged because I shot one too many bad people."

Hoot heard his father's disappointed voice inside his head concurring; "You're a hard nut, Ezra Hooten. You learn everything the hard way," and he knew the ol' man had nailed him. The way he'd dropped out of college and run off to Vietnam to get away from Donna and her big plans – how stupid was that? All those long years chasing Norman Carpenter after the fucking nutcase had killed Donna and escaped – now we're talking stupid piled on top of stupid! It seemed that Hoot had managed to make life as hard on himself as possible, on his friends and family, too, and he figured that made him something of a certified shit in a category of shits well above and beyond the rest. He leveled his frustrated eyes at Chili, said, "All the things I've been called, the names I've been given:

Sniper, Troubleshooter, and now Skyshooter? All those less-than-noble gunslinger titles were exactly on the mark. I'm what they used to call a side-arm marshal, or a .40 caliber expediter. Ever hear those terms? They're what armchair marshals back in the bootlegging days used to call deputies like me – essentially bounty hunters with badges and itchy trigger fingers; we were the marshals who cared a bit too much about justice being served and not enough about how it was served."

"You're blunt; I'll give ya that," Chili said.

"Guilty as charged," Hoot agreed. "Lawman, Judge, and Jury all wrapped into one – Expediter. All those hats fit me too well, Chili. The TSA can't have a goddamned shooter like me on the loose. Too much bad press is hard on the PR department."

***

"Everything's fine here," Hoot lied to his ex, Linda. At least it seemed like a lie for some reason he couldn't quite put his finger on. He had not exactly mingled with scallywags since Jeremy's arrival. He had, in fact, done everything he could to keep his involvement with Jessica Vega and Chili's investigation of the murder of Harold Hesse at arm's length from the boy – so it couldn't be that. Thanks to Maddie's long-distance loose lips, Linda already knew about the stroke even if he was guilty of understating his symptoms now and then – so it couldn't be the stroke either.

"How's the divorce going?" he asked, changing the subject and already knowing the answer.

"Lawrence is being a complete shit," Linda answered. "How're you? That's what I wanna know," she said, refusing to be sidetracked, their long-distance satellite connection having a cleansing effect, blunting the emotional barbs. "You sure you still feel like having Jeremy around in your condition. Living alone in that cabin, I mean."

"Bet your bluejeans I do," he answered. "Remy's a big help. Besides, I'm not alone. Lots of people check on me all the time."

And suddenly there it was again – that cold prickly feeling spreading from the center of his chest like a wisp of dry ice, the chill of the truth hiding among honest words.

***

Remy quickly proved invaluable to Hoot's recovery. The boy's eagerness to be helpful to his grandfather was a big part of it. But mostly it was Hoot's bullheaded drive to push himself for the boy's sake that made all the difference. Refusing to expose the true extent of his weakened condition in Remy's presence, he worked out daily with the intensity of a man half his age. Figuring that if he gave himself a heart attack while working out, at least he'd go out fit; the doctor saying he shouldn't worry about a heart attack. Instead, he should worry about another stroke.

Thanks, Doc. I needed something new to worry about.

Hoot and Remy took walks – short ones at first, and then longer ones; three blocks to the Quick Mart, seven to the gym and back, or just for the hell of it. Once, then twice daily. Hoot had walked with a slight limp ever since being wounded the second time in Vietnam, so if it was a bit more pronounced since his stroke, at least it wasn't new, and Remy's mimic of it was spot-on and endearing.

His left hand remained a problem. It took effort, hard concentration, and often the help of his right hand for him to straighten the fingers on his left, and he had zero grip when he closed them. Unreliable if not entirely useless, he started keeping that hand tucked away in his pocket much of the time.

A common symptom of albinism is visual sensitivity to light, hence, Hoot's ever-present polarized glasses. The stroke hadn't changed that, but he was going to need a new prescription…and soon. "Certainly before I have to shoot somebody else," he confided in Chili, an old joke between them, not so funny anymore.

***

"There's something I've been thinking about: something that's been nagging my more-fractured-than usual mind, but it's hard for me to talk about it...to find the words," Hoot told his oldest friend.

"At a loss for words and you call me? Jeezus, Hoot – I know I run my big mouth a lot, but I don't say much when I do. I'm no more of a wordy person than you are. You want words you should be talkin to Maddie."

"I can't talk to Maddie about this. She'd try to understand, but she'd get the nut of it all wrong because she's never worn a badge.

"Thing is...I'm losing my religion, Chili. About what I've been. What I've become. The things I've done..."

Chili took a long look at Hoot, reading him and seeming to realize that Hoot was being dead serious, that he needed support and was reaching out to him for it. He gave Hoot's shoulder a bearlike one-handed squeeze, an expression of camaraderie transforming his grizzled face, and said, "Every lawman comes t' that crossroad eventually. The good ones do, anyhow. Some never get past it." He gave Hoot's shoulder a parting pat that would've crushed a lesser man's collarbone, said, "My only advice is to keep movin. Always keep movin – it's all you've really got in the end."

"Okay. What direction?"

"That's the rub, ain't it?"

"Precisely," Hoot agreed. "The suits want to label me a shoot first, ask questions later expediter? They're wrong. Truthfully, I'm a beamwalker," he said. "My whole fucking life I've been walking the beam, straight and narrow and above it all. I never had to make any real choices about direction because the only direction I knew was straight ahead, the only direction that mattered. Anything else and you fell off the beam. Now, I see that the choices were always there. I just didn't notice them overmuch at the time. I ignored them; concentrating on only keeping my balance and reaching my objective, I made choices without seeing them. Career choices. Family choices. Life choices. I never even bothered to look too closely."

Chili threw his hands in the air in exaggerated exasperation, cried, "Hell's bells and buckets a-blood!" He gave his scalp a deep mauling with sausage-like fingers, asked, "Was it the stroke that got you started thinkin 'bout all this horseshit, or what?"

"Might've crossed my mind once or twice before the stroke," Hoot said. "But, let me tell you, old buddy; sweating bullets just to wipe your own ass has a way of making you think differently about all sorts of things."

Chili eyed Hoot from beneath eyebrows showing the strain of holding back a deeply furrowed brow, said, "So…you're a beamwalker huh? Yeah, I knew that. I'm gonna go out on a limb here since I've come t' know you 'bout as well as anybody, and I say that whether you're a beamwalker or a bullshitter makes no difference. I 'spect the truth is that you're just feelin scared."

"Scared? About dying?"

"Nope." Chili grunted a laugh, said, "Not you – you don't know what that kinda fear tastes like, or have the good sense to miss it. I figure with you it's more 'bout the fear of bein responsible for others, the fear of leavin others in the lurch if you let yourself die.

"It's nuthin but vanity, thinkin like that, Hoot. But it's you. It's the way you are right down to your toes."

Let yourself die? Hoot took a deep breath and felt something shifting inside his chest. A tumor in track shoes, suddenly in a hurry to turn malignant? Or maybe it was another fucking blood clot cutting loose, looking for a place to get stuck and start some more shit.

Chapter 34

"She's here, in Port Tim," Hoot told Chili over the reheated dregs of an earlier pot of coffee that Grace Marvel, who seemed a good deal more sympathetic to his peculiarities since his *incapacitation* as she called it, had set aside just for Hoot.

"Jesse? Here? That'd be damned bold of her," Chili replied. "You sure?"

"I've felt her presence off-and-on the last two days. In the shadows near the cabin. Just off the roadside when I go walking. But I didn't trust the feeling until now."

"Could be you're just gettin your gut back, your instincts, and you're feelin fidgety about it. You just need to work it out..."

Hoot smiled sagely at his oldest friend. Yes – this was why they had remained friends for so long; no matter how far out on a limb he found himself, Chili had always been within reach. Miles and years notwithstanding, Hoot always knew he could tag Chili and be good for another round or two. "I've considered that possibility," he said. "You know as well as I, it's no mean feat for a man to build up enough trust in his own instincts to get him to the endgame, and I confess that I've been somewhat unsure of mine recently, thinking that my gut needs a little kick-start since my stroke. I think I just got it – I saw her for sure this morning. At the AM-PM. On my walk with Remy. We were inside the store and I saw her buying gas through the storefront glass. I'm certain it was her, even though there was glare on the glass and my eyes aren't quite up to par yet. And...well – you know, I had Remy with me so I didn't try to approach her."

"Approach her!" Chili exclaimed, both eyebrows scrambling for his hairline like a caterpillar version of a Chinese fire drill. "I hate bein the one t' tell ya this, Hoot, but you're in no goddamned condition t' do any such thing. Remy or no Remy. I don't care if you have a whole goddamned busload of Remy's with you; if anybody approaches her, it'll be me when I arrest her for the murder of Harold Hesse, speedin, jaywalkin, passin bad checks, or any other damned thing I can conjure up – not you!"

"It has to be me," Hoot said, his remaining voice soft and calm.

"Why you?" Chili demanded, his eyebrows reluctantly finding their way back home and hovering like thunderheads over a stern expression in case they might be needed again. "You plannin t' shoot her?"

"If I have to."

Hoot inconspicuously helped his left hand out of his trouser pocket with his right and massaged the wrist, bent and pulled the fingers – therapeutic warm-up exercises. He said, "She wants something from me. She hinted about it in Mexico. This is something on her father's behalf, I expect. And now, here she is. Bold of her, as you put it. And foolish."

He pressed a small foam ball into his left palm and squeezed – uselessly. Used his right hand to help, and pressed the foam egg again with all his might as if pressing a feather through bone. Giving up, he clamped his fingers shut and returned the troublesome paw to his pocket, said, "The Jesse I know is plenty bold enough, but she's no fool, so whatever it is she came to get, it must be damned important."

"More important than spending Christmas with your grandson?"

"I sure as hell hope not…"

***

Alison Wonderland paced the threadbare carpet behind the reception counter at Mom's Motel. Alison was never what you might call a relaxed person without significant herbal assistance, and she was considerably more agitated than usual this morning. This morning she couldn't take her attention off C wing. There was trouble over there – trouble just waiting to happen. Biting her lower lip, she parked her antsy butt on a stool at the counter just long enough to refresh her Facebook page on a computer that was sitting next to the phone.

…The phone – all those unlighted lines!

She stood and paced some more. Checking the sludge that was lying dark and thick in the lower half of the ever-hot glass coffee carafe like a toxic terror, she dismissed the idea of making a fresh pot and turned the coffee maker off.

10:00 in the morning? Normally she'd be halfway through pot number two by now. The transients who used to be loggers, but were mostly low-end salesmen and truckers needing a shower nowadays, always stopped by to check out before getting the fuck out, always wanting their free continental breakfast with coffee to go. Mom's used to have a half-dozen long-timers staying at a time, weeklies and a few monthlies, and they could be relied on to want their coffee and pastry, too. But now, this close to Christmas…

She poked one of the three remaining pastries, past their pull date to start with, they were very close to being squirrel chow, now. Merry Christmas my furry friends, she thought. She replaced the pastry dome. And then, trying very hard not to look over toward C wing, she returned to her cockpit behind the counter and the thin veneer of companionship that was the internet.

She didn't know what she expected. Police with SWAT bashing doors in, snipers in the treeline? God smiting Mom's Motel off the face of the earth with a lighting bolt? She had no idea, but ever since her not-so-sweet daughter Jessica had quietly slipped back into her room over there in C wing, Alison Wonderland had been expecting trouble. The last thing she expected to see was the tall pale man who was opening the lobby door and coming in out of the weepy morning drizzle, saying with a voice as smooth as an undertaker greeting the bereaved; "Hello Missus Mackey. Do you remember me?"

"Marshal Hooten! Of course, I remember you," she replied, her mood immediately perking up. She put an exaggerated frown on her face, said, "I remember you and my Jessica – running off in a big thank-you-very-much hurry before I could even say goodbye. Besides," the frown transformed itself into a beaming smile as if a floodlight switch had been hit. "How could I not remember you, your skin so…un-tan compared to mine?"

Hoot only smiled in response.

"I've have a difficult time keeping my tan with the dreadful weather recently. Just look," she added with deep concern etched into finely-plucked eyebrows, pulling the hem of her sweater up to her chin to share the proof of her dilemma.

Watch out! Saddlebags are on the loose…again! Hoot thought, steeling himself against Alison Wonderland's ample display of pulchritude. He didn't want to gawk, but couldn't help noticing that Mom's mams weren't the same shade of deep cinnamon brown he remembered them being – they were more an orange-y shade of tan this time. Yup, he thought. Just ask any albino; ultraviolet light, with nowhere near the normal curies of natural thermonuclear energy, will do that to you. They were still huge and heavy-looking, however. Skin the texture of tooled leather, and armed with the deadliest non-pierced nipples on planet earth, he was sure. Those bad girls should be pierced, he decided – pierced and chained to restraints.

"Look at us!" she said, beaming and leaning into the counter, pressing the soft flesh of one over-tanned mammary against the back of Hoot's pale white hand. "If we were a couple we'd look absolutely interracial!"

"Is she here?" Hoot asked, courteously dislodging his hand.

"Yes," Alison replied, glancing out the window toward C wing. "In her room." She shrugged, turning from the window and lowering her sweater. "Don't wanna talk to her mama, evidently. I don't know why she came back, marshal. Honestly, I've never understood why she does half the things she does…"

***

They sat together on the isolated deck behind A-wing at Mom's Motel. Heavily overcast, the sky hunkered dark and low on the surrounding mountainsides, fog creeping up the valleys and thru woods to hover over wet places; windless, damp and chilly.

Hoot thought the weather was perfectly appropriate, underscoring the mood of their tête-à-tête. "You know what happened to me. So, what do you want from me?" he asked Jesse. "Why are you here?"

"Whoa, lawman!" Jesse said. "You drove all the way out here in your condition on the drizzly-ass day before Christmas Eve just to ask me that question, sounding like we aren't even friends?"

"Friends? You always fuck your friends, do you?" Hoot said while looking Jesse in the eye with the same hard gaze used to melt the resistance of countless reprimands.

But was it really the same?

Was he the same since his stroke? Was he still dauntless?

He didn't think so.

"Yeah!" Jesse slammed her answer back at him with defiance. "If I'm lucky I do."

"Or if your father tells you to." Hoot countered in a soft tone, gaining control of his escalating blood pressure and looking away, westward – toward the sea; toward better weather and another day as his ol' man, the quintessential fisherman used to say.

"Tight family you have. Very tight."

"What do I want from you?" Jesse parroted with a hostile grin that made Hoot think of a pit bull on a leash, her eyes betraying something Hoot would've never expected – fear.

Fear of what? Or of whom?

Certainly not of him. He thought that she should be afraid of him. She would be if she had a brain in her head – he wasn't so sure at the moment.

She fiddled with the propane heater, the contraption looking like a gargantuan bug zapper on a post; it ignited with a low whoosh! immediately radiating warmth.

"You could have called and asked me that," she said, returning to her seat close to Hoot and taking his hand in hers. "Sent me a text? But instead, you set family and friends aside to drive all the way out here and see me in person? It's me you came to see, isn't it, and not my mother who is much closer to your own age?" she taunted like a flippant adolescent.

Hoot regarded her with a scowl, but no answer. The comment didn't deserve one.

"Or did you come to shoot me?" Jesse prodded.

Hoot sat back and massaged his left elbow, basking in the radiating heat. He knew she couldn't see the loaded SIG tucked under his belt in the small of his back, but he refused to underestimate her, so he assumed she knew it was there.

"You have a death wish? Just give me a good reason," he said.

"How about because I'm a bad person?"

Hoot laughed, a genuine laugh that broke the tension, saying in a quiet voice, "Yeah. That much I know…"

***

"It's unheard-of for jihadists to enlist infidels without first converting them to Islam. Yet it appears that a very nasty ISIL group may have done precisely that and approached your father regarding smuggling something into the country for an event on US soil. We must stop whatever they're planning at all costs," Mr. Kenneth told Jesse. "I don't care if it's a dirty bomb in Las Vegas or a quiet lunch at the In-N-Out in Anaheim – it has to be stopped before it happens. I want you to stop it…"

Jesse considered the little she knew of her father's plans. It wasn't much – Felix Vega was considered to be a secretive man by rivals and foes alike. What they didn't know was that he was more off-the-cuff than secretive. Jesse thought her father was basically a lucky bastard who couldn't make a plan if you gave him paper, scissors, and glue – he was just a very lucky badass…so far. He had said it was critical the wire go down precisely as planned. He said Hoot would make the perfect inside man to bring it down.

"The Blue Rose wire in Texas?" she had asked her father, assuming that he meant the prototype ground radar segment that had been tested in Texas.

"No," Felix Vega had said. "A different one…"

258

Chapter 35

First thing Christmas Eve morning, Hoot and Remy went for their usual walk – straight into town to Piglet's Diner for breakfast. Marty Pigg, the proprietor, waiter, cook, and busboy, having no local family other than his regular customers, was reliably open for business with a pot of thick coffee waiting just for Hoot, fresh-squeezed orange juice for Remy. Next, instead of next walking over to Chili's office like they had been doing after breakfast, they went instead to Harlan's 24-hour IGA where there were still a few scraggly shrubs leaning against a dumpster in the corner of the Christmas tree lot.

Negotiating a deal with an unenthusiastic attendant who was otherwise busy gathering up signage and the last few tree stands, Hoot nabbed a scrawny 4'-tall Charlie Brownish cedar and immediately handed its management off to his grandson.

"Now, listen up," he told Remy; "Anybody asks, we went deep into the woods off Mud Bay Road and rescued this poor shrubbery from the encroaching tide. We did not pay a wino five bucks for the privilege of his aroma mixed with the tree's – got it?"

The gleam in Remy's eye sparkling wickedly, he nodded his head in eager complicity.

Hoot gave the boy's shoulder a conspiratorial hug. "Technically, this is not a lie," he said, his A-fib kicking-in and churning up erratic palpitations in his chest, his voice seeming to fade away along with his train of thought. "Not one that counts, at least," he added, suddenly feeling a fundamental shift in his equilibrium. Pinocchio's curse, he thought, the smallest of falsehoods exacting its toll. Or maybe another blood clot bouncing around inside the old cranium?

Careful Hoot! he told himself – no lies allowed. No lies…no stress.

"This is just part of a long…luh… Shit!" he said, the frustration of trying to speak almost knocking him down. Instead, he sat down on a nearby stack of pallets and dug his fingers into his white hair, massaging the demons away. "Wait. Don't help me. I've almost…

"You mean longstanding? I know that word."

"Yes, that's it! I was trying to say it's all part of a luh…longstanding male tradition. Certain things; a guy needs to learn by example. Things about stuff like hunting and fishing. How much you p…paid for your truck versus how much you tell everyone you paid. Beer. And where to get the best Christmas tree. Manstuff – not complicated. Just tricky."

"I understand."

"Good. You either figure it out or you don't," Hoot muttered. "Most do, but some…" Can't teach a young man to keep his dick outta the dirt, he thought. Everybody has to learn that one by example – good examples and bad ones.

Hoot stood, and they walked on in silence for a while, his grandson proudly managing the tree without assistance. "If it's all the same to you," he finally said to Remy, his tone soft and casual, vowels and consonants sorted out, diphthongs under control; "Maddie and Chili don't need to know about what just happened back there."

"Don't worry. I've got your back, G-pa," Remy said with a grin, adding, "Even if you were out kinda late last night, I didn't pay attention to the time when you went to bed – if anybody should ask, I mean. And I've hardly noticed any stuttering. But what about your limp?"

"My limp? What about it?" Hoot asked.

"You really figure you could get far enough into the woods to rescue this tree with your limp?"

Hoot considered the boy's question, smiling. Grandfather and grandson in cahoots – gotta love it! And then he said; "You did it. You rescued the tree. I stood guard…"

***

260

Christmas decorations were a lean commodity at Hoot's cabin, so Maddie took pity on the scrawny tree and baked some sugar cookies to tie on its branches. "It's a resinous twig, and contributes to a fresh aroma, at least" she said. "With a bit of creative ornamentation it'll serve." Hoot popped corn the old-fashioned way over the woodstove, and Remy made what popcorn he didn't eat into garlands. Chili grilled a salmon for their holiday feast. There were very few wrapped gifts, but Hoot had fastened a red bow to the scarred leather case of his old 100' engineer's tape measure and placed it under the tree – no wrapping paper to disguise what it was, no gift tag to identify the intended recipient: none were needed. Jeremy went straight to it as soon as he saw it, crying, "Wow! Thanks, G-Pa! You wanna come outside and help me measure some big stuff?"

"Sure. I'll hold the dumb end," Hoot answered, proudly. "You can roll the tape and do the math."

Remy and Chili had been keeping themselves busy with sneaky elf business the past two weeks, the end result being a clearly-visible glow of satisfaction in the boy's eyes when he presented Hoot with the gift of a hand-made maple boot jack to make removing his boots easier now that he had balance issues, and, for Maddie, a clever adjustable yarn swift, also handmade of maple.

"Old-fashioned woodbutchery. Eat your Etsy hearts out, Etsy people!" Chili commented with toothy pride.

***

It went that way: Christmas at Hoot's; his first as a grandpa, while outside, lurking in the dark monochromatic softness of ever-present fog, Jesse waited and watched with uninvited eyes; observing it all, just like her daddy had told her to do.

But not because he told her to.

No, she was doing this because she wanted to – Jesse was doing this for herself.

You are sooo not doing this for yourself! You're doing it for them! the Billievoice inside Jesse's head said. *You're a chickenshit, scared to death of your father. You always have been. And now you want to sell him out in a deal?*

After all this time? You're crazy to trust them – they can't be trusted. Trust me...

I'm not afraid of Papa Felix, Jesse thought. I'm Jesse James Vega. I have an agenda of my own, and I'm not afraid of anyone!

Oh sure! The voice said, bated, *Repeat it 'til you believe it...*

Chapter 36

"Wait and watch," Felix Vega whispered into his fourteen-year-old daughter's ear. This was in 1994, toward the end of Jesse's visit to Mexico, and on the cusp of Raoul's sudden disappearance. Jesse remembered that day. Every relentless detail of it. She remembered smelling tequila emanating from her father, on his breath and in the perspiration beaded among the wiry black hairs on his chest. She would never forget the flat of his hand between her shoulder blades; pressing her down as if planting a seed in the hard-packed caliche.

It was dark, and they were waiting for Raoul to meet his maker.

A scruffy neighborhood even by Jalisco standards, it neither welcomed nor rejected them or anything else that hunkered close to the ground and stole about in the dark: including rats, cats, and an unbelievably ugly opossum. An hour passed, and then another, time infinitely patient with itself while the moon slowly climbed higher. Nearly full, it illuminated the surrounding scrubs and tumbleweeds like ghosts at a bonfire, deep shadows at their roots.

There was a weather-beaten metal warehouse. Then there was Raoul, one of several assigned to guard the warehouse, walking a cluttered path between the shadows...

"Don't look away, Gota. You caused this. You need to see it," her father whispered, his breath tickling the small hairs inside her ear. Felix Vega ever the seducer, as if sweet-talking an ignorant-but-horny young thing into witnessing an execution somehow expunged presumed sins by committing more sinful acts – ultimately atrocities if need be.

Papa Felix seemed to be forgetting that Jesse had singlehandedly bludgeoned a grocery store clerk to death while supposedly defending herself from rape long before she ever met Raoul. He might have considered how that and this amounted to an awful lot of gristly first-hand experience for anyone – even a drug lord's daughter.

Jesse had liked Raoul. He was a pervert, but in a romantic way. Twice her age yet utterly helpless in her hands. He would flirt shyly with her, and she would flirt right back at him, let him wallow in his perversions. Didn't matter in the least that he was almost certainly one of her stepbrothers by blood or by marriage – she wasn't sure which was most likely in Raoul's case, and she didn't care. Didn't matter that he was married, and a father to who knows how many cartel-bound young Raoul Junior's, either. She called him cousin instead of brother so neither of them would feel too weird about what was going on between them. Would give him veiled looks and pouty smiles. Let him peek at her nonexistent assets. She found countless excuses to get close to him. Sometimes she would let him pull up her shirttails, fondle tomorrow's promises and slobber on her. And, if she wanted the whole world and the box it came in, all she had to do was let him reach inside her shorts and find dampness; turned his brown Mexican cockroot into a geyser every time.

And then her fucking father had to go and kill him just to make a point?

If Felix Vega had given credence to how much like her father his only daughter truly was, he might have realized what a horrible mistake killing Raoul would be, what an unforgivable error forcing her to watch the execution would be. Obviously he did not, resulting in Jesse's first man-toy going to meet his maker with twenty-three very ugly bullet holes in his once-beautiful body. A sight like that stays with a fourteen-year-old, no matter how tough she thinks she is.

Jesse resolved that night to kill her father. It was the only right thing to do…

***

The Billievoice was comforting in the beginning, coming to Jessica after the trestle incident when she was weak and vulnerable. When Jesse was full of a fifteen-year-old's flair for life in the extreme, the manifestation of her friend's voice inside her head had seemed perfectly logical – desirable even, because she was holding on to a tenacious glimmer of hope that the flower of her life might somehow recover and not simply wilt away like one of her mother's broken promises. The voice of Billiejean Wisdom – the one other person who knew the whole truth about that day on the trestle – first came to Jesse during the long dark hours after midnight a few feverish days immediately after the incident; after Billiejean had died and Jesse's face had been lacerated to the bone. It came during the time of night when reality was off the clock and only the Luckraven kept watch. It coddled her in the beginning. Told her she wasn't to blame.

Must be the drip talking, Jesse had thought. There's no ghost here in the room with me, or inside my head – haunting me...

She wasn't frightened. She knew all about ghosts. Knew how to deal with them. Knew how to suffer them, at least. But the Billievoice was different. Unlike other 'ghosts' that simply manifested as thoughts and images in her mind, shadowy breezes and ruffling curtains, this was more nightmarish; this was an actual three-dimensional voice that she would hear with her ears just as she would hear someone speaking nearby, an unnerving experience that she quickly attributed to the intravenous drip fastened to her wrist.

Yes, it had to be the drip! Jesse thought. Something very powerful slithering through clear vinyl tubing and straight into a vein, holding her pain at bay. Something that left her feeling numb far beyond the point of feeling tingly. But her pain still remained alive...inside her and all through her. It had to be managed. The drip did that at least; it managed the pain, but it also pinned to the bed like a collected specimen, right through the gut, cold and nauseating. She could squirm but she couldn't escape, so she concentrated on lying very still.

...And that's when the Billievoice spoke up: telling her to relax, telling her she wasn't to blame. *I'm not here 'cause I hate you*, it said as clearly as if Billiejean herself were sitting in the room and speaking. *Wasn't your fault that I'm dead, was it? So what difference does anything make now? You're the one who has to live with it. Not me.*

"What do you mean I have to live with it?" Jesse had asked, aloud, without stopping to consider the questionable state of her sanity that engaging this manifestation in conversation implied. "Live with what?"

The answer returned to her in full living stereo: *With being you, of course,* the voice said. *With the bad things you've done. Bad things you'll continue to do for as long as you live.*

...As long as you live, it had said as if it were a judge pronouncing a sentence, but Jesse hardly paid attention. Certain that she was hallucinating, she was a bit unnerved because she couldn't simply turn it off – confirming her suspicion that something in the drip had set her off on this tangent, peeking into dark places that were better left dark while her cheek ached insanely, slowly healing behind a barricade of Oxycontin .

Have you sacrificed friendship? the voice had asked.

Yes, I've sacrificed friendship, Jesse answered.

Love?

Yes...love too.

Nothing required Jesse to pay attention to any of it of course, but the voice would not be ignored.

It taunted her in Billiejean Wisdom's pouty insecure whine; *Was it Raoul that set you off? Things I said when we were riding on the train about you and him and what a little whore you'd become? You think I shouldn't've said those things, huh? Maybe you think I only said them to make you mad?*

If so, it worked. I'm mad...

Jesse recalled that it had worked very well indeed, memories flooding back with enough force to knock her off balance, memories of how furiously she had screamed at Billiejean to shut the fuck up or the Luckraven would hear and come knock them both off the train. Dizzy memories of what Billiejean's Mamma Wisdom always said – that bad luck hangs around, and good luck runs out.

Chapter 37

"There are two ways to bring terror to the United States – the hard way, and the easy way," Papa Felix told his daughter. "My new friends have had some success with the hard way. But it keeps getting harder, and they have finally come to realize that I control the easy way."

"I don't understand. Why would you terrorize a country that feeds you?" Jesse asked.

"I wouldn't. Except terror found America without my help."

"And now you want to be a part of it?"

"I feed myself and mine, Gota," Felix Vega said with the rawboned sincerity of a true old-world Don. "Me and mine and no one else – understand?" He made a small ritual out of trimming and lighting a cigar, said, "Once this thing is done, everything will change – everything!" He snapped his fingers, saying, "Like that! The Big Game will be a whole new game with new rules. And if I'm not one of the players making it happen, I'll end up being one of the ones it's happening to."

Taking a long drag on his Cohiba, he concluded from behind an exhaled cloud of sweet smoke, "That is not my path. The decision is mine and I've made it. So tell me now; where do you stand?"

On your grave, The Billievoice offered without hesitation.

Jesse said nothing to her father, of course, wearing her scarred face like a Festival Queen; but, the hate for her father festered, eating at her like a cancer. If she were only a bit more her mother's daughter she would've righteously blamed her father for everything that was wrong and dark in her life. But it would be a lie.

Jesse lied to everyone without a second thought. But not to herself – she refused to lie to herself; not even about her father...

The truth was that Jesse had liked it: the first time Felix Vega had watched her pleasure herself. Beyond the burning shame, she had tingled. And she'd liked it the first time he participated. The same way she'd liked it the first time she had killed: it was the same tingle. She had wanted these things to happen. She would forever feel guilty for that, the wanting part of it. She could never forgive herself for being weak, but she could accept who and what she was, and that would have to do.

As for Hoot's part in her father's scheme: Hoot and Jesse were to use their experience and credentials to fake a DHS unannounced inspection of the Okanogan border control station just outside the old mining ghost town of Molson Washington on the border with Canada. They were to sabotage the underground sonar cable at precisely seven minutes after midnight, New Year's Day; a much easier plan in theory than in execution, certain to be made worse by Hoot's extremely unlikely cooperation no matter the motivation. Except for one possibility – Jesse's hours spent in the dark watching Hoot's cabin had not been entirely fruitless. On the contrary, she thought she'd found a sizeable chink in Hoot's armor.

***

"Your father is a brutal man," Mr. Kenneth said to Jesse. "Killed one of his brothers. Killed a stepson. At least two nephews that we know of, and who knows how many other family members? Tough family. Must be a real bitch to be grow up in such a family. I can understand how you might hesitate to cross him."

"Nobody crosses Felix Vega. I dare you to find anyone who has, and lived to brag about it," Jesse said, her chin held high as if to take a blow.

"My point exactly," Mr. Kenneth said. "Now here is my problem, and my offer to you, Jesse: DHS fears that your father may be getting tangled up with some true believers from the Middle East, the Khorasan Group in Syria perhaps – ISIL extremists. And that arrangement puts a whole new focus on border security. These true believers are the new al-Qaeda. They hate America and the West more than they love life, and they are known to have their eyes on our border with Mexico. Your father is known to be very efficient at smuggling everything from drugs to people and weapons across that border – it represents little more than a toll gate to him. And, there is reason to believe the Khorasans have contacted your father about smuggling a dirty nuke into the US. We simply can't allow that to happen…"

Mr. Kenneth offered Jesse a slender black cigarette from a fresh packet. She declined with a shake of her head, and he continued, "We need better intelligence about your father's involvement, and considering your unique relationship with him – especially in light of certain issues that you may need some assistance with – I believe we could help each other."

Jesse was unmoved by Mr. Kenneth's concerns. She didn't trust him any farther than she could throw him; but she was nonetheless curious what he knew of her father's business, what he thought he might do about it, and, especially, what he could or could not do for her. She certainly knew there had been lots of men of Middle-Eastern descent visiting the Playa Rocosa compound in recent weeks – she had seen them gathering around the pool in their robes and headgear, business suits and dark glasses; always dark glasses to hide their scheming, and ogling, and lust.

"I don't have issues I need help with," Jesse replied with a double dose of pumped-up bravado like a humming bird standing up to a hawk.

"Please Jessica, we'll get along so much better if we're honest; don't you think? For example, regarding the coincidence of your cousin's urgent extradition on your assigned flight? I expect your father's Mexican Mafia attorney friends must've set that up. But I wonder; were you supposed to kill him, yourself, if your other cousin didn't do the job? Doesn't matter. Did you know, by the way, I'm the one who put Ezra Hooten on the plane, just in case?" In an aside, Mr. Kenneth said, "The whole thing going sideways, it's a good thing I did…

"How about a certain grocery boy in Forks? Do we really need to dig him up again after twenty years? I think you may have more…*current* issues at hand than you want to admit right now, considering that your name has recently surfaced in connection with a couple of murders in Washington state – a Mr. Harold Hesse and Mrs. Soozy Wickerman. Those names mean anything to you?"

Fists on his hips like a true action figure, Mr. Kenneth said, "Don't answer that question, Jessica. I warned you that I already know everything, and I hope you won't make me prove it. Now, we've been through all this before – I can't promise to make felonious evidence disappear, or close open investigations with a snap of my fingers. But I can influence the process and the results, and that I promise to do. Now, do we have an agreement or not?"

"If I do this, I'll never be able to return to Mexico," Jesse said matter-of-factly.

Mr. Kenneth smiled a toothy smile and said, "Are you serious? If your father is in bed with the Khorasan Group you won't be safe anywhere!"

"You said these people are true believers who want to cleanse the earth?" Jesse's nails dug into her palms. "If what you fear is true, I'm just an afterthought to them, but I don't know about Hoot. Get him involved without letting him know the game plan and there'll be blood, bet on it. With my father and Hoot both involved, there could be bucketfuls."

Mr. Kenneth said "This is one of those fewer-who-know-the-better deals, and I'm afraid that Air Marshal Hooten isn't one of the few. I don't like it that we need to keep him in the dark, but we must. Watch out for him. And whatever you do, don't let him fuck it up…"

"When will I see your end of the deal?" Jesse asked.

"Don't worry, I keep my promises. Just get me the information I need."

Thus far blissfully silent, the all-grown-up and mature version of Jesse's Billievoice spoke up, saying; *Holding Felix Vega in some dark cell awaiting extradition won't cut it. You know that, don't you? Your father needs to be dead,* and Jesse knew it was true – she'd never be free of him as long as he lived.

Misreading the expression that crossed Jesse's face when Billievoice planted her father's kiss of death in her mind, Mr. Kenneth reiterated "I said not to worry, Jessica."

Jesse stood and helped herself to a cup of coffee from Mr. Kenneth's thermos, sat back down, and replied, "I'm not worried.

And I'm not hesitating, either. In case you haven't noticed, I'm negotiating…"

***

Sometimes Jesse would fondly recollect her first stepfather, Christine's real father, Vincent Hay, who liked to be called Hey Vincent. She remembered how Hey Vincent had an amazing singing voice, and loved to sing along with opera LP's played loudly on the stereo in her mom's cramped apartment behind the motel office. He would sing The Marriage of Figaro at the top of his lungs in the shower. Aside from that, the man was a total limp dick kowtowing to Alison Wonderland's every desire and demand.

Hey Vincent had been installed like a routine man-feature at Mom's as soon as it became clear that one of his frisky sperms had managed to hurdle both a well-placed diaphragm and a homebrewed herbal barricade to land in paydirt. And then he was an ex before his daughter turned five, paying support without bitching, stopping by for birthday parties and weekend visits. He lived in Port Angeles, close enough to show up unannounced now and then to make sure Alison Wonderland was doing right by Christine – so different from Papa Felix el Lobo Vega, Jessica's own father. It was the only father-daughter relationship she'd ever seen that made her jealous.

In many ways Jesse knew her father entirely too well; well enough to detest him, the man a living paragon of familial irresponsibility. Not that it mattered much to Jesse – he could strut and crow all he wanted, make demands as if he were a demigod, and he didn't fool her; she knew his secrets, she did his laundry…and more.

Felix Vega thought himself irresistibly romantic – hah! Growing up, Jesse had seen and experienced more than enough of Papa Felix's idea of romance, and she knew the dark, humiliating underside of it; consequently she had little use for romance, thank you very much.

Jesse put her head in her hands and wondered for the zillionth time why she was the way she was. But how she could've turned out any other way given her headcase mother and her drug lord father?

She wondered; had Billiejean's Luckraven pecked her on the head when it made her her father's daughter? Now that she was grown-up and carrying her own load of guilt that was, to put it mildly…substantial, she was finding herself with fewer and fewer options that didn't end with her lying dead on a slab instead of her father – and it really should be him.

These feelings Jesse felt for her father on the cusp of betraying him were in a class all by themselves. He had, after all, betrayed her first, and often; any chance she might've ever had at a remotely normal life killed the instant his sperm cleared the head of his cock and went racing ahead inside her mother's cunt. But he was still her Papa Flix, and she was his Gota de agua, or simply his *Gota* – his raindrop; and while raindrops are always anonymous and generally harmless, they are also known to become torrents. He would see about that soon enough; she was about to rain on her father's parade in the worst way, and goddamn him if he didn't have it coming…

Chapter 38

"You come around right now and agree to help, or you go down with the rest of them," Mr. Kenneth had said. "Isn't that the way your father plays it?" He spoke with crossed arms as if scolding a truant. "So what's it gonna be, Jessica? We're out of time."

And now it was early morning December 31st, New Year's Eve, and Jesse truly was out of time...

First, she disabled an antiquated alarm system at the big Victorian-style Presbyterian Church in the Diamond Point neighborhood by cutting its power. She heaved a brick through a stained-glass window. And then she called 911 and reported a nonexistent break-in and fire.

Next, satisfied that an adequate amount of confusion would soon reign at Chili Hilliker's police station and keep the old busybody busy, she drove to the Port Timothy Telegraph newspaper office only a block away from the station, and parked in the alley.

Maddie was alone in the office with Hoot's grandson who was helping by answering the phone while playing an aerial combat game on the front desk computer. He was a small boy. Tall, but thin like his grandfather and kind of fragile-looking, he was kicking ass on the computer. Jesse walked up to him with a crocodile smile pasted on her face and put the barrel of her pistol against his temple, saying "Don't make me shoot you, kid," and he froze.

Jesse turned and pointed the gun at Maddie and said, "Sorry to interrupt, but I have a chore to perform tonight that will require your cooperation in order for me to win your friend, Hoot's, cooperation. Understand?"

"No," Maddie answered, "I don't believe I understand at all."

"That's okay. You don't need to. Just look me straight in the eyes, Mizz Marvel, and tell me if you see the slightest indication that I'm bullshitting when I say that I'll shoot this boy if either one of you do or say anything to arouse suspicion. Do you understand now?"

Maddie said nothing, but slightly nodded her head.

"Good. I'm making it your responsibility to keep the boy's lips sealed," Jesse said and then turned to Remy. "Remember this, kid. I don't want to shoot you or this woman, and I'll feel real bad about it if I have to do it. But I'm a pro, just like your grandpa, and I'll pull the trigger without a second thought if I have to, just like he would."

Jesse flashed Remy a big carnivorous smile and gave him a fist bump to the shoulder as if they were members of the same posse, then she turned her attention to Maddie and said, "Now, Mizz Marvel, please be sensible and grab your coats. It gets cold where we're going…"

**

As a grown woman Jesse had come to the realization that she had always been unsociable and that she'd never taken pains to hide it. Truthfully, she did have thin memories of being a different self, a younger, more fragile, and entirely different self from the person that she presently was. She called these memories daydreams because that's exactly what they were. Notably, there were no tears in her daydreams because she was happy there. She was also shy and naïve, but she couldn't remember how it felt to be that way, so her shyness and naïveté felt vacant and contrived. She couldn't imagine her life without wanting to control as much of it as possible.

It had been easy for Jesse to throw up a hostile front while living at home with Alison Wonderland, her mother's head perpetually ensconced in a fog of cannabis. And it was even easier in Mexico, with her largely absent father and his disinterest in anything remotely scrupulous or moral. Consequently, Jesse's goals and aspirations were a bit skewed. Whatever noble goals she may have once possessed, she took pains to hide behind a mask of overplayed boredom. And truly…she really was bored. Boredom made her restless. And restlessness is what eventually led her to kill the first time. It only makes sense...

Her mother was a real piece of work who'd contributed heavily to Jesse's angst. So often Jesse had wanted to say something soft like; "Don't worry, Mother, I'm here, I just need some space." But she never dared lay down such a vulnerable bridge, a simple span unlikely to hold up under the weight of her mother's idiosyncrasies. Instead, she held firm until the passing years broke whatever caring she'd once felt for her mother into jagged little pieces of spite for her half-assed efforts at child rearing, her whorish efforts to find and keep a man. What Jesse would inevitably say instead was something like; "Hell of a role model you are! Why can't you keep your own shit together for two consecutive minutes and let me have a real life of my own?" or; "Is there a mechanic in town you wouldn't fuck for a brake job or a bartender for the tab?" Her love for her mother reduced to drudgery, she gave it to her by rote; just another chore at Mom's.

Jesse's obstinate application of willpower had ultimately broken her mother's macramé hemp yoke, and she grew a backbone capable of withstanding any load – except her father's load. Felix Vega had borne down on his daughter in every possible way for her entire life, emotionally and physically. His parenting style had more in common with guerrilla warfare than familial fondness; the sort of abuser who gave abusers a bad name. But no matter how heinously he might've treated Jesse as a child, he was still her father, and would always be.

Truly, she had been made in his image – that was the rub...wasn't it?

She would kill him if only she could. She thought it ironic that she could so easily kill anyone else on the fucking planet, but not him. He was el Demonio del Diablo, the Devil's demon...a evil man – and how do you kill evil? He was the glue that had long held entirely too much of Jessica Vega's world together, and she feared she was about to pull a Humpty Dumpty.

How could she possibly kill Felix Vega?

She had a plan...sort of; the hitch being that her plan would probably get Hoot killed if she didn't end up killing him, herself.

Shit...

***

Jesse knew there was no possible way to coerce Hoot into performing his role in her father's plan. One way or another, Hoot had to want to play along. She had an idea, but she was going to need help, and there was only one person she could trust without question...

"Not the brightest bulb on the string, and ugly as sin," Alison Wonderland had often said about Vincent Hay, Christine's daddy, "but he sure could sing and dance!" Jesse remembered Hey Vincent as a decent guy, even if he was boring to the Nth degree. He was the only man Jesse could recall her mom ever hooking-up with who didn't have it in his head that Jesse and her sister were part of the deal in certain unsaid ways. He had been quick to make his escape from Mom's Motel, but he was always cool about regular visitation when Christine was little, and he still visited her at Western.

Hey Vincent had always seemed squeamish about the girls' situation. He'd once made the mistake of criticizing Alison Wonderland for sending Jesse to Mexico sans chaperone and was very nearly served his balls on a platter for his effort. He stood his ground and made it clear that he didn't think Jesse's father was an appropriate custodian for children, earning him points with Jesse, but not going over so well with Felix Vega. In time, he hardly missed the tip of his pinkie finger compared with how he would've missed his balls, and it seemed that he grew more of a backbone as a result.

Jesse later learned that the real reason for the missing pinkie wasn't her father's retribution for her mother's indignity, as she had told the story; rather it was because Vincent had refused to co-sign the paperwork that would allow Alison Wonderland to send both her daughters outside the country. Down to nine and a half digits, Hey Vincent had mustered the cash and courage to hire an attorney, ultimately persuading a judge to agree that Felix Vega was an unsuitable role model for a minor child and deny him unsupervised visitation with Christine and Jesse. Of course, the court's finding was ignored by Jesse's parents, but Hey Vincent was having nothing to do with Christine playing a role in Felix Vega's debauchery.

Hey Vincent was the only person Jesse knew who'd ever bucked her father and got away with it, making him the only person she knew who could help with her Hoot problem without alerting others...even if he wasn't quite as pliant as Jesse remembered him being, wanting more answers than Jesse could give.

"So what's the plan, again?" Hey Vincent asked her.

Alison Wonderland was right about Vincent's unappealing appearance – splotchy bald head, ruddy jowly cheeks, and big ears with fleshy lobes, knitting his brows in concentration made him look like he might be passing a kidney stone. "You want to sneak-up on a Border Patrol station in the Okanogan highlands...tonight?" he reiterated in disbelief.

"Yes. A surveillance station near Molson. But no sneaking," Jesse said. "We simply drive up to the front door and walk in like we're supposed to be there – and we are...sort of. We have credentials, at least. That's why I need to borrow your Hummer. It's heavy, looks official, and I figure my Mini won't get far on those roads this time of year."

"If this is Homeland Security business, why don't you just use an official vehicle?"

"Actually, this visit's a little bit off the radar."

"And you're taking the woman and boy with you?" Vincent nodded toward his kitchen where Maddie was looking rattled serving a steaming cup of hot chocolate to Jeremy.

"Yes. And picking someone else up on the way. The boy's grandfather."

"Does Felix Vega have anything to do with this?"

"Actually, this could get me out from under my father at last. Will you help?"

"Okay," Hey Vincent said, pondering. "I'll drive."

"Whoa! Hold up a second..."

"Do you realize that H-2 Hummers are no longer being manufactured?" Vincent said. "Makes each one still on the road a little more special, I think, and I'd like to get mine returned home in one piece, or, at least I want to be the person who was driving if it isn't." He grabbed his coat and said, "C'mon, then...let's go!"

Chapter 39

You're back?" Hoot said to Jessica Vega in unfeigned surprise. He had answered his cabin door in bluejeans and sweatshirt, shying away from the dampness outside. "I've had computer viruses keep coming back like this…uninvited, that is." He glanced over her shoulder at a silver Hummer with dark windows idling in his driveway like a huge getaway car, nothing else out of the ordinary. He asked, "Whose tank?"

"That's our ride. Belongs to my sister's father."

"Our ride?"

"We need to talk, Hoot. May I come in for a minute?"

Discretely slipping his left hand into his pocket, Hoot stepped aside. He knew that he looked like shit, and he didn't care; figured the quickest way to get Jesse to go away was to let her say whatever was on her mind – then he'd shoot her if she didn't get the fuck out.

"I take it you stopped by to find out if my aim is still good?" Hoot said. "Try pulling the piece that I know damn well you have in your coat pocket and we'll find out."

It was pure bullshit, of course; Hoot had no idea if he could still hit the side of a barn while standing inside of it. Truthfully, he hadn't fired a weapon since he shot the floss assassin on the plane, and wasn't sure he could even pull a trigger without dropping the weapon. He'd only challenged her to plant the idea in Jesse's head that he was armed with his own pistol, a ruse to keep her guessing.

Handicapped as he was, it would've been impossible for Hoot to serve coffee without rattling the cup like a beggar, so he waved toward the coffee maker and said, "Help yourself. It's decaf, and a little fresh for my taste. Terrible stuff, actually." He stood aside, near his refrigerator, where he always kept his .25cal Beretta in the bin with the cold cuts when not strapped to his ankle.

"How are you feeling, Hoot?" Jesse asked, sounding concerned.

Very touching that she'd bother to ask, Hoot thought, holding the possibility that she actually might give a shit at arm's length.

"I've had better days. And worse," he answered frankly.

Hoot told himself that humor is always the best defense when you're out of bullets, but bullets were definitely better. He could feel his nerves sounding the alarm, panic impulses barely held in check – Ah-oooga! Ah-oooga! Dive! Dive! – and he knew he'd better get his stress under control if he didn't want another popcorn stroke to take him down right here in his own kitchen; maybe a whole bagful of popcorn this time.

"How about you?" he said. "Is life on the lam all you hoped it would be?" taking care to imagine the words before speaking them.

Jesse flashed an exaggerated smile made gruesome by the scar on her face, and it occurred to Hoot; this was the first time that he'd ever noticed it and thought that it was ugly. *Unveiled eyes see the truth in a glance;* he heard his mother's voice saying in the back of his recently prone-to-wandering mind: thinking that careful application of foundation makeup would surely make Jesse's lacerated cheek less noticeable, and yet she took no pains whatsoever to hide it. Interesting. He remembered that she had called her scar her *penance* once.

He wondered; penance to the bone? – people like us are born to penance. It seemed to Hoot that Jesse took hers straight-up, the same way she took her liquor.

Hoot knew from personal experience exactly what the weight of penance felt like, how relentless it was. It had taken him twenty-eight long years to corner his own nemesis in a hellish spate of self-inflicted penance for failing the love of his youth, and he could still feel Norman Carpenter's knife in his gut stirring-up the bile of self-disappointment residing there; his only reward. He knew that, in spite of blind hope and assumed promises; penance does not equal absolution...ever. Yes, they were both deeply scarred people, he and

Jesse – maybe that's why he felt empathy for her in spite of being more than ready to shoot her.

"I'm not here to confess killing Harold Hesse, if that's what you're expecting," Jesse said. "For what it's worth, Harold and his brother were both perverts, so you shouldn't waste too much concern on either of them, anyhow."

"And the Wickerman woman?"

Jesse raised an eyebrow. "Her either…"

"Are there others?" Hoot asked. "How many have you killed, Jesse?"

Jesse didn't answer.

"We were both soldiers," Hoot said. "We both know the difference between killing someone because you have to and murdering them because you want to."

"And we both know how finely those hairs can be split in the heat of the moment, don't we?" Jesse said. "The random finality of luck? Knowing that even the sharpest skillset can leave you as dead as bad karma in a firefight, but constantly honing yourself anyhow? Combat separates the real killers from the ordinary killers every time. People who've never experienced combat know nothing about that; the awful thrill of triumph over another human being who was every bit as determined to kill you as you were to kill them. Once you've had a taste – the next step…"

"There is no next step, Jesse."

She looked him in the eye, said, "Do you remember ever not knowing? I don't."

"Combat doesn't make murderers out of soldiers. It doesn't work that way."

"You sure about that?" Jesse asked, her eyes looking feverish.

"You're a sick woman, Jesse."

"Yeah, I know. It runs in the family."

"Seriously. You need help…"

"I also happen to know that *help* doesn't help. I swear to God Almighty, Hoot…I'm trying to make things right the only way I know how. Will you help me do it my way?"

"If you're joking, I'm not laughing," Hoot answered with a grunt of disgust.

"How about your grandson? Are you willing to help him?"

"What are you talking about?" Hoot said, the small, transparent hairs on the back of his neck suddenly standing at attention.

"You still got your sniper rifle?"

"My old M-21? The rifle that my CO gave me with my second Silver Star? How do you know about that?"

"I'm sure everyone knows about it. It's one of your favorite don't-tell-anybody-I-told-you stories when you've had a few – I know about it and I've only known you since Thanksgiving!

"Now, here's the deal," Jesse said. "I thought young Jeremy might like to visit the Border Patrol drone post at Molson. At night. He's waiting in the car outside. So is your friend, Maddie. They'd like you to come along – probably to keep me from doing something stupid."

Remy! And Maddie!

A chill of alarm ran up Hoot's spine. Something in Jesse's businesslike tone made him understand that now would be a very bad time to do anything rash. "Why'd you ask about my old sniper rifle?"

"Because we probably won't get a chance to get close to my father."

Hoot realized Jesse was being serious – she was planning to kill her father! "This is New Year's Eve...what are you up to, Jesse?"

"It's complicated, Hoot. Like I said, I'm trying to set things right, but there's a whole lot of shit on the wrong side of the line. I need your help, and I knew you wouldn't help me without a little motivation. So...tell me; are you motivated? Or is someone in the car about to get unnecessarily hurt?"

"Goddamnit, Jesse! I hope you understand that I'll kill you as dead as Julius Caesar and make it hurt in the worst possible way if you harm so much as a hair on my grandson's head," Hoot said.

"Yeah. I know that."

"Or Maddie, either."

"Ever valiant, Hoot...it's a damned shame we've gotten off on the wrong foot – you're actually a pretty decent old fucker once you get past all the shoot-first shit."

"What do you want from me, Jesse?"

"Understanding and forgiveness?"

Hoot fumed at her flippant reply, but forced a bitter smile and said, "What else?"

"For me…nothing much. Unfortunately, my father has different ideas. Now, do you still have your sniper rifle, or not?"

"I have it."

"Knew you would," Jesse said with satisfaction. "Go get it. And your coat and your meds," Jesse said. "We're going for a ride, and we can talk on the way…"

***

Hoot expected the man driving the Hummer to be Jesse's father – he was not.

Vincent nervously offered his hand after Hoot was settled in the spacious passenger seat next to him, saying; "Hey, friend. I'm Hey Vincent, Christine's dad. Did you get drafted, too?"

"Evidently," Hoot said, taking care to avoid a tendency to underestimate people based on first impressions. It was going to be a long ride to Molson.

Jesse climbed into the Hummer's huge rear passenger seat next to Maddie and Jeremy.

"Grandpa?" Remy said.

"I'm here," Hoot said, giving Maddie a sincere look of gratitude for being at his grandson's side. "You guys okay?"

"We're all right," Maddie said, looking anything but.

"Okay," Jesse said. "Here's the deal." She made a show of drawing her pistol out of her pocket and chambering a round. "I hate being deceitful, so I'll come right out with it…you are all my hostages tonight, and we have a job to do. Now…please, everyone look me in my eyes and let me know if you have the slightest doubt that what I'm about to say is true." She gave the Hummer's occupants a moment to comply, and then continued; "Serious shit's going on in the Okanogan highlands, and that's where we're going. Like it or not, we're all part of it." She focused on Hoot and continued, "We can talk more about it on the way. But I want everyone to be fairly warned; if any of you even look to me like you are about to make the

282

slightest trouble," she put her weapon in Jeremy's ear and cocked it, said, "I will put the first bullet in this young boy's head."

Jeremy turned almost as pale as his grandfather, sat very still, and said nothing.

"It's a seven-hour drive to Molson if we're lucky. So, let's go!" Jesse told Hey Vincent.

Gripping the wheel in stunned silence. With a fearful glance at Hoot, Vincent's oversized Adam's apple bobbed with a big swallow of courage, his brow scrunched with determination, and the Hummer took to the road like the gas-guzzling thoroughbred it was.

***

"It's about the wire," Jesse told Hoot. "Papa wants it to go down right after midnight on New Year's Day. That's all I know."

"What wire?"

"You recall the Blue Rose project?"

"I remember. Underground sonar technology in a buried cable umpteen miles long, tested on the Texas border with Mexico a couple years ago. I was assigned to the apprehension team supporting the project. It was supposed to be able to tell the difference between an armadillo and a dog crossing over it, a deer and a drug smuggler with a backpack, a pickup and a four-wheeler, stuff like that. More expensive to set up than aerial surveillance, but a lot cheaper to operate. I was there when it went online, and I remember that it worked well enough."

What the hell is going on, here? Hoot wondered…and then inspiration struck; he said, "I remember reading somewhere that DHS wanted Congress to budget enough money to plant one on the Canadian border with Montana."

"Very few people know there's a wire all ready in place on the Canadian border," Jesse said with a sharp sideways glance at Hoot.

"A prototype?"

"Exactly. On the Washington border with British Columbia through the Okanogan highlands. Unofficially called the Okanogan Rose, it was installed last year to test if it works in the rough terrain and cold. That's the one my father wants shut down."

"He's planning to smuggle something special across it for New Year's," Hoot speculated.

"Drugs?"

"Unlikely. Drugs aren't special. Plenty of those already here, and nobody knows that better than Felix Vega. It's very likely a dirty bomb, considering that he's in bed with jihadists, now. Very big trouble – don't you agree?"

"My father has smuggled weapons, people, and drugs across the border his whole life. He's a drug dealer, and he has posses in place on both sides of the ditch for all of that business. This is something new, and I can see that he's unhappy with the date and other details in the plan. It's all a big bother for him, so apparently someone else is making the agenda."

"Who would that be?"

"Someone with exceptionally serious money."

Hoot shrugged his shoulders. "Terrorists with nukes don't care about money."

"Doesn't matter what they care about," Jesse said. "If someone else is calling the shots, setting dates and locations without Papa's approval: it has to be someone with enough cash and clout to bump my father down a notch to a lesser middleman position – that's exceptionally serious money because Felix Vega is hardly a peasant. Of course, he'll never be rich enough to satisfy himself, so he's a sucker for a big payoff. You were wondering about my father's concern? It has to be money. Or power. They're the same thing to him, and it's all he cares about.

"Papa sees himself as a businessman, a focused and successful businessman – a middleman providing a service, that's all he is; certainly not a terrorist. He's practically legit in his own eyes. He hobnobs with politicians. Spends big money in the community. Every criminal thing he does is justified in his opinion simply because everyone knows it was going to be done sooner or later by someone anyhow, he just does it better. Bolder and bloodier. People in the know, know this. Innocent victims are simply unlucky bystanders who put themselves in harm's way."

"A middleman in a high-stakes game?" Hoot said.

"Exactly. My father currently sits at the top of the Mexican drug lord heap, making him one of the top smuggling honchos in the world. If that's true, for him to elevate himself another notch, he has to go outside the drug community, start again with new cronies and work his way to the top of that heap. Whoever he's working for, it has to be someone wanting to move something worth even more than drugs, something that is substantially more dangerous."

"In what way?"

"In any way and in every way. The morality of my father's business or his business partners' businesses, their politics or the specific agenda of their business? These matters don't concern him other than their impact on profit. Whether it's drugs, prostitution and white slavery, or wholesale murder, it's all business, and nothing is part of the equation other than profit potential. It's a very simple equation: illicit, immoral, and dangerous endeavors = big money for big risk, legitimate ones = less risk, but with little or no money – not enough to warrant the startup and overhead costs, the potential for loss. Papa likes his profit margin well over 300%. If there's little profit, there's little interest where el Lobo is concerned. In this case I'd say that it's very big money, the way he's been acting."

"How big?"

"My guess? More than a hundred-million dollars…maybe a lot more. It's causing him to operate differently. Do unpredictable things."

"Like what?"

"Like using you, for one thing. He doesn't trust outsiders. He doesn't trust family, either, for that matter. But he knows how to control family. How to bend us, and how to hurt us. He can hurt family so much more easily and effectively than he can hurt strangers. And that's what it's all about in his world; controlling the hurt."

"Ours, too," Hoot said. "And for your information; he's not using me."

"Believe that if you want, but know that he uses everyone. I told him you were on the US Marshal's team assigned to the original Blue Rose project in Texas, and he figures you must know it well enough to shut it down. Now…can you shut it down, or not?"

"Maybe. If it's like the Texas wire, a power interruption will cause it to shut itself off. It'll automatically reboot, but it has to run a diagnostic first – that takes some time."

"Good enough…"

***

"You say Molson Station has drones but doesn't use them? Why not?" Hoot asked Jesse.

It was after 8:00pm and it was snowing. Hey Vincent, much to Jesse's irritation, was conscientiously driving five miles below the speed limit as precisely as human reflexes would allow. "Everybody with half a brain knows using cruise control on slippery roads is a good way for even a four-wheel-drive vehicle like this one to end up in the ditch!" he explained to the car at large as if conducting a driver's education class.

"It was political," Jesse said. "The drone program in Arizona was costing the Border Patrol a shitload, and wasn't meeting expectations by a long shot, so a month ago the IG took away two of their nine Predators and sent them to Molson Station. Molson has no budget for them, so now they're just sitting there, waiting for activation."

"And you intend to activate them?" Hoot said.

"I'm hoping just one will do it."

"You're nuts!"

"A Predator-savvy nut thanks to two tours in Afghanistan," Jesse said.

"Don't expect me to help," Hoot said. "I won't."

"I don't need your help, Hoot. My father does. I thought we discussed all that on the way – somewhere around Wenatchee, if I recall. I'm looking forward to Jeremy helping me with the drone if it comes to that."

"Me? You want me to fly a real, full-size drone?" Jeremy spoke up.

"Sure," Jesse said. "It takes two to fly a Predator and work the optics. I saw you playing Assault Horizon on the computer in Mizz Marvel's office, and you were kicking ass! – a natural drone pilot if I ever saw one."

"Leave Jeremy out of this," Hoot said.

"I will if I can," Jesse said. "That may depend on you and your rifle. But first, you have a different job, Hoot – shutting down

286

that stupid wire so my father can smuggle his dirty little secret across."

"You mean, so he'll show himself…is that it?" Hoot said, understanding that Jesse's real intention was to kill her father. Would that even be possible with his ever-present posse? Of course…a trained sniper at 500 yards is an impossibility to guard against – that's why she asked about the M-21. But the drones? Border Patrol Predators were unarmed as well as unpiloted.

"Why the precise timetable?" he asked. "What happens at seven minutes after midnight?"

"In addition to the wire and drones, DHS has been running a feasibility study on using satellite imagery for border enforcement, and this little chunk of it drops off the grid for exactly twelve minutes at seven minutes after midnight to re-task. Without the wire backing up the satellite, and with the drones down, the border will be wide open for those twelve minutes. A herd of anthrax-infected elephants could cross over, and nobody would know."

"Your plan is to launch a drone and follow the contraband?"

"If necessary," Jesse said. With a hard expression, she added, "Look, Hoot, we've both got our parts to play. You play yours, and I'll play mine, and we'll both leave here heroes. Just don't forget…I've got Jeremy."

"What about your father?" Hoot asked from the Hummer's front seat. "Do you seriously think this will make anything that he did to you un-happen?"

Jesse glared silently.

"Who's he working for?"

"Nobody I know."

"How about you, Jesse? Who are *you* working for?" Hoot challenged. "Who's the man behind the curtain making sure that we have access to take the wire down, insuring that your father is drawn out?"

Jesse set her jaw and said nothing.

"Is your tall dark friend at the TSA providing activation codes for the drones while staying in the shadows and keeping his hands clean?" Hoot queried.

"Just keep looking straight ahead," Jesse warned. "Straight ahead…"

Chapter 40

Hey Vincent parked his Hummer behind a low snowdrift. The Molson Station US Border Patrol headquarters building hunkered in an eerie high-pressure sodium glow less than a mile ahead. The Unmanned Aerial Vehicle hangar was out of sight behind a utility building a quarter-mile to the east.

Maddie and Remy stayed warm in the car. The other three stepped out to reconnoiter.

"What now?" Hey Vincent asked Jesse.

"First, we drop off Hoot so he can shut that fucking wire down precisely on time. And then you take me, Mizz Marvel, and young Jeremy to check out those drones." She pocketed her pistol and crossed her arms against the cold.

"You're not taking my grandson anywhere without me," Hoot protested.

"Well now…that's where you're wrong, marshal Hoot" Jesse said. "You're in no condition or position to make demands, and you damned well know it." She smiled wickedly and added, "Just relax and know that he's in experienced hands."

Hoot said, "I can't let you take him…"

"Yes, you can," Jesse fired back. "And, what's more, you will, because you don't have a choice in the matter."

Hoot glared. Feeling his a-fib starting to flutter behind his ribs under his left arm, he said, "Just don't forget that I'll kill you and make it count if you hurt that boy in any way," and then he returned to the car with his hand pocketed, his fist starting to tremble. Pressure building in his temples, he could feel his core temperature rising and knew that he was turning red in the face. Perspiration was beading on his forehead.

"Are you all right, Hoot?" Maddie said as soon as the Hummer was under way, evidently concerned about his appearance.

…Whoa! Hoot told himself, gaining a grip on his mounting tension – Doc had warned him to calm down until the blood thinners and blood pressure medications he'd prescribed had had a chance to work. Otherwise, Hoot put himself at serious risk for another stroke, possibly a massive one. "I'm fine," He lied, then truthfully added, "I'm sorry you had to get dragged into all this, Maddie…but I'm thankful you're here."

Frustrated, Hoot needed his head to be in much better shape than it was.

But then, he thought, that's been the story of my life, hasn't it?

***

Hoot's experience told him the most expedient way to shut down the Okanogan Rose wire would be to cut its power – not exactly rocket science. This was precisely what electrical storms had caused to happen three times the first week that the Blue Rose went on line in Arizona. So, that's exactly what Hoot did without concern for hitting Felix Vega's damned timeline precisely on the button, walking over to the utility building and letting himself in the quick and dirty way by breaking a window. Inside, he saw a bank of likely-looking electrical transformers, and started pulling Emergency Shutdown levers as fast as he could, the transformers groaning into silence while security alarms blared as if the apocalypse truly was imminent.

Making a hasty retreat, Hoot met an armed security team at the door to the station headquarters. Hands raised, he said, "I need to see the person in charge."

A young woman wearing fatigues, a Kevlar vest, a helmet, and pointing a very lethal-looking Heckler & Koch UMP45 submachine gun at the center of Hoot's chest, stepped forward and said, "What a coincidence…"

***

Hey Vincent drove up to the UAV hangar as if he owned the place. A large, white, inflatable structure with an aluminum frame bolted to a concrete slab; it was unlocked and unguarded as Jesse had expected it would be. She and Remy entered, and Remy immediately sucked in a breath, saying, "Wow!" in an awestruck tone. He stood transfixed by the much larger-than-expected size of two MQ-9 Reaper drones sitting side-by-side under the hangar's floodlights. Upgraded from Predator 1's, the Predator Reapers were bulb-nosed, silver-gray aircraft with the distinctive blue waistband and red stripe of the U.S. Customs and Border Protection Agency. Each rear-powered turboprop aircraft had a 66' wingspan, no windows, and a back end with an inverted tail fin that looked like it had been designed by a video gamer.

"We're gonna fly that?" Remy said, whatever fear for this whole insane 'adventure' of Jesse's that he might have in his heart momentarily held in check by awe.

"Yeah...we are," Jesse said. She stuck her head out the hangar door and signaled Hey Vincent and Maddie to join them. "You two get the hangar doors." she said. "We're gonna have to exit under prop power, so they both need to be open."

Jesse thought that Hey Vincent looked like he'd just been anally probed by little green men, but he nodded, and headed for the nearest hangar door, Maddie for the farthest.

"Come on, Remy, we need to hurry!" Jesse called, and started walking toward the other side of the hangar. She quickly found a door marked Control Mod, opened it, and started flipping switches.

***

"You shut the wire down four minutes early," Mr. Kenneth told Hoot. "I expect el Lobo will be displeased – do you have an extra finger you won't miss too much?"

"I should've known you would be involved in this...seems that you're everywhere nowadays."

"Ah...if that were only true," Mr. Kenneth said with a sigh of confession. "But, I'm not...involved. Just ask the lovely ICE officer who brought you to this room if she knew why she was told to bring you to me, or even if she knew who was waiting for you. She didn't need to know, so she didn't. You see, it's important that my involvement in field matters is kept out of the spotlight."

"I get it," Hoot said. "I was conveniently drafted by Felix Vega to douse the wire, and then you allowed me to do so because you couldn't order it done yourself without raising curious eyebrows. You're the Invisible Man: ever there – but never there. Multiple degrees of separation. That's your game, right?"

"Precisely." Mr. Kenneth said. "Do you realize the job of a US Border Patrol agent is the most dangerous job in all the US armed services? I'm surprised you aren't a Border Patrol agent, given the statistics and your propensity for violence."

"I wonder…would you be good for a job reference?" Hoot prodded.

"Controlling this country's borders has become of paramount importance in our post-911 world, a daunting task that should be mission-focused and apolitical, yet made intolerable by politicians more worried about immigration than annihilation: unfocused, under budgeted, and mismanaged," Mr. Kenneth said with apparent distaste.

"That's where I come in," he continued. "I'm apolitical. You see, nobody pulls my strings because, officially, I don't exist. Were it not for a handful of behind-the-scenes people like myself at DHS, this country's anti-terrorism efficiency would be entirely at the mercy of politicians far more concerned about reelection than national security." He smiled broadly. "Can you imagine?"

Mr. Kenneth may be a zealot, Hoot reasoned; but at least he seemed to be the sort of zealot who gets things done, and something could be said for any man who gets it done.

Mr. Kenneth said, "I hope we're on the same side in this business, Air Marshal Hooten. Because I fear our mutual friend may have gotten us involved in a real mess; much deeper than either of us would like."

Mr. Kenneth was interrupted by the blaring security sirens – Armageddon all over again! He calmly said, "I expect that alarm means that Jessica has successfully absconded with a drone. We'll move out as soon as the excitement dies down."

He was interrupted again by one of his aides knocking. Mr. Kenneth stepped out for a brief aside, and Hoot heard a man in the hallway say, "There's a problem, sir…"

Mr. Kenneth immediately called over his shoulder to Hoot, "Felix Vega was just spotted near the drone hangar! Come on!"

***

There was an explosion, and the night suddenly crackled with flames. The drone hangar had been a fire resistant inflatable structure – not a fireproof one– especially not when the flames were being fed with hi-octane aircraft fuel from the exploded drone.

Remy! Maddie!

Hoot scrambled outside. He started to run in the direction of the fire, but was held back by Mr. Kenneth who was holding open the door of a Tahoe and telling him to get in.

Hoot did…thankfully – he'd have never made it on foot in his condition. Now, he looked all around the hangar site from his vantage point in the Tahoe for any sign of Remy and Maddie, and he suddenly realized that Hey Vincent's Hummer was missing.

Vincent Hay, himself, was found cowering behind a dumpster, rattled, but otherwise no worse for wear. He confirmed that Felix Vega's posse had shown up and sabotaged the second drone. But, before that, Jesse had borrowed his H-2 and taken Maddie and Jeremy to Molson.

"Molson?" Hoot said. "You sure? I thought it was a ghost town."

"It is," Mr. Kenneth said. "There's not much there but a few old buildings and a museum."

"That's where she said she was going," Hey Vincent said. "She and the boy played on the big video console for a little while, and then she jumped up and hollered, "I need to go to Molson now!" as plain as day. She took the woman and the boy and my truck – I sure hope her driving has improved since her high school days…"

"Vega's hiding," Hoot said.

Mr. Kenneth agreed, saying, "We know that two weeks ago a cell with suspected Islamic State backing hijacked a truck carrying a dozen drums of highly-radioactive medical waste in Calgary. We also have reason to believe that a package containing material salvaged from an unaccounted-for Russian nuclear missile arrived separately a few days later. As did a bomb maker. And a day ago a snitch told our man in Calgary that the resulting bad news was loaded into a 40-foot container van destined for the docks in Vancouver."

"It's not headed for Vancouver – that's our bomb," Hoot said. "Are there any structures nearby big enough to hide a rig that size? Warehouses? Tunnels? Or mines?"

Mr. Kenneth said, "The terrorists don't need a 40-foot container rig. Something the size of a dump truck would be big enough for a nuclear device and enough medical waste to make a mess of it."

"He's probably switching to something smaller – possibly multiple vehicles, an old trick among professional smugglers," Hoot said.

"If it's true, as Homeland Security now suspects, that Microsoft's New Direction kickoff in Seattle next week is the target, the delivery vehicle could easily be switched a couple more times before then," Mr. Kenneth said. "There'll be somewhere in the neighborhood of 40,000-plus Microsoft stockholders gathered under the closed roof of the Seattle Mariner's baseball stadium for that event."

"Felix Vega won't be anywhere near it," Hoot said. "His job is done – he's probably handing the device off to terrorists as we speak, and he'll be gone as soon as he's paid in full. Probably within the hour."

Hey Vincent cleared his throat and said shyly, "If it helps…he won't be using any mines around here. The old abandoned mines around here aren't that big. I grew up in Twisp, in the foothills, and I used to play with my friends in some of those mines: all dug by hand – the Okanogan gold boom didn't last long enough for any big commercial digs. There's a tunnel on Highway 97 that's large enough, but it's a good thirty miles away."

"Too far," Mr. Kenneth said. "Don't forget, Vega had less than twelve minutes to get his contraband under cover before the satellite came back on line, and he knew it."

"There's the old roundhouse at the Northern Pacific yard just west of Molson," Hey Vincent suggested. "Kind of an obvious spot, if you ask me, but plenty big."

"That's gotta be it," Hoot said, understanding Felix Vega's mindset and tactics; bold but practical. What's more, he knew like Hoot that the best place to hide anything was always right out in plain sight.

Hey Vincent grabbed Hoot's attention while Mr. Kenneth was using his phone to direct his team. "Think you could bring my H-2 back in one piece?" Vincent asked, looking deeply concerned.

Hoot shrugged his shoulders and said, "I'll see what I can do."

"Let's go!" Mr. Kenneth put the Tahoe in gear.

***

The old roundhouse outside Molson was an icon left over from the twilight years of the Age of Steam when Molson had been the yard and station with the highest elevation on the entire Northern Pacific line, the empty, semi-circular brick structure with a crumbling roof once a maintenance barn for the helper locos required to pull and push a train over Stevens Pass. The track, switches, and turntable had been removed for scrap long ago.

Jesse doused the headlights and parked the Hummer in a dark spot beside an abandoned warehouse in the rail yard. Lighting in the yard consisted of a couple of inefficient security spotlights: one at the gate, and one at the turntable pit in front of a semicircular front wall that consisted of one large arched portal after another; twelve total, most with their giant doors missing. In the dim light the structure had a Coliseum-like presence.

"Stay here," she told Remy and Maddie without argument from either. She chambered a round in her pistol, took the safety off, and replaced the gun in her pocket. Then she went ahead on foot, looking for Papa Flix...

If she'd only waited a few more minutes, she would've been there to see her father approach the Hummer with two members of his posse and politely escort Maddie and Remy to his car.

***

Last to arrive, Mr. Kenneth parked the black Tahoe next to the silver Hummer. Jesse, Maddie, and Jeremy were nowhere to be seen.

Neither was Mr. Kenneth's team.

"Backup in five minutes," he told Hoot.

Just then a two-ton box van truck with **Okanogan Scrap Metal Recycling** painted on the side pulled out of the roundhouse and Hoot said, "We don't have five minutes!"

The two men split up and began to advance across the treacherous rail yard as carefully and quickly as they could, Hoot following the old main line rail bed up the right side and Mr. Kenneth following the fence up the left. Snow made their footing uncertain, and lighting was essentially nonexistent. It was getting colder.

Two more scrap metal trucks exited the derelict building, a Mercedes sedan between them.

"Shit!" Hoot exclaimed, turning, and running back toward the Hummer.

Too late – he had already been seen! The driver of the Mercedes pulled out of line and brought the car to a skidding sideways stop, lowering his window, and drawing a bead on Hoot, exposed in the open.

Bam! Bam! Bam! Mr. Kenneth provided covering fire from across the yard, and Hoot was able to dive for safety. For his effort Mr. Kenneth caught a round from the driver in his thigh, another in his chest, and he went down waving at Hoot to keep on moving.

Gasping for breath, Hoot's heart was beating with arrhythmic insistence as if trying to escape from his ribcage. He rolled behind a pile of rotted railroad ties and wiped a handful of snow across his face, trying to keep his senses intact. Hoot was certain that he'd seen Remy's terrified face in the Mercedes' back seat when the driver's window went down: only a glimpse, but it was more than enough to fill him with dread at the same time that it rekindled his determination – Felix Vega could not have his grandson! Period!!

Hoot stood and steadied himself, refreshed the clip in his Beretta, and began walking toward the Mercedes.

The window went up, he car spun its tires, and Hoot was left standing in the middle of a derelict rail yard with his irregular heart racing out of control, his unfired pistol in his trembling hand...

***

Jesse ran to the front of the roundhouse barely in time to see her father drive away in the Mercedes. She turned and made a dash for the parked Hummer.

What a pisser! The voice inside her head said. *The fucking fucker's about to get away with it again! Truly a pisser!!*

Hoot saw Jesse reach the Hummer, throwing open the doors and slamming them closed. He started walking toward her, his pistol held as steady as he could make it and pointed at her head.

She barely glanced at him, said, "Put that down," while lifting a black resin case out of the back of the Hummer. "Don't you get it, yet? I'm on your side, Shooter."

"You're too late," Hoot said. "He has Maddie and Remy. They're gone."

"No they're not," Jesse said, unsnapping the case to reveal an MQ-9 Reaper remote control console nested inside. She removed an accessory bag, flipped the case over and said, "Help me set this up."

Hoot unzipped the black Gore-Tex bag to find four adjustable aluminum legs. He snapped them into place on the bottom of the resin case and returned it upright. There was a pair of joysticks inside, a keyboard, and a mouse ball. The lid of the case served as a dashboard. Jesse connected a cable from a separate rechargeable battery to the control module, and four notebook-size monitor screens mounted in the dashboard immediately came to life, showing real-time images from the drone that she and Remy had launched.

"What's your plan?" Hoot asked.

"Don't have one. The Reaper that Remy and I launched will soon be in a holding pattern at 15,000'. I can fly it, but I can only control the Nav camera," she said. "If I get lucky and spot the car or either of the trucks I can see which direction they go, even follow them, but I don't have tactical control, so I can't lock-on to them."

"We already know where the bomb is going," Hoot said. "But we don't know which truck it's in. Follow the car with Remy and Maddie."

Jesse said, "My father won't stay on the ground for long."

"What? A helicopter?"

"No. He hates helicopters. He'll have a nearby landing strip already picked out to make his exit. It'll be a twin engine plane with enough range to get him halfway home."

"You've checked this out?"

"I have. There are two landing strips in the area with long-enough runways, and one private airport. He won't use the airport."

And aren't you glad... the voice said. *You'll need a spot a bit more out of the way and private than a public airport if you want your nearly-dead boyfriend to kill your father for you.*

***

A half-hour later Jesse pulled the Hummer off the road at Mud Lake where no lake was visible. The airstrip was about a half-mile away on the opposite side of the unseen lake; lights in the distance showing Hoot where to look. A plane was idling in front of a shed: red and green navigation lights on at the wingtips, and taxi lights were on, strobes were off. Felix Vega's Mercedes was parked next to it, the headlights on.

"Get your rifle. This is as close as we get," she said.

Seconds later they found a good vantage on a slightly raised berm, and Hoot pulled an optical rangefinder out of his gun case. He ranged the shot at 820 yards, near maximum effective range for the 7.62mm sniper ammo that was loaded in his magazine. The temperature had continued to drop all night, and while Hoot was very aware that temperature wouldn't affect a bullet the way the dry humidity would, he was also aware that it could severely handicap the shooter...

"It's a bad shot," Hoot said. "Conditions the way they are, the bullet is bound to drop over the lake, and a gust of wind like the one you just felt from the east could move it sideways an inch or more at this range. There'll be two shots, minimum: your father and the driver, probably not the pilot. But we don't know who else may be inside the plane or the shed. I only have six rounds in the magazine, Jesse, and then I'm out of ammo."

"Should be more than enough for the great Troubleshooter. One bullet-one kill. Isn't that right?"

"Without a trial shot?" Hoot shook his head. "I just don't know."

"It's the best shot you're gonna get," Jesse said. "If you want your grandson back, it's the only one..."

Hoot's a-fib was kicking in again – a fluttering feeling in his chest that would leave his ribs aching afterward. He ignored it, spread out his shooting mat, adjusted his rifle pillow and hold-down, and then he lay down on his mat for the shot of his life, chambered the first round...and waited.

This was the worst part of sniper work...the waiting.

Hoot had a vision of a much younger Ezra Hooten in Vietnam, waiting in the sweltering muck and bugs for targets to show their faces – faces he had, thankfully, largely forgotten save those permanently etched into his skull; his own personal Vietnam War memorial in bone. He often reflected on how he had become the assassin that he knew himself to be? It had been his twisted friend, Norman Carpenter's, idea, and not a good one in hindsight.

Hoot wore mittens over his fingerless shooting gloves to keep his hands warm, but his trigger finger was still getting cold and stiff at the same time that his brow was beading with sweat, feverish. His breathing refused to regulate. He waited, trying to calm himself, looking through the scope with both eyes open, remembering his father's reaction when he learned that his oldest son was training to be a sniper; "Don't do it," his father had warned, saying, "It's too personal. There's no turning back once a man has killed..."

Hoot could see the driver in his crosshairs, a clean shot. And still, he waited.

He remembered the expression of horror in his girlfriend, Donna Messenger's, eyes when he told her that he was dropping out of college to join his friend in Vietnam. He could've told her that he'd decided that he wanted to become the devil's hairdresser and she would've been less shocked. He should've shot himself in the head right then and saved himself a world of pain and disappointment in the long run. Hoot had missed countless opportunities to turn himself around.

Finally, the passenger door of the Mercedes opened and Felix Vega exited the vehicle, followed by Maddie and Remy. They entered the shed. The driver stayed in the car, but not for long. He opened the trunk and began transferring bags from the car to the idling plane's cargo hatch.

The plane's strobe and landing lights came on, followed by lighted white markers along the side of the landing strip with a red one at the end.

Soon, Hoot thought…very soon.

He removed the mitten on his right hand with his teeth, and snuggled the rifle butt a little more firmly into his shoulder. He gently put his finger on the trigger, but he couldn't stop his hand from trembling, so he took his finger back off the trigger and blew into his fist to warm the joints and tendons.

The shaking in his hands was getting worse instead of better, and he was developing a slight nosebleed.

This was worse than a bad shot; it was an impossible one: long range, at night, untested ammo, old unpracticed shooter. He rolled aside on his mat, said "I can't!"

"You have to!" Jesse said. "Once my father leaves with your grandson and ladyfriend they aren't coming back, Hoot!"

Hoot was lying on his back looking up at Jesse, visibly trembling. He turned his head and spit blood in the snow, wiped his mouth on his coat sleeve, and said, "Can't you see, Jesse, I'm falling apart, here. I can't make this shot. You'll have to do it…

Jesse hesitated, and then she scrambled to take Hoot's position on the mat, and looked through the M-21's tactical scope, adjusting the focus to her eyesight. The driver was still loading bags into the plane while her father stood near the car; he was saying something to Maddie, who obviously disagreed with whatever he was saying. Remy stepped closer to Maddie, and she put her arm protectively around the boy's shoulders. The Bausch & Lomb optics were so fine that, even from over a half-mile away in poor light, Jesse could clearly see the sneer on her father's face as he rebuffed Maddie, gesturing toward the plane's passenger door.

Softly as a falling snowflake, Jesse placed her finger on the trigger.

This was it! She was finally going to be rid of her horrible father! A nervous butterfly rose from her gut, and Jesse caught her breath with a slight gasp when the voice in her head, the never-absent, always-opinionated Billievoice piped up and said, *If the famous shooter can't make this shot, what makes you think you can?*

Jesse ignored the voice, keeping her attention on the target. She applied a steady pull on the trigger until she felt a slight increase in resistance – the hammer release mechanism…

It's your father, you fool! Evil incarnate!

Hoot turned beside her and gently laid a hand on her shoulder, saying in a whisper, "Let your breath out – slowly."

She did that.

How do you kill pure Evil? the Billievoice fretted.

"Take another breath, and let that one out, too," Hoot whispered. She did.

Don't do it…you'll miss!

"Hold the next one…"

What if you miss?

Jesse kept her focus absolutely zeroed on the target and pulled the trigger.

The window glass at her father's elbow exploded – she had missed!

She took another shot. This one hit the target. But it didn't take him down.

Felix Vega grabbed Remy and cowered behind him, wildly looking around for any sign of the shooter, a muzzle flash from somewhere in the brush beyond the big pond.

Maddie stepped in and grabbed Remy out of Felix Vega's grip, clutching him protectively in her arms, shielding him from danger just as Jesse steadied her nerves, and took her third shot…

Madeline Marvel fell.

Last Chapter

It had started snowing again; tiny, powdery flakes. Hoot was keeping watch through splintery gaps in a small, mostly roofless, barnlike structure that must've been two-hundred years old, the last remains of a pioneer farm at the north end of Mud Lake.

Maddie moaned in his arms. He held her a bit closer, saying, "I've got you, Maddie. Don't worry; I won't let you die here."

"It's as good a place as any," she said with a slight cough squeezing another surge of blood through her favorite winter coat and a makeshift bandage of Hoot's mittens.

"Help is on the way," he said. "Just stay with me."

Maddie nodded her head and took a slow, deep breath, grimacing with the effort.

***

After her last shot Jesse threw down Hoot's rifle, took the Hummer, and rushed to the airstrip. Hoot could see through the rangefinder that Maddie was down and the plane was leaving, but he was unable to do much of anything other than to keep breathing – one breath at a time. He was miserably nauseous and trying to keep his empty stomach from heaving. Evidently his a-fib seriously wanted to kill him this time.

Stroke? Heart attack?

Take your pick, Hoot thought, lying beside the shooter's mat. Furious because he couldn't hold the rangefinder steady enough to tell what was happening at the airstrip across Mud Lake. Furious that he was so fucking weak!

By the time Jesse returned in the Hummer with Maddie, Hoot had managed to get his basic shit together well enough to be sitting up. His pulse had settled into a sustainable rhythm, and his hands had quit shaking – almost.

Hoot felt...*different* inside, as if his body had been filled with gas: probably something with a comical name chosen to make replacement-grade insulated windows sound bulletproof: Argon? Krypton-2? He realized he couldn't remember the last time he'd eaten, and thought, No wonder I feel like shit...

"Can you walk?" Jesse asked, grabbing the M-21 and the rifle pillow. "I saw an old barn around the end of the lake. It's not much, but Mizz Marvel needs shelter, adding with a glance at Hoot, "And so do you..."

***

Most of the barn's roof was gone, and much of the siding, but there was no other structure in sight. Jesse improvised a compress bandage for Maddie's wound from Hoot's mittens and held it in place with a webbed nylon tie-down strap that she found in the Hummer. The bleeding had slowed, but not stopped – a bad sign.

Hoot limped around and managed to find enough dry wood to make a small fire.

After helping make Maddie as comfortable as possible in an old army blanket from Hey Vincent's mishmash of emergency gear, Hoot asked: "There was no sign of Remy at the airstrip?"

"My father took him," Jesse said with a fierce expression of pent-up rage.

Her fists were clenched. She stood and raised them like a woman possessed, said with a snarl, "God damn him!"

Then she took a deep breath and a step back. "The bomb is still heading for Seattle...and I have no idea if Mr. Kenneth has an eye on it or not," she said in an earnest tone,

"He doesn't," Hoot said. "Mr. Kenneth was shot at the roundhouse in Molson."

"Dead?" Jesse asked with alarm.

"No. He was wearing a vest, but he was hit a couple of times. He's sidelined."

Jesse stroked the scar along her jaw as if it ached. After a moment she glanced at Hoot and said, "It's a long shot. But there may be time…"

Still nursing an ember of lucidity to life, Hoot asked, "Time for what?"

Instead of responding, Jesse stormed off toward the Hummer, came back a minute later, and tossed a flare gun in a soft case in Hoot's lap. She said, "No cell bars in this hole – I've checked. When I get to Fletcher Road, I'll call for help. The closest medical center is in Oroville and I don't know if they have a helicopter, so it may be awhile. Stay awake, and use that to show them where you are."

"Time for what?" Hoot asked again.

"I have a drone circling, and I have about three hours left before it runs out of fuel. I may not have killed my father today, but with a little luck I can still kill his reputation."

"Go!" Hoot said.

Jesse turned to leave. She paused and said with a sincere expression, "I am truly sorry that I shot Maddie. I'm sorry for this whole fucking mess."

Hoot only nodded.

"I'll find Remy," she said. "Count on it. And I'll kill Felix Vega."

Jesse turned on her heel, and was gone.

***

For almost two hours, Hoot waited.

For what? For rescue? For salvation?

Hoot figured he'd spent the greater part of his life waiting. He realized there was a very good chance that he would die in this forsaken place. Perhaps he welcomed the idea.

Very little moved on the frigid Okanogan highlands this time of year without serious purpose, so whatever stirred was noticeable.

Presently, nothing seemed to be moving in their direction – certainly nothing with sirens and flashing lights.

Hoot thought this would be beautiful country if it weren't so harsh and unforgiving.

It had stopped snowing. There was a light breeze with powdery snowflakes lifting on the breeze like fine glitter, making the landscape look much softer than it was.

A thick mustiness loitered in the ancient barn in spite of its insufferable draftiness. Layers of frozen dust and frost on everything. Cobwebs that were surely antiques.

Much colder on this side of the Cascades than back home at Hoot's cabin on the strait; the sort of cold that won't quit until everything it touches turns to ice. Canada was nearby to the north, nothing else nearby. This was a barren, unwelcoming place, and Hoot wondered what sort of people would've had the gumption to try to scratch out a living here. How long had they lasted? Certainly a hellava lot longer than he and Maddie would, he figured.

Maddie stifled a moan and stirred beside him. Hoot peeked under her blanket at her makeshift compress. His mittens were now nothing but a gooey, blood-soaked heap of yarn.

Maddie's eyes were open, looking at him.

"It's a beautiful day. Cold…but beautiful," Hoot said, adjusting the cargo strap that was holding her bandage secure. "There's nowhere I would rather be right now than here with you."

"Liar…" she whispered through lips that were white with shock and cold.

"Okay. You caught me. The truth is I'd rather be back in Port Tim, lounging with you in your hot tub, so whaddya say we call it a day here and go heat up the Jacuzzi at your place?"

A grimace crept across Maddie's face. She hid it with a smile, but it remained in her eyes, and it wrenched Hoot's heart to see her in such pain. She said, "You need to get your grandson back."

"Don't worry, Maddie. I will. Jeremy's going to be fine," Hoot said, holding her in his arms, hoping to warm her and reassure her, but it was no use. The hard truth was the fire wasn't going to last long, and he had no idea if Jeremy was okay or not. But he was certain that if help didn't arrive soon to get Maddie out of here, she wasn't going to make it. Most likely, neither of them would.

"I am not afraid," Maddie said without a trace of panic, sadness, or bitterness.

Hoot knew that she meant what she'd said about not being afraid. Maddie had lived the fullest life she could've possibly lived, stayed true to her creative dreams, and created scores of characters who would outlive her. She was ready to make her exit.

She lay very still, barely breathing. Then, all of a sudden, she attempted to sit up, no doubt wrenching her wound open, saying, "Listen! Can you hear it? The music?"

Hoot laid her back down, spooning with her for warmth. He heard nothing but the breeze, occasionally a branch falling.

"I've plotted my best stories to music," Maddie said. "Sometimes I dance…"

Hoot gave her shoulder a squeeze of reassurance, asked, "Wanna dance?"

"Sure. Give me a minute," she said, "I'm having a thought." She was still creating, still writing in her head, new ideas every second.

Nodding her head slightly…rhythmically, she whispered, "Can you hear it?"

Hoot listened again and still heard nothing.

He said, "I'm sorry, I can't."

"You have to *listen*," she said with insistence.

Hoot listened harder. And then even harder, until he thought – or imagined – that he heard a faint melody as if from a distant violin. Low notes held on the breeze.

Maddie began to sway slightly with the music, nodding her head to keep time until Hoot could finally hear it, too – music! Hauntingly beautiful. And overwhelming.

Her hands fluttering, fingertips reaching for unseen keys, Madeline Marvel was dancing and typing, plotting her next Romance novel. She swayed, reaching for the moon and stars, her expression telling Hoot that she was going to dance up a great love scene…

Reaching around her with both arms, Hoot took Maddie's hands in his, and began dancing with her. Humming and swaying, they danced a slow waltz together…until she finally let go.

***

305

The sky in the east was lightening a bit, but sun hadn't yet shown itself above the horizon – just before dawn on New Year's Day in the Okanogan – when an explosion of significant force shook the ground with a rumbling noise. Loosened snow and icicles fell from everywhere...

Hoot had dozed off. Maddie was dead, her lifeless body still in his arms. He lifted his tear-streaked face and smiled grimly, knowing that Jesse had found the truck, and crashed the UAV into it. Felix Vega's dirty bomb wasn't going to Seattle after all.

But there was also another noise, an insistent noise, and it took a moment for Hoot to realize that what he was hearing was a chopper. He softly touched Maddie's cold cheek and said, "It's okay, Sweetheart. We're good now," then he reached for the flare gun.

***

Still very much alive, Hoot awoke in a hospital room...again! He was getting sick to death of hospitals, and he thought to himself; I should just go ahead and die so I don't have to wake up in another goddamned hospital room.

He had been dreaming. He couldn't remember the dream, but he knew that Linda, his ex, was in it. He could still hear her voice as if she was in the room with him, saying; "Ezra Hooten! If you don't haul your Casper-white ass out of that bed right now and go save my grandson, I'll come out there and choke you to death with my own bare hands!"

The End

ABOUT THE AUTHOR

Rod Lindsey is an indie writer with over 30 years of storytelling experience. Previously a Beamwalker in construction lingo, Rod has been a commercial artist and a professional photographer, a snake oil salesman of extraordinary guff, a carpenter, a soldier, a demolitions specialist prone to overuse of C-4, a motocross racer prone to spectacular crashes, and a nudist prone to gawking. *Skyshooter* is Rod's second Ezra Hooten novel. The first Ezra Hooten novel, *Troubleshooter*, won the Zola award for best Mystery and Suspense novel at the 2009 PNWA conference, and was picked Best Novel of 2012 by Blogtalk Radio Authors on the Air.

www.ingramcontent.com/pod-product-compliance
Lightning Source LLC
Chambersburg PA
CBHW070554260626
47161CB00002B/603